TEJALURA

TEJALURA

Gayle MacArthur

Violet Lantern Street
Publishing Company
2011

This is a work of fiction. All of the characters and events portrayed in this novel are products of the author's imagination.

Copyright © 2011 by Gayle MacArthur
All rights reserved.

ISBN-13: 978-0-9833275-1-6
ISBN-10: 0983327513

Printed in the United States of America

To Carole Peterson
Editor, Friend and Best Mom

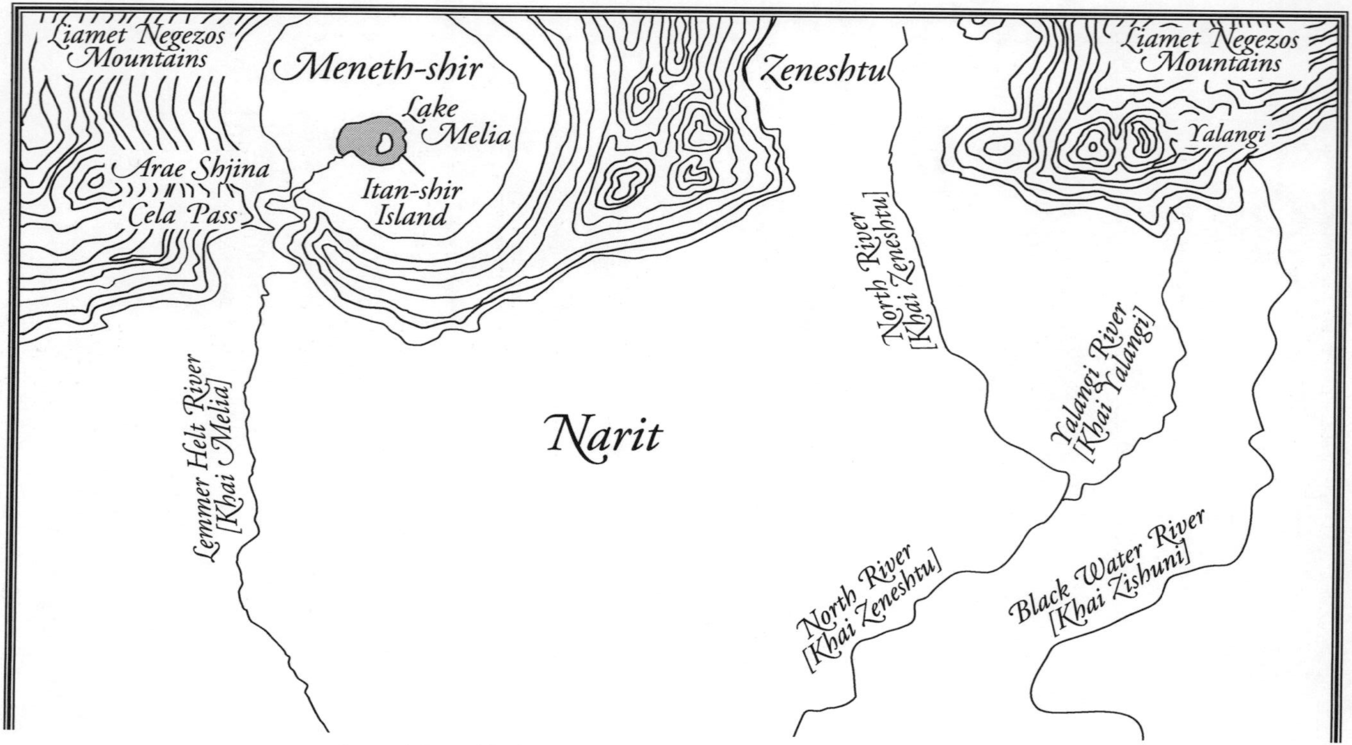
Liamet Negezos Mountains
Meneth-shir
Lake Melia
Itan-shir Island
Arae Shjina
Cela Pass
Zeneshtu
Liamet Negezos Mountains
Yalangi
North River [Khai Zeneshtu]
Yalangi River [Khai Yalangi]
Lemmer Helt River [Khai Melia]
Narit
North River [Khai Zeneshtu]
Black Water River [Khai Zishuni]

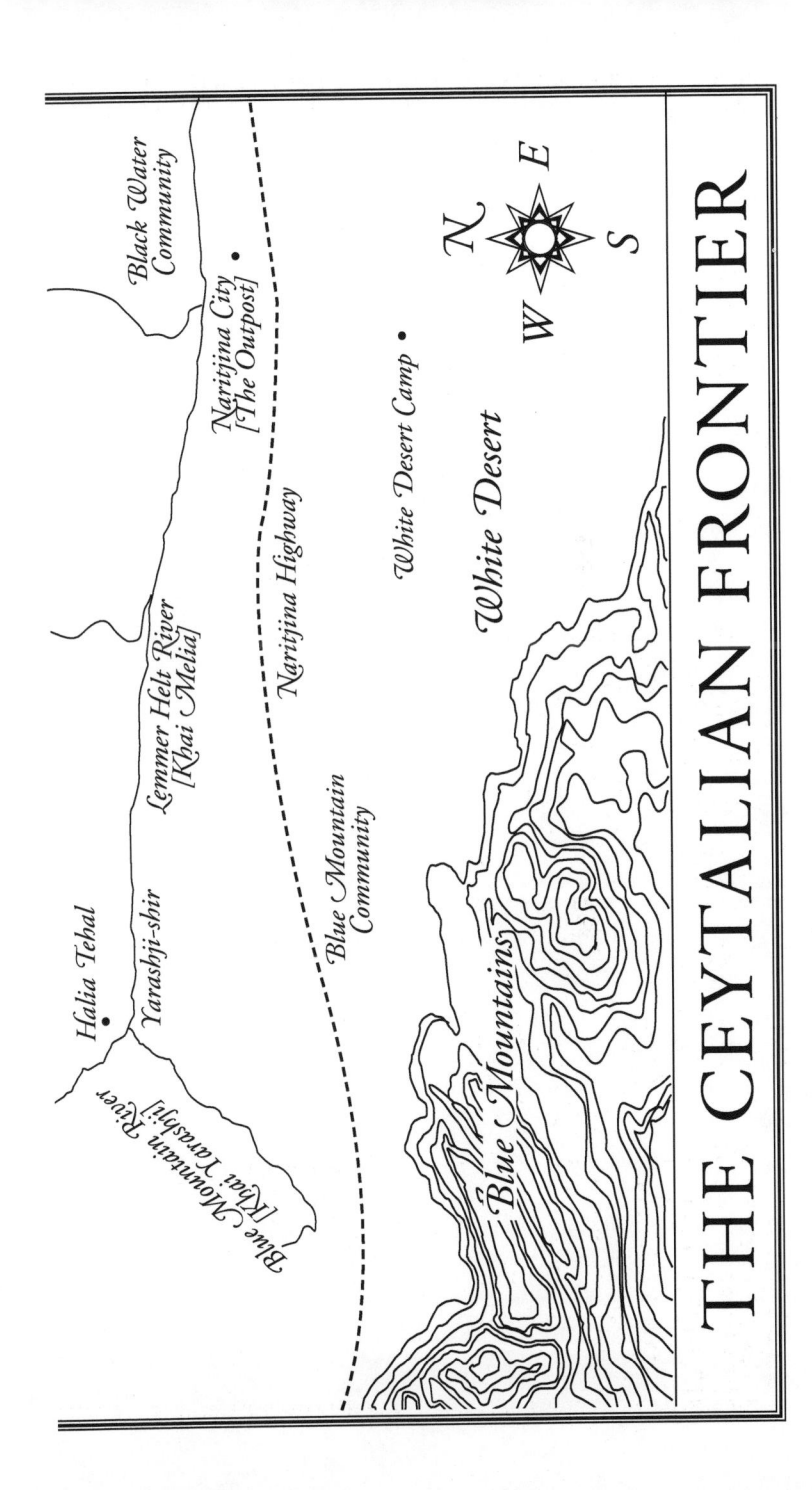

THE CEYTALIAN FRONTIER

- Black Water Community
- Naritjima City [The Outpost]
- Lemmer Helt River [Khai Melia]
- Yarashji-shir
- Halia Tebal
- Blue Mountain River [Khai Tarashji]
- Naritjima Highway
- Blue Mountain Community
- White Desert Camp
- White Desert
- Blue Mountains

N / E / S / W

Table of Contents

Map of the Ceytalian Frontier

1. The Soldier: Erten Zemmer 1317 EE 1
2. The Captive: Lillian Aleksandar 1317 EE 7
3. The Captor: Neve Ce 1317 EE 13
4. The Stranger: Lillian Aleksandar 1317 EE 17
5. The Daughter: Tejalura 1317-1323 EE 29
6. The Soldier: Erten Zemmer 1317-1323 EE 51
7. The Appaloosa: Tejalura 1323-1324 EE.................. 63
8. The Renegade: Terez Chevari 1325 EE 73
9. The Nejimenet Jevema: Tejalura 1325-1328 EE 83
10. Ceremony of the Chosen: Tejalura 1328-1329 EE 95
11. The Husband: Yari Tehalchev 1329 EE 111
12. The Blue Mountain Massacre: Tejalura 1330-1336 EE 117
13. The Enavian Agent: Erten Zemmer 1336-1338 EE 131
14. The Exile: Lillian Wolf 1338-1341 EE 143
15. The Tracker: Lemmer Kendal 1341 EE 165
16. Homecoming: Tejalura 1341 EE........................ 171
17. The Priest: Tehmu 1342-1348 EE...................... 177
18. The Queen: Divneve Ce 1348 EE 223
19. The Ambassador: Erten Zemmer 1349 EE 235
    Appendix 241
    Bibliography 259

Chapter 1
The Soldier: Erten Zemmer 1317 EE

> "The determined effort of the Enavian Empire
> to remain ignorant of the very people it rules is
> something that has never ceased to amaze me."
>
> — *Dr. Ura Jevetchev*

Spring 1317 EE

Thirty years ago Ceytal was a territorial planet and The Cela Rose was the only place a man could get a decent drink. I spent a great deal of my off-duty time there with my Ceytalian friend, Mheftu Padhari. He was a tall, blue-haired native with golden eyes. An old scar on his left cheek solved the problem of his too-handsome face.

Padhari could make himself at home anywhere in the universe. He was equally at ease with Enavian aristocracy or shiftless desert rats. I knew little about his origins for our friendship was based on the present, but I have always sensed there was real class there. At one time Padhari had known affluence and privilege. He had obtained a medical degree from a prestigious Enavian university, an uncommon thing for a Ceytalian. He had been in great demand as a general practitioner until he sold his business to lead expeditions of bored Enavian aristocrats into the wilderness—for a price.

He often served as a consultant to the DCNA (Department of Ceytalian Native Affairs). That's how we met. On our first case, we broke up a ring of slave traders trafficking in child prostitution. Padhari usually charged high consulting fees, but he had done that job for free. We stayed in contact after we closed the case. Whenever I was on leave and Padhari was between expeditions, we would go hunting together.

We were having a drink one evening at The Cela Rose when Dassar Nul, a Zenadishj slave trader, joined us. Although he worked in the "clean" end of the business, I have never liked the man. I couldn't justify my dislike for him; it was an instinctive reaction. He didn't care for me either, but we put our differences aside for Padhari's sake.

"Padhari!" Dassar Nul's voice boomed across the noisy room. "It's good to see you. And you, Zemmer, what are you doing here? You should be at the officer's club. You'll never make general if you continue to hang around provincials like us."

I stopped going to the officer's club the first week after my transfer to Ceytal. My fellow officers considered being stationed on Ceytal as so much wasted downtime in their military careers. There are only two topics discussed in that group: First, the hard-luck stories, the series of events bringing them to this godforsaken planet on the edge of the empire. Second, how bored they were now they're here. It was too depressing. I decided if I had to sit around and listen to that just to be general, it wasn't worth being general.

"'Join the Enavian Space Force and see the universe,'" quoted one bitter recruit. "Well I did and so far all I've seen are desert, swamp, and more desert. Treacherous mountains, hostile natives, and more desert. Disease, poverty, and more desert."

And what more could one want? I thought to myself. To a young man who had no specific plans for the future and no real military ambitions, Ceytal was an adventure. The officer's club held no interest for me; I'd take The Rose any time. Ironically, it was my mingling with the "provincials" that would gain me the practical knowledge of Ceytal that later furthered my military career.

Dassar Nul was still waiting for me to reply.

"The drinks are cheaper here," I said, explaining my presence.

Dassar Nul let out another belly laugh and slapped me on the back, causing me to spill most of my drink. He then turned to Padhari, deliberately excluding me from the rest of the conversation.

"And what brings you here, Padhari?" he asked.

"I'm meeting a client. We start out tomorrow morning for the White Desert."

"Is he Enavian?"

"Erteyan-Enavian. Not that it matters. Just so long as his money is good."

"I'll bet that's him over there," Dassar Nul said indicating a thin, uncertain young man, making his way through the crowded room. "He doesn't look like much. You'd better get him before some wind blows him away."

"He's got a mouth, let him ask for me. I want to enjoy my last drink in peace."

"Right. Hmm, he's Erteyan all right," Dassar Nul said contemptuously, forgetting (or perhaps remembering) that I myself was Erteyan. "One of those worms inflamed with the idea he's returned to his ancestral planet. Did he want to see those old ruins up in the mountains?"

"No."

"That's odd, isn't it?"

"Yes. Usually they want to spend a few weeks in one of those rubbles. Still, I can stand it because I make a good profit. It's the return trip I could do without."

Neither Dassar Nul nor I needed to ask Padhari about the return trip. He had told us often enough about his Erteyan clients. On the return trip he would have to listen while they outlined the evidence proving beyond a doubt Ceytal was the legendary Earth. With each Erteyan the speech never varied. Padhari could recite it word-for-word.

"Now about this client of yours," Dassar Nul continued. "If he doesn't want to go to the ruins, what does he want to do?"

"He just said he wanted to relax and enjoy himself. He wants to start at the foot of the Negezos Mountains and follow the North River through the Naritian Prairie until it meets with the Lemmer Helt River. If there's time, he wants to go south to the White Desert."

"How long did he hire you for?"

"Six months."

The slave trader laughed.

"He won't last a week. He'll go *meiklei* without any help at all. Mark my words. He's been pampered all his life by his father's money, and his mother brought him up to be a proper young gentleman to say 'please' and 'thank you' very nicely. Now when he comes up to you he'll say, 'How do you do? I'm afraid we haven't met before, but my name is—' what is his name?"

"Ral Hershem."

"'My name is Ral Hershem, you must be Dr. Padhari. I'm pleased to make your acquaintance.'" Dassar Nul caught the arm of the barmaid as she passed our table. "Here, Halia, another drink! Now mind you, I've nothing against Erteyans, it's just they're a queer, close-knit lot. Never a tenthpiece for anyone else, but a fortune to spare for their own kind."

"Well, at least they look after their own," Padhari said. "Have you ever heard of an Erteyan orphan—or a widow who had to be supported by the government?"

"No, you're right there," he agreed. "They're not all bad. Now take that Aleksandar family. Nicer people you couldn't find. They've been here almost twenty years, but do we know them? You're Lev's best friend. You have dinner with them all the time. But can you really say you know him? He and the others who live in the Black Water Community are . . . well, they're superior, that's what they are. Too good to share a drink with you, and they wouldn't know what to do with a good woman if they came across one."

"These people you speak of are my friends," Padhari said quietly. "And if you are still here when my client finds me, I suggest you leave if you can't speak courteously to him. He is Seraine's younger brother."

"Seraine?" I said aloud without thinking. The two men turned in surprise, as if they had forgotten my presence.

"Yes, Seraine Aleksandar, Lev's wife," he explained. "She's the mother of Jack Aleksandar."

I had met Jack Aleksandar briefly and wished to know him better for he had a pretty, dark-eyed sister named Gabrielle. I met her at a party, and although I only danced with her twice, she held my attention the entire evening. She was certainly a flirt, but a charming one, and I, as well as every other man present that night, found myself fascinated by her.

"Excuse me."

We looked up and saw Ral Hershem standing by our table.

"I'm afraid we haven't met before. My name is Ral Hershem. You must be Dr. Padhari. I'm pleased to make your acquaintance."

Winking broadly, Dassar Nul excused himself and left. I turned my full attention to Hershem. He looked a bit older close up, thirty perhaps. Yet he still had the unfinished look of those who have not quite found their place in life. Pale, nearsighted and bookish, he wasn't a man I normally would have sought out as a friend, but he was Gabrielle's uncle, so I smiled warmly. There was no way of knowing when I might see her again, and it wouldn't hurt to have the good will of one of her relatives.

·→※←··→※←··→※←·

I saw Gabrielle three weeks later.

Or rather what was left of her after, what later would be known as, the Market Place Bombing. The Aleksandars had visited the Outpost during a Ceytalian holiday and were caught in the crossfire of rival Zenadishj gangs. Although they were no more than smears of DNA on the cobbled stones of Mactil Street, Mheftu was able to account for the entire family based on forensic evidence. The fact that all Enavian citizens have ID markers implanted as a matter of course, also helped with the identification process.

Being the only officer within a two-hundred-mile radius who speaks three dialects of Zenadishj, the dominant language on Ceytal, meant I was detailed to nearly all field assignments. Normally it's nothing more than a break in routine, something to get me out of the office and give me a chance to learn more about Ceytal. But this incident involved civilian casualties of both immigrant settlers and Zenadishj natives. Both sides resented our efforts to investigate and refused to cooperate. To make matters worse, Enavian authorities weren't interested in long-term solutions. Our orders were to close each case as quickly as possible. It was a dirty, thankless job, and I wouldn't mind seeing a few of the senior officers do it for a change.

We passed several groups of Erteyans leaving the Outpost to return to their farms. They glared at us stonily. *Where were you when we needed you?* their attitude said. As a gesture of contempt, one of them spat with deadly accuracy at the soldier carrying the Enavian flag. I could have arrested him, but it wasn't worth the effort.

To hell with them, I thought. They immigrated to Ceytal of their own free will; no one forced them. Things are a lot different out here on the frontier than in Enavia proper, and they should have accepted that fact before they left in the first place, or not come at all.

While searching the debris for more evidence, a flash of color caught my attention. It was a picture of Gabrielle in a peach-colored dress holding a little girl dressed in yellow. I dusted it off carefully. Naturally it was Gabrielle's image that caught my attention. How was I to know the other girl beside her would one day change all our lives? At the time I saw only a little girl sitting in the shadow of her older sister.

For artistic reasons alone it was a pleasing composition, spontaneous and natural. I resisted the impulse to withhold the picture from evidence and keep it for myself. But what would I do with it? I had only shared a brief flirtatious conversation with her at a dance. Why should Gabrielle's image be so dear?

I walked over to Padhari who was sifting through the rubble with five other men.

"Here!" I said handing the image to him. "I found this over there by the wall."

He glanced at it briefly and pressed one of the corners to read the time stamp.

"This is good," he remarked. "According to the time stamp, it was taken just a few moments before the bombing."

"Who's the little girl beside Gabrielle?" I asked.

"Her sister, Lillian."

He eyed me closely. He had noticed my conversation with Gabrielle at the dance and was aware of my attraction for her. He pressed one of the other corners and produced a copy. He handed me the original.

"Gabrielle was a pretty girl," was all he said.

"The little one too," I remarked to draw attention away from my fascination with Gabrielle. "Was she among the victims?"

"I'm not sure," he said. "I found DNA to match all the ID markers except for Lillian and her younger brother, Johnny. Their markers are in perfect condition. Too perfect. It's more likely they were removed so the children could be sold to the slave traders without being traced."

"So they could still be alive?" I wondered.

Padhari thought for a moment.

"Perhaps," he said. "But only if they could be sold quickly. No matter what tribe these Zenadishj were from, they have a three-day journey of hard riding ahead of them. Children would only slow them down. It will be hard to find any buyers. They're too close to the Outpost. It would be easier to kill them."

What a waste it all was, I thought as I continued gathering the information I needed. Whatever grievances the Zenadishj might have, the death of these people, especially the children, solved nothing. I turned to my recorder to finish the report.

"And listed missing or dead are John Aleksandar, aged four, and his sister Lillian Aleksandar, aged seven . . ."

Chapter 2
The Captive: Lillian Aleksandar 1317 EE

> "I have fought the Enavians many times and have no love for them. But when two of their children came to live among us, the brother and the sister, my heart went out to them."
>
> — *General She Bear*

Spring 1317 EE

My father, Lev Aleksandar, had immigrated to Ceytal with his pretty wife, Seraine, and their two children, Jack and Gabrielle. I was there too, but I didn't count yet because at the time I was a small, three-inch translucent blue cube, which Gabrielle called her "little sister box." Gabrielle and I should have been twins, but our parents couldn't afford to raise three children then, so I had to wait for a more convenient time to be born. After several years of hard work and sound speculation, my father felt things were secure enough to let me out of my cube for Gabrielle's tenth birthday. I kept that cube for years until my younger brother, Johnny, broke it.

I spent the first seven years of my life on a farm much like the ones seen today along the Lemmer Helt River. It was an oasis of green surrounded by dry, barren desert. The Black Water Community (named in honor of the Zishuni natives who once lived there) was made up of eleven families who pooled their resources to purchase farming equipment and land from the Enavian government. The land was divided equally and each family worked their own section, but the equipment remained communal property.

Everyone had to work hard—everyone, that is, except Johnny, who didn't have to do much of anything except play. Mother said he was too little to work. When I did have free time there was no one my age to play with because the other families decided not to have children when I was uncubed. That left only Johnny who was to my disgust, a whole three years younger than me.

My older brother, Jack, used to spend time with me before he married and moved to another community. I liked Jack a great deal, even though he was a little wild. He drank a lot and spent most of his time with desert riders and mountain men. This made his wife, Cia, miserable for she was a religious woman. They had a baby, but Cia decided not to uncube it until Jack was ready to settle down.

Gabrielle was more of a second mother to me than a sister. I used to watch her while she dressed for a party or a trip to the Outpost. She may have been spoiled and vain, but she was very pretty. I couldn't wait to grow up because every one said I would look just like her when I did.

But I wanted a voice like my mother's. Her voice was the first sound I heard when I woke up each morning and the last before I went to sleep at night. I can see her now: her long, black braid swaying as she moved about the house, humming to herself. She was always happy; it was as if each day of her life she lived a dream come true.

I remember my father as a great bear of a man who was always good for a hug. For the most part he was easygoing, but there were some things he could be very dogmatic about. Words, for instance. He used them carefully and valued them differently than other people did. There was profanity, which other people thought was bad but my father didn't, and there were words you didn't dare say around him which other people thought were perfectly all right. He would have beat us if we ever called a native "dinge" or "yellow-eyes."

"You may not like someone," he would say to us, "but make certain it doesn't have a thing to do with the color of his eyes or the shade of his skin or the planet he just happened to be born on. Judge each person by his own merits. And when you hate, do it on an individual basis, rather than by groups. That way you will keep your enemies down to a manageable number."

"I suppose most people thought he was fanatical on the subject, but few openly disagreed with him."

I had no opinion of the natives one way or another. The only native I knew was Mheftu Padhari, but he wasn't a good example because he was a doctor and wore Enavian business suits. He also had an Enavian wife, Cia's older sister, Talamy."

I liked him because he used to bring us presents and tell us stories of the Zenadishj court where he grew up as a boy. He gave Jack a blue ring that had been given to him by one of the court nobles when he was a boy. Jack was so proud of it that he never took it off. Uncle Mheftu would tease me by calling me Princess Ceymar because I reminded him of the little dark-haired princess he played with in the palace gardens. He told me stories of the games they played and the adventures they had before he left Narit to see the world.

"What happened to Princess Ceymar after you left?"

"She grew up to be a very beautiful queen and now rules the Zenadishj Empire."

"You shouldn't have gone away, Uncle Mheftu," I said seriously.

"Oh? And why not?"

"You should have stayed. That way you could have fallen in love and married her."

Gabrielle and I had been watching Enavian romances, and I was proud of my grown-up knowledge of love, confused and incomplete though it was.

He smiled.

"No, Lillian. I couldn't have stayed. Princesses do not marry the sons of court physicians."

Uncle Mheftu was there at Johnny's birthday party; it was the last time all of us were together. Many years afterward I would try to recreate that day in my mind, the clothes we wore, the words we spoke, and details that would fade with the passing of time. I do remember being sent to bed early because I teased Johnny and made him cry. I went to my room under great protest because, after all, it wasn't my fault he was being such a baby.

·→※←··→※←··→※←·

The next day we went to the Outpost to do some shopping. Because it was the day after Johnny's birthday and the Zenadishj festival of the new moon, a routine errand became something of a holiday. We had to leave earlier than usual to get through the line at the gates. The festival wasn't the only cause for delay; security had been stepped up to handle the recent escalation of violence. New equipment had been installed at the checkpoints so visitors could be scanned for weapons. The line moved slowly that day and our mother kept the mood light by encouraging us to sing songs and play games to pass the time.

The guards were friends of ours from a neighboring farm and only gave our transport a cursory glance. They discussed crops with my parents, flirted with Gabrielle, and after a few teasing remarks to Johnny and me, waved us through the gates.

Once inside the Outpost, we ate at a Zenadishj food stand and discussed how to get through the shopping as quickly as possible. Leaving the Outpost might take longer than entering it, and we wanted to be home before dark. That left us with only a few hours to enjoy the market place. The men went to buy the tools we needed and the women went to Mactil Street. Mother found exotic spices and other luxuries that couldn't be produced on the farm. She bought me a pale green blouse and Johnny a pair of new boots. At the Enavian shops she paid by scanning the ID marker implanted in her hand. At the Ceytalian shops she paid in Zenadishj currency. After the last shop she gave us the remaining coins and told Gabrielle to take us to the kiosk by Mactil Park. Later we would all meet at the fountain before going home.

The kiosk was manned by a young Zenadishj merchant about Gabrielle's age. To win her favor he allowed us to buy at an enormous discount. Johnny bought candy and magazines and I bought a bracelet of red stones. Gabrielle selected an Oramaklete scarf and rewarded the Zenadishj youth with a smile and flirtatious conversation that promised nothing.

As we continued through the market place, the holiday spirit evaporated and the people we passed seemed alert and focused on a purpose other than the pleasant meandering of holiday shoppers. Some shops were closing early, Gabrielle glanced uneasily down the street looking for our parents.

We came to the fountain in the center of the park. Gabrielle washed the dust and the heat of the afternoon from our faces. We saw our parents across the park coming towards us. Gabrielle waved and told us to stay put while she crossed the grass to meet them.

That was when the bomb exploded and for a few minutes we could see nothing but smoke. Emerging from the smoke was an army of Zenadishj warriors on horseback. It was as if we were transported to a different world. An older one, ancient and mythical.

The flash of laser rifles cut through the air killing Enavian and Ceytalian shoppers indiscriminately. The air cleared revealing dust and rubble where our parents once stood. As Gabrielle ran across the park, a Zenadishj warrior caught her by the hair and I saw his knife cut into her throat. For a moment I could only stand there covering my face with my hands until I remembered Johnny.

"Johnny, Johnny! Come on, we have to hide."
"Why, what's happening?"
"Never mind, just come on!"

As I grabbed his arm, I heard the sound of hooves thunder behind us. I turned and screamed. The two warriors gathered us up without bothering to dismount or stop. For a moment the world was dizzying swirl of color: the glitter of his weapons, the bronze of his skin, and the magenta blaze of his hair. I squirmed and kicked, struggling to get away. When he shook me impatiently, I bit his hand as hard as I could.

"*Aii! Oramaklete!*"

He struck my face with casual strength. His companion laughed.

"*Tenukeh, Neve?*"

"*Hessante!*"

After getting me under control, our captors joined the rest of their group. The man who held Johnny pulled out a knife and cut into the palm of our left hands and removed the glassy orange ID markers and tossed them into the debris the bomb had created. They bound up our wounds to stop the bleeding, then everyone scattered into different directions. The men who held us rode northwest towards the Negezos Mountains. Straining my neck, I looked back to catch a last glimpse of the Outpost.

Several hours later my bones began to ache. At first I had decided not to complain, just to show that I wasn't any weaker than they were. But after it became dark and there was no indication of them stopping, I began to whimper, not caring who knew how miserable I was. We traveled two days and nights, only stopping to find a bathroom place. I didn't see how it was possible to keep such a pace. I dozed off several times, but each time I glanced up at my captor he seemed as alert and rested as ever.

At the end of the third day we came to the camp of the Zenadishj slave traders.

TEJALURA

Chapter 3
The Captor: Neve Ce 1317 EE

> "We all become slaves to something. Our jobs, our families, our friends as well as our enemies, bargain for or steal slivers of our lives. But to sell children who should be the freest beings in the universe? There can be no greater evil."
>
> —*Senator Neral Tariv*

Spring 1317 EE

"We should have killed the girl," Tarim commented as I flexed my sore thumb.

"She has strong teeth," I grinned. "She'll bring a good price."

"If we can sell her. The Nejimenets don't buy slaves."

"No, but we might get Dassar Nul to buy them." I had noticed the tents of the slave trader among those of the Nejimenets. "But it would be better to sell to the Nejimenets because they would give us a better price. Dassar Nul drives a hard bargain."

As we spoke, a tall, blue-haired gypsy approached us. His face was familiar to me.

"We may be in luck, Tarim. I know that man." As he came closer, I greeted him in traditional Ceytalian: "I see you, Zarkhon Tehalchev."

"And I see you," he replied. "Though I have forgotten your name."

"Neve Ce," I enlightened him. "But the name of my father, Lord Halim Usul, may be more familiar to you. You visited our estates just outside of Halia Tehal seven years ago."

"Yes, I remember your father well. You were just a boy at the time, so you must forgive me for not recognizing you at first. We are honored by your presence. What may we do for you and your friend?"

"We have some slaves to sell. Two Enavian children, a boy and a girl."

"We are a free people, we do not buy or sell slaves."

"You could adopt them."

Zarkhon's smile was cynical, but amused.

"For a price, of course."

"Of course," I smiled in return.

"You can try to sell them in the morning. Perhaps Dassar Nul would be interested in them. As for tonight, you are welcome to stay with my family."

There is nothing to compare with the hospitality of the Nejimenets. Tarim and I could not have been more warmly received had we been Zarkhon's brothers. Although I was charmed by his entire household, I was especially taken with his wife, Silverwoman, an Oramaklete with shining white hair and silver-gray eyes. When she heard we had come to sell two Enavian children, she urged her husband to buy them both, sight unseen. But Zarkhon was adamant.

"If we were to buy them, it would only encourage the slave trade."

"But we can't let Dassar Nul buy them. What if he sells them to the pleasure houses? Or worse, to the cannibal Oramakletes? Zarkhon, they are only children."

Zarkhon had no answer for her, but his silence closed all opportunity for further appeal. In spite of his opposition, I thought there might be a potential sale in Zarkhon. He and his wife had been married for many years and were childless. Also, many of their friends and relatives had died when the Enavian Plague swept through their camp, making their loneliness more acute. Hard and uncompromising as Zarkhon liked to think he was, it was obvious he was fond of his Oramaklete wife, who, for her beauty alone, would be hard to deny anything.

Dassar Nul showed little interest in purchasing them.

"The truth is," he said, "you would have to pay me to take them off of your hands. Those children are Enavian. I saw them with their parents at the Outpost. The last thing I need right now is trouble with the Enavian authorities."

Although there was truth to what he said, there was little risk getting caught by the Enavian authorities. Ceytal was a large planet. He was probably paving the way for making a low opening bid in the event he became involved in the transaction.

Late the next morning, we woke the children to present them to the Nejimenets. Tarim took their blanket and spread it on the ground and motioned for them to sit on it.

Everyone in the caravan came to see them. The boy, frightened by the crowd, clung to his sister, but the girl showed no fear whatsoever.

Blinking against the glare of the sunlight, she stared back at the Nejimenets with those very aware eyes of hers. She measured us with far more self-assurance than I have seen in many adults. Although a show of some timidity would have bettered her chances of being sold, I could not help but admire this miniature adult.

We sold the boy first to one of Zarkhon's relatives, a divorced woman. She came forward alone, walking with a pronounced limp that drew attention to the ugly scar where the back tendon of her leg had been cut. Such is the punishment for a woman accused of adultery on Ceytal. Divorced women seldom remarry, so if they are childless, there is no one to care for them in their old age. Guessing she wanted the boy for an adopted son, I decided to drive a hard bargain.

She cursed me venomously, but in the end she paid the price and led the boy away. His sister tried to run after him. I pulled her roughly back and she began to kick me and beat me with her tiny fists. The onlookers laughed at my inability to control an Enavian child. In anger I slapped her hard across the face and immediately regretted the action. After such a scene, it would be impossible to sell her. For a long time no one spoke or moved.

Without consulting her husband, Silverwoman approached us with a stately grace of a queen. Her eyes met mine as boldly as an equal. Her voice when she spoke was amused but edged with contempt.

"The secret of Zenadishj martial arts is at last revealed: you develop your strength by hitting little girls."

She studied the Enavian girl for a long time, but did not appear impressed with what she saw. Without comment to either me or Tarim, she threw a can opener and a length of rope to the ground at our feet. The expression on her face, her very attitude, left no doubt this would be her offer, take it or leave it. She would not bargain.

Angry, I started to pull the girl away but Tarim stopped me.

"A little is better than nothing," he reasoned. "Haven't we made a good profit off the boy? Sell the girl. What will we do with her if we don't? Be wise and be rid of her now."

A quick glance in Dassar Nul's direction confirmed there would be no sale there. Any interest the slave trader may have had in the Enavian girl, however remote, had completely evaporated. Dassar Nul was deriving too much pleasure from my humiliation to end the game so soon.

I glared at Silverwoman, almost hating her. She was shrewd enough to know I could not kill the girl. She returned my glare with a seraphic smile. How I longed to say something, anything, to wipe that smile off of her face. I sauntered forward as if I were the victor and not she.

"It is a good thing you Nejimenets do not make your living in the slave trade, for you would certainly starve. In the market place I can get as much as two *zars* for the can opener alone. I would have accepted as little as four tenthpieces for such a disagreeable slave."

Silverwoman's smile only deepened.

"And if you had asked," she said, "I would have been willing to pay as much as seven *zars*. The girl has a strong heart. She will make a good daughter."

Chapter 4
The Stranger: Lillian Aleksandar 1317 EE

"A journey to Meneth-shir is a journey to another world that changes one forever. It takes less than a heartbeat for a foreigner to become a citizen."

— *Dr. Ura Jevetchev*

Spring 1317 EE

As I watched the Zenadishj ride away, a gentle hand touched my shoulder. It was the beautiful woman with pale hair. She smiled and indicated the camp with a graceful gesture of her hand.

"Dimmeh, khiseley."

I decided it was best to smile in return and allow myself to be led to camp. We were met by an old woman who, like many of the others around us, was busy packing. The young woman spoke with her, then pointed to me. The old woman glanced at me and shrugged.

"You speak Enavian, girl?"

I nodded.

"Good. I know Enavian. Your Lemmer Helt, the great general of your people, he teach me Enavian. You know Lemmer Helt?"

I shook my head. Lemmer Helt was a name from history books. I decided that she must be the oldest woman alive.

"Well, no matter. You listen now. This Silverwoman, she buy you."

The younger woman smiled and nodded, then spoke a few sentences that had to be translated.

"She say she love you. She say she want you to be happy. She say she want to be mother to you."

"I don't understand," I said. I wasn't trying to be difficult, but too much had changed too fast.

The old woman tried again.

"You listen now. When you learn to speak right, you obey Silverwoman. But until then, you obey me. Here, you help Yari and Hushé," she said pushing me towards two boys who were both about twelve years old.

For the next few hours the three of us helped gather things to be packed by the adults. In the distance I saw Johnny playing with the smaller children. I felt resentment. It was no different here than it was at home. I had to work while Johnny played.

"You no worry about other little boy," the old woman said noting the direction of my glance but mistaking my thoughts. "Kiakashe paid plenty for him. He be all right."

"I'm hungry."

"So Khai hungry. What that to me? First Khai work, then Khai eat. Understand?"

"No, what does *khai* mean?"

"That's you. I just think of it to call you."

"Why?"

"Because *khai* mean 'rope.' That's what Silverwoman buy you with. So I call you Khai. That best name I think of except maybe Good-For-Nothing. Now get to work!"

After everything was packed, we gathered beneath a tree to wait while the other families finished their packing. I stood off to one side, uncertain of my welcome. Silverwoman, seeing me hesitate, held out her hand in invitation and I sat beside her.

There was a great deal of laughter and conversation; the old woman and the two boys seemed to be the center of it all. I heard the word *khai* repeated several times and guessed they were talking about me. Although they smiled when they spoke, I felt uncomfortable not knowing what they were saying. I heard two phrases, *"Nu, Zishu,"* and *"Nu, Tejalura,"* repeated several times. Feeling drowsy, I lay my head on Silverwoman's lap and slept until we were ready to start our journey.

Silverwoman and I rode on the same horse, and Ancient, the old woman, rode beside us. Between the two of them I was learning their language. Not that I wanted to, but Ancient refused to use Enavian words once she explained their Nejimenet meaning, so I was forced to speak in their strange tongue.

With Silverwoman to balance me, I was able to relax and view the scenery on this slow-paced journey that was so different from my ride with the Zenadishj. Friends and relatives of Silverwoman came to meet me. I studied them with frank curiosity. Before my capture the only natives I had seen, except for Uncle Mheftu, were the beggars who lived just outside the Outpost. But these Nejimenets carried themselves with pride and, although dressed in their traveling clothes, they were clean.

They all smiled at me, eager to be friendly. I returned their smiles half-heartedly and completely on my guard. Although I couldn't understand very many of their words, I guessed from the tone of their voices they were saying the same condescending things adults universally said to children.

"Why Khai not speak with people?" Ancient asked. "They think maybe she not like them."

"Maybe I don't. I'm just watching them."

"What you watch for?"

I shrugged.

"They're different. I've never seen natives like these."

"You mean free? Hah! We are not Outpost dogs," she said drawing herself up proudly. "We are Nejimenets of Meneth-shir. We are a free people and rich. My son-in-law, Zarkhon, richest man in whole valley. He so rich that Silverwoman wears twenty-five necklaces, many bracelets for each arm and ankle. Many rings for fingers and toes. And Turquoise, who is only the widow of his brother, has ten necklaces and her daughter, Laughter, has five. No, we are not Outpost dogs. We are *N'jim-ijeh*. Blue Human Beings."

I didn't see much of Johnny during our journey to Meneth-shir, except off in the distance with the other boys, riding a horse of his very own! He always got the best of everything, I thought resentfully. It wasn't fair. For a while I would be moody and silent, but this would pass when Ancient began to tell me wonderful stories that I pretended not to listen to.

The spring evenings were mild enough for us to sleep out in the open air. Tucked inside my blankets, I would watch the stars while Ancient explained their meaning and order. Each constellation had a legend about it and Ancient was determined to recite each one for me. That woman never seemed to stop talking, but continued telling her stories one after another, gradually replacing Enavian words with Nejimenet.

I liked the Oramaklete stories the best. They explained why birds fly and where the sun goes each night and what secrets the winds whisper as they pass by. Sometimes Ancient would tell me things that conflicted with what I had been taught by the Enavians, such as why Ceytalians and Enavians have different colors of hair.

The Enavians thought they had different colors of hair because their races had originated from different galaxies. The Ceytalians believed that Nor, the king and father of all the gods, had used the colors of the earth to tint the hair of the Enavians—the gold of the sun for blond, earth for brown, fire for red, and obsidian for black. Nor's wife, Lady Itan, chose the colors of her jewelry for the Ceytalians—the blue of the turquoise, the magenta of the fire stone and the white of the pearl.

If the Ceytalian myths were not accurate, they were at least entertaining.

The worst part of the trip for me was the trail through Cela Pass. It seemed the higher the road went, the more narrow it became. In the valley below, what had been huge boulders and forest trees days before, now appeared to be pebbles and moss. Ancient had to bully me into keeping quiet enough not to scare the horse over the edge. Sometimes the road was blocked and we would have to stop while the men cleared the way. I closed my eyes so that I would not become dizzy. We were still traveling through Cela Pass when night approached. Fortunately there was a full moon to see by.

I'll never forget the first time I saw Arae Shjina, Silver Falls. The reflected moonlight transformed the falls into a shower of molten silver against the black cliff. At the sight of such beauty my fear of heights left me, never to return.

Hours later, we entered the valley of Meneth-shir, the permanent home of the Nejimenets. In the darkness I felt, rather than saw, the vastness of the caldera and off to one side was a mirror-smooth lake. I was too tired to walk and had to be carried into the great stone house by Silverwoman. She spread my blankets before the fireplace to make a bed for me. I was asleep before she could cover me.

·→※←··→※←··→※←·

The first thing I was aware of the next morning was the house. I felt the strength and age of every stone. The stones spoke to me in their silence, telling me they had stood for a thousand years and promised to stand for a thousand more. I closed my eyes to block out the strange feeling, but the stones of blue-gray granite continued their song of untold centuries.

Then I heard another song that was lighter and freer. It was a woman's voice, a happy voice. Mother! No, Mother was dead, I remembered suddenly. Hot tears flooded between my tightly shut lids as painful memories returned.

"Tejalura," I heard Silverwoman call. The others hadn't liked the name Ancient chose for me and had decided to call me Tejalura.

"Tejalura? What's the matter darling?"

The sound of my new name, the softness of Silverwoman's voice, and the fact that I could understand the alien language, all helped to make my misery more acute. I hated to cry, especially in front of others. I wanted to be alone until I could stop. I saw the two boys, Yari and Hushé, standing together looking as if they wished they could do something to help. Hushé stepped forward and presented me with a doll he had made. He smiled as he held it out for me to take.

"Here, Taji. This is for you."

Later I would appreciate the doll for what it was, a work of art. Even then Hushé had a distinctive style all his own. The beautifully carved face of the doll needed only touches of paint to accent her features. Like her head, her hands and bare feet were carved of rich, brown wood and attached to a cloth body. She was clothed in a dress dyed a deep rose. Her curly, turquoise hair hung past her waist in a long, thick braid. It was real hair, someone had cut their own in order to provide it for my doll, but I was too self-centered to wonder who.

In a flash of anger, I struck the doll from Hushé's hand and it hit the floor with a crash. From the expression on Hushé's face, one would have thought I had hit him, not the doll. I glanced at Yari, and from the expression on his face, I knew it was me he would have hit if Hushé had not stopped him.

"Wait, Yari. Don't. You heard what Aunt Silverwoman said. We have to be nice to her."

"I'm tired of being nice to her! So what if her parents got killed. Mine did too and no one is being nice to me. Or you either and your father's dead. What makes her so special?"

"At least we had a family to turn to. She doesn't have anybody except us."

"Well, that wasn't my idea. If it were up to me we'd give her back to the Zenadishj. She's nothing but a brat."

"Yari!" Silverwoman's voice cut across the room sharply. "Yari, I'm ashamed of you. You are being unfair and you know it. There is a big difference between one's parents dying of fever, as yours did, and being murdered by the Zenadishj, as Tejalura's were."

Yari flushed.

"That may be true, but I also know that Ancient isn't nice to her, and if Ancient were here Tejalura would have never hit the doll like that."

"Yari," Silverwoman said in a stern voice. "Yari, do you know your way?"

Her words were more of a statement than a question and had a profound effect on the boy. He lowered his head for a moment.

"Yes, I do," he said quietly.

"Good. Enough said. Now why don't you take Tejalura out to the lake and catch some fish. Get about ten."

"Ten!" the boys exclaimed in unison.

"All right then, fifteen."

Yari and Hushé exchanged a look. They had been uncertain they could catch the ten fish Silverwoman originally requested. Now that she expected them to catch fifteen, they decided to remain silent rather than risk having their quota raised to an even higher amount.

"Now remember," Silverwoman continued. "Tejalura is your sister. You are her brothers and must watch over her."

Although the bonds of the Nejimenet family members are the strongest in the universe, to an outsider the structure of those relationships will seem fluid to the point of being nonexistent. A person may live in six different households during their lifetime or live in one from birth to death. The terms "brother," "sister," "mother," and "father" are used loosely, making it very hard to determine exact relationships. An aunt or an older sister might be referred to as "mother." "Sister" can be a term of endearment a man might use for his wife, while "brother" might refer to a close friend who is not even a member of their household.

Relationships are formally defined by how close family members are related to each other by blood. First-blood relatives are siblings of the same father and mother. Second-blood relatives are parents, half-brothers, half-sisters, aunts, uncles, and immediate offspring. Third-blood relatives are grandparents, grandchildren, or cousins.

First- and second-blood relatives are forbidden to marry; otherwise, little importance is placed on blood relationships.

The Tehalchev household, which I was adopted into, was as complex as any other in Meneth-shir and it was some time before I had them all sorted out.

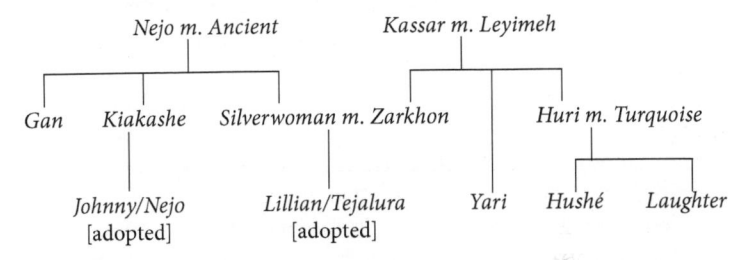

```
         Nejo m. Ancient              Kassar m. Leyimeh
        ┌────────┴────────┐          ┌────────┴────────┐
       Gan    Kiakashe   Silverwoman m. Zarkhon      Huri m. Turquoise
               │                      │              ┌────┼────┐
           Johnny/Nejo          Lillian/Tejalura    Yari  Hushé  Laughter
           [adopted]              [adopted]
```

Technically Yari was my uncle and Hushé my cousin, but they were close enough in age to make the word "brother" more applicable.

Hushé caught up my hand as they ran to the lake. I drew it back sharply, but I followed them outside. As the fresh air hit my face, I forgot my bad temper and gazed with wonder at the valley around us. Wild flowers of almost every imaginable color spread before us like a vast carpet. The dew from the grass was cold against my bare feet as I struggled to keep up with the boys.

"Do you think she understands us?" Hushé asked.

"A little, maybe."

"How much, I wonder?"

Yari shrugged. Over my head they exchanged winks.

"Do you suppose she's afraid of water?" Yari wondered aloud. "I sure would hate to get out to the middle of the lake and have her start screaming like she did back there on the mountain trail."

"She probably is. Those Enavians seem to have nervous children."

"Right. And look at her funny looking clothes."

"They're not half as funny as your clothes," I said hotly.

Yari and Hushé laughed, and I realized that I was tricked into speaking, which is what they wanted all along.

As we approached the lake I wondered if I would be afraid of the water. I hadn't been in a boat before and had only seen the Lemmer Helt River from a distance. Determined not to show any fear, I stepped into the boat with a studied nonchalance.

"Can you swim?"

I shook my head unable to speak.

"Don't worry, we'll *probably* be able to pull you out in time if you fall in," Hushé assured me.

"I'm not going to fall in," I said to reassure myself as well as them.

"All right, but if you do, take a deep breath," instructed Hushé.

"And make sure that you take a breath before you go under the water and not after," Yari added.

"I said I wasn't going to fall in!" I was angry they thought I was that stupid.

"Well, just remember if you do. Here, I'll show you how to fish. First, put some bait on the hook and throw it in the water."

I picked up the bug out of the jar. It was cold and slimy to the touch. They laughed at the expression on my face as I baited the hook. That done, I threw it in the water.

"Now what do I do?"

"You wait for the fish to come."

"How will I know when it comes?"

"The fish will pull on the line."

His last answer sounded so exasperated I didn't ask any more questions. I caught two fish before either of them caught their first. At the third fish, my line broke, leaving the rest to be caught by Yari and Hushé. Altogether, we caught eleven. I felt that I hadn't done too badly for myself, considering that it was my first time.

On the way back we were met by Laughter, Hushé's older sister. She waved to us eagerly. I noticed her tight, curly hair had been bobbed short and guessed she had been the one to provide the hair for my doll. Laughter, the most affectionate one of our household, certainly lived up to her name and was easily the most popular girl among the Nejimenets. I hoped she hadn't heard how I had hit the doll.

With her was Geysan, one of the farm laborers, but that wasn't unusual for he was often with her. He was a rather pleasant fellow, solid and predictable, always friendly and ready to laugh. Although he hadn't formally offered for Laughter, it was understood they would marry someday.

"We saw you three out on the lake. How did you do?" he asked. "Ah, Yari. Five! Hushé, four! And Tejalura—only two? What happened?"

"My line broke," I mumbled.

"Oh, well, that's bound to happen. Even to the best of us."

"She didn't do too bad," Yari put in. "She caught her two before Hushé or I caught any at all."

"When we reached the house, they taught me how to clean my fish. Yari took up a fish and his knife."

"Here, take the fish and slit its belly, like this. Now, put your fingers through, like that."

He took another fish and cleaned it with lightning speed.

"Now, you try," he said handing me the knife.

It was worse than baiting the hook. With my first fish, the guts squirted me in the eye, the next stained my shirt. I reached for a third fish, but Laughter stopped me.

"That's all right, Tejalura. You've cleaned your two. Let's go up to your room and change your clothes."

Until Laughter mentioned it, I hadn't known I had a room or even a change of clothes. During the journey I wore the cotton shorts and blouse I was abducted in, keeping them somewhat clean by washing them in the river. By now my clothes were in terrible condition.

My room was upstairs and it was large, at least it was much larger than the one I had shared with Gabrielle. The wooden floor was covered with a richly colored rug, and the few pieces of furniture were constructed of heavy, solid wood. There was a large tub filled with steaming hot water. I washed myself thoroughly then shivered as I dried myself off in the cold spring air.

Laughter opened the chest at the foot of the bed and pulled out a dress and a pair of sandals. My dress was made of soft, brown material that gathered at the waist and came to my knees. My sandals were made of red dyed leather.

Unable to brush the tangles out of my hair, Laughter was forced to cut it nearly as short as her own. I told her that I wished my hair was blue and curly like hers rather than being black and straight.

"Don't be silly, Taji. You have beautiful hair. It's so thick. No one in the valley has hair so thick."

"But I want blue hair."

"There are blue highlights in your hair when you stand in the sunlight, is that good enough? Tejalura, you must be happy with what Ce has given you."

It was still early in the afternoon when we went downstairs. Outside, people were sitting under trees taking a nap or in small groups talking and laughing quietly. I followed Laughter to a tree off to ourselves. I cupped my chin in my hands and gazed at the splendor of the valley before me. It was all so peaceful, so quiet, like a spell cast by a fairy. I felt my lids growing heavy, so I curled up beside Laughter and went to sleep.

Like a wild thing, not yet accustomed to new surroundings, I sensed someone approaching us and was immediately awake. It was Geysan. He touched his finger to his lips, signaling me to keep quiet. With a blade of grass he tickled Laughter's nose until dimples appeared in her cheeks. Her eyes fluttered open.

"Beast! You'd better be careful how you treat me from now on. I have Tejalura to protect me."

He studied me with mock seriousness.

"And a vicious looking guard dog she is too. She'll bear watching."

With a casual hand he mussed my hair and the three of us walked back to the house. As we entered the door I smelled the food and my stomach growled; I hadn't realized how hungry I was.

Silverwoman called a greeting to us and asked me to help her set the table. When all was ready the entire household gathered around the table and Zarkhon asked us, as he had each night during our journey to Meneth-shir:

"To whom does this food belong?"

"It belongs to Ce," we answered.

I was not exactly sure who or what Ce was, and I was almost certain my Enavian mother would have disapproved of me participating in a pagan rite, but I recited the words with the others just the same. Laughter smiled and squeezed my hand.

All around me was the warm glow of candlelight and bright colors, the blue of the Nejimenet's hair being predominant. A few had some green in their hair, others had dark royal blue, while still others, like Laughter's, shown pure turquoise. For the first time I noticed how pretty she was. Her skin was golden except where her cheeks and lips blushed pink. Her warm, topaz eyes were bright with interest as Yari and Hushé related our afternoon's adventure to her.

THE STRANGER: LILLIAN ALEKSANDAR

The conversations around me went so fast I could only understand a word or two. If I closed my eyes and didn't listen too closely, I could almost imagine I was back at the homestead along the Lemmer Helt River. I wondered what Johnny was doing.

Feeling vaguely empty and alone, I went to my room after dinner. There on my bed, waiting for me was the blue-haired doll. Climbing onto the bed I picked her up and with a tiny finger I traced her profile and smiled.

"You're not ugly," I told her. "You're just different. I'm going to name you Khai. That is my old name, but I don't need it anymore. You see I have a new name now. It's Tejalura."

Of course I had another name, Lillian, but it didn't seem appropriate to give a blue-haired doll an Enavian name.

TEJALURA

Chapter 5
The Daughter: Tejalura 1317-1323 EE

> A man's strength may be counted in his sons.
> But his joy and delight will be in his daughter,
> his jewel.
>
> —*Neve Ce*

Planting Season 1317 EE

As soon as our household was settled, we began the spring planting. We would rise in the morning while it was still dark and do the chores around the house, then as darkness became dawn, we all went outside. Yari, Hushé and I shivered in the icy mountain air as we ran barefoot through the wet grass. We threw dirt clods at each other as well as our dog, Bear Paw, who, barking, ran circles around the three of us. Ancient put a stop to it all by telling us to put our shoes on and get to work.

And work we did! There was a new field to be cleared on the west side of our property. We followed behind Geysan and the plow horse and gathered the stones as they were turned up in the soil. Zarkhon and the other men went ahead of us and pulled out the larger stones that were in Geysan's way. All the stones would later be used to reinforce the walls that divided the fields. No matter how hard I worked, Yari and Hushé were able to gather twice as many as I did. At midday Silverwoman called me in to help her prepare the food.

"Why can't I gather as many rocks as Yari and Hushé?" I asked her.

"You're not as big as they are. You can't expect to."

"It's not because I'm a girl is it?"

"No, that has nothing to do with it. Look at Ancient, she gathers more than any of us."

"But she's not a girl. She's old."

Silverwoman smiled.

"Besides," I continued, "She's mean and ugly!"

I don't know what caused me to say such a thing, but I immediately regretted doing so at the change in Silverwoman's expression.

"You must not say things like that, Tejalura. That is not our way."

It was the next day that I found the bone. At first I thought it was another stone. I grasped it firmly with both of my hands and pulled as hard as I could. It soon gave way, causing me to fall backwards. It was a human femur. I screamed and dropped it. The boys were the first to reach me.

"What's the matter with her? It's just a bone."

Ancient held me in her arms.

"Khai, Khai. Be still, be still."

My screams trailed off to a hoarse whimper as I dully watched Yari and Hushé gather the rest of the bones and take them away.

"There, that's better. The bone can't hurt you. That was probably my husband's grandmother. I remember she wanted to be buried under a tree that used to be here."

I shivered. I had come from a world where the bodies of the dead were kept in graveyards. But in Meneth-shir it was different, the ashes and bones of the deceased would be buried at the site they had indicated as their favorite place. It might be a shadowy spot in the forest or in the family garden or even at the crossroads where the paths of the living passed daily.

For the first time, death became very real to me. I had seen my family murdered, but the memory of it had the unreality of a nightmare. The finality of death had not fully registered in my mind until I held that bone in my hand. At that moment death became an assured fact; a frightening one. A few days later I decided to ask Ancient about it.

"What happens when we die?" I asked. "I mean, what do we look like? Where do we go? What do we do?"

She looked up from her work and smiled.

"So that is what you have been so serious about these last few days. You think about things for a long time, Khai. That is good."

For a time she was silent, until I thought she would not answer me, when she said:

"You have seen the bear worm spin his cocoon. He will sleep and at the appointed time he comes out, transformed into a creature with jewel colored wings. It will be the same with you."

"But the bear worm spins a cocoon, I get buried in the dirt."

Irritated that I had missed her analogy, she scowled at me and tried again.

"Yes, Tejalura, you get buried and so do seeds. And, in their time, they grow into something a thousand times greater than if they had never been buried."

"So dying is good?"

She shrugged.

"It is simply the way things are."

From then on we had a better understanding of each other. I could not truthfully say I loved her yet, but it was a start. The bond between us would grow until I can now say that knowing her was one of the richest experiences of my life.

Ancient was not a native of Meneth-shir, she was born in Yalangi, a village of Oramaklete cannibals. Her husband had ordered her to kill Silverwoman, their newborn daughter, one winter when they had no food. Instead she killed her husband and had to flee to the Naritian Prairie where she met the caravan of Nejimenets returning to Meneth-shir. Although she married a Nejimenet and adopted them as her people, to some extent she remained different from the peace-loving people of Meneth-shir. Yet, out of all my new family, it was this reformed cannibal tribeswoman who was to teach me the most about being Nejimenet.

"I am going to tell you the truth, Tejalura," she said to me one day. "Only the people of Meneth-shir are truly happy and do you know why?"

"Why?"

"Because only they understand how to live according to the ways of Ce. The Oramakletes do not, nor do the Zenadishj, and neither do the Enavians—gods help them all. Only the Nejimenet people appreciate and properly use the blessings that Ce has made available to us all."

"Who is Ce?"

"He is God, the one true god of us all. It is a good thing you came to live with us, Tejalura. Otherwise, you would never have learned about Ce."

"My mother used to tell me about a god who was the one true god of the Enavians," I said. "But His name wasn't Ce."

Ancient smiled. Her smiles were rare and difficult to win. She said to me teasingly:

"Well, either there is one god with two names or two gods making the same claim."

After the fields were cleared, it was she who taught me how to plant the different kinds of seed. We children would make a game of it, seeing who could plant the most rows. If any of us should finish a row at the same time we would race to the next one. I might have been slow at gathering stones, but I was able to hold my own planting seed. Ancient would laugh at our games.

"Why hurry?" she would say. "There is work enough for all and time enough to do it in."

It was she who made me aware of the miracle that occurred in the valley during the following weeks. It happened when we were repairing the leaks in our roof against the winter rains that would soon be coming.

"Look about you, Tejalura!"

With her hand she made the sweeping motion of a sorceress that encompassed the patchwork quilt of ripening fields Meneth-shir had become.

"Weeks ago," she said with wonder. "It was only weeks ago that all of this was but handfuls of seed in our hands."

I understood then why she used the planting of seed to describe death and rebirth. Whenever I have been threatened by death, I think of that clear autumn day on the rooftop with Ancient; and with the memory of those vast, golden fields, I lose my fear.

Autumn 1317 EE

After harvest, came school. Nejimenet children attend school as soon as they are able to speak and spend their first year learning their numerals and alphabet. As soon as they have mastered them, they learn to read and write simple words. Then they advance to sentences, which are usually excerpts of religious and historical writings. As they progress, their studies become more specialized and they are then given an opportunity to learn whatever they are interested in or talented at under the guidance of an older person.

School was held at Itan-shir, an island in the middle of Lake Melia. Centuries ago, the gray stone buildings on the island had been a temple complex used as a worship center, as well as living quarters for the priesthood. When the people of Meneth-shir became monotheistic, the priesthood was disbanded and the buildings were converted to studios, workshops, and classrooms. The main temple became the council room where a group of representatives (which must include at least one member from each household) would meet to discuss community issues. Only the library and the storage room retained their original purposes. Socially, as well as historically and geographically, Itan-shir Island is the very heart of Meneth-shir.

I could hardly wait to attend classes there, but first I would have to learn to read and write in Nejimenet. It was decided Johnny and I would be instructed privately by Laughter until we could join our age group. My brother seemed glad to see me, but he refused to speak Enavian.

"My name is Nejo Akashechev," he said loftily. "And I speak the language of Human Beings."

I felt like kicking him under the table, but I knew Laughter would not have allowed it.

Our first lesson was to learn to write our formal and informal names. My formal name was Ura Tehalchev, which meant "Light Moon Household." My informal name, Tejalura, meant "Moonlight." Johnny's formal name, Nejo Akashechev, meant "Friend Bear Household" and his informal name, Nejo, meant "Friend."

Not only was Johnny's Nejimenet more fluent than mine, his mind was quicker as well, so he was able to join his age group before I was.

"Don't feel bad, Tejalura," Laughter said. "Nejo had less to learn than you to catch up."

But that wasn't the only reason, I was simply a slower learner. At the Enavian school I had begun to learn to read and write. I hadn't been able to read very well, but I understood the difference between numbers and letters and could read simple phrases. Now I had to start over again with a new alphabet and a new set of numbers. Also Enavians wrote from left to right and the Nejimenets, as well as all other Ceytalian races, wrote from right to left. I was very confused and frustrated.

Each member of my household took it upon himself to help me with my studies. Even Zarkhon would patiently sit for hours teaching me to read and count. It was Hushé who was able to explain things to me best, so he was excused from his classes to tutor me. It seemed I would never learn, and often I found myself crying in sheer frustration. Then came the day it all made sense. When I was able to read through two short books and add and subtract simple sums, Hushé and the others felt I was ready to join my class.

It was an exciting day for me. I clutched my books tightly as I walked beside Yari and Hushé. It wasn't a long walk; the bridge to the island was just down the road from our home. It had snowed these last few weeks, winter was really here.

Before coming to Meneth-shir, I had seen snow only from a great distance on the Negezos Mountains. I will never forget the beauty of that first white morning. I ran outside to touch it and was followed by Yari, Hushé and Bear Paw. We played until Silverwoman called us in. Yari and Hushé told me the lake would become solid enough to walk on and soon we would be ice-skating. I had never heard of ice-skating and suspected they were making it all up to tease me. I was afraid to question them for fear of appearing ignorant, so I affected disinterest until their attention was focused elsewhere.

We were the first to arrive, so we helped the teachers and workers start the fires. We watched them set up their equipment for the day's work. There were all types of craftsmen: weavers, jewelers, blacksmiths, potters, carpenters, leather workers, etc. Some of them were permanent or long-term craftsmen, others were there working on a short-term basis to make special projects for their household. A few months ago, I had been there with Geysan and Hushé to make new furniture for our family. Hushé enjoyed it so much he decided to be a shift worker for a year and learn something about all of the crafts by helping out wherever he was needed.

As the fires began to warm the rooms, other students and workers began to arrive, so I sat on the floor with the others of my group.

Our teacher was Aunt Kiakashe. With her brother, she had served in the Zenadishj Army and fought against the Enavian Empire and the Oramaklete tribesmen. Upon retirement she returned to Meneth-shir battle-scarred, but very wealthy. Years later, when I told my Enavian friends the famous General She Bear had become a school teacher, they could not believe it. Actually she was a very good teacher and possessed the rare combination of discipline and sensitivity. Knowing that I was shy, she did not call upon me to recite the lessons, but assumed I was able to keep up with the assignments. As I relaxed enough to join in with the group, she discovered I was somewhat ahead of the others and considered advancing me to the next group. But when she saw I was making friends, she decided against a change at that time.

One day Yari and Hushé burst into the house and, stamping snow off of their feet, announced that the magic thing had happened. The lake was frozen solid, and no one would be going to school that day, not even the teachers. Geysan had been making me a pair of ice skates in secret and finished them just in time. They were beautifully made of light brown, hand-tooled Zenadishj leather. I could hardly wait to show the others.

"Don't put them on now, Taji. Wait until we get to the lake."

Imitating the way Yari and Hushé slung their skates over their shoulders, I followed them outside. The blue-green shadows of the pine trees peeked through layers of fresh snow. All about us was a world of utter stillness and peace. I smiled.

Suddenly Silverwoman ran ahead of us, laughing. Dressed in her gray furs, her pale beauty seemed a part of the silvery landscape about us. I tried to imagine how I appeared to the others. Was I pretty? I was wearing one of Hushé's old red shirts. Red had been one of Gabrielle's most becoming colors . . .

"Stop daydreaming, Taji, and get your skates on."

The boys controlled their impatience, taking time to make sure I had laced my skates tight enough and helped me on to the ice. Although I fell many times, I did not quit until everyone else did. I was determined to skate! We didn't return until late that afternoon. I was tired and bruised, but thoroughly in love with winter.

For the next few days there was no school. We would rush through our chores so that we could spend as much time as possible ice-skating. Late in the afternoon we would return home to find cups of steaming hot chocolate waiting for us. By the time we returned to school I was skating as well as the others.

Once we were snowed in for a couple of days, and the women of the Tehalchev household decided to pierce my ears.

"But let Mother do it," Silverwoman said to the others. "I couldn't stand to hurt her myself."

Ancient, grumbling that she always had to do the dirty work for me from the very first, placed ice behind my ears and quickly stabbed the thick needles through. I sat there stiffly, determined not to show the slightest sign of pain, for after all, I was a Human Being.

"Here, Taji. Look in the mirror and see how pretty you are now," Laughter urged.

The golden earrings made me look like an exotic gypsy—but was I pretty? My reflected dark eyes blinked back at me like a question, uncertain and hopeful. And what of the rest? The tiny brows, the nonexistent nose, the solemn mouth, and determined chin. Pretty? No compared with Laughter's brilliant coloring, I felt myself to be plain and dull.

But someday I would be pretty. After all, I was Gabrielle's twin sister.

Spring 1318 EE

As the weather grew warmer, we were encouraged to spend more time outside. I learned to play *mheftuli*, Ceytalian kick ball. The Nejimenet version we played was the most aggressive, I still have scars from those games. I was a lot smaller than the others my age, but soon, with their help, I developed my skill and speed to the point my size was not a hindrance. In fact, I was in demand as a team member in the general games—even Hushé and Yari wanted to have me on their teams.

It was time for planting again the fields had to be cleared of rocks that had come up during the winter. I still wasn't able to gather as many rocks as Yari and Hushé were, but when it came to planting I was able to plant a few more rows each day than they were.

I would usually spend my afternoons with Geysan and Laughter; they seemed to prefer my presence to being alone. I thought this was strange because Gabrielle had always chased me off when one of her admirers came to visit her. One afternoon Geysan and I, joining forces, teased Laughter mercilessly. Then, without warning, I took Laughter's part against Geysan.

"You have the true instincts of a mercenary, Tejalura," he accused.

"Isn't General Kiakashe my teacher?" I reasoned. "I've decided to join the Zenadishj Army, like she did, and make my fortune."

"Listen to her!"

"I will, I tell you. Just wait and see. I'll ride before a legion of hand-picked men and become a hero by driving the Enavians off the face of Ceytal."

I stopped, suddenly remembering that I was Enavian. I had been with Nejimenets a little over a year, yet I could scarcely remember another existence.

"I thought you were going to be a mountaineer like Yari and Hushé," Geysan reminded.

"Oh, well . . . that too."

That year the harvest celebration was a time of special happiness for our household because Geysan formally offered for Laughter. They would be married during the next *yaremida*. Each *yaremida*, or wolf winter, the Nejimenets form a caravan and go down to Narit for trade and to satisfy their need to travel and to avoid the bitterly cold winters that occur every third year. They meet with the Mountain Zenadishj to jointly celebrate a wedding festival known as the Ceremony of the Chosen. It is quite a display and Zenadishj tribes throughout Narit come to witness or take part in it.

We spent the following winter making our clothes for the wedding. Yari and I were to stand as *veshes* for Geysan and Laughter. Hushé and Tzeri were to stand for Dev and Liamet, who were members of the Sun household. To stand as *veshe* for a relative is the most important role a child can have in any ceremony. We each had a small speech to memorize as well as the words to the wedding song.

Yari and Hushé were fitted first. They would be fifteen next winter and felt very grown-up and important. Then it was my turn, and it seemed that everyone had decided to make as much of the occasion as possible.

"Now turn around and let us see you," Laughter commanded.

I turned around very slowly, holding my breath, and waited for their verdict.

"You were right, Grandmother," Laughter conceded. "Red is her color, she looks like an Urthic princess. What color should we embroider the edges? Gold?"

"No, silver," said Ancient decisively. "Silver with blue to match the turquoise jewelry she will wear. I will do the embroidering myself."

"You look beautiful, Taji. I'm certainly glad you are to be my *veshe* and not that fat pig, Tzeri."

"Laughter!" Silverwoman was shocked, and well she might be. Not only was Tzeri the great-granddaughter of Dejo, the Elder, but she was also a member of the Sun household. In ancient times their family formed the priesthood. Even though the priesthood was abolished long ago, the members of the Sun household were still highly respected.

"She merely speaks the truth," Ancient said. "Tzeri is a fat pig, and the grace of a *veshe's* dress is wasted on her. But Tejalura—look at her. She is perfection."

A few weeks earlier I would have spoken up in Tzeri's defense for we had been friends. But lately she had taken to ridiculing me and telling our secrets to the other children for no reason I could think of. I was too embarrassed to tell anyone in the Tehalchev household about it; I thought they would be ashamed of me. I realized then that I wasn't alone. I was a member of the Tehalchev household and they would always stand by me.

·→※←·→※←·→※←·

Winter 1320 EE

The next *yaremida* Zarkhon wouldn't allow me to ride my own horse on the journey to Narit because he thought I was too little. But in the distance I saw Johnny riding his own beautiful black pony. Apparently Aunt Kiakashe didn't think he was too little.

It was well past the fourth quarter of the day when we arrived outside the city of Halia Tehal. We sent two of our men ahead to obtain permission from Queen Ceymar to camp outside the city gates. The next morning I woke early to help Ancient start the fire. As usual, too late to be of any help, Yari burst into the tent all smiles. He hadn't been home all night.

"Good morning, Grandmother," he said cheerfully to Ancient. He reached into the pot to take a piece of meat, but Ancient shooed him away. "Good morning, Taji," he mussed my hair, causing it to fall in my eyes. Scowling, I brushed it back. Yari picked up his jacket and started to leave, and said almost as an afterthought to Ancient:

"Tell Zarkhon I'm going into the city with Hushé. We'll be back before dark."

Ancient grabbed him by the collar before he could duck outside the tent.

"Not so fast, Yari. You're taking Taji with you."

THE DAUGHTER: TEJALURA

"What?!"

"You heard me. Taji, get your *mahtil*."

"I don't want to take that baby with me," he protested.

"I didn't ask if you did. Taji's been doing a lot of work lately while you run loose all over the countryside. It won't kill you to watch her for one day."

"But, Grandmother—"

"I'm not listening."

"What am I going to do with her tagging along?" he wanted to know.

"You'll stay out of trouble for one thing. Maybe. Now I don't want to hear anymore back-talk from you. You may be the biggest boy in camp, but you're not too big for me to give you a good thrashing when you need it. Taji, hurry up."

"Oh, I'll just stay here with you. I really don't want to go into the city today," I lied. Well, I didn't really, not if Yari was going to hate my guts for it.

"No, you'll just be in the way," Ancient said. "Go with Yari. He won't mind—will you, Yari?"

"Of course not. I'm thrilled to death."

She shot him a glance.

"Go on, Taji. Get your *mahtil*."

"No, really, I'll stay."

But Ancient would not hear of it, so I wrapped the *mahtil* around my head and followed Yari through the opening of the tent.

"I'm sorry," I said when we got outside.

"Shut up."

I shrugged and we continued to walk in silence. I had a hard time keeping pace with him. True, he was a lot bigger than I was and could take bigger steps, but I was sure he was walking fast on purpose.

"Slow down, Yari. I can't keep up with you."

"Well, walk faster. You don't expect me and Hushé to walk slow just for you, do you?"

I tried to catch up, but he had quickened his pace even more.

"Yari, you're doing it on purpose."

"What?" He walked a little faster.

"You know what."

"No, I don't." Still faster.

"Stop that!"

"Taji, will you quit acting like a baby."

"Well, quit being so mean. It isn't my fault I have to go with you. I didn't want to go."

"Taji, if you cry I'll hit you, I swear I will. Here, I'll walk slower. How's that?"

I nodded.

"Good, it's probably that dress. You can wear some of Hushé's old clothes; they used to be mine anyway. But you have to promise not to get in our way or tattle on us when we get back."

"I won't."

We saw Hushé standing outside the tent, waiting. He waved to Yari, but his smile fell when he saw me.

"What's she doing here?" he asked.

"She's coming with us," Yari informed him. "Ancient made me bring her."

"Oh, great!"

"Don't worry, she'll be all right," Yari said when he saw my face start to crumple. "Why don't we let her wear some of your old clothes. She'll walk faster in pants."

"All right," he said resignedly. "Go on in, Taji. Only Mother is there."

I entered the tent and Turquoise showed me where to find the clothes. As I was changing I heard them talking outside.

"Why don't we leave her now while we have the chance?" Hushé urged.

There was a moment's pause.

"No," Yari decided.

"Why not? What's the matter with you?"

"Nothing. It's just—oh, she'll probably go crying to Ancient and Silverwoman. I'm in enough trouble as it is."

Swallowing my hurt feelings, I pretended I hadn't heard what Hushé said and joined them outside. I was determined to enjoy our excursion into the city. Perhaps I would catch a glimpse of the queen.

The line at the city gates was long but moved quickly. Visitors, as well as guards at the inspection point, were in a festive mood. During the *yaremida*, caravans of traders and entertainment troupes from all parts of Narit and beyond scheduled their routes to ensure their attendance at the Ceremony of the Chosen.

THE DAUGHTER: TEJALURA

How can I describe Halia Tehal? It was an enchanted city. The magenta-haired Zenadishj dressed in exotically dyed materials of clashing colors that by some miracle harmonized beautifully. The marketplace, with its coffee shops, produce stalls, and mysterious alleyways, fascinated me. Any merchandise imaginable could be bought or sold there. During the *yaremida* all the races under the Ceytalian sun were represented there so that my own black hair, as well as the blue hair of my brothers, brought us no special attention.

Soon we met with Tzeri and others who used to be my friends. They were with a group of sophisticated Zenadishj aristocrats. The Zenadishj girls in their group were old enough to veil themselves in public, but during the *yaremida* adult supervision was lax and the Zenadishj youth ran a little wild. The girls laughed openly with the boys their age and smoked cigarettes to show how grown-up they were. They began talking animatedly to my brothers as soon as we joined their group. Tzeri and her friends ignored me completely, except to "accidentally" blow smoke in my face. Their attitude towards me was not lost on their new friends. The prettiest Zenadishj girl, who seemed especially interested in Hushé, came up to me and said in a loud voice:

"And what is this? A boy or a girl?"

"She is our sister," Hushé said stiffly.

She tossed her head, a gesture of contempt that caused the glittering jewels in her hair to sparkle like sunlight on water. The tinkling of her earrings and bracelets filled the afternoon air.

"Sister? Ha! She looks like a *teyado*," she said using the derogatory term for Erteyans.

The others laughed but Yari and Hushé were dangerously quiet. Although they loved nothing better than to bully and torment me, this was their exclusive right as my older brothers and no one else's.

Guessing that, for once, my brothers' sympathy was in my favor, I became bold and kicked Tzeri's shin with my heavily booted foot. She screamed in surprise and pain and struck out at me with her fist. I was unable to duck fast enough so my left eye caught the full impact of her blow. But I recovered quickly and was able to hit her squarely on the mouth.

While I was busy, I noticed that Yari and Hushé were fighting the others. As we were both outsized and outnumbered, we did well to hold our own, but it was clear we would have gotten the worst of it if the authorities hadn't put a stop to it and returned us to our camp. Fortunately, the event caused no friction between the Zenadishj and our people, but was regarded with amusement by everyone.

The next morning Silverwoman and Ancient did their best to make me presentable for the Ceremony of the Chosen, but a neatly pressed dress and a freshly scrubbed face could not detract from the angry bruise on my eye. My only consolation was the fat lip I had given Tzeri. She must look just as bad, if not worse, than I did. But when she took her place among the other *veshes*, I saw that the swelling on her lip had gone down so it was hardly visible. Still I noted with some satisfaction, that she walked with a pronounced limp.

"Hey, Limp Leg!" I taunted as she passed me to find her place in line. Yari jabbed me with his elbow sharply for Aunt Kiakashe was nearby fussing over Johnny. Tzeri said nothing but glared at me as she limped by.

The Nejimenets and the Mountain Zenadishj have been friends for centuries and occasionally there is intermarriage. Kinsmen and friends, who may see each other only once every three years, have much to catch up on so the Ceremony of the Chosen is a major social event for both races. Enavians consider our weddings to be the most barbaric in the empire.

Understandably, the Ceremony of the Chosen must appear to be a rather brutal affair to the eyes of an outsider. The grooms, mounted on their horses, are lined up on one side of the field while the fathers, with their daughters, are lined up on the other side. Although the wedding arrangements are already finalized, each groom approaches the father of the bride and publicly offers for the woman of his choice. The father, just as formally, accepts and gives the groom the leather thong that binds the wrists of the bride. The grooms line up for the race. The horse race is the part of the ceremony Enavians find the most appalling, but it is not nearly so dangerous as it appears. The Nejimenets are excellent horsemen and the brides can release themselves from the leather thongs any time they wish. At the most, one is only a little scratched and bruised.

The origins of this ceremony can be traced back to the days when Nejimenet warriors chose their wives from war captives. But over the centuries, ruthlessness has been replaced by tradition. Today, the ceremony is completely controlled by centuries of rigid etiquette.

THE DAUGHTER: TEJALURA

The wedding song of the *veshes* is the most beautiful I have ever heard. The words are in Ancient Ceytalian and are almost unintelligible to either race, yet it has been faithfully memorized over the years so that the Zenadishj and Nejimenet *veshes* may sing in complete harmony each *yaremida*.

As we passed the queen, her glance fell on me and rested there for the briefest of moments; perhaps the color of my hair had caught her attention. She gave me a conspiratorial wink. I dared to smile in return.

Next came the brides, led by their fathers or male guardians. Then the grooms rode forward in their turn; Geysan looking especially magnificent on Silverwoman's dapple gray. Zarkhon and Geysan bowed to each other respectfully and recited the lines that have been repeated each *yaremida* for centuries.

"*Jevim*, your niece has found favor in my eyes. Her beauty is surpassed only by her gentle spirit."

"You are a proven warrior of many deeds of greatness," Zarkhon answered. "Take my niece and may she earn her bride-price."

Geysan took the wine cup as I handed it to him; it was scarcely half full. He gave the two of us a suspicious look. Yari smiled innocently, unaware that his upper lip was stained dark red. Belatedly, I wiped my own mouth on my sleeve.

During the race, Yari and I screamed ourselves hoarse so that when Laughter and Geysan won, we could hardly cheer their victory. Queen Ceymar presented them with a large amount of gold, and as a special sign of favor, she gave Laughter the ruby and diamond necklace that she wore. This is no small honor, for her people consider her a goddess.

The wedding feast was a complete blur to me. I was already dizzy from the wine Yari and I drank from the wedding cup. I might have been all right if I had remained under Silverwoman's watchful eye, but one of the duties of the *veshe* is to serve wine and make sure the cups of the guests do not go empty. This was a difficult job, for the Zenadishj are heavy drinkers and the Nejimenets were matching their pace.

The babble of voices surged about me like a rushing stream. I felt detached, as if I were underwater or in a dream.

"I know you have already married off five of your daughters, but this is my first. Thanks be to Ce, I have but two daughters left . . . "

"Did you see my Leyimeh? She was the most beautiful of all . . . "

"And the children, especially Yari and that little dark-haired girl of Zarkhon's, Tejalura. Isn't she a pretty little thing? And so tiny, she has the bones of a little bird."

"She scarcely looks five seasons old, yet Silverwoman tells me she will be eleven next autumn."

"Yes, but then I suppose Enavian children are smaller. The other one, Nejo, is small for his age, too."

"Isn't that wonderful about Geysan and Laughter? Oh, thank you, Tejalura. Yes, I would like some more wine."

"You look very pretty in your dress, Tejalura."

"Dasha, Jevema."

Suddenly Turquoise was beside me.

"Tejalura, have you seen Hushé or Yari?"

With an effort I made my eyes focus on her face and I shook my head. This was a mistake for the world began to spin and I thought for a moment I would lose my balance.

"Do you think you could find them for me? We don't want them to cause any more trouble with the Zenadishj. And if they are causing trouble, don't join them."

"I won't, Aunt Turquoise."

I wandered about for hours trying to locate them. I made my way through the genial crowd with a smile of beaming good will plastered on my face. It seemed that the whole earth had become my friend. At last I found them both off behind a tree being sick. Not only had they drunk too much wine, but they had tried to smoke Zenadishj cigarettes. I went to get help from the others. Passing a mixed group of Nejimenets and Zenadishj, I heard Aunt Kiakashe say to another:

"No, that is Tejalura. She is no Urthic slave! She is a daughter of Meneth-shir."

·→✻←··→✻←··→✻←·

It was good to come home to Meneth-shir and work in the fields and rest in the lazy afternoons. Harvest came and went, and it was time for school again. I was doing so well with my math Aunt Kiakashe thought I should be allowed to study it at an even higher level than Yari and Hushé.

THE DAUGHTER: TEJALURA

I was a fast runner and in demand as a teammate for *mheftuli*. My enemies had narrowed down to one, Tzeri. Yet, our traded blows and insults were done more out of habit than in earnest.

The first wash day of spring is always a special day, but it seemed even brighter than usual that following year. Sunlight sparkled through brilliant green leaves, nearly blinding my eyes. It didn't even bother me that my short legs had to run as fast as they could to keep up with the adults. The air was so fresh and sweet, I felt I could go on forever.

"That bundle you're carrying is nearly as big as you are, Tejalura," Turquoise said, smiling with amusement at my awkward progress.

I shot her a quick smile, much too out of breath to answer. Two identical little faces watched me with superior detachment from the backpacks on Turquoise's and Laughter's shoulders. Turquoise might have been the mother, rather than the grandmother, of Laughter's twin son and daughter, Imih and Teve. When we reached the river, the twins were freed from the backpacks, and the boys and I had to take turns watching them. We learned early that they were fearless and would have crawled into the river if given a chance.

It was during my watch that I noticed a strange man approaching us in the distance. I touched my aunt's shoulder.

"Aunt Turquoise, who is that man? He's looking right at you."

As she looked up her smile evaporated, and she tensed as if preparing to run. He smiled easily and waved to us. The Nejimenets are a tall race but he was the tallest man I had ever seen, taller even than Zarkhon.

"What, no greeting?" he said. "Aren't you glad to see me?"

"Of course I am," she managed to smile. "It's just that I'm surprised, that's all. When did you arrive?"

"This morning. And you are the first familiar face that I have seen. It seems half the valley was born during my absence. Who are these with you?"

"This is my daughter—"

"Your daughter?"

"Don't look so surprised. These two little ones are my grandchildren."

"Oh, no, Turquoise. You a grandmother? It isn't possible."

"It has been twenty years, Gan," she reminded him.

At the mention of his name, I looked at him sharply. Silverwoman had told me that she had a half-brother named Gan Akashe who was a general in the Naritian Army. So this was my Uncle Gan.

"Yes, it has been twenty years," he said. "Twenty years too long. And who are these three? I recognize the girl. You were one of the *veshes* at the Ceremony of the Chosen. I remember you not only because of your dark hair, but also because you had the biggest black eye I have ever seen. A trophy from that skirmish in the market place, am I right?"

I giggled and nodded proudly.

"That's Tejalura, Zarkhon and Silverwoman's daughter. And this is Yari, Zarkhon's younger brother. And this is Hushé, my son."

Gan helped us finish the laundry. He worked with us as easily as if he had done it all his life, although I am certain that as a general it wasn't a task he often did.

"Why don't you have dinner with us?" Laughter invited. "I'm sure that Ancient and Silverwoman are eager to see you."

"I should eat with Kiakashe and Nejo for they are alone. Tell Mother and Silverwoman that I will see them another time."

"Nonsense! Bring Kiakashe and Nejo with you. They often eat with us anyway."

"All right, you've persuaded me. We'll join you tonight."

With a final parting look at Turquoise, he left. We turned to Turquoise, but she quickly began folding clothes.

"You didn't have to be so insistent that he eat with us," she scolded Laughter after he was out of sight.

"Oh, Mother! Gan is very handsome, and he's obviously interested in you. You're going to be an old maid if you don't watch out."

"I've already had one marriage. A good one."

"So what's wrong with another one?"

Turquoise didn't answer.

Uncle Gan arrived with Aunt Kiakashe and Nejo late that afternoon. The boys and I had been practicing *mheftuli*. Nejo joined our game while the adults gossiped on the porch. I overheard Uncle Gan asking about Nejo and me.

"Nejo and Tejalura look much alike. Were they brother and sister before you took them in?"

"Yes, their parents were killed by the Desert Zenadishj."

He was silent for a moment.

"You should take them to the Enavian authorities," he said at last. "They could cause us all a great deal of trouble."

"I couldn't give up Nejo," Aunt Kiakashe declared.

"And we couldn't give up Tejalura," Silverwoman added. "We were without children for so long, Gan. She has become very dear to us."

"Besides," Ancient put in. "Who's to know that we have them any way? Who's to care?"

"You are probably right, Mother," he agreed reluctantly.

I heard no more, for Yari had hit the ball towards me and I had to pay attention to the game. We continued to play until Silverwoman called me in to help with dinner.

"Why is Mother acting so strange?" asked Laughter. "She's usually so friendly with guests, but she has hardly said a word to Gan."

Silverwoman smiled.

"Before your mother married your father, we all thought she and Gan would marry. But just before the *yaremida*, she announced that she would marry Huri, Zarkhon's brother. The next day Gan and Kiakashe left for Narit to join the queen's army. Why Turquoise married Huri no one knows. My guess is that Gan's military ambitions caused her to choose the safer, if not duller existence of a farmer's wife. Your parents had a good marriage, Laughter, but over the years I couldn't help being disappointed that things had not worked out between my brother and Turquoise."

"Oh, that's all right," Laughter said quickly. "I understand. In fact, I wish something would happen between Mother and Gan. She's too young and pretty to remain alone."

That night Gan's talk of Narit dominated the dinner conversation. Yari and Hushé hung on his every word. But Turquoise remained as silent and ill at ease as an uninvited guest. It seemed that the quiet peace she had built up over twenty years had been shattered by his presence. Either because of or in spite of her silence, Uncle Gan's eyes were often drawn to her.

I liked Uncle Gan from the start, as did Yari and Hushé. He took time to show us advanced techniques in mountaineering as well as drilling us in the fluid movements of *nutevek narashan*, Zenadishj sword fighting and self-defense. *Nutevek narashan* is a form of martial arts that has been refined to the formality of court dances but is no less deadly for its grace. We followed him about like puppies. For the most part he took our attention good-naturedly because it gave him a chance to be around Turquoise.

As hard as she tried to avoid him, Gan would not be put off. He had returned to Meneth-shir, and it was clear to all that he had returned to claim Turquoise.

That spring, to no one's surprise, Uncle Gan asked for and received permission to marry Zarkhon's sister-in-law, Turquoise. Turquoise declared that it wasn't necessary to have a formal ceremony because she had been married before and she was already a grandmother twice over. But Uncle Gan argued that it was his first marriage, and he wasn't going to miss any part of it.

It had been decided that Hushé and I would be their *veshes*. Since we had been *veshes* the previous *yaremida*, we did not have to learn our lines, but we needed new garments to replace the ones we had outgrown. With planting and harvesting and the added work of sewing the wedding clothes, we were a busy household.

·→※←·→※←·→※←·

When we journeyed down the mountains I had to ride with Silverwoman again. The fact that I was thirteen and one of the best riders my age, meant nothing to my adopted parents. I believe I fought that harder than anything else before, but Zarkhon and Silverwoman remained firm. I was too small to ride my own horse through Cela Pass and that was final.

After we entered the Naritian Prairie, I was given one of the pack ponies to ride and I had to be content with that. We rode further east along the Lemmer Helt River than we usually did, passing several deserted farms and houses. Where were the Enavians? The deserted Outpost was not far from the spot where we made camp. Hushé and I raced ahead of Yari in our eagerness to explore the deserted buildings.

I remembered the times I had been there with my Enavian family. There was the store Johnny and I used to go to and look at magazines. The owner would give me peppermints and tease me by saying: "Listen Lil, how about you and me going to the dance tonight?" Across the street was The Cela Rose where my brother Jack used to go.

THE DAUGHTER: TEJALURA

Mother had always told us to stay away from there. At the end of the street was the church.

I climbed the stairs and entered the doorway. I walked down the empty aisle to the patch of sunlight made by the stained glass window of purple, blue, scarlet and gold. I could almost hear them singing, my mother's voice among them, but the words weren't clear in my mind.

Where were the Enavians, where had they gone?

"Tejalura!" It was Laughter's voice. "Tejalura, come help us make dinner while the men set up camp."

I turned and went outside to join my family.

Chapter 6
The Soldier: Erten Zemmer 1317-1323 EE

> "Warriors of Meneth-shir and Zeneshtu share a bond that is centuries strong. Possibly because they both live in the Negezos Mountains and train for war all their lives. Not once have they started a war; but once engaged, they are never defeated."
>
> —*General Gan Akashechev*

Taen's decision to withdraw its troops from Ceytal couldn't have come at a worse time. When I received my orders, I was annoyed but not surprised. It was the latest of many short-sighted actions made by a disinterested government half a galaxy away.

After the Market Place Bombing of 1317, Enavian troops from Nevara had been transferred to Ceytal. These soldiers, hardened by encounters with Nevaran guerrillas, had little sympathy for the Zenadishj and slaughtered innocent and guilty alike. Entire communities were destroyed, creating a serious refugee problem. Just as the refugee camps were being established, the troops were transferred back to the Nevaran system because another revolution had broken out. This left Enavian settlements and refugee camps on Ceytal exposed and unsupported. To their credit, many of the emergency relief workers and volunteers remained. Unfortunately, many of them paid for that decision with their lives. The brutality of the Enavian soldiers had inspired anger, not fear. The Zenadishj didn't hesitate to attack as soon as the soldiers were gone.

It was hard not to be critical of a government unable or unwilling to support its own territories. Many suffered, but the ones who suffered most were the refugees, and of the refugees, no group suffered more than the Azakhanis. The Azakhanis had been among the first of the Zenadishj people to surrender to the Enavian government. They were half-dead with cold and starvation when they arrived at the Outpost and the help they received was not the best, but at least they survived.

The children laughed and played games as they had before, and the elders sat about the fire and spoke of the old days, as old men often will. But the young men and women chafed at the invisible bonds that tied them to the refugee camp. While their old way of life was forbidden to them, they were denied entrance into the Enavian world that was ever before them. Unable to make a life for themselves, self-destruction became their only form of expression. Within a few years, most of them were either addicts or prostitutes or both.

It made me angry because the Azakhanis were a beautiful and intelligent people; they were meant for better things than their dreary existence at the refugee camp. If the black market was able to smuggle drugs and alcohol into the camp, then the Enavian government should have no trouble providing proper food, clothing, medical aid, and educational training. I sent one formal recommendation after another to my superiors, but nothing ever came of them. In those early days my opinion meant little, so I could only fume with impotent anger at the tragic waste of it all.

Terez Chevari, the chief's grandson, was one of the rare ones who tried to make something of his life. Dissatisfied with his life at the refugee camp, he decided to do something about it. He joined the auxiliary branch of the Frontier Guard and served for two years as an interpreter and guide.

He saw little value in mourning for old times. Those days were gone, the dead were best buried and forgotten. The world belongs to the living, and being alive, he decided it was up to himself and not the ghosts of his ancestors, to make a place for himself in it. And if the Enavians have the upper hand . . .

"What of it?" he said after we had become friends. "You won the war, didn't you? It would be pointless to go on hating you while you control all the power and all the money—the very things I need to survive. The decision is a simple one. Learn the ways of the Enavians and live; remain too proud and die. That's why I'm working as a scout in the Frontier Guard."

He did his work well and gained the reputation of being efficient and dependable. Of course, some of the men didn't like him because he was a Zenadishj, but after a few assignments, they acquired a sound respect for his abilities. As his commanding officer, I took an interest in his career and began to help with his education in my spare time.

Women took an interest in him, too, which was understandable for Terez was a handsome young man and much older looking than he was. In all his contacts with the Enavian ladies he remained polite and charming—but distant. Terez was no fool.

THE SOLDIER: ERTEN ZEMMER

He managed to save most of his pay during his two-year enlistment because there had been little to spend it on. His food and lodging were provided and he had no friends to go to town with, so he deposited most of his money in a savings account I obtained for him. Three months before he left the Guard, I called him into my office. He entered the office and saluted smartly.

"Sit down, Terez," I said. "This is unofficial. I notice that you've just about served your enlistment, and if you're smart, you'll be leaving us soon."

He grinned.

"That was my intention, sir."

I nodded. Ceytalians were good men and I always thought it a shame they had no opportunity for advancement in the Guard, otherwise we might be able to keep more of them in longer. Someday, maybe.

"What are your plans now?" I asked him.

"I don't have any yet, sir. I thought I might buy some land and settle down."

"That sounds nice, but I don't think that would be a good idea. Not just yet anyway."

He frowned.

"I don't understand, sir. Why not?"

"Oh, you have enough to buy a nice-sized piece of land to make a good start for yourself. But what do you think will happen when some Enavian buys the land next to yours? What if he takes a liking to your water hole or just doesn't happen to like the idea of having a Ceytalian neighbor? He and his friends will try to run you off. I say 'try' because you don't strike me as one who's easy to scare, so you'd get your head blown off. As for getting legal help from the government—well, I'm sure you've seen enough examples of that in the Frontier Guard to know just how much help you can count on. Precious little."

I paused. Terez had listened but had made no comment.

"Look, Terez, I don't mean to interfere. I'm just trying to give you a little advice. I've seen too many of your kind getting kicked around, and just once I'd like to see a Ceytalian kick back and succeed."

Terez shook his head.

"I'm sorry, sir," he said. "I'm not interested in 'kicking back.' I only want to live."

"Yes, I know. What I meant was that I'd like to see a native dare to live like a human being and succeed. As things stand now, you have enough money to marry and settle down—if you were Enavian. But you're not. If you already have a girl in mind, and you're bound and determined to homestead, I suggest that you don't even bother to buy the land. Just find a nice place, settle there until someone kicks you out and then move on. But I don't think that appeals to you much, does it?"

"No, sir."

"I didn't think it would. In that case my advise to you would be to wait. Wait until you have enough money and influential friends so that your race won't matter to anyone."

"How do I do that?"

I smiled.

"Well, Terez, you are about to make use of your first influential friend. Me. I have a cousin who owns a ranch along the Blue Mountain River. His name is Ral Gavin, maybe you have heard of him. He's hiring now. I know working on a ranch doesn't sound very enterprising, but it will give you a chance to see how a successful ranch is run from the inside out. Also, you'll meet certain people who might prove useful to you in the future. Of course, I'll give you a good recommendation, but the rest will be up to you. What do you say?"

"Let me think about it, sir," he said, but I knew he would take the job.

*· →❊←· →❊←· →❊←· *

Winter 1323

Later I saw Terez during a visit with my cousin, Ral Gavin. Having relatives nearby was a luxury not all men stationed on Ceytal had, and I took advantage of their open invitation at every opportunity.

Upon my arrival I was greeted by his wife, Eialise. Before her marriage to Ral, Eialise Gavin had been one of the most celebrated beauties of the Enavian court. Again I found myself wondering how my cousin had captured her. He wasn't handsome or rich or witty or any of the things that would attract a woman of royalty. The most powerful men in the empire had courted her, yet he effortlessly won her against the rest of the competition.

"Erten, it's good to see you," she said as she hugged me. "Ral is in the back, but come on in. There's someone I'd like you to meet."

Since their own marriage they had conspired to get me settled. Each visit, however pleasant, was qualified by an introduction to "someone we'd like you to meet."

Their last one was the governor's daughter. Her blond Enavian beauty had rivaled that of her hostess's, but when I looked into her eyes, I found myself gazing into pure vacuum. I braced myself to meet their latest candidate.

I was surprised when Eialise introduced me to a sophisticated Ceytalian half-breed. Her mixed blood didn't bother me; in fact, I find half-breeds to be the loveliest women in the universe. Something happens when the races mingle. Something magical.

Her name was Pallas, which means "lioness" in ancient Enavian. The name suited her because of the Enavian gold of her hair and the Ceytalian gold of her eyes. Her father was a Zenadishj jeweler and her mother was the daughter of an Enavian merchant. She had just come in from riding, but even in her dusty clothes she had the queenly grace of her royal namesake. Unlike the others I had met, who were either too cool or too eager, Pallas regarded me with friendly interest when Eialise introduced us, then excused herself to change for dinner.

"Oh, I like this one," I said aside to Eialise as she led me through the hall. "She must be your idea, Ral would never have thought of her. Where did you find her?"

"Ral does some business with her father who controls the jewel trade in this part of Ceytal. And you're wrong, Ral is the one who invited her. I've only just met Pallas, but I like her."

Just then Ral greeted me as he entered through the back hallway dusting himself off with his leather gloves. Eialise disappeared into the kitchen to see how the servants were doing and Ral led me into the library. Ral had a parlor where formal guests were entertained, but the library was where he brought his closest friends. It was a comfortable room with enormous windows spaced between large book-lined walls and decorated with furniture that was worn. The temperature was always kept cold so the fire in the fireplace could warm it. The battle of the two contrasting temperatures is something even the most sophisticated room controllers are unable to duplicate. I felt each nerve in my body unwind and relax.

Ral and I had grown up together on Taen and were as close as brothers. We had escaped poverty, he by going into business and

I by enlisting. It was the letters I sent to Ral and Eialise that influenced their decision to immigrate to Ceytal and we have remained close to this day. During the course of our conversation I asked about Terez.

"Referring Terez to me was the best thing you've ever done for me," Ral said. "He's the best worker I have. I'd like to make him foreman, if he stays long enough. I told him you were coming today. He should be joining us in a few minutes."

"Good, I look forward to seeing him."

"Do you know that he was able to repair the watering system that broke down a few months ago? He didn't just repair it, he streamlined everything so that it works more efficiently than the original design. I thought I would have to send away for a whole new system; the company refused to send me a technician to repair it. They said it was too outdated. Well, I might have been able to afford a new system, but just barely, and it would have meant putting off some other plans I had. Terez offered to try to make it work, and since I had nothing to lose, I let him. I'm glad I did. He's saved me a fortune."

Since the Nevaran Revolution, problems like Ral's were becoming more common throughout the empire. The provinces had to rely more on their own resources and ingenuity as support for Enavian technology became less available. In some ways this was a healthy thing for the Ceytalian economy. It made us more self-sufficient—or, at least, made us realize we were capable of more than we thought we were.

"I'll be glad when the revolution on Nevara is over. Damned radicals! They only make things worse for the rest of us Erteyans and nothing will be changed. The Enavians will win in the end, and thank God for that. I'll admit the empire isn't perfect, but we would be in bad shape without it."

"You can't blame the Nevarans," I said. "They want their independence. Taen leaves us alone only because we have no real mineral wealth or anything else of interest to them. Otherwise, we'd be fighting against the Enavians too, instead of waiting the outcome on the sidelines."

"Don't tell me you're another one of those would-be rebels pushing to get us involved with the Nevaran Revolution."

"No, but I do understand and sympathize with their position. What about you? I suppose you want to blow the Nevarans out of the system to set an example for the rest of the territorial planets."

"No, I know as well as anyone else the Nevaran system has needed mineral wealth. But the benefits of being a territory of the empire outweigh the disadvantages and I think we should work with the government, not against it."

"Bravely spoken, Cousin. Especially considering your connection to the royal family. In Eialise you have reaped the greatest benefit of us all."

He grinned sheepishly. Of course I was teasing. Ral had never exploited his marriage to Eialise. As proud as he was of his royal wife, he was just as proud of being a self-made man.

To be honest, there was a great deal of truth to what he said. At one time the Enavian Empire was the power that held the scattered systems of civilization together with a stable government, a universal language, and organized trade routes. But whether or not imperial dominion was beneficial any more was debatable. In my opinion the empire was over extended. Rather than being the nurturing influence it once was, it was draining the lifeblood from its provinces. The empire took much, but gave little in return and someday an accounting would be required.

"There are rumors," Ral was saying, "that the empire is pulling its military support out of all the provinces and territories. Is that true?"

At the time, I hadn't heard anything official, but perhaps it wasn't too soon to tell him what I knew so that he would be able to plan for the welfare of his family. Although such information was classified, I didn't hesitate. Ral and I had been through a lot.

"During the past few months some of my men have been transferred to the Nevaran system. There may come a time in the near future when all military support will be withdrawn from Ceytal. If that happens, our settlements here as well as the neighboring planets, will be vulnerable to attack. If I were you, I would make plans to return to Taen, especially now there's that trouble with the petition."

In an effort to suppress Erteyan support of the Nevaran Revolution, a petition had been drawn up and presented to the emperor demanding the confinement of all Erteyans on detention planets throughout the empire. The emperor vetoed it, I suspect because his favorite niece was married to an Erteyan.

"No, Eialise and I built this place together. Ceytal is our home, we'll never leave. But we are sending Melisanne to a finishing school on

Taen, the same one Eialise attended. By the time she graduates, this will have all blown over."

Eialise abruptly entered the room, accompanied by the enchanting Pallas.

"If it were up to me, Erten, Mel would go to a good Ceytalian school. Enavian schools are a waste of time and money."

Eialise carried a tray of refreshments and set them down on the table as she spoke. Ral made no comment, but it was clear that he was irritated with her for carrying the tray in herself. He believed the niece of the emperor should let servants do such tasks. Eialise thought Ral was too pompous and did things for herself out of spite. This was the only discordant note in their marriage. Otherwise, Ral and Eialise are the most contented couple I know.

Eialise is a remarkable woman with unusual ideas. She has a talent for making small talk, but prefers to speak of interesting things. She is the only woman I know who brings up the subject of politics. Because she grew up at court where politics was the small-talk of royalty, it never occurred to her there was anything unusual about it.

"Erten, you've just returned from Narit with Senator Tariv. How did it go?"

"As well as can be expected. You know that Tariv was there to try to get Queen Ceymar to abolish slavery in Narit."

"Really," Pallas spoke up for the first time. "Isn't slavery already forbidden by imperial law?"

The innocence of her statement surprised me.

"Weren't you born on Ceytal?" I asked.

"Yes, but I grew up on Taen. I returned to Ceytal only weeks ago. I've been studying medicine at the university. You'll have to fill me in on the situation here."

Her smile was warm and encouraging. I suspected she knew more about the subject than I did but feigned ignorance to learn my opinion.

"With pleasure," I said finding it easy to return her smile. "It's true slavery is illegal, but it's harder to enforce on the territorial planets. Tariv wanted to make the abolition of slavery a reality rather than mere words. Queen Ceymar was not cooperative; she does not acknowledge Enavian jurisdiction on Ceytal.

He did manage to get her to sign an agreement for the return of all Enavian captives."

"Are there that many?"

"More than we thought. Thousands have already been returned and those are only the ones on record. There must be thousands more who will never be found."

Ral shook his head.

"That's a terrible thing. Terrible."

"Many of them are kept in special refugee camps, because we can't locate their Enavian relatives. Programs are being set up to integrate them back into Enavian society. But because there is already competition for grants and government funding for Ceytalian refugees, things aren't going well. The whole affair was very poorly planned. It will probably go against Tariv's record. It's a shame because it wasn't his fault. He was just cleaning up someone else's mess. He's a good senator, I like his style."

"Oh, I wouldn't worry about Tariv. He'll sail through this crisis as he has others in the past. Tariv came by just before returning to Taen, but you weren't with him."

"No, I went hunting with Mheftu Padhari."

"Dr. Padhari is a Nejimenet isn't he? Where do those people live, I've often wondered about them."

"I have too. Mheftu is pretty closed-mouthed about his people. I have no idea where they live or come from."

"Now, the other Ceytalians call them 'gypsies,' yet they seem too secure, too affluent to be real gypsies."

"They're honest for one thing. The quality of their craftsmanship and the integrity of their merchants make them welcome in almost every city in Narit. That alone distinguishes them from the other gypsies. According to legend, they were born in the sky."

"Where did you hear that?"

"Not from Mheftu. From some Zenadishj I've worked with. I asked Mheftu about it, but he was as closed mouth as ever. My guess is they live somewhere in the Negezos Mountains. But even if a Nejimenet community did exist in the mountains, there are so many ruined cities there it would be hard to identify it on our aerial maps."

"Can't they do an infrared scan?"

"They have but the readings are confusing. Centuries ago, a pre-Ceytalian civilization dropped a chemical bomb there. It's impossible to get accurate heat readings on the Negezos Mountain area. All the abandoned cities record human life, but all those inspected are deserted."

Surprisingly, Pallas had something to add at this point.

"The cities aren't deserted. Bodies have been found wrapped in cloaking fields. Although the cloaking fields didn't protect them from the effects of the bomb, they did preserve them perfectly. Their heat factor and water content remain unchanged, but they are quite dead. Scientists are still trying to discover how the bodies in the cloaking fields are able to maintain the body heat without decomposing. Some of their bodies are on display in the museum of Taen."

I'd never heard of this, so I asked her to tell me more.

"In one of my classes I had to do some research on the pre-Ceytalian Wars and the long-range effect of chemical warfare on Ceytal. I did one report on the Great Yaremida Spot believed to be the residue of one of those ancient bombs. This invisible mass completes its orbit around Ceytal every three years, causing severe winters on the surface it covers. But you know this already, don't you. I must be boring you."

"No, not at all," I assured her. "Of course, I knew about the 'wolf winters' that occur every three years, but I never knew the cause. You also researched the cloaked bodies of the ruined cities."

"Yes. It was fascinating. Several of the preserved bodies have been dissected. In one, a living embryo was salvaged and brought to its full term. It was a girl. I believe she is living on Taen, but her identity is kept confidential so she can live a normal life. There were pictures of her and her progress. She is about twenty-nine now, she is married with children—even her husband doesn't know her origins. Here let me get my report. I have a picture of her."

The picture showed a young woman who was fresh and healthy rather than beautiful. Her dark coloring and bone structure would have passed unnoticed in any Erteyan community.

Mheftu and I used to joke often about the fanatical Erteyans who claimed to be returning to their "home"—now I wondered.

It seemed odd to be gazing into the face of a woman whose parents had conceived centuries ago. I remembered some of the cities we had explored in the mountains. The thought of those shrouded bodies, waiting in those buildings made me shiver.

I glanced up and saw a picture of my niece, Melisanne.

"Where is Melisanne, by the way?" I said in an effort to dispel the uneasy feeling.

"She's with Terez—yes, here they come now. She has become very attached to him, I don't know what she'll do when we send her off to school."

"When will she be leaving?" I asked.

"In a few weeks. Maybe the school on Taen will get her to wear dresses. I've almost given up hope of ever seeing her dressed in anything else besides scuffed boots and pants."

I frowned for I disliked hearing criticisms against Melisanne. Yet, as I saw her through the window coming in from the stables with Terez, I knew there was some truth to her father's words. Her face, though pretty, was sunburned and smudged with dirt. She could be such an attractive girl if she tried.

She was eleven when Terez came to work for my cousin and by that time her role as a tomboy had been established. From the time she could venture outside, she had spent her every waking hour with the workers. They had taken to letting her help with some of the work, partly because she amused them and partly to keep her from underfoot. But to Melisanne it was a serious matter, she considered herself to be one of her father's workers.

She attached herself to Terez on sight and followed him about like a shadow. As the other men before him had, he retaliated by assigning her little odd jobs to keep her occupied so he could get his work done. Although he found her a bit of a nuisance at first, he later became fond of her.

"He even nicknamed her Meiklei," Ral continued. "What does that mean anyway?"

"It means 'mirage nymph.' According to Ceytalian mythology, the *meikleis* are the illegitimate daughters of the desert god and the rain goddess." I smiled at a sudden thought. "The word *meiklei* is also used to describe someone who is mad or insane. Crazy."

"That must be why he called her that," Ral decided. "Can't blame him though. He's had quite a time with Mel. Seeing how well Mel minded him, Eialise thought he might be able to help discipline her. But I put an end to that. I told her I hadn't hired Terez to be a governess. Still, we often found ourselves asking him to help out with her when no one else could do anything with her. Of course, the other men can't leave that alone, they've taken to calling him 'nanny' or 'wet nurse.' He's been good-natured about it, but I'm sure he'll be glad when she goes to school."

At that moment Terez and Melisanne entered the room, bringing the freshness of the afternoon with them.

"Uncle Erten!" Melisanne ran across the room tackling me with a hug that almost set me off my chair. She had grown. In spite of her wind-tossed hair and old clothes, one could see she was blossoming into womanhood. I saw the glances she gave Terez when she thought no one saw her. I had seen the same look in the eyes of some of the older, more sophisticated women at the Outpost. But to see the same fire in the eyes of my little niece was frightening. I intercepted Ral's concerned look and knew the other reason he was sending Mel to Taen. Well, that was Ral's problem, the responsibilities of an honorary uncle didn't include this short of thing.

I returned my attention to Pallas, who was now seated next to me.

Chapter 7
The Appaloosa: Tejalura 1323-1324 EE

> O Turquoise Horse
> Shining we have seen thee rise
> Brilliant as the dawn
> Saffron and rose with fire
> Burning we have seen thee rise
> Above the mountains
>
> — *Zenadishj Folksong*

Spring 1323 EE

One morning Zarkhon announced that he was taking me to Zeneshtu Valley to buy me a horse. At last I was to have a horse of my own!

The owner of the horse farm was an old friend of Zarkhon's named Neve Chevari who had been doing business with the Nejimenets for years. He must have known that I was Zarkhon's daughter by adoption, but his greeting was no less warm than if I were Nejimenet-born.

The next morning I went out to the corral to inspect the available horses and saw the one that I wanted—the appaloosa. No one in Meneth-shir possessed a horse so fine.

"Your daughter has a good eye for horse flesh, untrained though it must be. A pity though, for the horse is not for sale."

Zarkhon placed a hand on my shoulder to stop the angry words I would have said.

"But my friend, why should this be?"

"The appaloosa hasn't reached her full growth," Neve explained. "She isn't ready to carry a rider yet."

"Even a rider so young?" Zarkhon placed his hand on me. "As you can see, my daughter has yet to reach her full growth. Even then, she promises to be small."

I started to be angry with Father, but I caught myself before I said anything. I understood that it was a game they played.

"That's all right, Father," I said airily. "I don't like any of these horses. Can't we buy one somewhere else?"

He laughed and ruffled my hair.

"She learns fast, my Tejalura, doesn't she?"

The Mountain Zenadishj have refined the etiquette and protocol of horse trading to an art. If they bargain for more than an hour, they must offer their customer tea or refreshment. If the bargaining continues into the early evening, they must invite them to a meal. After that, the customer must spend the night with their family and have breakfast the next morning. The longer the bargaining, the higher their esteem of their customer.

We bargained with Chevari for three days and when we left, I rode the appaloosa.

It was cold the day our caravan returned to Meneth-shir and the sky was a strange gray. Our household was the second in line after the Jevetchev's. I was glad of that for I often heard the others further behind complain of the dust. Ancient was riding beside me and I was glad of that, too. Sometimes Turquoise rode with me and she would gossip about things I had little interest in. This bored and irritated me, making the days of travel seem like so much wasted time.

But with Ancient, it was different. The old woman had the knack of making the hours pass easily. Much of the time we rode in silence, watching the changing shadows of the familiar view as the sun made its journey across the sky. She would point out some landmark and say: "See that cliff? There was a great battle fought there." or "See that river running through the canyon? There was a time when it was not there." Then she would proceed to tell their story. The words she used were simple and few, but with them she wove a tapestry of rich colors and beautiful patterns in my imagination. The legends and myths seemed to make the landscape we passed even more magnificent.

Once Ancient had told me that when people died they returned to the earth and became what they truly were. A strong warrior would become a mighty tree or a capricious maiden might become a flower that comes and goes with the spring. It was an Oramaklete belief rather than Nejimenet, but it pleased me. I like to think that when Ancient died she would become a tall, jagged cliff or mountain. Then one day someone would point to her and say: "See that mountain? Well, there is a story behind it . . ."

THE APPALOOSA: TEJALURA

Ancient watched me as I urged Melia Meiklei along the narrow path. Zarkhon had not wanted me to ride the appaloosa because she had not traveled this path before. Only the most sure-footed horses were mounted by the Nejimenets, the others were used as pack horses.

"She's doing well for her first time, isn't she?" I said to Ancient.

"Better than you did, anyway. What a time we had with you, remember? Screeching and clawing like a wildcat you were. I thought we would have to tie you down."

I laughed to think of my earlier fears and remembered it was my first sight of Arae Shjina that had taken them away and I grew eager to see it again. Beauty, I thought to myself, must be the most powerful force on earth.

"Ancient, I think I know how to make Zenadishj peaceful like us."

"How?"

"Well, if they spent more time looking at the land rather than staying in their noisy cities, they wouldn't fight so much."

"And then they would be peaceful like you and Tzeri are."

Stung by her words I said:

"It's her fault. She started it."

"But did you think that she might have a reason? Or that there was something you could do or say to put an end to it?"

Although I wouldn't say so aloud, I had to admit to myself that I hadn't.

"At one time," continued Ancient when she saw that she had made her point, "Tzeri used to play with Yari and Hushé quite a bit. But when they acquired a new little sister, they spent less time with her and she grew to resent the little sister. Her resentment may be unfair, but it is understandable."

"What do you think my way should be, Grandmother?"

"See if you can't make a friend of her. Ask her to go climbing with you sometime. You shouldn't go off alone as you do."

"She might refuse."

"She might."

We rode for a while in silence before she spoke again.

"Did you know that Tzeri has asked to study under Kiakashe to become a *nutevek narashan?*"

This was a complete surprise for I hadn't known Tzeri was interested in martial arts.

"Gan has told me that you are already practicing with Yari and Hushé. Perhaps it's time to start your formal training under your aunt."

That night when we made camp, I asked Aunt Kiakashe if I could study under her.

"You know that Tzeri is also training under me?"

"Yes."

"Well, it's all right with me, but on one condition: make peace with Tzeri. Come to terms with each other before next autumn when we start."

After we reached Meneth-shir, a few days before we were to clear the fields, I asked Tzeri to go climbing with me. To my surprise she agreed to go with me. Not knowing how much experience she had, I chose the easiest trail that I knew. We walked for a while in silence, then she asked:

"Tejalura, are you trying to insult me by picking the most baby trail there is?"

"Have you climbed before?"

"A little," she said. "Not as much as you have with Yari and Hushé, but I can manage better than this."

"All right, you choose the way."

I was surprised at the difficult path she chose, but the ease that she managed it proved she wasn't showing off. In some ways she made a more satisfying companion than either of my brothers. I could share things with her that I would never dream of speaking to Yari and Hushé about. I tell you that there is no sweeter feeling than to discover a friend in an old enemy.

That evening I had dinner with her family and spent the night. The Sun household and the Moon household have always been close and both were glad Tzeri and I were now friends. Tzeri's great-grandfather, Dejo, told us stories of the days when the Sun household had been the priesthood of Meneth-shir and the Moon household had been its statesmen and military leaders. Jevetura, one of Tzeri's cousins, recorded Dejo's oral histories in scribbled notes that later she would organize into a book. I often wondered why Jevetura spent so much time scribbling down the rambling words of an old man when every other girl her age was out playing *mheftuli* or riding horses. I suppose she knew best. Years later her works were to become famous, not only on Ceytal, but throughout the Enavian Empire.

Although at one time we were a fierce and warlike people, we have evolved into a peaceful nation. We have dispensed with kings and priests and are now governed by a loosely organized council.

The appointment of counselor is not a coveted one. The average citizen of Meneth-shir considers the job a nuisance that takes farmers away from their fields, housewives away from their homes, craftsmen away from their vocations, and fishermen away from their boats. Each citizen accepts that, at least once during their lifetime, they must serve as councilor for their household. There is no prestige or honor involved in the appointment, it is an inevitable, but necessary, task that ranks about the same as burning garbage. It is important to understand this attitude before one can begin to grasp Nejimenet politics.

The Nejimenet council meets once a year to collect the tithes and to distribute the goods to each household and to estimate the future needs of Meneth-shir. For some time the council considered appointing a treasurer to keep the records organized so the annual council meetings could be even briefer. Jevetura was the first to be nominated for the position because she had a brilliant mind and could solve problems almost as quickly as an Enavian computer, but she declined saying that she was too busy recording Dejo's stories.

"Besides," she said, "I don't like math. Why don't you ask Tejalura to do it? She loves math."

"She makes mistakes," Aunt Kiakashe said.

"Not as many as the others do," Jevetura insisted. "I wouldn't mind going over her figures once in a while to make sure they are correct."

I wasn't even sure I wanted to be a treasurer, but there wasn't any reason not to try it. The council decided to ease into the process gradually. At first, I would only be responsible for the financial records of the Tehalchev household. This would allow them to measure my abilities, as well as define the task while it was on a smaller scale. A few more households would be added each year, until my report included the whole valley. I placed little importance in being the treasurer, because, at the time I was far more interested in other things. Years later, my appointment would play a significant part in my life.

Tzeri and I saw little of each other during the planting and harvest. What time we had we devoted to rock climbing and *nutevek narashan* workouts. By the time school started, our friendship had become a strong and precious thing. We would meet Aunt Kiakashe at Itan-shir Island hours before the other students to begin our training. Our *mheftuli* games now had an added dimension and it didn't seem to matter whether we played on the same team or not. In fact, we were happier when we pitted our skill against one another.

·→※←··→※←··→※←·

Spring 1324 EE

That spring Turquoise and Laughter each had a child so now Silverwoman and I had to take a more active part in taking care of the twins. Imih and Teve were three, almost four, and were as identical as two peas. They were also as mischievous as any two children I have ever seen. To keep them out of trouble, we had them help us in small ways in the field. They loved Tzeri and she could get them to do anything.

Tzeri's friendship was not the only thing I gained during our climbs together; I gained a sense of oneness with the land. It spoke to me in a language all its own. Whenever my eyes would fall on a familiar scene, I would find a surprise awaiting me. With a shifting sunlight, a beautiful tree would become a detailed silhouette that framed an arrangement of granitic rock and spring flowers.

Again I became convinced of the power of beauty and wished that I had blue hair and golden eyes like Tzeri so that I might better fit with my surroundings. I confided this to my friend and she laughed.

"But Taji, there is nothing wrong with being different. Doesn't Silverwoman have white hair and gray eyes? Everyone agrees that she is the most beautiful woman in Meneth-shir. Do you know I used to be jealous of you because everyone made so much of you that first year you were here. All anyone could talk about was how pretty you were. I wanted to look like you so everyone would notice me."

"Too bad we can't trade," I said.

"Oh, we'd only want to trade back, I don't think anyone is satisfied with what they look like." She studied me critically. "If you wore a lot of jewelry you would look just like an Urthic princess. Are you sure your parents were Enavian?"

"Of course. You don't have to have blond hair and blue eyes to be an Enavian citizen. Once I knew a Nejimenet who was an Enavian citizen."

I told her about Mheftu Padhari, but she shook her head in disbelief. Tzeri is convinced she knows everything and doesn't believe anything she has not seen or heard herself. But I love her anyway. After a long comfortable silence I heard her say in a very careful voice:

"Is there going to be a special dinner for Yari and Hushé tonight?"

"Oh, not really," I answered as casually as I could. "But there are bound to be extra guests to say good-bye to them. You're coming, aren't you?"

She shrugged.

"Oh, I suppose so."

I smiled and closed my eyes again and let the sun relax me. Yari and Hushé were leaving for Zeneshtu the next day to work on Neve Chevari's horse farm. I knew that Tzeri was desperately in love with Hushé and would miss him, but she was afraid to tell him. Not once did it occur to me to tell Hushé, for I loved Tzeri too much to expose her. Yet if I could use my knowledge to her advantage in the future I would. I sighed, and thought that it must be terrible to be sixteen and to be in love. I hoped this did not happen to me when I turned sixteen.

On our way back we were met by Yari and Hushé. For the first time I noticed how handsome they were. I lived with them, I fought and argued with them daily. How could I not notice they had become men. A phrase from *The Song of Two Heroes* came to my mind: "Their laughter rang through the valley stronger than swords." I started to hum it to myself. I glanced at Tzeri and saw her mixed expression of joy and dread.

How could Hushé be so blind as to miss the love written on her face?

Apparently men are a little more obtuse in some matters than we are, for as we approached them, Hushé ruffled Tzeri's hair thoughtlessly. As far as he was concerned she might as well have been twelve years old. How could he? Hushé, the artist who was so sensitive to other's feelings, how could he be so dense when it came to Tzeri?

During dinner I tried to keep up a joking conversation with Tzeri to cover up for her, but it was hopeless. She continued to look after him with calf-eyed wistfulness. Fortunately, Hushé never guessed a thing. He and Yari were too excited about their journey to notice her silence.

The next morning Tzeri left quietly, without explanation, so I went to the stable to help my brothers get ready to leave. I was a little angry at Hushé for his treatment of Tzeri, but with the two of them laughing and teasing me, my anger soon left. The only comfort that Tzeri had was Hushé knew nothing about the way she felt.

On impulse I told them I would miss them and I wished that I could go with them.

"Well, why not?" Hushé said. "We're all ready to go so it wouldn't take much more to get you ready too."

I hesitated. Although I had always been welcome to join many of their activities, I knew there were times when they would prefer to be on their own. I tried to be sensitive to that, thus always assuring my welcome at occasions such as this.

After making sure their invitation was a serious one, I talked it over with my parents. Knowing that Neve could always use an extra hand, they didn't see why I should not be allowed to go to Zeneshtu.

As fun as it was to go down the mountain pass during the *yaremida*, it was nothing compared with just the three of us alone, able to set our own pace. I was proud to be riding between my two heroes, to laugh and joke with them as an equal. After we left the Liamet Negezos Mountains, we followed the river the Enavians call the Lemmer Helt River and we call Khai Melia. It was almost like being on a holiday because we should have been working in the fields. But when we came to Zeneshtu, Neve made us work harder than we ever had in our lives.

I liked Neve Chevari. He was volatile and short-tempered as are most Zenadishj, but he was just as quick to show his affection. When I did well I was his Urthic princess; but when I failed at something, I was an ignorant, shiftless *teyado* and Zarkhon had been well cheated when his wife had paid a can opener and a length of rope for me.

He took the three of us to the city of Halia Tehal so we could learn by watching his business transactions. He could drive hard bargains and demanded high prices because his reputation for honesty was well established among the other traders. Many Naritian aristocrats would deal only with him or, if dealing with another trader, they would contract a member of Neve's household to act as an advisor.

As another part of our education, he took us to the market place and showed us how dishonest traders would cheat by making an older or sick animal appear strong and young. The other traders howled when Neve opened a horse's mouth and revealed where a hole had been drilled in its teeth to accommodate cloves to make its sour breath sweet or explain how they would force a drooping tail to lift by placing spice up its anus.

"In the long run," he told us, "There is no profit to be made in cheating customers, for a cheated man's memory is as long as his tongue is active. He and his friends will avoid doing business with you if it is at all possible. But if a man is dealt with honestly, his memory is just as long and his tongue is just as active—only it will be in your favor."

"Look at me and learn, I am rich and happy; look at them and learn, they are poor and miserable. Learn how to cheat so no man may cheat you, yet be yourself honest with all men. In this way you will succeed no matter what business you may take up."

I have always remembered his words, not only for their practicality, but also for the strange influence of Nejimenet thought on the Zenadishj mind. Nejimenets are thoroughly honest, despising dishonesty to the point they will not admit to its existence. With the Zenadishj, deceit is their only form of interaction, be it business or personal. Truth would not be believed if it were heard.

Because of Neve's friendship with my father, he had been exposed to Nejimenet culture and had applied many of our practices and beliefs to his own lifestyle. For instance he worshipped Ce, the one God of Meneth-shir, rejecting the complicated legion of gods and goddesses of the polytheistic Naritian Zenadishj. He still paid the temple tax, which was required by law, but not a tenthpiece more. He was quite vocal about his disgust of the priesthood.

"It's bad enough we must pay a government tax, but to pay an even larger tax to the temple for no other purpose than to feed, clothe and educate a group of parasitic priests is beyond bearing. I can stand it because I am rich, but what of the poor? Mark my words, there will be trouble someday."

Chapter 8
The Renegade: Terez Chevari 1325 EE

> "Equality is not a privilege to be earned, inherited, or awarded to a chosen few. It is an unconditional truth—a natural state of being that must be acknowledged and experienced by all if the Enavian Empire is to remain the power it is today."
>
> — *Senator Neral Tariv*

Spring 1325

Melisanne had been attending school on Taen a couple of years when Ral Gavin forced me to take a vacation.

"Terez, you haven't taken a single vacation in all the time you've worked for me." Ral Gavin said to me. "You have about three months' vacation pay as well as time off coming to you. Take it and go and don't come back until you've used it all up."

I grinned.

"Are you trying to get rid of me?"

"No, but I've been getting some nasty notices from the Labor Office. If you don't start using your vacation, I'll have to pay some very stiff fines."

So, suddenly I had three months to do as I pleased. I would have visited Erten Zemmer, my former commanding officer, but he had been transferred to Nevara. There was my mother, but I had no desire to see her for she had grown into a bitter, unhappy woman.

For the first time it occurred to me I was quite alone in the world. There was my father, Neve Chevari, but I had no memory of him for I had been young when my mother divorced him. Those who knew him, considered him to be a good provider and a successful businessman. If he spent his money on other women and wine, most agreed my mother had driven him to it. For lack of a better plan, I decided to visit him. If he would not receive me, at least the journey to his farm in the Zeneshtu Valley would help use up some of my vacation.

The Zeneshtu Valley is a province of the kingdom of Narit, but other than being subject to annual taxation and a draft of every tenth man during times of war, the Naritian Empire generally leaves Zeneshtu to its own devices. It was a joy to see the Zenadishj living in prosperity outside Enavian jurisdiction, instead of bleak confinement in the refugee camps.

Everyone in the valley knew my father, so it was not hard to find his house. He was standing on the front steps when I arrived. He scarcely gave me a glance.

"If you are looking for work," he said harshly, "You can just turn around and go back where you came from. I've no openings here."

I smiled.

"Hello, Father."

He stepped forward, squinting against the sun.

"Terez? Terez! Well, come in, come in boy. Don't just stand there."

I dismounted and followed him into the house.

"Forgive me for not recognizing you," he said. "You were barely able to walk the last time I saw you. How is your mother?"

"Well enough. You know that she is living in a camp outside the Outpost don't you?"

"No, I'm sorry to hear that."

"It was her own choice. I have offered to rent a small house for her, but she refuses to leave the camp. I think she is afraid she would have nothing to complain about if she left."

He smiled and shook his head.

"Poor Nateheh. I wish you could have known her when she was young. Your mother was a good woman. She had a good sense of humor and was a lot of fun. What could have changed her so?"

We were silent for a moment and I wondered which had first shaken the foundation of their marriage: my mother's bitterness or my father's indiscretions? Which had caused the other? But I kept my thoughts to myself. Abruptly he said:

"So tell me, Terez, are you married? Are you working? Where do you live? Are you going to stay or is this just a visit?"

I laughed.

"No, Father, I am not married. Yes, I am working for an Enavian who lives by the Khai Yarashji. No, I do not plan to stay, this is just a visit."

He nodded.

"I see," he said. "But I want you to know that this is your home whenever you want it."

At first I could say nothing, but my heart sang. I belong somewhere.

"Thank you, Father," I said quietly.

He coughed to cover his embarrassment and changed the subject.

"Now you were saying that you work for an Enavian. What sort of work is this?"

I told him about working at Ral Gavin's place. He asked some very astute questions and we compared different methods of caring for livestock. Our brief exchange gave me some new ideas to recommend to Gavin when I returned.

"Well, at least you have learned something from this Enavian," he said grudgingly, but his eyes were filled with pride.

We entered the dining hall and I was introduced to three Nejimenets—Geysan, Yari, and Hushé—who were finishing up their afternoon meal. Father did a lot of horse trading with the Nejimenets, and these three, in particular, were frequent visitors to the Zeneshtu Valley.

I liked them immediately, in fact, I like most Nejimenets I meet. We spoke for hours, but I learned little about them because of that Nejimenet trick of turning the conversation away from themselves. They asked a lot of questions about the Enavians. Since they seemed interested in learning more, I mentioned we were short-handed at the Gavin ranch and they could apply for work if they wanted to. As a further incentive, I told them the pay was good, although they didn't have the look of men who needed money. They seemed eager for a chance to live among the Enavians. When I finished my visit with my father, my new friends accompanied me.

Gavin was short-handed so he was more than glad to hire the Nejimenets. They enjoyed their work at the Gavin ranch and got along with the other men. Their positive attitude rubbed off on the others and any problem they encountered was treated as a challenge. Geysan, the oldest, was steady and unimaginative. Yari was the bold one who wasn't afraid to ask questions or give suggestions. Hushé was quiet and deceptively gentle; he could work harder than any man among them.

Gavin wanted to make me his foreman. This I thought was a mistake and I told him so.

"But Terez, you are one of the best workers I have. The other men look up to you and when Mandt isn't around they go to you for advice. They respect you."

"That may be true now, but if you put me in a position of authority over them, they will resent me. Mandt's two sons, Dax and Kiral are going to have the strongest objections."

"And since when has the position of foreman become hereditary? Look Terez, I want my next foreman to be someone I can trust. All that I have built up is going to belong to my daughter and the man she marries. I hope she marries someone responsible, but since I can't depend on that I have to make sure there are competent people working under them."

"But why did you choose me?"

"I've checked you out. My cousin, Erten, speaks well of you, and your military record is impeccable. Your father is a wealthy man with strong ties to Enavian business community. You have no reason to cheat me."

How odd. I'd never considered myself as a well-connected man, yet that's how Gavin had described me. I understood then the wisdom of my friend Zemmer's advice years earlier.

"Why don't you teach Melisanne to run the place."

"In a few years maybe, but she's too young yet. All she thinks about are boys. As they say, there's safety in numbers, so I won't worry until she settles down to one. Why are you fighting me? A man your age should be eager to settle down to a career."

"I have plenty of time," I said unconcerned. "I'm only twenty-three."

"Really? I thought you were older than that." He thought for a moment. "You must have been underage when you enlisted in the Guard."

I shrugged.

"There are less restrictions in recruiting auxiliaries. They never asked my age, so I never told them."

"I see. Well, that does make you a bit young to be made foreman. I'll see if I can keep Mandt on for a while longer and you can be his assistant. That will give the other men time to adjust to taking orders from you. By the time you take over the men will accept your appointment as a matter of course—or those who don't will be replaced by others who will."

I still thought it was a mistake, but I didn't argue the matter. I could always find another position somewhere else if it came to that. I like

Ral, but he acted as if I made a life-time commitment to work on his ranch. I knew I should be grateful, but it sometimes irritated me. I rose to leave and said:

"I'll get back to work."

"Oh, by the way, my daughter is coming home next week and I'd like you to take Eialise out to the Outpost to meet her. I have to meet with some buyers so I won't be able to myself."

No one called it the Outpost anymore. It was now known as Naritjina City, but I didn't correct him.

"Certainly."

"Oh, and Terez—be sure to wear your good suit. Eialise will want to take Mel to The Cela Rose for lunch and you'll be expected to join them."

Had I been an Enavian employee they would never have dreamed of inviting me to dine with them in a public restaurant, but the Gavins insisted on treating me "equal." This made me feel awkward at times, but their intentions were good and, in the end, I suppose that's what mattered.

Eialise Gavin is one of the most unself-conscious women I know. Unless her personal maid rises early enough to choose a coordinated outfit for her to wear, Eialise will wear whatever she lays her hands on first, and the results could be ghastly. Her delicate, blond beauty and her unmistakable good breeding attest to the fact she is an Enavian lady of highest rank, but there isn't an artificial bone in her body. Many have wondered how she came to marry an Erteyan rancher. I believe the answer is: she looked at him, Ral Gavin the man, and loved him. Their social positions never entered into it.

Only a woman with her social blindness could have stood by me in the spaceport, oblivious to the stares we received. Had I worn my work clothes, my position as her employee would have been clear. But because of my youth and my expensively tailored suit, I could only be the paid escort of an Enavian woman of few morals. When she did notice the stares, she glanced down at the dress she wore.

"My dress is all right isn't it, Terez? Helvah picked it out for me."

I smiled. She honestly didn't know why they were staring.

"You look well, Evimeh Eialise," I answered, placing the Zenadishj term of respect before her name.

At that moment she spotted a friend some distance away.

"Why it's Dr. Padhari," she said. "Mheftu! Over here."

If people stared when there was one Ceytalian native standing beside her, you can imagine the attention she drew with two. But she remained oblivious as ever.

"Eialise, it's good to see you," he said using her first name with the same casual warmth she had used his.

"Mheftu, this is Terez Chevari, our foreman. At least he will be when Mandt retires."

"We've already met. Hello, Terez. What are you two doing here?"

"We're meeting Melisanne," Eialise explained. "She's coming home from school now. We're expecting her to arrive on the *Zenith* at any moment."

"I have bad news for you then. The *Zenith* has been delayed. I know because I'm supposed to meet Hershem and Cia, they're returning from their honeymoon."

"Honeymoon? I didn't even know they were married. That's wonderful. I always thought Cia was too pretty to remain a widow. I remembered how alone she was after Jack died. She and Jack had a son who was cubed, do you know if they plan to uncube him?"

"Not right away. They want a few years to themselves. Look, since we all have to wait for the *Zenith*, why don't we have a drink together in the lounge?"

Dr. Mheftu Padhari was proof a Ceytalian could succeed in any society, for he had done so twice. First, as a doctor and then again as a wilderness guide. He treated his success casually, almost carelessly. Though his suit was informal, its cut and material were expensive. In contrast, my own suit must have made me appear as stiff and formal as a waiter. Someday, I promised myself, I would have Padhari's self-assurance.

Soon we were joined by Melisanne, escorted by Hershem and Cia Hershem. At the sight of me, Melisanne waved to me eagerly. I smiled in return, but felt a little out of my depth. Mel, who had been an enchanting child, had grown into a disturbingly beautiful young woman.

Hershem and Cia looked as happy as any couple I have ever seen. I remembered Cia as thin lipped, stern and a little priggish, but now there was a new glow in her eye and a blush on her cheeks. She looked years younger. The three of them had become close friends during their return trip to Ceytal, and it was decided we should all go to The Cela Rose together.

Since Taen's withdrawal of imperial troops, Enavian services and goods had become difficult to obtain. The Outpost had been deserted for a time but soon enterprising Ceytalian businesses, many with home offices in Halia Tehal, had taken over the empty buildings, including The Cela Rose.

The Cela Rose proved not all things civilized depended on Enavian sovereignty. Although great care had been taken to preserve its current Enavian elegance, architectural features dating back to days it was a Zenadishj tea house were subtly enhanced. The menu had been expanded to include Zenadishj and Urthic dishes. It was even rumored that, for a price, an authentic cannibal Oramaklete plate could be ordered. But that was just a rumor.

Much of the management staff remained the same and wealthy Enavians were shown preferential treatment, especially old customers like the Hershems. We were seated at a triangular table so we paired off: Ral and Cia, of course, Padhari and Eialise, and Melisanne and myself. I was glad of Padhari's presence, because I wouldn't have been treated with such respect and courtesy if I had been the only Ceytalian present. Again, the wisdom of Erten Zemmer's advice was reinforced. Someday I too would have enough friends and money so that my race would not matter. Someday.

I turned to Melisanne and caught a glimpse of her clear profile. As a girl her skin had been burnt brown by the sun, but now she had her mother's pale, fairy queen beauty. Only the pink stain on her cheeks against skin of purest porcelain, hinted she might be real and not a dream. She laughed at some joke Mheftu had made, then turned to face me and I felt an unexpected confusion. I heard Ral Hershem call to me as if from a great distance. Relieved, I turned to speak with him.

Get a hold of yourself!

I managed to avoid direct conversation with her during the rest of the meal and the ride back home. As soon as we arrived, Gavin called me into his office.

"I just wanted to tell you it's official now. You are being trained for the position of foreman. Starting now, there will be an increase in your pay and benefits. I want you to be in my office before light tomorrow morning. Mandt and I are going over the books with the auditor, and I want you there."

I left the office and started to make my way outside when, as I half-hoped and half-dreaded, I saw Melisanne coming down the stairs. I walked by as if I hadn't seen her.

"Terez, wait!"

I stopped and turned.

"What is it, *Evimeh*?"

I had used the Zenadishj title of respect in an effort to remain impersonal, but being her mother's daughter, Melisanne laughed.

"*'Evimeh!'* Oh really, Terez, since when have I become *'Evimeh'* to you?"

"Since you have become an Enavian lady."

"Have I changed so much?" she asked anxiously. "How?"

I stood there waiting as she skipped down the staircase. Sunlight streamed from the window behind her, catching the light of her silver-blond hair. She was a vision. Little Meiklei had disappeared without a trace.

"How have you changed?" I made a motion with my hand. "Your hair, your dress—" I decided not to mention her skin. I smiled. "But then I was expecting a little girl, instead I see the woman you have grown into. My compliments to the Enavian girls' school. If I ever have a daughter, I will send her there."

"Don't," she smiled and shook her head. "Don't." She hesitated, uncertain what to say next.

"You wanted something, *Evimeh*?" I reminded her politely.

"Yes," she said with exasperation. "Time with you."

I smiled.

"We've just dined together at the most expensive restaurant on Ceytal."

"But everything was so rushed at the station. Mheftu didn't give you—or anyone else—a chance to speak. And as soon as we came home you disappeared. Why did you run off like that?"

"I had work to do."

"Oh, work," she brushed the word aside as if it were nothing. "Daddy would have let someone else do it. I've been away so long and you were one of the people I wanted to see most of all."

I stood there for a moment, unable to think of a proper response. It was then an Enavian, a young man about my age, entered the room. He did not seem pleased at all to see Melisanne speaking to me with easy friendliness. Before a word had passed between us, we were rivals. Melisanne's training at the fashionable girls' college had not been wasted. She smoothed over the awkward moment with the effortless poise of a diplomat's wife.

"Hello, Lonnor. I'd like you to meet a very old friend of mine, Terez. Terez, this is Lonnor Weldon, Jr. Lonnor attended the University of Taen, which was next to my school."

"I am pleased to make your acquaintance," Weldon said and held out his hand. He too had learned etiquette.

I had not. I looked at his hand puzzled. Melisanne, seeing my dilemma, laughed easily and said:

"Terez, you are about to have your first lesson in deportment. Here, take my hand—no with your right one. Now, we shake them and say, 'I am pleased to make your acquaintance.' Now you shake Lonnor's hand."

"I am pleased to make your acquaintance, Mr. Weldon," I said. An Enavian graduate couldn't have done better. Still, I decided I didn't like Enavian etiquette, nor did I like this Enavian named Lonnor Weldon Jr. And, for all his courtesy, I didn't think he liked me either.

"So, Terez, you're an old friend of the family. Do you live on one of the nearby estates?"

"No, I live here. I work for the Gavins."

He looked puzzled. I was still dressed in my Enavian suit.

"Are you an accountant or lawyer, perhaps?"

"No, I'm one of the hired hands."

Something in Weldon relaxed and dismissed me as unimportant.

"I hate to interrupt this touching reunion," he said turning to Melisanne, "But the others are having tea in the parlor." He bowed mockingly. "Shall I escort the lady Gavin down the hall?"

She glanced aside to me. "Will you come, too?" she asked.

"No, *Evimeh*. I have much to do."

The truth was I had nothing to do, but I could imagine the fool I would look in the parlor.

Her smile slipped only fractionally.

"That is unfortunate. Perhaps later," she suggested.

She slipped her arm into Weldon's and allowed herself to be led away. I stood watching them as they turned down the hall and thought how well they looked together. She was so graceful in her long dress, and he was—what was the word?—dashing. And what was I?

Weldon's laughter echoed down the hall.

"Mel, you're too much. To think of giving a filthy dinge a lesson in etiquette."

I turned away. Yes, that was what I was—a filthy dinge. To the Enavians I could be nothing else and I would be a fool to think otherwise. It was a small moment, as most pivotal moments are. I saw clearly what my place in the world was and it was not with the Enavians.

Without a word to anyone I packed and left the Gavin Ranch. I returned to my father's people in the Valley of Zeneshtu.

Chapter 9
The Nejimenet Jevema: Tejalura 1325-1328 EE

> "A woman's heart can be more challenging than any frontier. But only if she is the right woman."
>
> — *Neve Ce*

Summer 1325 EE

I arrived at Zeneshtu Valley only to learn Yari, Hushé and Geysan had left a few weeks earlier with Neve's son, Terez, to work on an Enavian ranch. At first I felt abandoned, but the feeling soon passed. I fell in easily with the familiar routine of Chevari's ranch and found myself extending my visit through summer and most of autumn. I made new friends among the workers, but I missed my brothers. It was the longest time I'd been separated from my Nejimenet family since they adopted me when I was seven.

Although I missed my brothers, I enjoyed the fact that I was no longer standing in their shadow. I felt I was becoming a person in my own right, an adult who was taken seriously. As a test of my new incarnation, I announced to Neve Chevari I would travel alone to Halia Tehal to meet my family for the *yaremida* gathering. My brothers would have forbidden it, but they were miles away at an Enavian ranch, so they had nothing to say on the matter. Chevari himself said little at the time. He was only concerned that I pack enough provisions for the journey. At last, I was free to do as I pleased!

Or so I thought.

As I was ready to leave, Chevari dispatched five of his agents on some invented errand so they could accompany me to Halia Tehal. During the past six months, Chevari made a fine show of treating me the same as any of his other hired hands. But I had never been anything other than his ward, the only child of his best friend. He allowed me my illusion of a summer adventure, but, in reality, I couldn't have been more sheltered than if I had been closeted in a harem.

Still, why waste time worrying about what couldn't be changed? It occurred to me there might be worse fates than being escorted by five handsome Zenadishj warriors. With such an entourage I took great pleasure playing the great lady. I could have easily grown used to it, but it all ended when they delivered me to my brothers. Yari and Hushé quickly put me in my place and showed absolutely no remorse for deserting me that summer.

Geysan, eager to return to Laughter, left without us. My brothers and I stayed a few days, lodging in the guest rooms at the Horse Trading Office on Queen Street. It was fun at first, but I soon tired of having to wear a veil every time we left Chevari's offices. Also, I thought perhaps my presence kept them from activities they couldn't do with a younger sister hanging about. I thought they'd be glad to see me go, but when I made plans to leave, they protested me going off alone.

"But Geysan went alone," I protested. "And don't you dare say it's all right for him because he's a man. I'm a *nutevek narashan*."

"You may be a *nutevek narashan*." Yari said. "But he's five times bigger than you are and looks like a slayer of *nutevek narashans*. No one would even think of crossing Geysan. If you wanted to leave without us, you should have left with him."

I left the next morning before they woke up. This had been easy to do because they had been out late carousing with the other horse traders. By the time they discovered my absence, I would be miles away. After leaving Halia Tehal I crossed the bridge outside the city gates and realized I was truly free for the first time in my life.

Late that afternoon I smelled a camp fire. Through the trees along the river I saw a young Zenadishj who had made camp for the day. I remembered it was Neve Beltehal, a holy day of rest for the Zenadishj. He was young and handsome, his magenta hair was thicker than most Zenadishj and his body was well muscled. I judged him to be a little older than Yari and Hushé. When I saw the design on his saddle, I knew he was a member of Neve Chevari's household. I remembered Yari mentioning Chevari's son would be in this area, but I couldn't recall what his name was. As Chevari's son he would be safe to approach, but for some reason I was shy and unable to step forward and introduce myself. I watched him for a while then went my way.

I turned and went upstream, knowing I would soon meet with our caravan. My pace was slow and meandering so I could take time to look at whatever caught my fancy. At night I would lay awake watching the stars, and the sound of the river was like music.

After several days I met with the caravan from Meneth-shir. The first person I saw was Tzeri. After we talked of my journey, she asked some very careful questions about the welfare of Yari and Hushé and the Chevari household. I answered with a knowing smile that *Hushé* was quite well. At once she knew her secret was out.

"Taji, you knew all the time! Why didn't you tell me?"

"I didn't want to embarrass you in case he didn't feel the same way. I thought it would be easier if you thought no one else knew. But he bought you a present when we were in the city, so now I'm pretty sure he does."

"What did he buy me? Jewelry? A dress?"

I had been afraid she would ask, still, I thought, I had better warn her.

"A flint."

"A what? Oh, Taji, that's terrible!"

It was, but Hushé was Hushé and his sensitivity was rarely expressed outside of his art.

"It's a very nice flint," I offered.

"That may be, but it isn't a gift for a sweetheart. What makes you think he likes me?"

"Because he didn't buy anything for anyone else. He swore he wouldn't when Yari had to buy another horse just to carry all the presents he bought for us. At the last minute Hushé bought the flint for you."

"Well, I suppose that's something. Are you sure that he didn't buy you or Yari something?"

"Nothing. Yari bought me something, but I have to wait until he gives everyone else their presents. You know how he likes to make a big ceremony out of everything. Don't worry, I'm certain Hushé likes you."

"It's easy for you to be so casual," she said. "Just wait until you fall in love."

"Never!" I declared laughing. But I remembered the young Zenadishj I had seen by the river and wondered.

His name was Terez.

I was gathering wood for the fire when I saw him ride into the camp with Yari and Hushé. My heart stopped at the sight of him. He was and still is one of the most beautiful men I have ever known. He was not vain, but there was an arrogance about him, and that, combined with a winning smile, had a devastating effect on my emotions. The thing I feared most had come to pass: I was sixteen and I was in love.

He caught me staring at him and smiled. I lowered my glance and carried the wood over to the fire where Ancient and Silverwoman were cooking the evening meal. A small distance away, Yari unloaded his pack horse and began handing out presents while Hushé and Terez led their horses away.

I overheard Yari tell the others Terez was Neve Chevari's son. After serving in the Enavian Auxiliaries, Terez became assistant foreman of an Enavian ranch along the Blue Mountain River. Terez had either quit or been fired—something to do with a scandal involving Gavin's daughter. Although I would have liked to have learned more about Terez, the others were eager to receive their gifts, so Yari concentrated on handing them out.

Each female member of our family received a piece of turquoise and silver jewelry, a bolt of cloth and a blanket. Uncle Gan and Geysan each received a steel axe and Zarkhon was given a music box. An Enavian would consider a music box a womanish gift but my father was quite pleased with it. Since possession of it made him the owner of the only mechanical device in Meneth-shir, it gave him a certain prestige among the others.

He gave Nejo a Zenadishj spear. It was a beautiful weapon and well made. It had a metal point, the shaft was of dark wood inlaid with turquoise, white and magenta stones. To everyone's amusement, Nejo couldn't lift it.

"This is not a play weapon," Yari told him. "This is a spear for a man. You will carry it when you are old enough to join the Naritian Army."

Yari could be so annoying; *he* had never served in the Naritian Army. He had no business encouraging Nejo to enlist. Nejo was just a boy, he was far too young for such a weapon.

"And for Tejalura, bracelets and a red blouse. Of all the women in Meneth-shir, only she can wear this color so well."

I was still angry with Yari, but I had to admit it was a fine shirt. It was cut in the Enavian style and must have cost him a great deal. Enavian goods had become difficult to obtain.

"Try the blouse on," urged Tzeri. "Let us see how pretty it looks on you."

But Ancient had other ideas.

"Wait, Taji. I want you to get some water first. I'll get no work out of you once you put that shirt on."

"Can't one of the boys do that?" Laughter asked. "Let her try it on."

"No," I said quickly as I saw Terez and Hushé approaching. "I'll do it."

"Good. Here's the bucket and here's a knife to cut some flowers with. Cut the red ones by the river in honor of our guest."

I left as Terez joined the group. I was relieved to be off alone with a chance to gather my thoughts. But instead of forcing him out of my mind, I dreamed foolish dreams about Terez, just as Tzeri must have dreamed about Hushé. I dreamed of a life as his wife helping to raise horses with my father-in-law, Neve, and raising a son who looked just like Terez.

I shook my head to clear my mind of this impossible, happy picture. Such a thing could never be. After all, he was older than Yari so he might already have a wife. Even if he did notice me, which was doubtful, as a Nejimenet I could never be happy as a second wife. And there was the affair with the Enavian woman. It sounded like Terez already had enough women in his life to be interested in me.

Aunt Kiakashe had married a Zenadishj while she served in the Naritian Army. The marriage ended in divorce, she never explained why. The severed tendon on her left heel might be an old battle scar, but some of us speculated it might have been the price of her freedom from an unhappy marriage. Among the Zenadishj adultery is the only grounds for divorce and only women, not men, could be charged. A Nejimenet woman did not marry a Zenadishj man lightly.

Still, I found myself thinking of Terez's smile.

I tossed the bucket into the water to fill it, taking a moment to see the stars reflected on the smooth surface. With my knife I began to cut the thick stems of the red flowers growing along the bank. I sang to myself, being happy for no particular reason. Behind me I sensed a movement. I straightened and turned, tightening my grip on my knife.

It was Terez, I could see him clearly for the moonlight was a revealing as the day. It was he who spoke first for I could say nothing.

"I'm sorry, I didn't mean to frighten you."

Relaxing, I smiled.

"How is it you know a song of the Mountain Zenadishj?" he asked.

"Yari and Hushé taught it to me."

"That's right, they have been working with my father. Yet they have only returned today. How could you know this song?"

I was so unnerved I couldn't explain that I had also worked for his father and had visited Zeneshtu many times. He brushed my faltering words aside.

"It doesn't matter. You know the song and it pleases me. I have been away from my people for a long time. The song brought back many pleasant memories."

Again I smiled.

"I am glad it pleases you. But now I must return with the water and the flowers. Ancient will wonder why I've been gone so long."

"No, stay. There are things I would say to you."

This was my first experience with the attentions of a man. To the others of Meneth-shir I was still a child, not much older than when I had first come to be among them. It did not occur to them I was old enough to be thought of in such a manner. I found Terez's interest to be most flattering.

"First tell me your name," he asked.

"Tejalura."

"Moonlight? Yes, of course. You are called so because the highlights on you hair are like moonlight against the blackness of night. Did you know we Mountain Zenadishj consider Urthic women to be the most beautiful on earth? You would fetch a high price in Zeneshtu."

He touched my cheek and I trembled.

"Are you afraid, Tejalura? Don't worry, I won't take you for just one night. I will buy you from your master and take you back to my household."

I backed away in confusion.

"Buy me?"

There were no slaves in Meneth-shir, all were free men. Up to this time I had assumed my status was that of a true daughter of Zarkhon and Silverwoman, but now I began to wonder just what my position was. After all, Zarkhon did buy me.

"Yes," he said. "Wouldn't you like that? My father's house is large and he has been after me to settle down. I cannot marry you because you are a slave, but you would be shown every courtesy and right due a first wife. Now tell me your master's name."

Humiliated, I took another step back. So much for my dreams of being his wife in Zeneshtu Valley.

Impatiently he grabbed hold of my arm.

"It's a fair offer," he said. "More than fair."

I tried to pull away from him, but he held me tightly. In my panic I forgot all of Aunt Kiakashe's training. I screamed. He covered my mouth, but I heard the sound of others approaching and he was pulled away from me.

"There is no reason for this," Terez was saying. "The girl is unharmed."

But the two men still held him and the others' knives remained unsheathed.

"But Yari," he continued. "She is a slave. The Nejimenets cannot value the honor of a slave so highly."

"Tejalura is no slave. She is a member of my household."

For a moment no one spoke. I sat there, my body racking with sobs that made no sound. I sensed Yari kneeling beside me.

"Are you all right?" he asked gently.

I nodded.

"He didn't harm you—in any way?"

I shook my head violently. He turned to face Terez.

"Your father is our friend and for his sake your life will be spared. You may ride out of this camp in peace."

Yari glanced at the other men. Reluctantly they put their knives away.

"You may go," he repeated. "But if you return, your blood will be on your own hands. *Nu erevna, N'jim-aza.*"

Yari gathered me up and carried me back to the tent. By now the whole camp had come out to see what had happened. Questions were asked and answered, the story spread and grew with each telling. I heard the sound of many voices and heard the word "Zenadishj" repeated several times. Many of the women touched me as we passed and murmured in sympathy. I buried my head in Yari's arm, I couldn't stand to look at them. I was relieved when at last we were inside the tent.

"Leave her alone," Yari told the others. "She's all right. The best thing for her now is to just let her cry for a while."

"What happened?" Laughter asked. "Was that Tejalura we heard screaming?"

"Yes," he said. "It seems our friend has taken advantage of our hospitality."

"Poor Taji."

"You mean poor Terez," Yari corrected. "You should have seen him. He looked as if he had been fighting with a wild cat."

The others laughed at his exaggeration and it became a joke, nothing to be taken seriously. I smiled weakly as Silverwoman handed me warm mug of tea.

"In a week or two he'll be back to offer for you, Taji. If you want to get married, here's your chance."

"What do you mean?" I asked Yari sharply.

"Neve is a man of honor. He won't let a matter like this go unresolved. For friendship's sake he'll make Terez offer for you."

"But I don't want to marry him," I said. At least I didn't if his father was forcing him to offer for me.

"Well then, turn him down—but do it politely because we still need Neve's trade," Zarkhon advised.

Weeks later, as expected, Terez did offer for me. The members of the Chevari household, Neve Chevari among them, accompanied him. With formal politeness, Terez made his offer of marriage to me and, with just as much formality and politeness, I declined. He looked relieved and I felt an unexpected disappointment.

"Good!" he said with feeling. "Now we are all friends again. Here, let me give you a kiss just so we know what we are going to be missing."

Swinging me up easily, he whirled me about while everyone cheered and clapped their hands.

It was decided to celebrate the event by holding a dance in a nearby field. Zarkhon felt our household should not join in the party. Laughter was furious because Geysan agreed with him.

"The Mountain Zenadishj are a little more wild than we are and there will be a lot of drinking," Zarkhon explained. "It is better to stay home."

"We have things that we can do," Silverwoman said, cutting off any more objections.

The distant sound of music and laughter drifted by as we worked. Looking up, I watched them for a while. At that moment I wished I were out there with them.

I remembered something from my Enavian childhood. It was the first dance Gabrielle attended—how many years ago?—I had lost count. Too young to join the party, I was allowed to watch from upstairs on the promise I would make no noise. She had flirted to see how many admirers she could acquire before the evening ended. Within an hour she had captured every eligible bachelor present and made enemies of all her former girlfriends. How jealous they were as they sat gossiping about that "terrible Aleksandar girl." I can hear them yet:

"See how low her neckline is."

"Look at how high she lifts her skirt."

"She thinks she is so pretty."

But Gabrielle continued to dance, not caring in the least what was said about her. Enavian dances of the court, ancient Erteyan waltzes, Ceytalian folk dances—they were the best, especially if one had a pair of long graceful legs to display, which Gabrielle did.

How proud Daddy and Jack were of her that night, even though Daddy had to speak to her about her "disgraceful" conduct. But I could tell he was just as proud of her as we all were.

Gabrielle . . .

I remembered her dress, it was made of deep red material that shimmered in the light. How lovely she had been, and soon, because I was her identical twin, I would look just like her. I remembered the dances she had begun to teach me so I would be able to dance well when I went to my first party. And all the advice she had given me.

"Now Lillian when a man proposes to you, you must reject him; politely of course, but you must reject him."

"But what if he is the one I want?" I had asked.

"You may accept his proposal, but never the first time he asks. Make him ask again, that way he will appreciate you."

Would Terez ask again? I wondered as I watched him and the others dance around the fire. The music was wild and fast, I knew that dance well.

"Why don't you join them?" suggested Laughter, who had been watching me. "Zarkhon won't even notice—Tejalura?"

I had been watching Terez dance with a pretty girl. I turned my attention to Laughter.

"No," I said. "There's work to do."

"Don't be foolish! Silverwoman will let you go—won't you?"

My mother nodded but added, "If she wants to."

"See there? No, Taji, put it down, I'll let you wear my light green blouse and my turquoise necklace. You'll be the prettiest girl there."

"No, I don't want to go."

"Tejalura, you will never catch a husband that way. I'd go if I weren't married." Her eyes scanned the gathering. She gasped, "Look! My husband! And Uncle, too! See them there, flirting with all those Zenadishj girls as if they were single. We'd better get out there before we each have a second wife to contend with. Come on, let's get dressed. You too, Ancient."

The old woman scowled.

"I'll not make a fool of myself, I'm staying here."

"Of course you're going, Grandmother. You can dance with all those other old relics sitting about the fire gathering dust." She winked and jerked her head in my direction. "And Tejalura can sit here by herself and pout if she wants to."

Ancient chuckled slyly, put her work away and followed them into the tent.

I glared at them as I set to work again. I hated it when they tried to manipulate me. Stubbornly, I decided I would sit there the whole evening rather than give in to their schemes.

The four women emerged from the tent arrayed in their brightest clothing, giggling like adolescents. Ancient wagged her finger at me.

"Watch out. I might catch some young man right out from under your nose. I was pretty fast in my day."

"In your day, Grandmother," I reminded her. "In your day."

Laughing, they went out to join the others. Someone had run out to meet Ancient. She said something to the others but I couldn't make out what it was. A few heads turned in my direction.

Coolly, I turned away and returned to my embroidery. I tried to do a sober job of it, but at last I gave up. The threads were so tangled it was impossible to straighten them out. Irritated, I threw my work down. Let Ancient untangle it tomorrow! That would teach her not to act like an old fool.

I started to enter the tent to go to bed, but I cast a backwards glance. I wasn't tired yet and it wouldn't hurt to watch for a while.

Stealthily, I made my way to the fire. It was almost dark now, no one would be likely to see me. And if they did, I had my old, faded dress on to attest to the fact I had only come to watch, not to participate. I sat down on the outskirts where a few others, mostly the elderly, sat.

For a while my presence went unnoticed and I began to feel a little indignant. Well, I was here, isn't that what they wanted? Maybe not. Maybe they had just used my reluctance as an excuse to get out themselves. Ancient! And at her age too! Then:

"Taji!"

It was Laughter.

"Come on and dance with us. Oh wait, you can't, at least not dressed like that."

She caught the attention of a few friends and against my feeble protests, they guided me back to the tent.

"You must wear your red blouse, the one Yari gave you. You haven't worn it yet and he'll be heartbroken."

"Well, let him be. I'm wearing my leather shirt."

"Taji, you can't! It has a stain on it. See? You must wear the red one. Besides all the other girls will be jealous of you. They can't wear red because it looks so awful on them. Here's the jewelry. Put as much on as you can."

Reluctantly I obeyed. As soon as I was through, they pushed me outside. Only then did I allow my excitement to show. At last I would dance. And if the others laughed, what of it? I was going to have fun.

I had come in the middle of a dance but Turquoise allowed me to finish the remainder of it with Geysan. When that was over, I was swung expertly into Yari's arms. But tonight I couldn't be angry—even with him. I gave him my prettiest smile and laughed at everything he said. He was a good dancer.

I had a wonderful time. Young men and older ones too, who hadn't given me a moment's glance before, now sought my company as if I were a favored equal. I flirted, but not seriously, as did my partners and not at all with married men. With them I was attentive, charming, even flattering, but nothing more. It was like being at one of Gabrielle's dances, only better.

I noticed that Ancient herself was doing quite well. All the other men who were not otherwise occupied, hovered around her for a dance, and surprisingly she was quick on her feet. I decided to remember this the next time she complained about her bones not being what they used to be when there was work to be done.

The wine skins were passed around and everyone, including me, made sure they received their fair share. Soon I was feeling a little giddy. My laughter was gay and came easily but my steps were as sure as ever.

"I think you are a little drunk," Yari said aside to me the next time we danced together.

"And I feel wonderful."

"Yes, but I think you should go home now."

"Now?"

"Yes, now."

"But I've only been here a little while."

"You've been here since sunset and it's past midnight. Now go home before you fall and make a fool of yourself."

"Oh, Yari, I won't fall. I only get dizzy when I stop dancing, so if I keep dancing—"

"Tejalura, you're drunk," he said bluntly.

By now those around us had stopped dancing and stood listening.

"I'm not dru-unk!"

The others, except Yari, laughed when I hiccupped. Zarkhon stepped forward.

"Leave her be, Yari. She's having a good time, don't spoil it. So what if she is a little drunk, we all are."

"That's right, Brother. We all are a little drunk. And in a few hours we will be very drunk and anything can happen."

Everyone's face came into focus. They were all smiling, amused at the scene before them. The over-protective Yari arguing with Zarkhon, the indulgent father. No one was acting like themselves tonight. Zarkhon, Yari, myself, any of us.

Confused, I ran back to our tent. I sobbed for a while then fell asleep.

Chapter 10
Ceremony of the Chosen: Tejalura 1328-1329 EE

> "Marriage? We have no choice but to tolerate it.
> Believe me, were it possible to devise another
> system, it would have been done by now."
>
> — *Neve Ce*

Autumn 1328 EE

It was an exciting day for me when Aunt Kiakashe tattooed the blue mark of the *nutevek narashan* on my cheekbone. Yari, true to his autocratic nature, objected by saying he considered it a barbaric custom that was more typical of the Oramakletes than Human Beings.

"Leave her be, Yari" Hushé defended. "It may be a good thing. That trouble with Terez would never have happened if she'd had a tattoo."

With that, Yari was silent.

Since the incident with Terez, our household had been accustomed to receiving visits from many of the young, unmarried men of Meneth-shir. They came with Yari or Hushé, but it was obvious to all, embarrassingly obvious, it was me they came to see. It was an awkward time for me. I had no interest in them and had nothing to say so I kept silent in the background, leaving the others to entertain the visitor as best they could. While working in the fields or playing *mheftuli* it was easy to speak with the young men my age, but when they approached me as suitors I became uneasy and shy.

For a while one could come to visit, then give up and another would take his place and then another in a long procession that spanned two years. At first my family said nothing of the matter beyond a few teasing remarks. If I was happy going to school, rock climbing with Tzeri, training to be treasurer, and doing my share of the work on the farm, then they were happy for me. All except Ancient. One night after the latest of my suitors left, she was unable to stand it any more in silence.

"That one won't be coming again, I'll wager," she said. "And why should he? That one there," she pointed to me, "sat as if she had swallowed her tongue."

"I didn't have anything to say."

"'I didn't have anything to say,'" she mimicked in cruel imitation. "Well, you had better think of something to say the next time, because the rest of us have run out of things to say."

"She doesn't have to say anything to them," Yari defended. "She doesn't invite them over."

"Do we?" she asked. "No, they invite themselves. But I don't blame them for how else can they meet her? She never goes to any of the dances."

"She went to one," Yari offered as a pitiful scrap of defense.

"If I were you, Yari, I wouldn't be the one to bring that subject up. I could have killed you for the way you embarrassed poor Taji. It's your fault she isn't going to any of them now."

He raised his hands in mock surrender.

"Peace. Enough. I'll say no more."

Ancient renewed her attack on me.

"You don't want to be an old maid do you? No. So why don't you go to the dance this week and have some fun for a change? Yari won't bother you." She fixed her eye on him. "Will you, Yari."

"No," he said quickly. "I wouldn't think of it."

"See?" she said to me. "Come on, Tejalura, why don't you go?"

"I'll think about it," I answered evasively.

"No, I won't let you off so easily. Tell me now, yes or no."

"No."

I blocked off her steady stream of reproof and concentrated on the blanket I was making. One more row and it would be complete. Out of the corner of my eye I saw Yari start to leave. Zarkhon entered at the same time.

"What is all this?" he asked Yari, motioning to the ranting and raving Ancient. Yari shrugged and spread his hands helplessly.

"Ancient, what are you carrying on about?"

She proceeded to tell her son-in-law, at great length, about my horrible fate as an old maid.

"But that's ridiculous," he said. "She's only eighteen."

"And she will soon be nineteen."

"Ancient, you are being Oramaklete. We are Nejimenets, not savages who marry their daughters off at puberty. Tejalura is too pretty not to marry and she'll marry when she's ready. Now where is my dinner?"

From this statement I thought I had an ally in my father, but that *yaremida* he betrayed me. We had met the Mountain Zenadishj and had traveled with them for a few weeks when he called everyone together to make an announcement before the evening meal.

"Today, before we came back to camp, a man called me aside and asked me to give him Tejalura for his wife."

"Did you accept?" asked Silverwoman apprehensively.

"Yes."

Laughter hugged.

"Oh, Taji this is wonderful. Who is he?"

"I don't know," I answered.

"Don't you have any idea?"

I shook my head.

"Nor will she know until the wedding day," Zarkhon interjected. "This is to be a marriage after the old custom."

Laughter protested.

"Oh, Uncle Zarkhon, that's not fair. I don't believe they followed that custom even in the old days."

"Nevertheless, it will be followed now."

The others rushed up to me excitedly, laughing and hugging me. I saw Nejo run outside to spread the news all over the camp. Everyone seemed happy except Silverwoman who stood to one side. Her eyes measured Zarkhon with a steel-gray inspection he chose to ignore for the moment.

"How much did this man pay for Tejalura?" she asked.

Zarkhon frowned disapprovingly.

"A very great deal, though it is none of your concern. Four excellent horses, ten unused lengths of cloth, seven good skins, and two hundred gold Enavian credits."

We all stared. It was a fortune, especially when one considered twice as much would be given on the wedding day. Never had we heard of such an offer.

"Who could afford to pay so much?" Laughter asked. "You didn't sell her to one of the Zenadishj did you?"

Terez. If it has to be anyone, let it be him, I prayed. But Zarkhon shook his head.

"No, he is a man of Meneth-shir, a respected man. I'll say no more."

"You must give it back," I said.

They all looked at me in astonishment.

"You can't Taji."

"Don't be a fool," Laughter advised. "There has never been such an offer since the Journey. No woman in Meneth-shir can boast of such an honor."

"I don't want to get married."

"I have already given my word," Zarkhon said. "But don't worry, he is a young man and well respected as I have said before."

I started to protest, but I found it hard to put my feelings into words. I wasn't ready to marry yet. Although I might have gone along with it if it were Terez. I had thought of him a great deal lately, but I wasn't sure I wanted to marry even if he had been the one to offer for me. Suddenly my freedom seemed a priceless possession that should not be surrendered lightly, and then only in exchange for something greater value. But not now, not yet. I tried to convey this to Zarkhon, but he silenced me with an abrupt motion of his hand.

"Before you say anything else, there is a question I must ask you."

He looked at me so sternly it was a struggle for me to meet his eyes.

"This is a very important question," he continued, "And it will concern your marriage. Answer it truthfully for you may have to come before the council and answer it again and I will have to hold you to what you say today. Do you understand me?"

Unable to take my eyes from his, I nodded.

"Good, now answer me. Tejalura, are you my daughter—"

"Zarkhon!"

Impatiently he motioned for Silverwoman to be still.

"Answer me, Tejalura. Are you my daughter or are you related to any member of the Tehalchev household?"

He had used the word *jameshe*, my flesh, my blood. He could have used *jamesh* which means 'mine' or 'my own' for he had bought me and I was technically his property, but I was not a daughter of his by blood. I was afraid he would be angry if I said I was, but then again I was afraid he would be angry if I said I wasn't. I chose my words carefully.

"No, you are my father. You fed me, you clothed me, and helped teach me the way of Human Beings, but you did not give me life. Though I call you my father, I am not of your blood."

I relaxed when he nodded and seemed pleased.

THE CEREMONY OF THE CHOSEN: TEJALURA

By the next morning everyone knew of my offer. They smiled and told me how happy and excited they were for me. I was treated more as an adult than a child. Women told me what marriage had been like for them; giving birth to children, raising them, different ways they prepared their meals, what pleased their husbands and what did not.

At those times I thought it wouldn't be so bad to get married, yet, would it be the right thing to do? I was happy with my life the way it was. There was no man I wished to marry, although sometimes I thought of Terez. Of all the men in Meneth-shir there wasn't a man I didn't respect. They were fine men, all of them. But was there one I could love? And what of the man who had offered for me, how did he feel about me? The size of his offer must indicate something.

On bath day I decided to stay behind for a while to catch up on some unfinished work but I promised to join the others soon. About an hour after they had gone, I saw Yari leading his horse to the tent he and Hushé shared. I smiled and waved him.

"Hello, Stranger," I called out to him. "When did you get back?"

"Just now," he said. "You seem to be in a good mood today."

"I am."

"What no problems to tell me?"

"None," I said, then hesitated. "Well, there is one but—"

He waited for me to continue. I could tell Yari, he would understand. Hadn't he remained unmarried? Perhaps he could help me against the others when I told them of my decision not to get married.

"Oh Yari, someone wants to marry me. You haven't heard because you've been away for a while."

He laughed.

"Is that your problem? I could name several girls your age who would be happy to have your problem. What's the matter? Was the bride-price so small?"

"No. They say it's the biggest offer ever."

"Well, what then?"

"Nothing," I said. "I just don't want to get married."

"To this man?"

"No, I don't even know who he is and I don't care. I just don't want to get married."

"Don't be ridiculous, Taji. Every girl wants to get married. What would happen to this world if no one ever married?"

"Hah! You're a fine one to talk about the virtues of marriage."

"A good point," he agreed with a smile. "But still, I think you should accept the offer."

"Why? You've never married. I thought you would understand, Yari, you of all people."

"I do understand," he said. "But there is one major difference between our situations. I support myself, I am a burden to no one, while the household benefits from my services as a hunter, warrior, and farmer. Can you say the same for yourself?"

I thought for a moment.

"Yes, I can. I offer the same service you or any other member of our household can. In fact, I have two skills you don't: I am a *nutevek narashan ce* and soon I will be the official treasurer of Meneth-shir."

"I see I have not made my point," he said, as usual ignoring anything I had to say. "But you will marry like a good Meneth-shir girl and give your husband many children like a good wife."

I shook my head stubbornly.

"No, I'm telling Father tonight. I won't be forced into anything."

His mouth tightened in anger.

"Do you know what you are, Tejalura? You are a spoiled little brat. Well, it's time you started taking on the responsibilities of a woman instead of acting like a five-year-old baby and I'm going to see that you do."

"How?"

"If you cheat my brother out of the bride-price I will take you as a concubine after the old law."

I sputtered like a wet cat.

"You wouldn't dare!"

He grinned.

"Believe me, Tejalura, I would. If you are not Zarkhon's daughter, then you are his slave. The choice is yours."

"I won't do it, do you hear me! I won't be pushed into anything!"

He didn't even bother to answer me but went to his tent.

Angry, I put my work away and went to the river only to be greeted by a radiant Tzeri who told me Hushé had offered for her so we would be married in the same ceremony. I tried to be happy for her, and I was, but it seemed so unfair. Tzeri knew who was to marry her and at least it was to someone she loved. I was depressed the next few days but, needless to say, I didn't mention my wanting to stay unmarried to Zarkhon.

·→❋←·→❋←·→❋←·

Our household separated ourselves from the others to visit Neve Chevari and to invite him to the wedding.

"So," he said beaming at Hushé and me, "Who are you two marrying?"

"Tzeri Jevetchev," he answered proudly.

"And you, Taji?"

"I don't know."

"You don't know? So, it is to be a marriage after the old custom. That is good. And Yari, when are you going to get married?"

There was a small silence, and I knew. From the look on everyone's face, I knew! I don't remember the evasive answer he must have given Neve because I was so angry I couldn't see straight. I don't know how I made it through the rest of the evening without anyone sensing my feelings. Somehow I managed to choke down my meal and make some excuse to go to bed early.

As I was leaving the washroom and going to my room, I heard my parents discussing me.

"She should be told," Silverwoman said.

"They will be married in a few days and that will be the end of it," Zarkhon assured her. "There is nothing to be concerned about."

"I'm sorry but the happiness of my daughter concerns me very much. It is very cruel the way you have left her wondering. And asking her if she was your daughter! Well, let me ask you this: Are you Tejalura's father? Could any real father treat his daughter as you have treated her?"

I didn't want to hear any more. I had never heard Silverwoman speak to Zarkhon in such a manner. Yes, Yari would pay dearly for this. Some way, some how I would make him pay.

·→❋←·→❋←·→❋←·

A few days after we had returned from Zeneshtu, Tzeri and I needed to go into the city to do the final shopping. With us came Silverwoman and Laughter, who brought the twins with her. Imih and Teve were eight now and felt themselves very important because they were to be my *veshes*. They still looked alike, but now because of their different styles of clothing and different lengths of hair, you could tell them apart.

It was a hot, dusty day and I had no interest in shopping as the others did. The fact they were happy made me even more miserable. Off in the distance I saw Mheftu Padhari, the friend of my Enavian father. It had been many years, but I recognized him instantly.

"Mheftu!" I shouted, forgetting those who were with me.

He looked about him to see who had called him. I had to wave my hand to draw his attention. He stared at me in disbelief.

"Gabrielle? No, of course not. You must be Lillian."

"Yes," I nodded laughing. "I am Lee-lee-yan."

Tzeri came up behind me.

"Who is that man, Tejalura?"

I ignored her and ran out to the street to meet him. I threw my arms around him and we both laughed.

He said something in a once familiar, but now forgotten, language. I struggled to understand the meaning of the words he spoke but could not. I shook my head in confusion. He was speaking Enavian.

"Nu creda, Mheftu."

"I said you have grown much over the years," he repeated in Nejimenet. "And how is Johnny? Is he with you?"

Nejo. It took me a moment to realize who he was talking about.

"No, he is back at camp," I said. "He is nearly a man now. If you think I've grown, you should see him. You wouldn't recognize him."

Behind me I could hear the voices of my family discussing my strange behavior.

"Here, Mheftu. I want you to meet my family."

"Tejalura, your conduct was shameful," Turquoise scolded me. "Who is this man you all but made love to in the middle of the street for all to see?"

I laughed.

"Mheftu, this is my Aunt Turquoise. This is my mother, Silverwoman; my grandmother, Ancient; Tzeri, my friend; Laughter, my cousin; and her children, Imih and Teve. Everybody, this is Mheftu Padhari. He was a friend of my Enavian father."

Instantly everyone was all smiles. When Mheftu was a boy he had lived in Meneth-shir and the older ones in our group had been friends

THE CEREMONY OF THE CHOSEN: TEJALURA

of his parents so it became somewhat of a reunion. We invited him to the wedding ceremony that would take place in a few days.

・→▨←・→▨←・→▨←・

Silverwoman awakened me before sunrise the day of the wedding. She and the other woman dressed me carefully attending to every detail of my hair, make-up, and jewelry. I let them for it was important I look my very best to make my vengeance complete. If my plan worked my marriage with Yari would last less than an hour. How humiliating it would be for him to have his wife divorce him on his wedding day.

When the ceremony began, we marched out to the open field. Tzeri and I held each other's hands while our *veshes* sang the wedding song. I could not help being proud of Imih and Teve, for not making a single mistake.

When the grooms came forward one at a time, I began to feel uneasy. Tzeri, who was ahead of me in turn, smiled her welcome when Hushé came to her. I saw the love in their eyes and felt a pang of jealousy. I held my breath when it was my turn.

Yes, it was Yari. He rode his magnificent stallion as if he were lord of the earth. Enjoy it while you can, I thought to myself, for in a few hours you will look the greatest of fools. He dismounted and walked—no, sauntered towards us.

"*Jevim*," he bowed, respectfully to Zarkhon. "Your daughter has found favor in my eyes. Her beauty is surpassed only by her gentle spirit," he recited in the face of my icy glare.

Zarkhon returned the bow.

"You are a proven warrior of many deeds of greatness," he answered. "Take my daughter and may she earn her bride-price."

They bowed again and Yari remounted his horse. We stood there in silence while the next wedding group recited their lines. I could sense him watching me curiously; he had not expected me to fall into everything so easily.

"Tejalura, what are you thinking?"

"What does a bride usually think of on her wedding day?"

"I asked you a question—which requires an answer, not another question."

I remained silent.

"Tejalura, what are you planning?"

I smiled sweetly.

"You'll see."

"If you make a scene or cause embarrassment to our family—"

"You should have thought of that before you bullied me into this, Yari."

"Tejalura—"

He was interrupted by the announcement for the race to begin.

Yari knew I was a fast runner for my size, but there was no reason for him to pace his horse as fast as he did except for that mean streak of viciousness he gives in to frequently. We left the others far behind us at the beginning of the race and there was no way for them to overtake us. I called to him several times to slow down, but he affected not to hear me. Soon I gave up and concentrated on keeping pace with his horse.

We won the race, but everyone expected that from the beginning. Our household had won every wedding race that we competed in for the last seventy-five years.

As I stood there gasping and wheezing for air, Yari threw the reins of his horse to me and instructed me to tie it with the others. I obeyed simply because I did not have the breath to argue with him. That done, I went to the river to wash the dust off of my face and make myself as presentable as possible. So far my plans for vengeance hadn't worked out too well.

I found him with the other men who were congratulating him on our victory. We had won the prize money from the queen and, as with Laughter and Geysan, the queen's personal jewelry had been included.

I walked over to where Yari stood.

"Yari, I want you to call the council together. I'm getting a divorce."

He lowered his wine jug.

"You can't be serious," he said.

"I am. Very."

"On what grounds?"

I smiled.

"You'll see."

He shrugged and went off to gather the council members, which was no small task for most of them were far gone with wine. But they

THE CEREMONY OF THE CHOSEN: TEJALURA

managed to form a half-circle, stumbling over each other to find their proper places. Dejo Jevetchev, who had been the first to find his seat, had already dozed off and Zarkhon had to nudge him awake. Finally orienting himself, he turned to us.

"Ah, my children. You wish to address the council? State your case."

"I, Ura Tehalchev, wish to annul my marriage to Yaremida Tehalchev."

Dejo smiled patiently.

"But Tejalura, you haven't been married an hour yet," he reasoned. "Give it a few weeks. Things will sort themselves out. Now, if there is nothing more to say—"

I cut in before his dismissal.

"There is. Our marriage is not according to law."

"What law?"

I looked at Yari smugly and said:

"The law that forbids second relatives to marry."

Dejo nodded.

"This is a very serious matter," he agreed. "Yari, have you anything to say?"

"Yes."

I began to feel uneasy for he was as sure of himself as ever.

"But I must call on one of the council members to recite the testimony given by Ura Tehalchev, herself." He turned to Zarkhon.

"Brother."

Zarkhon stood.

"On the day I announced my daughter's engagement, I foresaw this complication—though I didn't think it would be Tejalura who would dispute the marriage. In order to avoid this, I asked her if she was my daughter and she answered she was in no way related to me or any member of the Tehalchev household by blood."

He sat down and the council was adjourned. The marriage was legal. I stood there watching them as one-by-one they returned to the feast. There was nothing I could do. I had lost. Yari came up beside me.

"Don't worry, Taji," he said. "I promise I won't beat you too hard for this one. Not this time."

"Get away from me, you pig!"

"A shrewish wife is sometimes sold to the Zenadishj if she can't be tamed. I would advise you to—"

I turned on him.

"Sell me then!" I screamed for all to hear. "Better them than you!"

His smile disappeared. He studied my face to try to judge just how serious I was. I returned his look defiantly. After a long moment, an uncomfortable one for me, he said aside to Teve who was nearby:

"Teve, bring me the blanket off my horse."

When Teve returned, Yari turned to me.

"Give me your cord."

He rolled the blanket and tied it with the leather strap that had bound my wrists. He picked up his jug and went off to the tent. The others had become silent now, watching the scene before them. We younger ones didn't have the slightest idea of what was going on, but the older ones nodded among themselves.

"Now what's this supposed to mean?" I asked half irritated, half embarrassed. I had lived among the Nejimenets most of my life, but there were times I believed I would never understand them. Where did all these traditions come from?

"He is leaving the decision up to you," Aunt Kiakashe said. "Sometimes a girl is not pleased with the husband of her parents' choice. This used to happen with marriages after the old custom. If a man had any pride he would give his bride a chance to annul the marriage. That is what Yari has done. If you don't want him, leave the blanket there and you will stay unmarried as before. Zarkhon can keep the bride price in honor and nothing more will be said of the matter. If you want him, pick up the blanket and follow him. It is as simple as that."

As simple as that. Everyone watched me with anticipation. I gathered up the blanket and ran after Yari.

·→※←··→※←··→※←·

Winter 1329 EE

Many times over the years I have wondered why I picked up that blanket and during our many fights I would wonder aloud. Some inner instinct must have told me he would make a good husband.

Even during our most troubled times I have never regretted this choice.

But only later was I to realize this. Our first few weeks of marriage were precarious. As many fights as we had, there were many we avoided by a caution we had acquired in our attempts to test each other's strengths and weaknesses. I had known Yari nearly all of my life, but at times he seemed a stranger to me. When things were going well between us I felt a happiness I had never known before. When things were bad, I was so miserable I wanted to die.

One afternoon when the women of our household went off to do some sewing, Turquoise called me aside and said:

"Come on, Taji. Let's go away from the others for a while and have a talk."

Unable to politely decline, I followed her. When we were out of sight of the others, we sat down in the grass. I waited for her to begin.

"What's the matter, Taji?" she asked suddenly. "Since the wedding you have looked so unhappy. Why?"

"There's nothing wrong," I answered stiffly. "Everything is fine."

"That's not true. Aren't things working out with you two?"

Unbidden, the tears began to slide down my cheek.

"Has Yari been saying things?" I asked.

"No, of course not," she said quickly. "He doesn't seem to have anything to complain about. To look at him no one would think he owned the world. But you, Taji, you look so unhappy all the time. Everyone has noticed it. The wedding night—it wasn't at all what you expected was it?"

I blushed furiously at her meaning.

"No," I muffled. "It's so messy and it hurts and—ugh!"

She smiled understandingly.

"I know but believe me, Taji, it will get better after a while."

She brushed my hair with her fingers as she used to long ago. I pushed her hand away.

"I'm not a child!"

"With your attitude you are hardly a woman."

I began to cry harder.

"It's just that Laughter and everyone talked about it as if it were something fun or beautiful or—"

"And it is," she consoled me. "It is all that and more but only after a while. Oh, those girls have filled you with a lot of foolish talk. I shudder to think of my first night. It was everything you said: Messy, painful and, as you so aptly put it, 'Ugh!' No, but there are other nights . . ."

She paused, searching for the right words.

"Oh, Tejalura, marriage can be fun. I have known Yari since he was born. He is a good man and he loves you, he has made that clear to all. I think it was a mistake to marry you so young. He should have waited, but this can be worked out. You must grow up very quickly, Tejalura, and make things work between you two. The choice is yours."

I regretted being so open with Turquoise. I knew how women talked among themselves and not only did I fear becoming an object of ridicule, but I was afraid Yari might hear of it. But as time passed and nothing more was said, I found myself relieved and glad for the knowledge that in some matters at least Turquoise could be discreet. Still, I made up my mind to keep such personal matters to myself in the future.

Yari and Hushé left with the other men for one last hunt before we returned to Meneth-shir. At first I thought I would be glad to be by myself for a few days, but now I had to admit I missed Yari very much. I was at the river bathing with the other women when Urali ran to us shouting that she had seen the men returning. Chattering excitedly, we threw our clothes on and ran to the village, I was in the lead.

"Look at Taji run!"

"Someone had better warn Yari."

"Run, Taji!"

I laughed as I raced ahead. I was certain now that I was pregnant and wanted to tell him as soon as possible. I had wanted to run into his arms and welcome him but I couldn't because there was someone with him, a Zenadishj. I stopped short. The man was Terez. Yari frowned at me and I couldn't blame him. My thin, cotton blouse and skirt clung damply to me, revealing my body as if I wore nothing at all. River water still dripped from my hair.

"Tejalura, we have a guest." His voice was quiet, but there was an edge to it I didn't like. "Make sure there is enough food and change your clothes."

I ducked into the tent and, obeying what I knew to be his most important command, I found some dry clothes that were presentable. I threw my wet clothes to the ground angrily. How was I supposed to know that Terez would be with him? Perhaps I should have married Terez when I had a chance. He was much better looking than Yari. Terez would have laughed at the incident instead of growling like a defensive wolf as Yari had.

By the time dinner was ready, both of our tempers had cooled and we were able to enjoy the evening with Terez. Terez now rode with the Desert Zenadishj and his father had disowned him.

"But when I get ready to settle down I'll marry and he'll forgive me and all will be well again. Until then, I'm free. You can't imagine what it's like to ride across the desert. I tell you there is nothing like it."

"So you are happy?"

"Yes, the Enavians are starting to keep us pretty busy though."

"The Enavians?" my husband said sharply.

"Yes, didn't you know they were back?"

"No, I didn't. How long have they been back?"

"A year, maybe more."

I could feel Yari's eyes on me, studying my reaction to this news. He seemed to be the only one who remembered I was Enavian. I often forgot it myself. I returned to the task of filling the bowls, careful to give Terez a few extra pieces of meat.

"We could use some extra fighters, Yari. Come and join us when married life becomes too dull."

"Oh, I don't expect that to happen for quite some time yet," he smiled at me. "Besides I have no quarrel with the Enavians. Our world is big. There is room for all."

"Just tell that to the Enavians. They will not be content with sharing. I don't even think there is such a word in their language. They will only be happy with everything."

"Do you know why they left in the first place?"

"The Enavian soldiers left to fight a war on another planet called Nevara. The Enavian settlers left because they were afraid to stay without soldiers to protect them. Also, Erteyans were being placed on detention planets and labor camps throughout the galaxy."

"Why?"

A shrug.

"Who knows? I have heard it is because they started the war—the one the soldiers went to fight—it doesn't make sense. Anyway, they're free now and they are all coming to Ceytal, even those who weren't here to begin with."

"Why Ceytal?"

"It was one of the few planets that didn't imprison them and also because they believe this is the planet where their race originated. Which is, of course, ridiculous. Our people have been here thousands of years before there was such a thing as Erteyans."

"I agree with you that their theory is fantastic, but I still feel there is no reason to fight them. As I have said before, there is room for all."

"That is easy for you to say. You have a fine protected valley that acts as an impregnable fortress, but we are out here in the open—even Zeneshtu Valley is vulnerable. If we don't want them to take over our land with their farms, we must strike now before it is too late."

Chapter 11
The Husband: Yari Tehalchev 1329 EE

"The heart of my beloved is a mystery I have pledged
to solve. Even if it takes the rest of my life."

— *Neve Ce*

Winter 1329 EE

Terez is my friend and he will always be welcome in the Tehalchev household, but I do not like the way he looks at Tejalura. It was the expression in his eyes as he watched her running from the river that made me angry, not her appearance. No, certainly not her appearance. I remembered how pretty she looked standing there, fresh and innocent as a child. She seemed happy to see me until I ordered her into the tent. Perhaps I had been a little short with her, but there would be no apologies. I must be firm with her now or I would never be able to manage her in the future.

During Terez's visit, she had mumbled something about visiting Tzeri and left. She was gone all afternoon. She still hadn't returned hours after Terez had left. When it became evening, my first impulse was to look for her, but I stopped myself for I knew if I gave in to her now I would loose what little control I had gained over her. If she wanted to behave like a spoiled brat, let her. I decided I would best establish my advantage by remaining at home, affecting unconcern rather than by chasing her down.

Where was she anyway? Oh, yes, she was with Tzeri. They must be off together somewhere gossiping about how horrible men were. But as the hours stretched on, I knew she must be somewhere else for Hushé would not have put up with that nonsense this long.

By the next morning she still hadn't returned and I was furious. She must have returned to Zarkhon's tent, which meant the whole family knew we were fighting. Well, as far as I was concerned it was all their fault anyway. They had done nothing but spoil her rotten since she was a child. I went to Zarkhon's tent to bring her home, but she was not there nor had anyone seen her since yesterday afternoon.

Could she be with Terez? I turned cold at the thought. I swallowed my pride and went after him. It took me two days to locate Terez's group only to find she wasn't with him either. After my initial relief, I became anxious again. Where could she be?

When I returned to camp I gathered some of the men and we formed search parties and tried to pick up her trail, but Tejalura made good use of her head start and left no trail. This wasn't a dramatic gesture or bid for sympathy. She didn't want to be found.

Could she have gone to the Enavians? Now that they were back she could easily have found refuge with them. If so, she was gone. I could only hope she was safe wherever she was.

"It's all your fault!" Silverwoman accused me through her tears. "You could have waited a few more years—until the next *yaremida*. But no, you wanted her now, so you must have her now. What Tejalura might have wanted was never taken into consideration. Selfish pig! I don't blame her one bit for leaving you."

"Let Yari be," Zarkhon commanded his wife.

"Don't you speak to me that way," she shrieked at her husband. This was a Silverwoman I had never seen before. "You could have prevented this whole thing and you didn't. It's more your fault than his."

"Can't you see it doesn't matter whose fault it is? Our daughter is gone. We all loved her and we all have lost her. Blaming each other won't bring her back."

But Silverwoman didn't listen to him. Blind with grief, she continued to reproach him bitterly. Unable to stand any more of it, I returned to my tent alone.

Throughout the day I thought of Tejalura. I remembered her as a child when she first came to us. It was during the Yaremida of the Enavian Plague, the one that took the lives of so many of our people. My parents died in that plague as well as my older brother, Huri, the husband of Turquoise. And not long before, Ancient's husband, Nejo, had died of old age so each of us had lost someone dear to us. And then came Lee Lee Yan, such a willful, stubborn thing she was, with no manners. But somehow she brought life back into our household.

When had I begun to notice her as something more than just another member of my household? I believe it was the summer she went with us to work for Neve Chevari. Yes, I remember how angry I had been with Hushé for giving her permission to come with us.

"That skinny little brat will only be a nuisance the whole trip to Zeneshtu," I predicted.

"She hasn't been so bad lately," he reasoned. "Besides, haven't you noticed? She's growing up and isn't skinny at all."

Such a flattering comment coming from Hushé (who either hadn't quite discovered girls or couldn't be bothered with them) caused me to look at Tejalura with new eyes as we rode down the Cela Pass Trail. She was laughing at something Hushé was saying when I first noticed it. Her laughter was that of a woman's, sweet and low. What happened to the girlish giggle that used to irritate me? There was a new glow in her eyes, a new warmth, where had it come from? And the queenly tilt of her small, stubborn chin would have been comical a year or two earlier, but now it gave her a new air of sophistication that made her almost a stranger to me.

When did it happen? I saw her daily, how could I not notice this change in her? It seemed only yesterday I found her off by herself, crying because she knew she was "never, just never" going to be pretty. And then, as the wind blew through her dark hair, she seemed carelessly unaware of her beauty and its power. The only feature that remained of that unhappy girl was a light sprinkle of freckles across her nose.

It seemed to me she directed most of her conversation to Hushé during our journey to Zeneshtu. With that first pang of jealousy, I realized just how dear she had become to me. All summer I watched her. Inwardly I was guarded, but outwardly I teased her as mercilessly as ever. Hushé and the others in the Chevari household came to her defense as often as not. Neve himself took an honest liking to her; I began to wonder if he might be thinking of taking a second wife.

I liked Terez a great deal when I first met him, but I could have killed him for the way he treated Tejalura. A week after the incident, she spoke to me about it.

"Yari," she said to me one day. "Yari, do you think I'm wicked?"

Her face was so serious and her dark eyes so large and earnest I had to laugh.

"Of course you're not," I said. "What brought this on, Taji?"

"When Terez kissed me I—well, I liked it."

"Shameless!" I exclaimed in mock horror and she giggled nervously. "Well, now that you are a woman of the world there are a few things you should know. It's normal for a young girl to enjoy a man kissing her. But don't get any serious ideas about Terez."

"Oh, why?" she asked a little too casually.

"He already has a woman," I said cruelly. "A beautiful Enavian woman with blue eyes and blond hair."

"The woman at the Enavian ranch?"

"Yes. Terez is returning to Blue Mountain to marry her." It was a lie, but I convinced myself it was for her own good. "I'm just warning you, Tejalura. I don't want to see you hurt."

"You don't have to worry about me, Yari," she said airily. "I'm not in love with anyone and I never will be."

Since she showed no interest in any of the suitors who courted her during the next two years, I was content to let matters be. By then I had decided I wanted her for my wife, but she was so young for her age I felt it best to wait a few more years. At the next *yaremida* Terez was among the other Mountain Zenadishj who came to join the Ceremony of the Chosen.

"I'm glad to see you, my friend," I greeted him. "Pleased but surprised. You've never attended these gatherings before. Is there someone you know who's getting married?"

"Yes. Me, I hope."

"Oh? Who are you marrying?"

"Tejalura. I plan to ask for her again, only this time properly. Where is Zarkhon? I'd like to speak with him about it as soon as possible. What's the matter, Yari?"

I thought quickly.

"Nothing. It's just that—well, I'm glad you met me first for it will save you some embarrassment." I paused. "You see, I've already offered for Tejalura myself."

There was a silence.

"I see," he said running his fingers through his hair. His grin was a little strained, but it never slipped. "Well, that's great. She'll make a fine wife, Yari. I'm sure you two will be very happy."

I never saw Terez so caught off balance or at a loss for words. Briefly my conscience bothered me. Did I have the right to interfere? What if Terez and Tejalura were meant for each other? But selfishness won out and I approached my brother to offer for Tejalura. Zarkhon didn't seem at all surprised, it was as if he knew.

"Of course I knew," he said. "All of Meneth-shir knew. Give her time, Yari, she'll come around."

"I'm not so sure. She avoids men and swears she will never marry."

"They are the ones who long for it the most. Marrying her is the best thing you could do."

"I might have trouble convincing her of that."

"Don't even try," my brother suggested. "Marry her after the old custom and she won't have a chance to say anything at all."

Silverwoman protested at first, but she reluctantly agreed to go along with it when Zarkhon pointed out that if we didn't go through with it she might marry Terez and move to Zeneshtu. But we lost her anyway, so it was all for nothing.

Evening was approaching. It was time I started to prepare the evening meal.

"Yari."

I turned to see Silverwoman. The afternoon sunlight reflected on her hair like strands of brilliant white crystal.

"Yari, I'm sorry for the awful things I said this morning. I was as much at fault as anybody. There is no need for you to eat alone, Yari. Why don't you join us tonight."

I did but it was a mistake, because Hushé and Tzeri were there too. Watching their happiness was painful, but I postponed as long as possible returning to my empty tent. When I returned I saw Tejalura's horse tied outside.

Quietly I entered. Tejalura was sitting by the fire, her profile towards me, mending the seam of a shirt I had torn. Although she must have heard me enter she continued her task in silence.

"You came back. Why?"

Instead of answering me, she asked a question of her own. This is her favorite tactic and is one of the things that irritate me most about her.

"Yari, why did you marry me?"

"What?"

Taken by surprise, I didn't know what to answer.

She looked at me directly.

"You heard what I said. You went to a great deal of trouble to marry me, why?"

I took my jacket off and began to gather my things for tomorrow's hunt.

"Tejalura, what are you talking about?"

"I am talking about the rest of our lives . . . Yari, please put that down and listen to me!" She paused. "I want to know how things are to be for us from now on." Another pause. "Yari, do you love me?"

Her voice broke at the last two words. Her lower lip trembled and tears slid down her cheek. In two moments she had changed from an angry woman to a hurt child. I smiled.

"Yes, Tejalura. Very much."

"Then why did you marry me after the old custom?"

I sighed and drew her into my arms. How much should I tell her? Should I mention Terez? No, not even when we were very old would I tell her of Terez. I chose my words carefully.

"I married you after the old custom because I was afraid you would reject me as you had your other suitors. Tejalura, if you are unhappy, you don't have to stay with me."

"No, Yari, I'm happy—very happy."

She giggled and hugged me harder.

"Besides, it's a little too late now."

"What do you mean?"

That was when she told me about our child.

Chapter 12
The Blue Mountain Massacre: Tejalura 1330-1336 EE

> I have seen them coming
> Ever closer, ever near
> Like thunder, yes like thunder
> Swift as death and cold as fear
>
> —*The Legend of Div Kassar*

Yari and I named our baby Ceymar, but no one called her that. Instead they called her Trista and so Trista she became. She was a fat butterball of a baby with dimples in her cheeks and a pretty mouth. We liked to tickle her because she would press her lips together as long as she could hold her breath and then burst out laughing, giving us a glimpse of her seed pearl teeth. Yari said that she was me all over again, except for her golden eyes. Her black hair was a disappointment to me but she was so perfect in all other ways I couldn't help but love her.

By winter she was walking and I had trouble keeping up with her because by then I was pregnant with the twins. They were born that summer, two boys. Khai, the eldest twin, looked like Nejo and Akashe, the youngest, was the image of Yari.

The following spring Ancient died. One day she was working in the fields, the next day she was gone. I looked for her spirit among the flowers and trees and stone cliffs but never saw her. Well, after all it was just an Oramaklete superstition.

We saw Terez during the next *yaremida*. He was as restless as ever and was the leader of a mixed tribe of united Zenadishj, Nejimenets, Urthics, and Oramakletes. He had a regular woman now, a young Urthic girl named Tamai. Although Terez told us she was as fierce a fighter as any of the men, her manner seemed quiet and shy. She was a pretty thing and I wish I had been able to speak with her but she didn't know Nejimenet and I knew little Urthic. Terez did enough talking to make up for the both of us.

"Three children? But you were only married last *yaremida*. That's what I call fast work, Yari."

Terez gave me sudden smile that caused me to blush in spite of myself. "And I must say motherhood becomes you, Tejalura. Tamai is expecting a child. She continues to fight with us. I'm trying to get her to stay out of it but she won't."

"Can't you just order her."

"I do, for all the good it does. Tamai never openly disagrees with me, which is a blessing. She simply does as she pleases. Stubborn!"

He fondly brushed a strand of her hair from her cheek. She smiled and caught his hand like a playful kitten.

"So the fighting is still going on?"

"Yes, the Enavians grow stronger with each day. Now they want us to live in their camps and become farmers."

"Is that so bad?"

"Being farmers, no. Living in their camps, yes. Have you seen those places? I grew up in one. It is easy for you to talk, you have Meneth-shir. But I tell you, my friend, there will come a day when even Meneth-shir will not be safe from their greed. Even the queen fights them."

"I thought there was a treaty."

"There was but the Enavians have broken it time and time again. Fight with us. With the Naritian Empire and Meneth-shir behind us we cannot fail."

Yari shook his head.

"No, I disagree with you. All they wish is a place to live. I say let them."

"On our lands!"

"The land belongs first to Ce the Father," Yari pointed out. "Besides, what did we ever do with the land along the river? Let them have it."

"But someday that will not be enough. Someday all of the land will be filled and there will not be enough for us and the Enavians. What then?"

"Then together we will work out the problem, if the problem arises."

Terez smiled and shook his head.

"Just remember your words when they demand Meneth-shir of you."

Yari raised his hand.

"All right, you win. Enough of this. Tell me how your father is."

"Well enough, but he thinks like you and wants me to settle down and get married."

"And you're not ready yet."

"No, there is too much to do. I cannot relax and forget about the way things are down here simply because I have Zeneshtu Valley to hide in. You're right in saying the land is ours only as a gift from Ce. But unless we love this land enough to fight for the right to keep it, He will give it to the Enavians who love it enough to fight and take it."

He laughed suddenly as if he found his speech too serious.

"There I go again. You are right, let's talk of other things."

Autumn 1334 EE

How swiftly the years are passing, I thought to myself. Fourteen, now, Imih considered herself quite grown up and spent a great deal of time watching the children. She was a pretty girl with tight curly hair like Laughter's and promised to grow into a real beauty like her mother and grandmother.

I was made official treasurer but it was to have little effect on my daily life. Whenever any of the households had a question or an update for their budget, a member of that family and I would refer to the records I kept in the archives on the island. A month or so before the annual meeting, I would organize the material for my financial report to the council. Ura would check my math. It only took her a few hours out of one afternoon, depending on the number of mistakes, to audit my reports. How I envied her that gift!

All surplus crops and manufactured goods were sold to the Zenadishj and other *shemetul* and the profit from these sales would be banked in the treasury with the tithes. I was amazed at the vast fortune that had accumulated over the centuries.

"What are we supposed to do with all of this treasure?" I asked.

Zarkhon shrugged.

"Whatever Ce wants us to do with it. If anyone has need of it, whether they be Nejimenet or *shemetul*, they are to have it."

We learned while trading horses with some Mountain Zenadishj that Terez and most of the men from his band had been killed by the Enavian soldiers only months after we last saw him. It was a terrible blow for Yari. Although they had not always agreed with each other's views, they had shared a deep friendship.

The next *yaremida* we saw that the Enavian settlements had flourished in the absence of the desert fighters. We had always been indifferent towards the settlers.

"Let them come," we had said. "There is room for all."

Yet now they had a free reign, many of our campsites established for centuries, had been plowed and irrigated or had small towns built on them. It is one thing to speak of tolerance and quite another to practice it.

Once we passed a small farm and I saw a young girl in a cotton print dress running barefoot, her long black braids flying in the wind. She might have been me twenty years ago. She sat on the fence and waved as we passed. As Trista and I waved back, I wondered what my life might have been as an Enavian.

Unable to camp at a familiar site, we were forced at times to camp near Enavian settlements. We would double our guards at such times but they never approached us. Oddly enough it was at one of our old campsites, far from any Enavian settlement, that the soldiers attacked us.

It began when a small band of Zenadishj desert fighters came to our camp seeking refreshment and refuge. We gave them food but would not let them stay for we could see from their collection of bloody scalps that they had recently attacked an Enavian settlement. The soldiers came two days later. We had guards out but even so they caught us unprepared.

At the first sign of trouble, Yari grabbed the twins and shouted for me to follow. Struggling to hold Trista close to me, I ran as fast as I could. But soon I was separated from my husband in the crowd fleeing the camp. I felt a strong arm grab me and pull me into the bushes but before I could scream I saw it was Aunt Kiakashe.

"You had better put Trista down, Tejalura. There's no use carrying her now."

"What?"

I glanced down at Trista and saw a hole had been burned through her head. There was blood all over me as well as her. I uttered a cry that was half a scream and half a moan. Aunt Kiakashe shook me hard.

"Get a hold of yourself!" she hissed. "We have a lot of work to do. We are going to get us a transport. You used to be Enavian once. What do you know about transports?"

I tried to gather my thoughts, but I wasn't much help to her. I had forgotten the Enavian word for transport until she said it. I was surprised that she knew it, although I shouldn't have been. As a former general of the Zenadishj army she was an expert on all military weapons and equipment. I had seen transports on the farm where I lived with my Enavian family and I could remember being allowed to ride in one as a special treat. I knew that you started and stopped them with a key, but that was all I could tell her.

Aunt Kiakashe was one of the greatest military geniuses of our time and during this crisis all she had was me. Her frustration must have been great but she acted as if she were in charge of professionally trained unit instead of a shell-shocked mother who had just lost a child. Something in me responded to her direction. That is what makes great generals. Not because they are heroes, but because they have the ability to make heroes of others.

"All right now," she said. "We'll jump the next one that passes by. Here's a knife. Kill them, but keep the bodies. They'll have burners, ammunition and other useful items. When we take it over we'll drive it away so fast their friends can't stop us. I'll drive and you'll take the rear gun. And when we do that—"

As if on cue, while she was talking, a desert transport not only passed us, but it stopped a few feet away with its back almost directly facing us. Their rear gunner was dead. We looked at each other in amazement.

"Good," she smiled grimly. "Perfect. You take the man on the left, I'll take the man on the right. *Ja creda, Taji?*"

"*Di creda.*"

We split off according to plan, silent as two shadows as we moved across the hot, dusty ground. Aunt Kiakashe attacked her man a moment before I could reach mine. He turned and looked me full in the face. He was just a boy, younger than Nejo. My appearance, covered with Trista's blood, must have shocked him for the necessary seconds it took me to kill him. Aunt Kiakashe started the engine and I took my place at the gun. Although my mind was clear and my eyes saw everything sharply, there was an unreality about it all. It had all been too easy and I thought I would be killed at any moment. She drove to where some of the men were gathering. I saw Yari among them.

"Tejalura, are you hurt?" he asked as he gathered me in his arms.

I shook my head.

"It's not my blood."

He nodded. I think he knew then Trista was dead, but neither of us said anything for fear we would break down.

"Tejalura, Kiakashe, both of you go with the other women. We'll take the transport."

My aunt was furious.

"Get your own transport!" she snapped. "We fought for it, we should be the ones to drive it."

Unable to order Kiakashe, he turned on me.

"Tejalura, obey me. Go with the other women."

At the sound of my husband's voice, Aunt Kiakashe's influence over me vanished. Wordlessly, I joined Silverwoman who was watching the boys. Aunt Kiakashe had stubbornly remained in the driver's seat. Yari didn't argue with her because I don't think he knew how to drive it. Stripping the bodies of their burners and ammunition, they pushed them off to the ground and told me to search them.

First, I searched the boy I had killed. There were some letters and identification papers. His name was Otain Nikkuvvar. The letters, Aunt Kiakashe told me later, had been written to his sister. He had been so young he didn't have a sweetheart. The other appeared to be about the same age. On him I found a medallion, some cigarettes and a lighter. They were just boys. I could not even hate them. How could the Enavians be so cruel as to send them out here to die so far from their home?

My dress and my arms were caked black with dried blood. In a daze I allowed Turquoise to lead me to the river to wash me. As I sat in the sun drying my hair, the boys ran up to me with flowers clutched in their hands. I absently placed a hand on each shinning head, one black and one blue. I was thankful they had been spared the horror of the battle. They hadn't realized this was something more than just another outing.

"Here, Mother," Akashe said, placing both bunches of flowers in my lap. "We picked these for you. And here's a pretty stone for Trista—Mother, what's the matter?"

"She's crying," Khai whispered.

"Leave your mother alone," Silverwoman chased them off. "Go play with the others."

Exchanging guilty looks, they obeyed their grandmother. Silverwoman put her arms around me but I would not be comforted.

We won the battle, but at a great price. One hundred and fifty-six of our people were killed, three of them were from our household: Hushé, Laughter and Trista. We were only able to win because of the youth of the soldiers and the inexperience of their commanding officer. It was not a victory to be proud of for there is no honor in killing boys.

We learned from our prisoners they had attacked us because they thought we had been responsible for the raid made on the settlement a few miles up river. Their leader, Commander Halumne Ceven, was shocked to find he had attacked the wrong Ceytalians.

"But we followed their tracks here."

"Yes," said Uncle Gan, who spoke Enavian. "Two days ago a band of Zenadishj came to us and told us of their attack on the Enavian settlement. We sent them on their way. They went in the direction of the Blue Mountains."

"You aren't Zenadishj?"

"No, we are Nejimenets. You Enavians call us Neshamin."

The young man's face had gone a sickly gray under his tan.

"You mean this was a mistake? A mistake!"

Uncle said nothing.

"Damn!" the young commander muttered as he turned away to regain his control. It was a long time before he spoke again.

"I will take full responsibility for the actions of my men. Punish me as you will, but I ask that you let my men go free."

Gan smiled sadly.

"We have no wish to kill you. Go."

"You mean you are letting us go, all of us? Just like that?"

"There are so few of you and killing you will not bring back our dead."

"You make me ashamed," the Enavian said simply. "Is there anything we can do?"

"Help us bury our dead."

Our camp had been burned so badly there was little left, but we salvaged what we could. It was too late to return to Meneth-shir before the first snow blocked the pass, so it was decided to spend the winter with the Mountain Zenadishj. Their valley was lower in altitude than ours and the North River Pass that led to Zeneshtu was open even during the worst *yaremida*.

During our journey to Zeneshtu Valley, I moved as one dead. I spoke to no one and had to be forced to eat. At night I woke up screaming the name of the Enavian boy I had killed. Once I was almost left behind when I had wandered away in a daze during a rest period. It was my father who found me.

"Do you realize that you have held up the whole caravan for nearly two hours?" He was angry with me for the first time since I was a child. "You are not the only one who has suffered. We all have."

"But Trista!" I sobbed. "My Trista."

"You seem to have forgotten you also have two sons and a husband who need you now more than ever." He paused to continue in a gentler voice: "Not to mention a father who loves you and is worried about you."

Blubbery mess that I was, he hugged me anyway and tried to ease the pain.

"Be patient and wait," Zarkhon told me. "Wait to see what good Ce can make of this situation."

"Good?" I said incredulously. "What possible good can come of Trista's death? Or Laughter? Or Hushé?"

I regretted my words as soon as I spoke them. What right had I to snap at him? Their deaths had brought him just as much anguish; he was only trying to comfort me.

"I'm sorry, Father."

We were silent a moment.

"You do not know this, Tejalura, but a few months before the Zenadishj brought you to us, there were only two people living in the Moon household, Silverwoman and myself. We had been married many years and still there were no children to bless our union. The fact our house was one of the largest in the valley only made our loneliness more acute. We truly thought Ce had forgotten us, but this was not so. He not only knew of our needs, but also the needs of the others. He knew my father-in-law, Nejo, was about to die and Ancient would need a home. He knew there would be an epidemic that would take the lives of my parents, leaving my younger brother, Yari, orphaned; and Turquoise, the wife of my older brother, was left widowed with two children. That was the same winter the Zenadishj brought you to our camp. You see, Ce even knew of your needs, even though you were Enavian.

"In the space of a few weeks, our household had grown from two to eight. When Laughter married Geysan and had Imih and Teve, that made eleven. Turquoise married Gan and then Kiakashe and Nejo joined us that made fourteen. My daughter married and had children that made seventeen. Make no mistake; Ce does not forget His people. He can turn any misfortune to a blessing if we let Him."

I could not be as optimistic as Zarkhon, but I made a special effort to be more considerate of those around me.

Neve Chevari put us up for the winter. He made light of his generosity by saying he did so only because he knew we would more than reimburse him for his help when we were able to return to Meneth-shir, for the wealth of the Nejimenets was well known.

Life had been good to Neve. He was fatter and richer than when we saw him last. The light of his life had become his little granddaughter, Khai, the child of Terez and the Urthic girl, Tamai. Though orphaned she did not lack affection; the whole valley loved her as they had loved her father. Except for the darkness of her hair, which was a deep rich purple, she looked much like Terez and had the same carefree, sunny disposition.

When Chevari spoke of Tamai, one could tell by the tone of his voice there had been little affection between the horse trader and the woman his son had loved.

"Terez sent her up here to have the baby. She was an animal! She didn't even know how to sit in a chair or eat properly. She ran away after Terez was reported dead."

He may not have cared too much for Tamai, but he worshipped his granddaughter. She was denied nothing and I feared his indulgence would spoil her. When I spoke to Chevari about it, he sighed:

"You are right, Tejalura. She needs parents, not a grandfather she can twist around her little finger. I have been thinking it would be a good thing to give her to you and Yari to raise."

"But we couldn't take her from you! Khai is all you have left of Terez."

"And I would have you take her because she is so dear to me. I have always had a special love for Zarkhon and Silverwoman it is natural I pass this love on to their daughter. I don't think you realize how much you have blessed their lives. They were so lonely before you came to them. That summer you spent working on my farm I noticed you and thought you would make a good wife for my son. It all might have worked out if my son had not been such a fool."

So I had not been the only one who envisioned me as Terez's wife living in Zeneshtu. How different our lives might have been had I married Chevari's son.

"But it was not to be," he continued. "Ce had ideas of His own, and perhaps He knows best. I came to think of Khai as the child you and Terez might have had, if things had been different. So please, take her. Besides, what sort of life could she have on a horse ranch with a bunch of scruffy, dirty ranchers?"

I knew he had heard of my grief over Trista's death and he was trying to help. We took her with us to Meneth-shir that spring. In order not to confuse her with my son Khai, we called her Yanahna, which means, "replace her."

Upon our return to Meneth-shir a council meeting was held and it was decided we would cut off all communication with the outside world. With a few exceptions, such as visits to Neve Chevari and the Naritian queen, Ceymar Ce, our caravans would cease. The *yaremida* winters would be hard, but always there had been a number of our people who had stayed behind, the old or disinterested, and if they could survive it, so could the rest of us. We would live our lives in peace. Let the rest of Ceytal fight, kill and die. We would not, we had our mountain refuge. There was not even a council meeting for all were in agreement.

All except Yari.

He said nothing at first, but I could tell something troubled him. At first I assumed it was Trista's death. One of the men had told me how Yari had found her body and buried it with his own hands. I tried to speak to him about it once, but he cut me short, ordering me to never mention her name again. He felt her loss deeply, but that was not what was bothering him.

"I have been thinking," he said one day. "I have been thinking Terez was right."

"About what?" I asked. "Terez said many things."

"About the Enavians. We can't ignore them. We must come to terms with them." A small pile of personal items taken from the bodies of the Enavian soldiers lay before him on the table. He picked up the medallion and handed it to me. "Here, Tejalura, look at this."

I glanced at it briefly and shrugged.

"It is just a medallion. What about it?"

"It's not just a simple medallion, Tejalura. It is much more complicated than that. Look at the tiny mechanisms inside. You were Enavian once, what would they use this for?"

I shook my head unable to remember. It was Aunt Kiakashe who answered him:

"The Enavians use it to tell time, but I'm not sure how it works. I think when both of those little bars reach the top mark—I think it means midday."

I resented her for being able to explain something to Yari that I couldn't. I also resented the respect and confidence he had for her knowledge.

"It is of no real use," I said trying to undermine her authority. "All we have to do is look at the sun to know when it is midday."

Impatiently Yari brushed my words aside.

"Do you know how to start it?"

"No," I frowned, trying desperately to remember. "Wait, that thing—there, at the top. I think you turn it."

"Which is the top mark, the one that stands for midday?"

"I don't know."

Yari seemed fascinated by the moving parts in the timepiece. He wound it up and held it to his ear to listen to the ticking noise it made. He shook it and then listened again. I smiled. In that brief moment I saw a glimpse of Yari, the boy.

"It will make a fine toy for the twins," I commented.

"Hmm."

Forgetting Kiakashe was near, I reached over and tickled him in the ear. He brushed my hand away.

"Taji, please. Try to be serious."

Kiakashe entered the room; I sighed and picked up my sewing again.

"Look here," he indicated the inside of the lid. "There is something carved on the inside. Can you read it, Kiakashe?"

"It reads: 'For my son, Otain Nikkuvvar.' It is only a keepsake, Yari, an antique pocket watch. There are other kinds of timepieces that are more valuable and accurate. You are making too much of it. Tejalura is right, we have but to look at the sun or stars to know the time of day or night."

"Unfortunately that would be the opinion of most Ceytalians and that is the difference between the Enavians and ourselves. For us time passes when it passes, but for the Enavian, this is not good enough. He must mark and calculate each moment with these machines. Look at it, Kiakashe, our finest jewelers could not forge something as intricate as this 'keepsake' of theirs."

"Is this so important, Yari?"

"Yes. Even I could devise several uses for it. Suppose in battle we had to divide our men into two groups. If we had two of those medallions you could have one and I the other and we could agree to attack simultaneously when our time pieces reach a certain mark."

Kiakashe nodded. "Yes, it would be like commanding two positions at one time."

Yari nodded.

"Exactly. And if we had knowledge of the Enavian's plans before hand," he picked up the papers on the desk, "such as these. We could counterattack them more efficiently if we understood the scale of the time on which they base their plans."

"Then we will simply steal all the time pieces we need."

Yari shook his head.

"No, you are missing the point. It is the genius behind the timepiece that is important, not the time piece itself. We could steal time pieces, but if they broke or became lost we couldn't replace them."

"We don't have to," Kiakashe said patiently. "We simply steal more."

Yari started to speak again, but changed his mind. Kiakashe placed her hand on his shoulder.

"It's late, I'm going home. You should rest, Yari. Tejalura, make sure he eats well and goes to sleep early."

Yari was silent for a long time after she left.

"Do you understand, Tejalura?" he asked quietly.

Tears filled my eyes.

"I'm trying to, Yari. I am trying very hard."

He glanced up at me and smiled briefly and placed his hand gently on my arm.

"Kiakashe is right," he said. "It's late and we need our rest."

He brooded darkly for the next few days and then called a council meeting. I attended, not only because I was treasurer, but also because I wanted to hear him. I wanted to understand the husband I could no longer speak with, the husband who was quickly becoming a stranger.

Yari had never been the type of man to call council meetings or to think deep thoughts. He had always been so happy and easygoing, content to take each day as it came. Now he spent a great deal of his time in seclusion that was only broken by strange questions no one could answer. Often he would ask me about my Enavian childhood, but I never seemed to remember anything useful. I would spend whole days trying to remember something about the Enavians just to give me a reason to speak to him, but this only seemed to irritate him. My husband had changed since the attack, and I wanted to understand what it meant for us.

He began his speech by stating we could no longer maintain our detached attitude with the Enavians and outlined several reasons why. I noticed many of his words were the words of his friend Terez, but he used those words to a much different end.

"We must not fight the Enavians," he said. "At least not yet. Rather, we must learn from them. Our ignorance is their best weapon against us and we must change that. The Enavians have requested that all Ceytalians move to a refugee camp so we can adapt to a new and better way of life.

"We are not deceived.

"They only wish to keep a better eye on us or, at best, train us to be second-class citizens of a new society in which the Enavians are dominant. Let us use their system for our own purpose. Let us go to these camps and learn of the Enavians. We can always come back to Meneth-shir whenever we want and use what we have learned against them. But we must learn more about them. The Tehalchev household will go to the Outpost. Any who wish to join us are welcome."

Although I had misgivings about leaving Meneth-shir, I said nothing for I was certain Yari would have gone without me. I was surprised at the number who went with us, nearly a third of the valley. We were to pass ourselves off as true nomads and no mention of Meneth-shir was to be made to anyone from the outside. When I left, I did not realize it would be five years before I would return.

Chapter 13
The Enavian Agent: Erten Zemmer 1336-1338 EE

> "Gentlemen, let us be frank with one another.
> The purpose of the refugee camps is to provide
> a socially acceptable method of exterminating
> the Ceytalian aborigines."
>
> — *Dr. Halumne Ceven, Jr., Mayor of Naritjina*

Winter 1336 EE

"I'm sorry, but the answer is still no. Once I received my promotion, I promised myself I would never set foot on another refugee camp."

"But you're the best agent we've got," insisted Ceven. "There isn't a man in the field who can handle dinges the way you do. You've performed miracles with the tribes you've been assigned to."

"Oh, there's really nothing to it," I explained blandly. "Decent food, fair treatment, and I don't allow my men to bother their women. Anyone can do it, Ceven. Anyone."

"Then you'll do it," he said ignoring the sarcasm in my voice.

I shook my head.

"No, I'm all through wet-nursing natives. Besides, I'm too old for that sort of thing. Why don't you get some bright young man for the job. What about your nephew, Hal? It would be good experience for him."

Too late, I remembered that young Hal Ceven was up for trial. I always liked the boy. I often thought he might make something of himself, provided his royal family didn't spoil him by making everything too easy for him.

"I'm sorry Ceven. I forgot about Hal's trial. In spite of what the news reports say, I think you have every reason to be proud of him."

"Proud of him! What for? Not only does he attack a tribe of peaceful Ceytalians, he manages to lose the battle, all of his equipment, and most of his men. And having that accomplished, what does he do? He reports back to his station and turns himself in to the authorities when he could have easily covered for himself. I tell you the boy ought to be shot!"

The worst part is Ceven meant every word. And he wasn't the only one who felt that way; young Hal had been disowned by his entire family. As bad as it looked for the boy, I believed in the long run it would turn out to be the best thing that could have happened to him.

"But we've strayed far from the issue," Ceven continued. "You still have not given me a reason—a good reason—for turning down the assignment. Might I remind you a promotion can easily turn into a demotion."

He'd have to do better than that, I thought. Although the empire may be partial to its royal sons—Ceven's high rank was proof of that—it was not in the habit of demoting competent officers, namely me, at the word of incompetent parasites, namely Ceven.

Actually, I do Ceven an injustice, for he is an excellent general. Shrewd and efficient, but lacking in backbone. This is probably due to the fact that he didn't have to work his way up the hard way as others do.

"The answer is still no."

"Don't be tiresome, Ertie," he said knowing full well how much I despise that diminutive to my name. Not even my wife, Pallas, calls me Ertie. "You know family connections have nothing to do with a man's rank. We all have to work our way up, regardless."

I let that one pass.

"Speaking of royalty," he continued in a tone of voice that told me his next approach would be blackmail. "Speaking of royalty, remember when we went to Narit to meet with Queen Ceymar? Remember that amusing little establishment called the Flower of All Delights? Now you wouldn't want your wife to hear of that, now would you?"

"You don't know Pallas very well. After eight years of marriage to me, there is little that would surprise her. And since that happened several years before we met, she would have little interest in it."

Now that blackmail and threats of demotion had failed, he would try to intrigue me, to capture my interest so that I would beg him to let me do the job as a favor. That should have been his first approach, after all the years he's known me you would think he'd learn that by now. I think he only does it on the off chance I'll knuckle under. After all, why go to the bother of gaining a willing worker when it is so much more gratifying to make him your slave by holding an axe over his head.

"I know overseeing a refugee camp is a bit beneath you, but this job requires special handling. Have you ever heard of the Neshamins?"

"Isn't that the tribe your nephew attacked?"

"The same. They have requested placement on one of our camps."

"What's wrong with that? Isn't that what the empire wants?"

"Yes, but there's something odd about this tribe. Up to now most of the natives requesting placement have been made up of destitute orphans, widows and grandmothers who come to us because they had no other choice. But these Neshamins, there isn't a grandmother or baby in the lot. All are young and healthy. Another curious thing is there are many young men of military age among them. They come to us, not out of desperation, but by choice."

"And the question is, why should a prospering tribe of Ceytalian nomads come to us by choice."

"Exactly. Now if their request is sincere, I don't want some butcher to ruin this opportunity. But if the Neshamins have some ulterior motive for entering a refugee camp, I want a strong man in charge."

"What ulterior motive could they have?"

"Retaliation."

"I don't understand."

"Remember, they were attacked by my nephew's men."

I accepted the job because it promised to be an interesting change from my previous assignments. But I didn't accept a cut in pay even though I was only doing the work of an DCNA agent.

I did some research to find all the information I could about the Neshamins, or the Nejimenets as they call themselves. The only reference I could find of them was an article about the Blue Mountain Massacre, and that dealt mostly with Hal Ceven and the few of his men who survived. According to the most recent publications, the Ceytalians all practice cannibalism, but any DCNA agent can tell you that isn't true.

I visited the camps I had formerly been in charge of and questioned the natives. All I could learn about the Nejimenets was that they were a rich, powerful people who were respected for their military skill. Although they had no armies of their own, they had served with distinction in the armies of other Ceytalian nations.

The most famous generals of the Naritian army had been Nejimenet. There was a General Ten Bears, or Gan Akashe, whom I have personally fought against, and his sister General She Bear. Once every three years the Nejimenets and the Mountain Zenadishj would meet at Halia Tehal for trade and a joint wedding celebration. But beyond that, there was little else I could discover about these mysterious people.

I visited Hal Ceven in prison to get what information I could from his brief encounter with them.

"It was the damnedest thing," he said. "They could have easily killed us and they had every reason to, but they didn't."

"Did you talk with any of them?"

"Yes, a man named Ten Bears and a younger man named Wolf."

Ten Bears is a common name, so I didn't realize he was talking about the same Ten Bears I had fought against. And the name Wolf was even more common.

"Were they the leaders?" I asked.

Hal shrugged.

"They spoke Enavian, that's all I know."

"Were there any old people among them? Any children?"

"Yes, quite a few as a matter of fact. Why?"

"I was just wondering. After the battle, how many of them were there?"

"Oh, about three thousand. I'm just guessing."

Now that was interesting. According to General Ceven there were less than nine hundred Nejimenets at the White Desert Camp. Where were the other two thousand?

My years at the White Desert Camp were the most rewarding of my entire military career. It turned out to be a quiet job, and located as we were in the desert far from the cities, it was almost like an early retirement. The few problems that came up were easily overcome after a short conference with their leader, Wolf. If a Nejimenet needed to be punished, I let Wolf handle the matter. As for the soldiers, I kept them in line by severely punishing and transferring any trouble-makers who mistreated or harassed the natives in any way.

Many thought my methods ridiculous, but I was determined the tragedy of the Azakhanis and Terez Chevari would not be repeated. The record showed that while the White Desert Camp was under my authority, there wasn't a single incident, nor did any of the natives turn renegade. The record also showed that within two years the White Desert Camp had become entirely self-supporting, able to buy its own supplies, rather than being dependent on the meager allotment given to them by the government. They sold jewelry, blankets, leatherwork, woodcarvings, and ceramic ware to the visiting tourists and shopkeepers in Naritjina. And from miles around homesteaders found good bargains at the Nejimenet produce and meat markets set up along the Naritjina Highway.

Yes, I was quite pleased with the program's progress and had good reason to be proud, even though I knew its success lay with the cooperation of the Nejimenet people. But then there was that business with Lillian Aleksandar, which was most frustrating. I wish I could have done more for her.

A year after the Nejimenets had been in the White Desert Camp, I discovered a woman among them by the name of Moonlight who, because of her black hair, was either Urthic or Erteyan-Enavian. I called Wolf into my office to discuss the matter with him, not only because he was their leader, but also because he was the woman's husband.

"I should turn your wife over to the authorities, but I won't. My main reason for not doing so is that she is obviously staying with you of her own free will. She's had plenty of opportunity to make her presence known to us if she wasn't. As far as I'm concerned she's a black-haired Nejimenet. But word might spread and if higher authorities step into this, I won't be able to help you."

"Why should the authorities be concerned about my wife?"

"In the past few years, captive Enavian citizens have been discovered on these camps and a program was started to return these captives to their families."

"They would take her away to live among the Enavians?"

"Yes, but believe me, I will do all I can to prevent that."

He accepted this without much comment and left. The next day, Moonlight came to my office with some presents: five honey cakes and some very good leatherwork. She was a charming little thing and was obviously happy to know she would be allowed to remain with her Nejimenet family. Enchanted, I sat back and watched the play of expressions on her face while she thanked me in excellent Zenadishj. It was almost with a shock I realized I was looking into the eyes of Gabrielle Aleksandar.

When Moonlight shyly asked if she could visit my wife, I immediately consented. Although making friendships with the natives is considered bad for the discipline, I felt it would have been rude to turn her down. She might have been hurt and my small opening into the tribe would have been lost. Also, Pallas would never have let me live it down. Pallas had wanted to learn the Nejimenet language for years.

As soon as she left my office, I went through all my drawers until at last I found what I was looking for, the picture of two pretty dark-haired girls in their summer dresses. I smiled as I remembered a party I attended eighteen years ago and the lovely young girl in a red dress with whom I danced. I turned the picture over. The time stamp and copy option had long since worn out, but I could still read the hand-printed notation written on the back.

Gabrielle 17 years, Lillian 7 years
Mactil Street Park, 1317

From then on, relations with the Nejimenets improved. Moonlight wasn't the only woman who visited Pallas. There was her adopted mother, Silverwoman; her aunt, She Bear (imagine General She Bear exchanging recipes with my wife!); a woman named Turquoise; and Turquoise's granddaughter, Song. Within months, Pallas was able to speak the language more fluently than I. After a while the inspection at the gate became a mere formality the guards soon dropped altogether, letting the women come and go as they pleased.

For two years Moonlight's presence at the White Desert Camp went unquestioned, but when I received a dispatch telling me to expect a visit from a representative from the DCNA office in Naritjina, I knew it was only a matter of time until she was taken away.

I had expected the investigator to be slightly uninformed about the native situation, but not to be so totally ignorant as this Kirat Sleevan was. I doubt he had taken a step out of his office since his arrival to Ceytal about a year ago.

"I'll come right to the point," he said. "I've come for the girl and the sooner you release her to me the sooner we'll be done with the matter."

"Excuse my ignorance, Inspector, but your dispatch only said you would be coming, it didn't state why. You'll have to be more specific. To what girl are you referring?"

"The Enavian girl, Moonlight."

I scrolled through the dispatch, barely giving it a glance before handing it back.

"We do have a woman by the name of Moonlight here and she might be Erteyan-Enavian, but I assumed she was Urthic. I don't believe she's the one you are looking for. This release is for a 'captive' Enavian. Our Moonlight is not a captive but a happily married mother of two children." I smiled sympathetically. "Moonlight is a common name. A mistake is understandable."

The corner of Sleevan's mouth tightened impatiently.

"I don't know what game you are playing or why, but it won't get by me. They told me all about you at the Naritjina office. I've come for the girl and I will take her with me when I leave—by force if necessary."

"Now, now—mustn't get upset," I said lightly. "Excuse me while I call Chief Wolf in."

"What do we have to talk to him for?"

"If you've heard so much about me at the main office, then you know I treat Ceytalians like human beings. Not only is Chief Wolf our Nejimenet liaison, but he is also Moonlight's husband. Excuse me while I send the guard to ask if he is available."

Wolf came, but he took his time about it. He greeted Sleevan coolly in perfect Enavian. Sleevan seemed surprised a Ceytalian could learn the language.

"You speak Enavian," he said stupidly.

"Yes," Wolf said. I noticed he did not include the usual "Sir" or "*Jevim*."

"Well, I suppose you know why I'm here."

The man is babbling, Wolf must have really unnerved him.

"Yes, I know why you are here. You wish to take my wife. Why?"

Sleevan coughed.

"Well, I wouldn't put it quite that way—"

"But I would. Please, we waste much time and I have many things to do. Let us be frank with one another. You want to take my wife from me. Please explain why."

Sleevan had to take a minute to revise his approach.

"Well, she should be returned to her family, her real family."

Wolf didn't argue the statement. Instead he said: "You have found her family then?"

"No, but I'm sure we will soon."

"I see. And where will you keep her while you look for her family?"

"Oh, you needn't worry. We have built many homes for the displaced—for people like Moonlight."

"To build these many homes, you must have many displaced persons. Perhaps these homes are crowded, no?"

"Well, yes we are a little crowded, but she will be well taken care of. You can be sure of that."

Wolf was silent for a moment.

"I have a better suggestion," he said. "As chief of this tribe, I will give you permission to leave Moonlight here until you find her family. I think that would be a much better arrangement. That way your homes for the displaced would not be so crowded. Of course, you have to receive Jevim Erten Zemmer's permission first." He turned to me. *"Zemmer Ce?"*

"Er—certainly, certainly. Moonlight is welcome to stay."

"Good, the matter is settled," he said rising from his seat. "Now, if there is nothing more to discuss, I will leave. Good day, Sleevan."

Sleevan had not expected anything like this. Wolf's actions and words were not those of an ignorant savage. He had handled the matter in a most professional manner.

"You have trained him well," he commented.

"Trained him? Hardly. Oh, I've helped him brush up on his Enavian grammar a bit, but he is essentially the same man he was two years ago when he came here. I am as surprised as you are. He shows a real flair for this sort of thing."

"Did his wife teach him to speak Enavian?"

I laughed.

"I doubt it. She only knows a few simple phrases. My wife, Pallas, tried to teach Moonlight Enavian, but has given her up as a hopeless case. Would you like to have lunch with us? Moonlight is over there now if you'd like to meet her. She promised she'd make us a delicious native dish."

"No, no thank you," he stood to put his hat on. "I'll be back for the girl, Zemmer. You can count on it."

Determination. You will find it in all these worms who populate the offices in Naritjina. Their pathetic little egos demand satisfaction for even the smallest slights.

"Oh, really?" I said squinting my eyes against the sun as I looked out across the desert. "We've been having terrible weather lately. I hope you don't have to make another long, hot, dusty trip out here."

·→▩←··→▩←··→▩←··

Sleevan returned about a month later; with him was Dr. Mheftu Padhari. I had always liked Padhari, although I hadn't seen him in years, I remembered him as an excellent doctor. I couldn't imagine what business he had with Sleevan.

"He's here to identify Lillian Aleksandar." I waited, forcing Sleevan to add, "You know, the girl, Moonlight."

He seemed very pleased with himself.

"But where is her family?" I asked.

"They didn't come. There wouldn't have been any point. They have never seen her so they couldn't very well identify her."

Padhari and I went outside to identify Moonlight. I grinned at him.

"Well, that's the government for you," I said. "They send a native to identify a twenty-seven-year-old Enavian captive. Then they take her away from her husband and children and 'return' to a family that has never laid eyes on her."

We walked on.

"You knew Moonlight?" I asked.

"Yes, as a young girl. I was a friend of her Enavian parents, Lev and Seraine Aleksandar. You remember them don't you?"

"Yes. When was the last time you saw her?"

"About eight years ago, in Halia Tehal. She was engaged to be married to Wolf at the time."

"You're against all this aren't you?"

"Yes."

"Then why are you here?"

"Because she is the daughter of an old friend and she may need help."

At least I knew where his sympathies lay.

"Couldn't you just pretend not to recognize her?" I asked.

"It wouldn't do much good. Cia, the woman married to Lillian's uncle, used to be married to Lillian's older brother, Jack. Cia could identify her."

Moonlight saw us as we approached; her dark eyes regarded us anxiously. Padhari was the first to speak.

"Hello, Lillian."

"Hello, Mheftu." She turned to me. "Am I to be taken away now, *Zemmer Ce*."

"No, not yet, but soon. I'll stall as long as I can."

She relaxed and smiled, inviting us into her house. It had originally been a cheaply built barracks, but with a rug and a few pieces of furniture, Moonlight had transformed it into a home. As she gracefully moved about the room preparing our tea, children flew in and out like young birds making contact with their mother before setting off again. She was the image of a woman fulfilled. She belongs here, I thought. After a brief, but pleasant visit, we returned to the office. On the way back, Padhari told me how impressed he was with the White Desert Camp.

"I have never seen anything like it," he said. "Clean houses, healthy children. How do you manage it?"

"Most of the credit lays with the Nejimenet people themselves. Oh, I've pulled a few strings to get certain things arranged, but all this couldn't have been possible without their willingness and hard work."

Kirat Sleevan was fit to be tied when we returned.

"What took you so long and where is the girl?"

"She's at home with her family. Dr. Padhari has identified her, but I can't release her to you until your documentation is in order and a member of her family must be present so she can be released to their custody." He started to bluster, but I cut him short. "Look, it isn't my fault you can't process your own documentation properly."

He was back in a few days and with him were Ral Hershem, his wife Cia and Padhari.

"Here is your documentation," Sleevan tossed the order on my desk. "And here are her relatives. Now where is the girl?"

I glanced at him briefly, but said nothing to him.

"Perren!" I called to the guard outside. "Get Chief Wolf."

Sleevan protested.

"Zemmer, these people have come a long way. They came for Lillian Aleksandar, not to listen to some dinge's double-talk."

"Don't worry, Sleevan, you've got her all right. But there are certain formalities that must be observed."

"Formalities be damned! These people have come a long way and you are wasting government time and money."

"And I don't care if the government has me shot for it!" I said slamming the orders on the desk. "I am going to give that girl a chance to say good-bye to her family."

"Those natives? Her family is right here."

I glanced at the small group. Cia Aleksandar-Hershem hadn't seen Lillian since she was a girl of seven, and Ral Hershem, who was her uncle on her mother's side of the family, had never laid eyes on her. Mheftu Padhari was the only one who could recognize her and he was a Ceytalian native. It seemed a poor trade indeed.

Wolf and Perren entered the room.

Perren shouldered past Sleevan without ceremony. Sleevan's reason for being here had spread among the soldiers, so he was not a popular figure. I turned to Wolf.

"He's got the orders, Wolf," I said in Nejimenet. "I want you to know that every man, every officer petitioned the main office with my approval and support. It was turned down. There's nothing more we can do. I'm sorry, very sorry. You'll have to bring Moonlight here. Tell her she can take as long as she needs to say good-bye to the others."

Wolf nodded.

"I understand," he said before leaving. "Thank you."

I crossed the room to the window. I watched as Moonlight hugged nearly everyone in camp, even the soldiers. And last of all her twin sons. It was almost as if I were out there among them. I could hear Pallas's voice in the back of my mind: *"You're getting too involved with these people, Erten."*

"Sleevan, come here. I want you to see something; it will do your soul good. Look out there."

He was unmoved.

"She'll forget them in time."

I glanced at him.

"Really? Those people represent twenty years of her life. Is it so easy to forget twenty years?"

He shrugged.

"Perhaps not." He continued to watch. "That dark-haired boy, the one she's holding now. Who is he?"

"That's her son. The blue-haired boy is too."

"It's the dark-haired one I'm interested in."

I turned to face him.

"Sleevan, you listen to me and listen to me closely. Don't even think about sending a warrant for that boy. If you lay one finger on him or breathe one word to the main office of his existence, I'll kill you, Sleevan. I swear I'll kill you."

Chapter 14
The Exile: Lillian Wolf 1338-1341 EE

> Have you seen my homeland?
> Have you seen my love?
> The many years apart have made me
>   foreign and unknown.
>
>   — *Nejimenet Folksong*

Winter 1338 EE

"But Yari, I don't want to go!" I could feel the tears slide down my cheeks. I knew by the stern expression on his face they would do me no good, but I could not stop them.

"We have no choice," he insisted with a trace of impatience.

"Yes we do. We could go back to Meneth-shir."

"Without having accomplished what we came down here for? That would mean the years we have spent among the Enavians would be completely wasted. Now you have the opportunity to live with them, be one of them. You could learn more in a few months than any of us could learn in ten years living here in the White Desert. Tejalura, this is important."

"I'm your wife. I should be important. Yari, what has happened to you? Is it Trista?"

His expression hardened.

"As your husband, I order you to go. We are not going back to Meneth-shir. Now pack your things."

In that moment my heart became hard and cold against him. I might feel pain later, but now there was only an icy anger.

"There is no need to," I said. "After all, I am going to be an Enavian lady now and the clothes of a dinge would hardly be appropriate."

I had resolved to appear coldly detached from it all, but at the sight of my two boys and Yanahna Khai, I started to cry again. After I said good-bye to everyone—everyone except Yari—we went to the office.

I recognized Mheftu, of course, but I had no idea who the other two were until Mheftu introduced them. Ral Hershem was my uncle on my mother's side of the family. His wife, Cia, had once been married to my brother, Jack.

I stood stiffly beside Yari while he spoke with Erten Zemmer. Then, without a word to me, he left the room. I have never felt more alone in my life. My heart cried out for him not to leave me, but I said nothing. Controlling the cold, sinking feeling inside of me, I went with my Enavian family to my new home.

It would have been a long, hot, dusty ride by horse, but in our enclosed and temperature-controlled transport, it was not only a relatively short drive, but a comfortable one as well. I studied the stylish Enavian dress Cia wore and determined to obtain similar clothes as soon as possible. I did not want the Enavians to laugh at me. I listened to them speak to each other in that forgotten language and wondered how I would manage in this new way of life. Fortunately, Mheftu would be staying until I had learned enough Enavian to communicate with my new family.

Sensing my mood, he tried to cheer me up.

"There's someone who is very anxious to meet you."

"Oh? Who?" I asked without interest.

"Jack."

"Jack? Oh, you mean Jack's boy." I did some quick calculation. "He must be nearly twenty now. Why should he want to meet me?"

"Actually he's eight years old. Jack and Cia had him cubed about a year before the raid. You were too young to remember. Cia had him uncubed a few years after she married Hershem. Up to now he has had a carefully regimented upbringing by conservative parents. Suddenly he has a long, lost Aunt Lillian, raised by a tribe of savage, bloodthirsty Ceytalians, come into his life. You're the most exciting thing that's ever happened to him. He's been pestering me with questions about you since he heard you were coming to stay with his family."

I smiled.

"What is he like?"

"He's a bright boy. He looks a lot like Jack did when he was that age, except he has Cia's blue eyes."

My smile deepened. My nephew would be about the same age as the twins and he probably resembled my golden-eyed Khai a great deal. If we became friends, I would not be so lonely.

When we entered the house a group of women descended on me like nervous hens, cackling in a language I did not know. I glanced back at Mheftu.

"The welcoming committee," he explained briefly. "You have suffered a fate worse than death at the hands of savages. Let them make much over you for a while. It does no harm."

Stoically I bore their attentions until they were through. Cia led us all to the parlor for tea. They seemed amazed I was able to sit in a chair and hold a teacup without disaster. I could feel their eyes on my tattoo whenever they looked at me. I felt stiff and uncomfortable not knowing what they were saying.

Just then I saw two blue eyes blinking between the railings on the stairs. I smiled. Encouraged, he came down the stairs to join the group. I saw a slight frown on Cia's face. Apparently she considered this to be an adult gathering. I remembered how stern and disapproving she had been of me when I was a child and my sympathy for Jack deepened.

He stood before me and made a small formal bow.

"Erevna, Tejalura."

My heart warmed to him, not only because of his resemblance to Khai, but also for his own sake. He had been the only one of my family to try to speak to me directly in my own language. His mother looked as if she would have willingly crawled under the rug to escape the questioning looks of her friends.

"Erevna, Jack Aleksandar," I answered.

Then, with only a few promptings from Mheftu, he recited a little speech of welcome in Nejimenet. He had apparently been practicing this for quite some time. In spite of Cia's certain disapproval, I would teach him Nejimenet. Such efforts should be encouraged.

"Dasha," I thanked him. "And I am glad to be here."

He formally greeted the other guests and his mother instructed him to return to his room. With a final impish wink of one blue eye, he left. I sighed as the adults resumed their conversation. I found I was able to endure the tedious afternoon because of that one bright interruption.

Later I met with my uncle in the library; he said that he had matters to discuss with me. Mheftu was there to translate. My uncle's first personal words to me were:

"All right, Lillian. Just what have you been planning to do for money?"

I blushed as Mheftu translated his words. All at once I felt unwelcome and insecure.

"I had not thought that I would need any," I answered.

"Nonsense! Women always need money. Did you know that as an orphan of an Enavian frontier settlement you are entitled to a monthly allowance and free medical care? Well, now you do. And, if you press the issue—and you will—you can receive payments, retroactive to the time of your parents' death. As soon as your Enavian citizenship is established, I'll see to it the government lives up to its responsibilities to you."

And he did. We met with a rather nervous Kirat Sleevan and his superior officer at DCNA headquarters in Naritjina. Sleevan suggested that, since my uncle was wealthy, government aid was unnecessary in my case. Uncle Ral disagreed.

"It doesn't matter if I am the richest man in the empire. My client, Lillian Aleksandar-Wolf, is entitled to her rights as an Enavian citizen and I am going to see that she exercises them. And I might remind you gentlemen she wasn't the one to make an issue of her citizenship. She was a married mother of two beautiful children and would have been perfectly happy to remain so if the government hadn't taken her away from her Nejimenet family. Nor was it due to any action on the part of my wife or myself, but rather due to the pettiness—excuse me—the thorough research of one of your agents." A keen look to Sleevan at this point. "I tell you the government is the cause of this and I intend to see that it fulfills its responsibilities."

Sleevan suggested I be returned to the Nejimenets, thus solving the problem altogether at no cost to the government. By now I had picked up enough Enavian to follow what was going on so I replied to him in perfect, though heavily accented Enavian:

"But I am just beginning to enjoy the advantages of being an Enavian," I said gracefully crossing my legs and adjusting the hem of my skirt. "You cannot expect me to go back and live among utter savages. Please, be reasonable, sir."

"Of all the—" Sleevan began, but his superior cut him short.

"You've got us into enough trouble, Sleevan, so shut up. All right Hershem," he said resignedly. "Lillian Wolf will receive her benefits with back pay." A pause. "And interest. Anything else?"

"Well, now that you mention it," my uncle said. "I believe Lillian is eligible for a scholarship of some kind, isn't she? Her enrollment at a university would help her assimilation a great deal."

He shrugged.

"Why not? Now that she's in the system, she can register anytime."

We left the office, leaving an anxious looking Sleevan to face his displeased superior. We never saw Sleevan again. When we returned for some follow up visits, we noticed someone else occupied his desk.

My uncle located the land that had been my parents' homestead, which was now owned by a successful textile manufacturing company. I relinquished my rights to the property and received a small share of the profits as compensation. As a result of his efforts, I had become wealthy in my own right, making me feel a guest in his home, rather than a dependent. For this consideration I was most grateful.

My uncle was not a stingy man by nature, I'm sure he would have gladly supported me, but he had keenly felt the unfairness of my situation and had been serious when he intended to make the government pay and pay dearly.

It wasn't long before I was able to speak fluent Enavian. Mheftu remained for about a month to help ease the transition, after that Jack became my teacher. He taught me Enavian and I taught him Nejimenet. To my surprise Cia made no objection and even encouraged us to study together.

There had been a great change in Cia. My childhood memories were of a stern, coldly beautiful woman who spent a lot of time arguing with my brother and reading about religion. I think that's why Jack was away so much. Her beliefs were as strong as ever, and she could be formidable if crossed, but there was a new warmth in her now. She had a love and a tolerance for others that had not been there before. Either Cia had changed greatly in the last twenty years, or my memories of her were at fault.

"It is probably a little of both," Mheftu said. "Children always overreact to the villains in their lives, but to be honest, you were quite a handful then. Cia had to come down on you hard to keep you in line. Also, she was a very unhappy woman at the time. I'm sure that had a lot to do with it."

"Unhappy about what?"

"I know you thought the world of your brother, Jack, we all did, but he wasn't a very good husband. He drank quite a bit and spent money foolishly and ran around a lot. Oh, he loved Cia, there was never another woman or anything like that. But Jack just wasn't ready to settle down. He was a good man to have on the trail, though."

Then young Jack and I sat wide-eyed while Mheftu recounted adventures he shared with my brother in the wilderness of Ceytal. I could tell he missed Jack, which I could understand because his stories reminded me of rock climbing and exploring with Tzeri. I wondered how she was. She had been so lonely after Hushé's death and she did not even have children to comfort her.

"—but he never did. Lillian? Lillian, where are you?"

"I'm sorry, Mheftu. That was rude of me not to pay attention."

"That's all right. What were you thinking of?"

"Oh, nothing important," I said quickly and changed the subject. "I'm curious about something, Mheftu. Why do you choose to be a guide? According to Erten Zemmer, you are one of the best physicians around, even better than Enavian doctors."

He smiled broadly.

"Financial reasons."

"But don't doctors make more money than expedition guides?"

"That all depends, Lillian. A general practitioner must settle in one place long enough to establish his reputation and build a clientele—a faithful following of runny-nosed hypochondriacs—eighty percent who can be depended on to pay their bills. My problem is I can never stay long enough in one place. Guiding expeditions suits me better and my medical skills have often come in handy. Treating cases of hypothermia and fractures are more rewarding than prescribing placebos to bored housewives and stressed executives."

"Then you'll be glad to get out again. When do you leave?"

"Next week. I'm meeting a party of tourists in Naritjina who are joining an archaeological expedition into the White Desert."

"The archaeologists don't mind being with them?"

"They mind very much, but they have no choice because the tourists are footing the bill. Archaeologists are always short of money." He paused. "By the way, we'll be passing by the Nejimenet camp, are there any messages I can deliver for you?"

I told him there was and went to my room to get my letter to Erten and Pallas. When I handed him the letter he glanced at the name on the envelope.

"Is that all, Tejalura?" he asked in Nejimenet.

"Yes, that is all," I answered in Enavian.

THE EXILE: LILLIAN WOLF

Spring 1340 EE

"*... My dear people, I hate to disillusion you but the vast majority of your ancestors were the scum of the Enavian Empire, thieves and murderers out of slums and debtor's prisons. Forget the quest for religious freedom and social equality your lower division instructors told you about. Bravery? You can forget that, too. As misfits and failures they had nothing to lose by coming here. Pioneers have always been of this breed and always will be . . .*"

Angrily I switched off the lecture of my Ceytalian history class and turned to my uncle.

"Now do you see what I have been telling you about? That's the sort of garbage they're teaching today. It's bad enough this is a required course, but they could at least get someone who knew what the hell he was talking about."

Ral smiled lopsidedly and rubbed his chin.

"I see you've broadened your Enavian vocabulary since your enrollment at the university."

"You're changing the subject."

"All right, what's your main objection to what he said?"

"Why it's lies, all lies!"

"Really?"

"Yes. My parents weren't criminals. They weren't failures either. As a matter of fact they were pretty well off and everyone thought they were crazy to immigrate to the frontier. They came because they wanted to. Didn't they?"

"Yes," he said. "Their immigration, I think, was Seraine's idea. My sister always had been a little odd and independent in her way of thinking. At the time I couldn't understand it, they had everything a couple could ask for: a happy marriage—never have I seen a more devoted couple, each had promising careers, good friends. What more could they want? Seraine tried to explain it to me. She said life on Taen was too fast, too regimented and the activities of her family were so fragmented she scarcely saw them."

I remembered excerpts of letters my mother had written to her family in Taen:

"I want to have time to enjoy my husband and my children. I want us to lead richer, fuller lives. I believe that by living on Ceytal we will have this chance."

My uncle continued:

"I thought they were crazy, our whole family did, but now I believe I understand. I am glad that at least you and Johnny were able to grow up the way she would have wanted you to although I'm sure she didn't anticipate you being raised by Ceytalians."

I started at the mention of Johnny's name, but I hoped my expression did not change. I have never discussed Meneth-shir or Johnny with anyone.

"The point is," I said before he could say anything further, "Their decision to immigrate was a matter of preference, not desperation. You came to Ceytal and you certainly aren't a failure."

"Thank you, Lillian. But you must admit that, if not the majority, at least a sizable chunk of our population is made up of the undesirables your teacher referred to. His views aren't incorrect as much as they are one-sided. How did the rest of the class receive his statements?"

"Very coolly, but very quietly. Except me. But I only spoke up because he started needling me again."

"What do you mean "again?'"

"Oh, I've told you about it before. He was going through his usual routine of calling me your 'royal highness' or 'Lady Wolf'—that sort of thing."

"Yes, I remember you mentioning it before, but I don't know how it started."

"It began when he lectured on the Ceytalian aborigines. You wouldn't believe the—the stuff he was coming up with." I had started to use another word to describe it, but I made an attempt to tone my language down. Hershem has some very old-world Enavian ideas as to how a lady should speak. "He thought that because there were a few cannibal Oramaklete tribes on Ceytal, the whole native population practices cannibalism. I corrected him on that point and he didn't take it too well. He asked me by what authority I said this and I answered I had lived with the Nejimenets for twenty years. When he realized who I was, he was very sarcastic about the whole thing, commenting on how honored the class was to have her royal highness, the wife of Chief Wolf in their midst."

"Lillian, you have to remember that your experience is unique. As ignorant as you may believe him to be, he has spent years of intensive research on the history, and culture of Ceytal. You can't expect him to appreciate being told by one of his students—a female at that—all his years of study were wasted."

I shrugged. One of the first things I was taught in the school on Itanshir Island was to be prepared to unlearn anything I had been taught. I considered my Enavian instructor's attitude petty and self-defeating.

"So now you've argued with your instructor and have been expelled from the university. We could petition to have you reinstated. It's not as if you weren't provoked."

"I'm not sure I want to go back."

"Are you sure of what you want to do?"

I shook my head.

"Well, then take my advice and go back to finish your education. I realize you are at loose ends now—trying to decide what to do with the rest of your life. But until you decide, get all the education you can. A good education is a possession you'll never regret."

"Even if it means taking useless classes like Ceytalian Cultural History?"

"Yes. Make a special study of that class; find out why it missed the mark. What was the object of the instructor? Did he fail? If so, why? Having graduated from an Enavian university as your teacher did, I think I can make a fair guess at part of what the problem is."

I waited while he lit his pipe.

"Enavian students," he continued, "Tend to be rather spoiled and rich and, since there is little to challenge them, more than a little bored. To gain a reputation as a good instructor, a teacher has to excite them, wake them up. Any radical statement will do, especially if it is critical of their parents' generation. At Naritjina University he found himself a little out of his depth because the Ceytalian students are of a different breed altogether. They tend to be older due to many interruptions in their education, such as military service or lack of money for tuition. They're tough, hard-working and serious about their studies, and not simply taking up time because they don't have anything better to do.

"Families and communities are too united and far too busy building a home for themselves on a hostile planet for your teacher's iconoclastic speeches to strike a responsive cord with the frontier students.

Your teacher should come back in, say fifty years, when we are more settled and secure and have the leisure to indulge ourselves with such diversions."

I returned to the university to please my uncle, but I was restless. I felt the need to take hold of my life and direct the course of my future. Yet, I could not decide on a specific goal.

Cia was shocked when I had adopted the casual dress and manner of the second-generation colonists, which contrasted sharply with her stylish Enavian dresses. I owned one or two fashionable gowns so I wouldn't embarrass her at formal gatherings, but otherwise I wore modern Ceytalian garments.

Jack was a comfort to me, often we would go horseback riding or drive to Naritjina City, the newly built capital located where the Outpost once stood. I loved Naritjina City. It was alive and exciting, it bustled with noise and activity, as the quiet valley of Meneth-shir never did. We would drive in my transport and, if the road was clear, I allowed Jack a turn at the controls.

Mactil Street, a popular tourist attraction, was the heart of Naritjina City as it had been of the Outpost. Mactil Street boasts of many restaurants and cafés located near an authentic Ceytalian market place.

The market place on Mactil Street dates back to pre-Ceytalian times and the arrival of the Enavians made very little impression on the merchant class. Throughout the ebb and flow of Enavian colonization, it has always been business as usual for the trade on Mactil Street. The attempt of the Enavian government to change the Ceytalian market days, because it conflicted with their own galactic timetable, met with complete failure. The merchants ignored the revised schedule of "new" market days and continued to trade on the same days they had throughout millennium. Enavian vendors who showed up on the wrong day, found no one to trade with. Eventually, at great expense and inconvenience, the Enavians changed their own schedules to accommodate the Ceytalian market days.

In its crowded cafés and shops all of Ceytal was represented there. Soldiers of the Naritian Army, the Imperial Space Force, and the Frontier Guard milled about in different colored uniforms, eager to spend their accumulated pay. There were workers from farms, Oramaklete nomads from the desert, Zenadishj horse traders from

Zeneshtu; an occasional mercenary in Naritian uniform represented the Nejimenets. For a tenthpiece you could sit in a café for hours. The cafés are so crowded often tables have to be shared with strangers, but that makes it all the more interesting.

On one visit to Mactil Street, every table at our favorite café was occupied. The only available seats had to be shared with two young frontier guardsmen—a handsome young man and a woman sharing their brief leave together. I would have left them their privacy, but Jack had run ahead to secure a seat for us. We have learned you have to move fast on Mactil Street.

"Jack, must you be so rude?" I asked in exasperation. "I am sorry," I apologized to the couple. "We'll find another place."

The man stood up from his chair with unexpected formality.

"There is nothing to apologize for," the dark-eyed captain insisted. "Won't you please join us."

I hesitated.

"We insist," he turned to the girl. "Don't we, Irima?"

The young woman smiled and nodded in agreement.

"Let us introduce ourselves," he said in accented Enavian. "I am Lev Kedhari and this is my sister, Irima."

I smiled with extra warmth, unreasonably glad they were brother and sister. Tejalura, you are a married woman, I told myself. Don't let this Lev Kedhari melt you with his beautiful dark eyes.

"It's a pleasure to meet you," I said striving for detached politeness, but failing miserably. "My name is Lillian Wolf and this is my nephew, Jack Aleksandar."

Irima said something aside to her brother in a language I guessed to be Urthic. Lev nodded and turned to me.

"Irima has noticed your tattoo and would like to know under whose instruction you received it." At my stunned silence, he continued: "It is the mark of a *nutevek narashan* is it not?"

"Yes, it is," I said. "I'm just surprised because you are the first Enavians to know what it signifies."

"We are not Enavians," he said mildly. "We are Erteyans."

"Oh," I said at a loss until I remembered something I had overheard during the many discussions Yari had with Terez. "Are you also called *teyados*?"

They both stiffened at the word.

"Only by our enemies."

"I'm sorry," I said hastily. "I don't even know what the word means."

He spoke briefly to his sister in Urthic. She laughed and nodded, then spoke and laughed again. By this time my embarrassment was acute.

"*'Teyado'* or *'teyadinj'* is the Urthic word for animal dung," Lev explained. "More specifically, 'the dung of an unclean animal.' The Zenadishj coin insults in the language of those they are offending to ensure the insults are understood."

I should have known better than to use the word before I knew its meaning. But they seemed to find it amusing and we all had a good laugh at my expense. By then it was impossible to return to my former role as the courteous but distant stranger.

This was my first meeting with the new generation of Ceytalian-born Erteyans and I was impressed. Their direct manner and healthy good looks, combined with an air of optimistic determination was refreshing. Until recently, they had been second-class citizens of the Enavian Empire. Being dissatisfied with that position they demanded a world of their own and that world was Ceytal, which they claimed to be their legendary Earth.

We spent several hours talking with them. Jack was impressed with their uniforms and asked about their weapons. I was interested in their farms because I had grown up on one before the Nejimenets had adopted me. My interest led to an invitation to visit their farm. We exchanged addresses so we could arrange to visit them during their next leave.

"And you must come and visit us too sometime," I also offered politely.

Lev and Irima exchanged a look.

"Could we visit you now?" he asked abruptly. "You see, we have little money left. It would help not to have to rent rooms in the city."

Their forwardness surprised me. I have since learned to never make an insincere offer to an Erteyan for politeness sake, because they will take you up on it. On the other hand, I have learned the offer of an Erteyan can be taken at face value. They are not in the habit of mouthing empty pleasantries.

I called Cia to give her some warning that we would have guests for several days. Surprisingly, Cia welcomed them warmly.

Although Irima's shorts and cigarettes must have shocked her, she gave not the slightest sign. Irima's hair was bobbed short, which is the style of prostitutes among Enavian circles, but Cia seemed only to notice that the glossy black curls made a beautiful frame for the pretty Erteyan girl's face. Cia's standards have not changed over the years, but she had acquired a tolerance for those of another background.

Hershem and Lev got along from the start. They spent most of their time discussing politics. They disagreed on everything, but in the same friendly manner that reminded me of Yari and Terez.

"Now I'm not an Imperialist," Hershem assured Kedhari, "But I believe you and your rebel friends are trying to go too far too fast. Ceytal is a raw wilderness of undeveloped swamp and desert. We simply are not ready for independence yet."

Kedhari shook his head.

"No, don't you see our lack of development is a factor in our favor. The empire will be more willing to let us go now because, after all, what is there to lose but a barren wasteland. But with each new farm and factory, we become more precious to them. If we wait too long, they will consider us too valuable to let go because they have invested so much into us."

"But if the empire should desert us, the Ceytalian natives would tear us apart."

"Or we could unite—work together with the Ceytalians to build a strong, free planet."

Now it was Hershem's turn to shake his head.

"It's a beautiful dream, Lev. I only wish it were possible."

・→※←・・→※←・・→※←・

Months later, I received a call from Lev. Arrangements had been made for Jack and me to spend a week with his family on the Blue Mountain Farm. We met Irima in Naritjina, but her brother was nowhere to be seen.

"We couldn't get off at the same time," she explained. "But five days of our leave overlap each other; we were lucky to get even that. Anyway, you'll be staying at Blue Mountain Farm for fifteen days instead of ten. Will that be all right?"

"Of course," I said quickly. "I'm flattered you invited us to your home during your leave at all." The time they spent with their family must be precious indeed, but she shrugged and said with typical Erteyan honesty:

"It was Lev's idea, not mine." She glanced sharply at my tattoo. "You never did mention who your instructor was."

"Oh, Aunt Kiakashe. You know her as General She Bear."

"She served in the Naritian Army? Yes, her name is very familiar to us. Many of our parents and grandparents fought against her."

Her statement made me feel terribly old and I realized that she had not been born until after I had been among the Nejimenets for four years. How old was Lev? He looked about my age. But then, why should his age matter? He was merely a friend and I was a married woman with two children. I must remember this.

"Am I speaking too fast for you?" she asked. "Lev told me that you had learned Urthic at the university, but I could not believe you spoke it so well."

"Thank you, Irima," I said, flattered for she did not give complements lightly. "No, I understand you perfectly."

Irima and I took turns at the controls, so we could admire the beautiful scenery. We followed the Naritjina Highway and by the next afternoon we were passing through Yarashji-shir. Its familiar beauty made my throat ache with unshed tears. I realized we were very near the campsite where the Enavians attacked us. Trista would have been nine now.

Near the end of the journey we passed by the Gavin ranch where Yari and Terez had worked. At last, we arrived at the Blue Mountain Farm. I was impressed with the farm. For better protection and more efficient farming, it was communally owned and worked—there were no servants or slave labor. Guests of several months were expected to help with the work. Because our visit would be a short one, Jack and I were not expected to work but we did anyway. My tattoo was noticed and respected, especially among the older Erteyans who had fought against my aunt.

Four days later, Lev arrived. Jack and I had been helping the others hang out the laundry when I saw him walk towards us. I smiled and waved. As he returned my greeting, I discovered again how handsome he was. My cheeks grew warm under his gaze, Terez had once looked at me like that. It would have been so easy to return his glance, but instead I lowered my eyes and picked up another article of clothing to hang.

"Put that down, Lillian," he commanded. "This is supposed to be a holiday. You shouldn't be working at all. You are our guest."

"I know, but I felt so guilty just sitting around. Besides, working on the farm is the best way to get to know the people and well—there just wasn't anything else for us to do."

"There is now. You know how to ski, don't you?"

"Yes, but—"

"A friend of ours owns a cabin in the mountains. Our whole family is going to ski there and you and Jack are going with us."

"But Lev, we couldn't."

"What have you to do instead? Stay here and shame us by doing chores? Is that what we are to expect when we visit you?"

"No, of course not! All right, you win."

Ced and Mar Winters, the owners of the cabin, were there to meet us. They ran a general store at the foot of the mountains that seemed to be doing good business. I had a hard time keeping Jack under control. I have never seen that boy so wild, but since Cia kept him in such a tight reign, I suppose this was to be expected. I spoke sharply to him in Nejimenet, not once thinking any of the others understood.

"You speak Nejimenet well," Ced commented. "How did you come to learn it?"

"I lived with them for over twenty years," I answered. "How do you know it?"

"We used to get a few Nejimenets out here every so often for trade. Haven't seen any for the last few years, though. Too bad, they were nice people. Good customers."

The matter would have stopped there except Jack seemed intent on making the most of the situation.

"Aunt Lillian's real name is Tejalura and she has two sons that are my age. Akashe and Khai. Someday I'm going to go hunting with them."

I could feel Lev's eyes on me.

"Oh, when?" he asked lightly.

"I don't know," Jack answered. "I guess when she goes back to her husband. He's a famous chief, you know. Yaremida Ce."

"You don't mean Chief Wolf Winter?"

"The same," I said stiffly. "Please, let us talk of something else."

Later I overheard Mar whisper to Ced:

"She's the one we heard about on the news report. How awful, she must miss her family so."

"She seems to be doing all right. Have you seen the way Kedhari looks at her and the way she looks at him?"

Ced's words shamed me, but he was right. It would have been all too easy to forget my Nejimenet family and make a new life for myself among the Enavians. I was attracted to Lev and, although he never said so in words, there was no doubt in my mind how he felt about me.

When Jack and I returned home, I was moody and irritable. I did not owe Yari any loyalty, yet I knew I would not be able to go through with a divorce. Why? What was it bound me to him? At an early age he had bullied me into a marriage that I would not have wanted on my own and the way he allowed the Enavian authorities to take me away from him was unforgivable. Yet the fact remained I was bound to him and I could not find the strength to break free. My moodiness did not go unnoticed by the others.

"It's that Erteyan boyfriend of hers," remarked Mrs. Weldon, one of Cia's busy-body friends. "When are you two going to get married?" she teased.

"I already have a husband," I said coolly.

Hershem looked at me sharply. Later, when we were alone he said:

"If you want a divorce it can be easily arranged."

"I know that, but that's not the problem. The problem is I'm twenty-nine and my life so far has been a complete waste. I haven't accomplished anything." I paused. "And I haven't seen my husband and children in two years."

"I'm sorry, Lillian, but it never occurred to me you considered your Nejimenet marriage as legal and binding. Do you still love him?"

I shrugged.

"I don't know. I suppose we had a good marriage in the beginning, but he changed after the soldiers killed our daughter. I can't even be sure he loves me. I mean if I have noticed Lev, how do I know Yari hasn't remarried or taken a second wife during my absence?"

"A divorce might be the best thing," he said after a moment's silence. "After all, there is little chance you will see each other again."

That wasn't true, but I couldn't tell him about Meneth-shir. So my decision depended on whether or not I loved Yari.

"Maybe you are right," I said at last. "A divorce might be best. I'll think about it."

I had Hershem draw up the documentation and a copy was sent to Yari, but weeks passed and there was no reply. Mheftu came to visit after his return from the White Desert. He brought two letters for me, one was from the Zemmers and the other was from Yari. I seized Yari's letter and tore it open.

> *Tejalura,*
>
> *All of us here in the White Desert are well and in good health, and all send you their greetings and wish you well. The boys have grown a lot in the last two years. They also send their love to a mother who is daily remembered.*
>
> *A great deal has happened since you left. Your mother has had a baby, a girl named Melia. Your friend, Tzeri, has become the third wife of Neve Chevari and they are expecting a son—Neve is certain it will be a son. They also send their love, as does Yanahna-Khai.*
>
> *A new agent is being assigned to our camp, so Erten and Pallas will be leaving soon. The government is not pleased that we have been doing so well. Erten said that our trade with the merchants in Naritjina has resulted in a remarkable profit for us—better than most Enavian businesses. Why the government is not pleased, I don't know. Erten has tried to explain it to me, but I still do not understand. Since you have become Enavian again you may understand better than I. If you do, try to explain it to me.*
>
> *I received the divorce papers, but before I could decide what to do with them, your little sister, Melia, tore them up. I think she is wiser than the two of us so I have decided that if you send me any more papers I will give them to her.*
>
> *Your husband,*
>
> *Yari*

I suppose I should have been angry his letter included no apology for sending me away to live with the Enavians; instead, I felt ridiculously happy he had not signed the papers. Enclosed was a picture one of the soldiers had taken of Yari kneeling with his arms around the boys. They had grown. The camera had caught Yari's smile, that careless, happy one that was so dear to me. It was the old Yari from before the massacre. After reading the letter from the Zemmers I immediately wrote Yari a reply. I also enclosed a picture of my Enavian family.

>Yari,
>
>All is well. My Enavian family send you their greetings. The man and the woman who stand beside me are my uncle, Ral Hershem, and his wife Cia. Of course you know Mheftu. The young boy who looks like Khai is Jack Aleksandar Jr. He has been a great comfort to me. He has also written a letter to you, which I have enclosed with the picture. Jack is learning Nejimenet and I think that he has done a good job of it. If you wrote back to him, it would be such an encouragement. You are a hero to him.
>
>There is so much to tell you, but I can hardly do it in one letter so I will concentrate on what is most important.
>
>Remember the Erteyans Terez spoke of? They are wonderful people and I have come to admire them a great deal. They are a minority group of Enavians and have come from all parts of the empire, many from penal colonies, to settle here on Ceytal. Terez was right when he said they believe Ceytal to be their legendary planet, Earth. I have talked with some of their leaders and their intentions are peaceful. They only want to settle the land and feel as you do that there is room enough for all. I know they settled on our campsites, but they claim that if they had known they were our campsites they wouldn't have settled there. I believe them.

> *They have accomplished miracles with the land. Their agricultural methods are bringing a new life to our planet. There is a freshness about them, an optimism that is contagious. There is much we could offer each other. It is the Enavians who are our enemies, not the Erteyans. We must try to work together.*
>
> *For the most part I do not like the Enavians. They are a loud, rude, and arrogant people. Enavian authorities only tolerate Erteyan settlements because they believe their presence will give them control of the frontier. Erteyans have tried to remain independent, but with every Zenadishj attack, they become more dependent on imperial armies. If only there could be peace, we could gain independence from the empire.*
>
> *I have read Erten's explanation for the government's suppression of the success of the White Desert Camp and I am as puzzled as you. I suppose I will never be a real Enavian again. But one thing is clear, they are our true enemies and for some reason they do not want Nejimenets to succeed. The camps must be a cover for some terrible purpose of their own. Be very careful.*
>
> *Your wife,*
>
> *Tejalura*

The following year was my most enjoyable among the Enavians. I had decided to remain Nejimenet and as soon as Yari returned to Meneth-shir, I would join him. From the tone of Yari's letter, I felt it would be soon.

Hershem was pleased when I changed my major to law and helped me with my studies. We had many long talks about the different aspects of the law. Our debates drew us closer together and I learned that more than knowledge, my uncle had wisdom.

I chose to study law because I thought if we understood their legal system, we would be able to negotiate with the Enavians as equals. But I was to learn the Enavians tended to disregard their own laws when it came to dealings with the Ceytalians. We were a weak and divided people who, since we posed no threat to the Enavians, inspired little respect. We could only negotiate successfully with the Enavians from a position of strength. That would be best accomplished if we established friendly relations with not only the Zenadishj and Oramaklete nations, but also the Erteyans.

I received a call from Lev asking me to join him in Naritjina for the afternoon. It had been a day when I was especially happy with things as they were, but the sound of his voice shattered my peaceful world.

"No, Lev," I said awkwardly. "I can't meet you. In fact, I don't think we should be seeing each other any more."

He was silent for a moment.

"Lillian, I know you are not the kind of woman to have affairs. You are faithful and I respect you for that. If you were any less than the woman you are I would not feel as I do about you. I have accepted the fact that you will never be mine. I will not worry about what is not possible between us and enjoy what is possible."

"And what is that?" I said teasingly.

"Your friendship and the pleasure of your company," he answered seriously, "Without which I would be a much poorer man. Now that we understand each other, will you meet me in Naritjina?"

There are some men who would say that without meaning a word of it, but not Lev. He had said he would respect me and he did. I think I was a little disappointed. Lev continued to be my escort among Enavian society and our friends began to accept us as a couple. We were often complimented on how well we looked together—and when was it we were planning to get married?

Lev fielded such questions with a smile and a graceful shrug and said:

"I have asked her many times, but she prefers being my temptress to being my wife."

One evening he took me to see an excellent production of *Ceymar Ce*, a play based on the life of the Zenadishj queen. During the performance, I remembered she was the queen Mheftu told me stories about when I was little. Liet Kassar, a promising young actress of Urthic decent, performed the part of Queen Ceymar. *Ceymar Ce* had received interplanetary awards for the high quality of its holography.

During intermission the transmission of the entire cast continued while they relaxed, broke into small groups and loosened the collars of uncomfortable costumes. The audience was allowed on stage to mingle with the actors' holograms as they gossiped, drank coffee, and companionably lit each others' cigarettes. A group of college students pretended to take part in the actors' conversations, some had even dressed in special costumes. A week earlier one student had continued to stay after the play had resumed and wasn't discovered until the end when he was left standing alone. The audience gave him a standing ovation before he was escorted off stage.

Afterward we dined at The Cela Rose. I wondered, and not for the first time, what it would be like to have an affair with a man like Lev Kedhari. I defy any woman to remain aloof in the presence of a man who adores her—especially when that man is as attractive as Lev.

On our way home we heard a news report that the Nejimenets had gone renegade and all citizens living in the White Desert area were warned to be on the alert against possible attacks. Lev said nothing until we arrived at my home.

"Good night, Lillian," he said to me at the door. "And good-bye."

As soon as I closed the door, I ran upstairs to my room. I was going home. Now, more than ever, I was certain my home was Meneth-shir. The opportunity I had to make my home among the Enavians had taught me that my place was with the Nejimenet people.

I executed a deed transferring my Enavian wealth to Jack. I packed what few things I would need for the journey, mounted my horse and left. How easy it all was—no tickets to buy nor transport schedules to consult. I was free.

Two days outside of Naritjina, I glanced up to see a tracker hovering above me. I took my burner out of my belt and, taking careful aim, I fired. There was a crash of metal as the tracker hit the ground and I looked at the twisted silvery mess the tracker had become.

They were such cute little machines, it was a shame I had to shoot this one. I should have waited longer before leaving for Meneth-shir, it was stupid of me not to guess the Enavians would use me to locate my husband and our people. Satisfied that I had successfully thwarted their efforts, I rode on admiring the scenery around me.

TEJALURA

Chapter 15
The Tracker: Lemmer Kendal 1341 EE

> Once I dreamed of an Urthic maiden
> Who loved me with a love so true
> She sang a song of the river...
>
> —*Ceytalian Folksong*

Autumn 1341 EE

After following Lillian Wolf's trail for three days, I found her camped beside the Lemmer Helt River just a few miles upstream from where it is joined by the Blue Mountain River. She knelt by the fire with the accustomed ease of a nomad, cooking something that smelled delicious. Her thick, blue-black hair was casually pinned out of the way except for a few strands against her cheek, which she brushed away with a sunburned hand. From a short distance away she might have been a young girl of fifteen, but as I came closer, I saw the faint dryness around her eyes and guessed her to be about thirty.

"You must be hungry," she said. "Come and join me."

I hesitated before accepting the bowl she offered me.

"This is good," I said after tasting the food. After a few chews, I asked: "You know why I'm here, don't you?"

"Of course. So far you are the seventh tracker to find me this week. The Enavian government is nothing if not persistent." Her smile deepened. "I must say the present model is an improvement over the mechanical ones. What made them decide to send a human?"

She was actually flirting with me. Not seriously, but teasingly, as very good friends do. I relaxed and smiled in return, I couldn't help it.

"The government does have a budget to meet," I explained. "Do you realize how much a mechanical tracker costs? By the way, I notice you have two of them tied to your horse. What do you plan to do with them?"

"Oh, I'm taking them home to my boys. I thought they might enjoy playing with them."

I nearly choked on my coffee. One tracker alone cost the government thousands of credits, and she thought they might make cute toys for her children.

"No doubt they will," I said casually, deciding to get them back from her as soon as I could catch her off guard.

"What is your name?" she asked suddenly.

"Lemmer Kendal. Call me Lem."

I rubbed my hand against my forehead, suddenly exhausted.

"Why don't you go to sleep," Lillian said softly. "You are tired. More tired than you know."

At her suggestion, my eyes seemed to grow heavier. I have been hypnotized, I thought to myself. Or poisoned.

· →※←· →※←· →※←·

The first thing I saw when I opened my eyes was the morning light dancing on the river. Lillian was already awake and cooking the leftover rabbit from the night before. That with some fruit and water made our breakfast. The moment was so rare and perfect I said nothing for fear of spoiling it.

I saddled my horse when she did, half expecting her to protest my following her, but she said nothing. In fact, she seemed to assume that we would be traveling together. Her destruction of the six mechanical trackers proved she wished her destination to remain secret, yet she was completely unconcerned by my presence. Did she plan to kill me? I smiled to myself as I watched the landscape around us. That was one of the reasons I like Ceytal. It may be a little wild and unpredictable, but it was never dull.

"What are you thinking about?" she asked, also smiling.

I looked at her briefly, then returned my attention to the landscape around me.

"I'm wondering just how you are going to try to kill me," I said.

"And so you smile?"

"Why not? The sun is shining, the sky is clear, I'm in the company of a beautiful woman," I decided two can play at flirting. "A man could die worse off."

She shook her head, but continued to smile.

For the next few hours we rode in comfortable silence, content to watch the beauty of the prairie. But soon I found myself telling her of my childhood and what it was like to grow up in the Blue Mountain Community. I worked on the farm with my parents and my nine older brothers until I was twelve and then I got my first job working at Ced Winters' general store. I also told her of my early years in the Frontier Guard. At first I was afraid I had bored her but she insisted it was not so.

"You have helped me imagine what it would have been like had I remained Enavian. I have often wondered."

By then I had talked myself out and it seemed to be Lillian's turn to speak as we sat by the fire drinking our coffee, not yet tired enough for sleep. She spoke, not of herself but of her country, Meneth-shir.

"There is no place like it on earth," she assured me. "It is a large, beautiful valley of rich farmland and dense forests. Our houses are built of gray stone. In the center of it all is Lake Melia, which is the source of the Khai Melia—the river you Enavians call Lemmer Helt. And the center of Lake Melia is Itan-shir Island where we have our schools and workshops. Life is good there, complete."

"But don't you work?"

"Of course we work, as a matter of fact, we work very hard. But our attitude about work is different from Enavians. Here let me explain: in the Enavian language there are different words for 'work' and 'play,' but we Nejimenets make no distinction between the two, using one word interchangeably. That word is *iraveh*, which literally means 'activity.' We take joy in all we do, whether it be dancing, hunting, or working in the fields. I think that is one of the major differences between Enavians and Nejimenets."

"Surely you have problems."

"Of course we have problems, many problems. But our approach to them is different. Problems are challenges, not obstacles."

"What about criminals? How does your legal system work—your courts?"

"Courts? We have no courts. Nor do we have prisons, for we have no need of them. There hasn't been a crime committed in Meneth-shir for hundreds of years."

"But I'm sure that even the Nejimenets disagree about something occasionally; land ownership, water rights, damaged property—something."

"Certainly, we are human after all. But as I said before, our approach is different. When two Enavians disagree about something, they take it before the council and their attitude is 'I can't win unless you lose.' But when two Nejimenets disagree it is, 'I can't win unless you win also.' A solution is reached that will not put either at a disadvantage."

"But what if such a solution can't be found?"

"I don't know. So far, there hasn't been such a problem."

I was silent for a moment.

"My mother used to speak of a place like that. She called it 'Paradise.' I never thought such a place existed."

"Believe me, it exists."

It sounded so impossible, yet I longed to believe her. It would mean so much to me to know there was such a place as Meneth-shir.

"No wonder you Nejimenets are so fanatical about keeping its location a secret from the rest of Ceytal. I almost wish you hadn't told me where it was. You know I'll have to report it to my superiors."

She smiled.

"But you won't."

"You sound so sure. How do you plan to stop me? By killing me?"

"No, that won't be necessary." she suddenly stood and stretched. "I think I'll turn in now. It's going to be a long day tomorrow."

I tried to stay awake that night in order not to be caught off guard, but against my will, I drifted off to sleep anyway. As a result I woke up late the next morning. Lillian had already packed both horses and was leaving me.

"You can't just leave me here unarmed with no supplies or even a horse."

"But I can. I'm not too worried about you, you're young and healthy. There's plenty of water in the river and fruit on the trees. You'll make it back all right."

"But I know the location of Meneth-shir. All I have to do is follow the Lemmer Helt River to its source, Lake Melia. You told me so yourself."

She smiled and shook her head.

"By tomorrow you won't remember that there is a Lake Melia or such a place called Meneth-shir."

"What do you mean?"

"Do you know what *nathaja* is? No? Then you may be more familiar with its Zenadishj name, *nateheh*. Or perhaps cela rose?"

"Yes, it's a prairie flower the Ceytalians use for poison. Did you poison me?"

"Not exactly. We Nejimenets have discovered that if the powder ground from the seed of the *nathaja* is administered in small amounts, it merely prevents the brain from recording information as long as the victim has it in his system. For the last three days this drug has been in your food and water. By tomorrow you won't remember a thing that has occurred during that time." She paused to let me absorb that. "Good-bye, Lem Gavin. Ce be with you."

I stood there for a moment then began my long walk back to the Naritjina City. As I walked I kept repeating to myself: "The source of the Lemmer Helt River is Lake Melia, and Lake Melia is the center of Meneth-shir, the nation of the Nejimenets. The source of Lemmer Helt River is Lake Melia . . . "

・→✷←・→✷←・→✷←・

I sat on a rock gazing into the rushing waters of the Lemmer Helt River wondering just how I came to be there minus my horse and supplies. Just a moment ago I was by the Blue Mountain River speaking with a dark-haired woman who handed me a bowl of food, smiling.

Chapter 16
Homecoming: Tejalura 1341 EE

> Sing a song of the mountains
> A song that is strong and brave
> A song that will ring through the valley
> And say: "You are home again!"
>
> — *The Return of Gan Akashe*
> *Nejimenet Folksong*

Late Autumn 1341 EE

The thundering roar of Arae Shjina was the sweetest sound I have ever heard. Like a beautiful song, it soothed every nerve of my body. I did not hurry my horse along the trail, I wanted to hear and see everything. It was as if I had been asleep during my years among the Enavians. The wind was fresh and smelled of spring, yet it was cold and silvery and would not quite let me forget winter.

When at last I reached Meneth-shir, I looked across the broad caldera and saw my people working in their fields and wondered at the quiet peace of our world. Tears came to my eyes.

I was home.

I led my horse to the field and watched her as she joined the rest of the herd and thought of how beautiful she was. Arae was a dapple gray mountain pony of Neve Chevari's breeding, a present from Hershem and Cia.

In the distance I saw a group of boys playing, among them were Khai and Akashe. I did not reveal myself, I didn't know what to say to them, but was content to watch them unobserved.

As I followed the path that led to the house, I saw a graceful young woman standing in the doorway looking so much like Laughter she might have been her ghost. Imih continued to stare off dreamily into the distance until her eyes focused on me.

"Tejalura!" she cried out in surprise and pleasure. "Silverwoman! Turquoise! Come and see, it's Tejalura!"

Turquoise and Imih ran to greet me, but my mother preferred to welcome me with her own quiet smile. A little girl with pale, blue hair and silver-gray eyes toddled out to join us. With her coloring, she could only be my mother's daughter, Melia. She smiled at me and two dimples like Trista's appeared on her cheeks.

"Hello, Melia," I said as I knelt to hug her. I glanced up at Silverwoman. "She's beautiful, I'm so happy for you, Mother. I know how you and Father have wanted a child."

"As much as we have wanted your return," Silverwoman said. "And now that you are here our family is complete."

"All right, enough!" Turquoise interrupted briskly. "Let's get to work. You have been a spoiled Enavian lady and you must learn to be Nejimenet again. You can help Barije with the fire. You always could get the most out of a log and she could use a few pointers."

"Who is Barije?" I asked.

"My father's woman," Imih said briefly. "A Zenadishj."

Puzzled, I looked to Turquoise questioningly.

"On our return to Meneth-shir we were attacked by a band of Zenadishj. Barije was one of the survivors. She has not fit in well with us, but she causes little trouble so we allow her to remain. I think Geysan would leave our household if we didn't."

Barije didn't even look up as we entered the room. I was surprised at her youth; she didn't look much older than Imih. Against the firelight, the clean line of her profile appeared as defenseless as a cameo of a lost child. At first glance I thought her pretty, but I revised my opinion of her as her hard yellow eyes examined my friendly smile with little interest. I refused to let her stony silence disturb my mood. I sat there looking into the fire, the warmth of it relaxed my body while the light of the dancing flames hypnotized me. The soft sounds of the others moving in the room brushed against my ears.

As if from a great distance I heard the scuffling and stamping of feet and the rough laughter of men coming in from work. Then there was a small silence.

"Tejalura?"

At the sound of his voice I turned and smiled.

"Well, Yari?" inquired Turquoise sharply. "After all this time aren't you going to even kiss her?"

He grinned and shook his head.

"Later."

During the meal everyone plied me with questions about my experiences with the Enavians, everyone except Yari, who simply watched me. I answered them as best as I could, but I felt suddenly shy under Yari's gaze. As the conversation changed to other things, he joined in the laughter and casual talk. No longer the center of attention, I took this chance to study the man I had married twelve years ago.

The laugh-lines around his eyes had deepened, he looked older and more mature, but still the most handsome man in Meneth-shir. He was no longer the careless youth I had married, nor was he the dark brooding stranger he had become after Trista's death. There was a new strength in him, a deeper warmth. He had been listening to someone half-smiling, then sensing my look, he caught my eye and his smile deepened. I flushed and looked away in confusion. It was a pleasant feeling to discover that I was still in love with my husband.

After dinner we drank coffee by the fire, Yari and I sat a little apart from the others. Our conversation was awkward at first; we spoke only of the safe and familiar.

"I saw Khai and Akashe earlier today. Where are they now?"

"They are spending the night with friends. You'll see them tomorrow."

"They have grown to be fine boys. I could not believe how big they have become. Three years is a long time."

"Much too long," he agreed with a rueful smile as he brushed aside a strand of hair from my cheek. "I must say your forgiveness has come much more easily than I had a right to hope. I want you to know that if I had it to do over, I would never have let the Enavians take you from me. There never was a day that passed I didn't miss you."

It wasn't often Yari apologized so I didn't mention there had been weeks and months I hadn't thought of him at all. I simply put my head on his shoulder and squeezed his hand. I knew Yari well. His words had been a little too practiced, which indicated that either he was hiding emotions he felt too deeply to reveal or covering the fact that he didn't care at all. How simple this man could be; how complex. And yet I loved him beyond all reason.

He and the others filled me in on the important events that had occurred in Meneth-shir during my absence. We spoke of the council and how they still disagreed with Yari's views.

"But didn't you show them my letter?" I asked.

"No, but I told them you had some more information that might change their minds. Now that you have returned, they will call another meeting and you can tell them what you have learned."

"Good. But first I want them to read the report that I have compiled. I have had a copy made for each household. If they read it first then we can better discuss things with less argument and more understanding."

At the mention of my report he asked to see a copy of it. I wasn't eager to leave the warm fireside, but I didn't want to break the fragile link that we had established, so I ran up the stairs and pulled a copy out of my traveling bag and ran down the stairs to give it to him.

"I am impressed," he said as he quickly scanned the report. "You did this yourself?"

"My uncle helped a lot. He's a well-known lawyer with quite a bit of influence. I was able to interview politically important people to give me a clear idea of the situation."

He nodded.

"Good, we'll call for a meeting next month."

"Why next month?" I asked. "Why not call a meeting next week? It won't them take that long to read it."

"No, but it will take you at least until next week to pass the report out and I want everyone to get a chance to read it and think it over."

"But if I ride my horse I can have them distributed in two or three days."

"Tejalura, you have been away for five years. Do you expect people to allow you to pass by their homes without stopping to visit for a while?"

He was right. In fact, it took me more than a week to deliver them. Everyone was impressed with the report and the fact that I had lived five years among the Enavians (three of those years as an Enavian citizen) gave it more credibility. I was certain the council would vote to reestablish contact with the *shemetul*.

I couldn't have been more wrong. The isolationists held out by two-thirds. What hurt most was that my father, one of the few council members who went down with us, voted against us.

"I am impressed with the findings of my daughter, Tejalura, but they do not build a convincing argument for continued involvement with the *shemetul*. Have I not lost a niece and nephew and a granddaughter to them? Is there a man here who has not lost a relative or loved one? We have been self-sufficient for centuries and have had no real need for outside contact. I say that, unless Ce should dictate otherwise, we should keep to ourselves."

The outcome of the vote indicated that the others felt the same. The council asked Yari and I, as well as the others who had lived at the White Desert Camp, to compile a book using my report as a guide so that what we had learned could be used at a future date if needed.

"By then it will be so outdated it won't even be worth the paper it is written on," I fumed. I also suspected that the purpose of the book was to placate us for the five years of work we put into this project.

Yari was more philosophical about it.

"As Zarkhon said, it is in the hands of Ce now."

"Men! It is so easy for you to make a mess of things and then blame it on a god. If we stand by while the Zenadishj, the Oramakletes, the Urthics, and the Erteyans are taken over by the Enavians, we will have no allies to help us when the Enavians come for us."

"That seems a very remote danger. Meneth-shir is too difficult to reach and we have no mineral wealth for them to covet."

"We have good farmland, and on a planet of swamp and desert, that is something."

"Tejalura, we have already gone over this at the meeting."

"But five years of our lives, Yari. Such a waste! I know that it doesn't bother you so much, but you're a man. Do you realize that I'm over thirty! I'll be a grandmother soon."

He laughed and hugged me.

"You have a few good years left."

"It's not just that," I said with a sigh. "It's just that—oh, Yari, how can our people be so blind? When will they see that we can't remain cut off from the rest of the world?"

"I don't know Tejalura."

Except for our trade with Neve Chevari, Meneth-shir remained isolated from the rest of Ceytal. But a year later, Queen Ceymar of Narit sent two Zenadishj priests to deliver an important message to our people. The council sent four of us to meet them and find out what they wanted: Gan Akashe, Yari and I were chosen because of our experience with outsiders and our knowledge of Zenadishj and Teve, now a young man, because he made a special request to go with us.

Chapter 17
The Priest: Tehmu 1342-1348 EE

> I have seen the wind
> I have listened to its secret in the trees
> Of a far, hidden place within my soul
>
> — *Song of the Solstice,*
> *Ancient Ceytalian Hymn*

Late Autumn 1342 EE

"It's about time," Metul said through chattering teeth. "I'm frozen stiff. Now listen, Tehmu. You keep quiet and let me do all of the talking."

His last admonition was unnecessary, but then, most of what Metul said was unnecessary. How he loved the sound of his voice, even if he was merely stating the obvious. Of course he would do the talking, for he was senior priest while I was merely a disciple.

Still, his anxiety was understandable, for this was the most important assignment in his career. The survival of the Naritian Empire depended on obtaining the aid of the Nejimenets. If successful, it would strengthen his candidacy for high priest. But would the Nejimenets help us?

Everything hinged on the response of the Nejimenets to our request for their aid. Already we had wasted precious time waiting for the Nejimenet leaders to meet with us. No outsider entered the land of the Nejimenets and they could only be contacted by message. Although the Nejimenets were our most trusted allies, they remained elusive and mysterious. They served in our armies, but only on a volunteer basis, they could not be conscripted. Nor could they be taxed. If we needed money, it would be borrowed with the understanding that it would be repaid. We have always been able to depend upon their help when needed—but only on their terms. They were an entirely independent people and could neither be bullied nor bribed.

I glanced up at the stars and smiled. Never had I seen the stars so clearly. The lights of our own city, Halia Tehal, often blocked them out. But here in the pure mountain air, they appeared as sharp points of crystal light against a background of black ice.

Metul rose stiffly to meet the Nejimenets as they approached. There were three men accompanied by a small, dark-haired woman with a tattoo on her cheekbone that indicated she was of the warrior caste.

"Ah, General Gan Akashe," Metul said to the oldest man. "It is good to see an old friend."

"Metul," the general nodded courteously, but did not appear to share Metul's enthusiasm at their reunion. "What do you want?"

"We have an important message to deliver to the king of the Nejimenets."

"Give it to us, and we will deliver the message."

"I'm sorry, but the queen instructed us to give it personally to the king and no other."

They hesitated. The woman said something in Nejimenet to Gan Akashe and the old general nodded.

"Very well," Gan Akashe agreed. "But we will only take one of you. The young man who came with you."

"If you are to take only one of us, it must be me. I am the senior priest—"

"You are fat and you are old," the woman said bluntly. "You wouldn't last an hour on the trail."

In the end, Metul had to agree to their demands. He was in a foul mood when he came back to inform me of their decision.

"You are to go with them."

I frowned.

"As senior priest, shouldn't you be the one to go?" I asked. I thought it would be better if he didn't know that I had overheard how a woman had dishonored him.

"I didn't argue with them. We're lucky they're allowing us to go at all. They'll drug you, but don't try to argue with them. They're fanatical about keeping the location of their homeland secret. You'll spend the winter with them at least, perhaps longer, depending on how long it will take them to decide on our proposal. While you are there you must learn all you can about these people and you will do that best by keeping your eyes and ears open and your mouth shut. Do I make myself clear?"

I nodded, hating him so much I didn't trust myself to speak. Painful memories of my dark childhood came back to me sharply.

Metul had been my watchdog during those years; I could still feel the cold stone floor beneath my knees as I spent hours praying for the forgiveness of some minor infraction. And those many nights I spent staring wide-eyed into the darkness, fearing he would come and rape me as he had other boys my age. Yes, I hated Metul and he has always known this.

"Here, I'll give you my horse," he said. "Yours is too good an animal to risk on such a journey."

I kept my hand tight on the reins. He actually thought I would give up Wind Song that easily.

"You have no right to that horse," he said sternly. "All property is communally owned by the brotherhood."

"Then you have no right to take him," I answered.

"As your senior priest, I order you to give me the horse."

"And I appeal to the high priest," I countered insolently.

Not only was the high priest my uncle, and hundreds of miles away at the moment, but it was the high priest himself who had given Wind Song to me as a present. Metul had no real power over me, especially since I would be gone possibly several months. He knew it and the knowledge galled him. Without a word or a bow, I turned from him to join the Nejimenet group.

The tallest of them greeted me in perfect High Zenadishj, as did his wife, the black-haired woman, Tejalura.

"Here, drink this please," she said with a smile. "I am sorry, but it is necessary for security's sake. It isn't harmful, and there won't be any unpleasant aftereffects."

I had wanted to ask her where she and her husband had learned to speak such beautiful Zenadishj, but I was out cold before I could form the sentence. The next thing I knew, it was night, and I was watching Tejalura feed the fire. She looked up and smiled.

"I can tell by the puzzled look on your face, that you are back with us again."

"Was I unconscious?"

"No, you were fully conscious, you had to be. The trail is too dangerous. The drug we gave you temporarily prevented your brain from recording information."

"Where did you learn to speak such fluent Zenadishj?" I asked abruptly.

She laughed.

"You asked that question before, but the drug had already taken effect, so I will tell you again. As a young girl I worked for some time with the Mountain Zenadishj on a horse farm. Also, from General Kiakashe, who was my *nutevek narashan* instructor. Have you heard of her?"

I nodded.

I liked Tejalura immediately, and she managed to convey that she returned the feeling without suggesting anything more than friendship in the future. There was little vanity in her straightforward manner.

Because Nejimenet woman do not wear veils, they are considered no better than prostitutes by the priesthood as a whole, but privately I find them fascinating. Nor am I the only Zenadishj who has gazed at a distant caravan trying to catch a glimpse of their proud and independent, bare-headed women. Not only are they very beautiful, but they are chaste. I have never known one to be unfaithful to her husband, nor have I known a husband to be unfaithful to his Nejimenet wife. There must be a good reason, and whatever that reason is, it has every Zenadishj male secretly desiring a Nejimenet woman for his own.

"Is he with us yet, Tejalura?"

I turned to see her husband approaching us with a smile on his face. He said something to her in their own language that made her blush, then he hugged her and gave her a light kiss on the cheek. Their open affection surprised me. Were these the fierce warriors I had heard about all my life?

When the meal was finished cooking, we sat around the fire and I was given a chance to meet the others of the party. Each spoke fluent Zenadishj and I asked if all Nejimenets did.

"No," a youth named Teve answered. "But a great many of us do. What about the Zenadishj, do many of your people speak our language?"

I was forced to admit there wasn't anyone I could think of who spoke Nejimenet. If there had been, the priesthood certainly wouldn't have sent me.

Teve had first guard duty, and since I was unable to sleep, I sat up with him and talked, mostly about his family. Yari and Tejalura were related to him by some obscure connection which he tried to explain, but, at last giving up, said they were members of the same household.

As a member of an extended family, I presumed him to be of the poorer, lower class. But I revised my opinion when he showed me a rather expensive piece of jewelry he had purchased for his twin sister.

"You must love her a great deal," I commented. "For such a present would more likely be given to a sweetheart or a wife."

"I have no sweetheart, so the dearest girl in the valley to me is Imih."

"Ah," I said knowingly. "You mean you are between lovers."

"No," he insisted. "I have never had a lover, and there is no woman that I want yet."

I looked at him in astonishment, for no Zenadishj youth his age would ever admit he was a virgin—he would die first! Yet this young, very masculine Nejimenet acted as if there were nothing unusual or shameful about it.

He smiled at my unbelief.

"But then," he said, "Things are different with your people."

We changed the conversation to more impersonal matters such as sports, fishing and hunting. He said his household often hunted together, and if time permitted, I would be welcome to join them.

Tejalura told me there was nothing to compare with the sight of Arae Shjina, a large waterfall that marks the southwestern boundary of Meneth-shir. She made the others agree not to drug me on the last day, so that I might see it. I'm glad she did, for I have never seen such beauty. I could almost believe that I was entering another world, and, in a way, I suppose I did.

·→※←··→※←··→※←·

"We have decided," she told me later in the afternoon, "That you are to live in the storage house at the end of our property. We thought you would like your privacy. Living in a crowded household would make it a very long winter since you are used to being alone. The storage house is small, but it has a fireplace and is quite comfortable. It was the original home of our family centuries ago. But for the first few days, you'll have to stay with us until we clean it out."

When we entered their house they told me to sit by the fireplace while dinner was being prepared. Yari and a dark-haired man named Nejo kept me company. Out of the corner of my eye I saw Teve speaking earnestly with a pretty girl with tight curly, blue hair. Their features were so similar that I knew her to be Imih.

That night I enjoyed spending the evening with a Nejimenet household. Although I was not the center of attention, I was not left out, but included in the conversation matter-of-factly, as if I were one of them. It was a good feeling.

The next morning I heard the song of the birds and saw the early sunlight through the autumn leaves outside my window. Downstairs I heard singing and laughter. I was eager to join them, but reluctant to show my eagerness. It was Zarkhon's wife, Silverwoman, who noticed my presence first. Imih and a little girl with pale blue hair followed her look.

"Good morning, Tehmu," Silverwoman said. "Here, sit at the table, I'll get your breakfast for you."

In my own language, Silverwoman's name would have been called Halia Liet, which is also the name of the moon-goddess. She was not young, yet her inner beauty made her lovely beyond words. It was impossible not to return her smile.

"I thought you Nejimenets did not eat a morning meal," I said.

"We don't, but we knew that you were used to it, so we prepared something for you."

She set a plate of fruit and bread on the table. Beside it was a cup of tea. It was a strange combination, but I couldn't expect them to know what made up a decent morning meal. I smiled my thanks and ate. Surprisingly it tasted very good.

"Some of the others are clearing out the small house," she continued. "Imih is going right by there, so when you finish, go with her. She will show you where it is. It's secluded enough to be as private as you could want it, yet it is close enough to join us at meals or whenever you wish. I hope you like it."

"I'm sure I will. I appreciate all the trouble your family has gone to."

"It is nothing. Are you finished? Good. Join Imih outside."

I saw Imih sitting on a rock playing with the little girl, Melia. Beside her was the cart with an empty barrel on it. We started to go, but Melia demanded to go with us. With a sigh of exasperation, Imih said:

THE PRIEST: TEHMU

"Besedi, Melia. Dimmeh."

I found that if I listened closely, I could almost understand her. In Zenadishj that same statement would have been: *Besari, Marihe. Dimma.* Their language shouldn't be too difficult for me to learn. With a smile and a gesture, she indicated a small cottage Tejalura and some others were clearing out.

"Good, you're here," Tejalura said with relief. "You can tell us where you want everything."

I glanced briefly about the one-room building. There were a few pieces of heavy furniture—a bed, a wooden chest, a table and two chairs. There was also a fireplace with stacked wood beside it.

"I like it as it is," I said shortly. "Thank you."

Sensing I had dismissed her, she left me with an invitation to join her family for evening meal. Again, I thanked her and closed the door thoughtfully.

Suddenly, I was suspicious of their friendly manner. Why should they be so warm with me? I was nothing to them. Was all this an act so they could catch me off guard and learn politically useful information from me? Of course, it must be. I had been a fool to think otherwise.

From then on, I avoided all personal contact with the Nejimenets, but watched them warily from a distance.

Early one morning, Tejalura came to my door. It was hard not to respond to her friendly smile. Beside her were her two sons.

"We came by to ask you if you wanted to join us at the lake. We're fishing today."

"You think that I am not doing my share of the work," I said, intentionally misunderstanding her invitation.

She hesitated.

"No," she said quietly. "There is no question of work, for you are our guest. I simply thought you would like to get outside for a while."

"I will go hunting," I said stiffly. "That is unless it would not be proper."

"No, it's all right. Well, good-bye, Tehmu. Khai, Akashe. Say good-bye."

Dutifully they obeyed.

As I watched them go, I regretted not accepting her invitation. I heard a sound, and turned to see Imih coming down the road with her cart. I had watched her every morning from my window since the first day. I fought back the impulse to go back into the house, but she had already seen me, and it would not do for the Nejimenets to think a Zenadishj warrior priest was afraid to face a mere maiden. She offered a shy, pretty smile and raised her hand in greeting. Briefly I nodded, but did not return the smile.

At that moment her cart tipped over, and the barrel, as if by a will of its own, rolled practically to my feet. At first I made no move, then feeling it was expected of me, I bent to lift the barrel and return it to the cart.

"*Dasha*—" she paused, then began again in heavily accented Zenadishj: "Thank you very much, Tehmu."

"It is nothing," I returned in careful Nejimenet.

She smiled.

"You are learning our language."

"A little."

She hesitated, then:

"Well, again, thank you very much. Good day."

The next morning I sat in the doorway drinking a cup of coffee that had long since grown cold. I tried to convince myself I wasn't waiting for Imih, but when I saw her coming, my heart became light. I wondered if she would greet me with that same friendly smile. Yes, she did, but it was all I could do to nod casually as she passed. I found myself hoping the barrel would tip over again, but it didn't. Blushing under my steady gaze she continued on her way to the river. I threw the rest of my coffee into the bushes.

When she returned I watched her from inside the cottage. As she passed, she looked in my direction, but I knew she couldn't see me. I felt puzzled and frustrated at the same time. I wanted to speak to her, yet how could I meet her? Up to this time I had only known the company of the temple prostitutes, respectable women were closeted in harems or heavily veiled in public. There were no familiar guidelines to help me.

The following morning found me sitting on the doorstep drinking my morning coffee, waiting for her to appear. Her face was flushed again, but this time with anger.

"Why do you stare at me so? Have I suddenly grown two heads?"

I said nothing.

"Well, what's the matter? Didn't you understand what I said?"
"Yes," I answered shortly and moved to go into the house.
"Wait, Tehmu."
I turned.
"I'm sorry," she began. "It's just that you made me nervous the way you kept looking at me, without smiling at me or anything. You can smile, can't you?"

I said nothing until she turned to go.

"Wait," I said and she stopped. "I smile sometimes," I stammered, awkwardly groping for the correct Nejimenet words. "Now, with you. I walk to house with you."

Suppressing a giggle at my terrible Nejimenet grammar, she thanked me. I offered to pull the cart back; she could not know such a task was considered shameful to a Zenadishj man. And so a pattern was established. I would walk with her down to the river and back again. Gradually my Nejimenet improved and I became acquainted with the Tehalchev household.

One gray afternoon, snow started to fall and continued into the night. By the next morning all of Meneth-shir had been transformed. I decided to skip breakfast and enjoy the bright morning outside. Shortly I met Imih and Silverwoman. How beautiful they were together. Imih, with her bright coloring, might have been a summer fairy somehow trapped in winter, but Silverwoman was the Ice Queen herself.

I don't remember what the three of us talked about, I was too aware of Imih. After a while Silverwoman went back to the house, leaving us alone. We stood there in silence, she refused to look at me. On impulse I touched her cheek and she blushed, shy but unafraid. In an awkward rush she threw her arms around my neck and kissed me. Technically, Imih's kiss was the worst I have ever known, but the innocence of it touched my heart in a way the more expert ones of the temple prostitutes could not.

"Imih!"

We turned with a start to see a stern and angry Nejo standing there.

"Imih, go home," he ordered, eyeing me coldly.
"No!" she snapped defiantly.
"But he was—"

"He was kissing me, and I was thoroughly enjoying it. That is, I was until you came along."

Her words were insolent, and the expression on her face just itched to be slapped. Nejo's eyes narrowed in anger.

"Imih, you are acting like a tramp."

She rushed forward in anger, but I held her back.

"Leave it be, Imih," I said. "Go now and I will handle this."

She did as I asked without a word of protest. This seemed to anger Nejo more, his black eyes cut into mine like obsidian knives. I remembered how Tejalura had stood up against Metul at Cela Pass. As much as I hate Metul, I would be the first to admit he can cut a rather imposing figure, yet that little slip of a woman had barred his entrance through the pass. In that moment as Nejo stood there, glaring at me, the two of them seemed very much alike.

"Well," I said. "Are you just going to stand there scowling at me, or do you have something to say?"

"I mean to find out what your intentions are towards Imih."

"I don't see that is any of your business."

The anger in his eyes smoldered, but he managed to keep it controlled.

"You listen to me, Priest, and you listen well. It just so happens to be my business. Not only is Imih a member of my household, but it also happens I was going to offer for her this spring."

"It would seem she does not return your interest."

"Yes, and this I could accept, providing the man she loved treats her with honor. You do, of course, intend to marry her."

"Marriage?"

He smiled thinly with contempt.

"Just as I thought."

"It is but a harmless flirtation," I said, trying to convince myself as well as Nejo.

"Imih is no temple prostitute. She has never kissed a man before, and she would not have kissed you if she did not want you as her husband."

"But I am a priest."

"Don't try to play games with me. I know that Zenadishj priests are not celibate."

"No, but—"

"Then either you love her enough to marry her or you do not. It is as simple as that."

As simple as that. If only it were, I would have married her that instant. Nejo's words pointed out to me the difference between the honest, straightforward ways of the Nejimenets and the twisted, complicated ways of the Zenadishj.

"You do not know what you ask," I said quietly.

"I can accept the fact that Imih does not love me, but I do not want her hurt. If you will not honor the love she has for you, then stay away from her. At least have that much honor."

A few days later, Tejalura came to see me. She stood in the doorway hands on her hips.

"Just as I thought. You look as miserable as Imih. Listen, Tehmu, I don't like meddling in the affairs of others, but when two people I am fond of look as unhappy as both of you do, somebody has to do something. Now, you love Imih, don't you? So, why don't you marry her?"

I smiled and shook my head.

"You don't understand, Tejalura, there are so many differences between your people and mine, I would have to tell my life's story. You would tire of it quickly."

She sat down.

"Try me."

I don't know why I opened up to her. Perhaps I had drunk too much wine or perhaps it was because she was the first person who had cared enough to ask.

· →✻←· →✻←· →✻←·

"All of my life I have been alone, that is the way it is with us. To you Nejimenets, love of others is an everyday experience, but it is not so with us, especially with members of the priesthood. We grow up not knowing who our parents are or even our brothers and sisters, aunts and uncles. Marriages are arranged by the high-priest council, and children are taken away from parents as soon as they are weaned, to be raised in nurseries.

"My earliest memories are of that cold nursery and the stern guardians that were ever on the lookout for any transgression to punish. It was their job to cull out all children who were blemished or dull-witted, to be used for sacrifices. According to our beliefs, only the very best is given to the gods, but in reality, this is a convenient way to rid the priesthood of the unpromising as well as the dangerous rebels. We were a rather quiet and conservative group of boys, neither daring to show too much wit nor too little.

"Each year the numbers of my age group dwindled until there were only eighty. By then we were old enough to enter school, and during the first year, another twenty were 'chosen', and the year after that, another twenty, until there were only thirteen boys my age among the priesthood youth.

"I used to have nightmares about being chosen as a sacrifice. These dreams were so vivid I felt the cold surface of the stone alter against my back long after I woke. I felt the knife as it cut into my flesh, and the hand of the priest as it grasped my heart and pulled it from my chest. With my dying eyes I saw him turn to display my heart to the crowd in the plaza while it was still beating. Always that priest was Metul.

"The others never laughed at my screams when I woke up from these nightmares. They had dreams of their own.

"As the years passed and my education became more specialized, I realized that unless I angered the priesthood, I would remain relatively safe. The priesthood, whatever its failings, was not wasteful and too much had been invested in me to be sacrificed on a whim.

"My education consisted of theology, astronomy, higher math, chants, songs memorization and interpretation of sacred writings, dances, and martial arts. I had no talent for the creative arts, but it was required that I at least study one. So I chose ceramics, hoping my natural dexterity would cover my lack of talent. It was there that I met Neve.

"Neve was a real artist, unlike myself who had taken the class to meet a requirement. When he saw I was having trouble mastering the art, he would give me helpful suggestions to improve my work. This was strange in itself, for the usual attitude among us is that if we are superior in any way, we keep it to ourselves to give us an upper edge.

"From that our friendship grew. I don't think you can know what it is like to be alone all of your life and then suddenly to have someone to talk to, to confide in, to share your feelings without fear of betrayal. He spoke as no one had ever spoken. He did not think our country was being governed justly, and he had many ideas for the reformation of Narit. For the first time I began to question the society I had grown up in. It had never occurred to me another, better system than the one already in existence was possible.

"Unfortunately, the priesthood did not see Neve's ideas in the same light, and he was chosen for the next sacrifice. That same day I was called before the high priest. I was afraid because I could think of no reason for the holy father to take notice of me save for my association with Neve. I had heard that he was a hard and cruel man, but I was later to learn he was a just man caught up in a cruel, inhuman system. I did not know this at the time and had to fight to control my fear.

"'Holy Father,' I murmured reverently, bowing low, hands pressed together.

"He favored me with a rather long inspection. The harsh expression on his face did not give me reason to think he was too pleased with what he saw.

"'Well, Tehmu,' he said in a voice as hard and uncompromising as stone. 'You are as pretty as your mother, but you are also as stupid as your father. Boy, do you realize you almost got yourself killed?'

"'Forgive me, Holy Father, but I don't understand—'

"He waved my words aside impatiently.

"'Spare me, spare me. Sit down, Tehmu. We are quite alone and do not need to stand on ceremony. I am your uncle, Bari Usul. Your mother was my sister. Do you remember anything about your parents?'

"'No, Holy One. How could I? For are we not all taken from our parents at birth?'

"'Unless they are children of Those Who Are Called of the Gods, as your parents were and as my parents were also.'

"As I have told you, Tejalura, all marriages are arranged by the priesthood, but if a man and a woman love each other enough, they could declare their love sacred and are allowed five years together, after which they are sacrificed. If they have children, the children are allowed to remain with them until the five-year period is ended.

"'But such children are usually sacrificed with the parents,' I said to Bari Usul.

"'They are, unless their uncle happens to be a high priest. Up to now I have been able to spare you, but believe me, it has been no easy task for you have been marked from birth. Over the years some of the brotherhood felt you were a little too brilliant and you ought to be sacrificed. But each year I was able to spare you, and recently, before this business with Neve came up, your origins had been all but forgotten. Do you realize how close you came to being chosen? You may have been marked before, but you are doubly marked now, for you were spared for no other reason than because you are my nephew and all know it. You had better watch yourself and keep a low profile, for I may not be able to intervene again.'

"I did as my uncle bid me, but I saw things with new eyes. Never before had I dared to question the way things were, but Neve's death and the discovery of my parents' identity changed my attitude. Outwardly I became the most efficient of apprentices, and five years after my talk with Uncle Bari, I was ordained a priest of the junior order. That was five years ago. I believe it was my uncle's influence that allowed me to come to Meneth-shir so I could prove myself, as well as get me safely away from the priesthood for a while.

"And I must tell you this, Tejalura, I am impressed with you Nejimenets as a people. For the first time, I have seen people live as I think the gods meant them to live. And another thing, I love Imih as I have loved no other. But you can see the difficulty in deciding to marry her: not only would I die in five years but so would she. I want so much more for her than that."

"But both of you could be safe up here, or at least Imih could be."

I was doubtful, and she saw it.

"How could they hurt you?" she asked.

"There are ways, Tejalura, there are ways."

She snorted.

"Zenadishj superstition! A curse can have no power unless you allow it to. Couldn't you marry her in the Nejimenet way? They would never know."

"Perhaps not," I said deciding not to argue the matter. "But I want her to be my wife before my gods as well as hers."

We were silent for a moment until she put her hand on my shoulder.

"I am glad you have told me these things, for I understand better now. I still believe there can be a way for both of you."

THE PRIEST: TEHMU

I was alone again but it was harder after experiencing the open friendliness of the Tehalchev family. They didn't avoid me, but rather, I avoided them. I no longer joined them at dinner because I could not face Imih. During the following weeks I only saw Tejalura or Silverwoman. Sometimes they brought the younger children with them, but that was all. At first I watched for Imih as she made her daily trip to the river for water, but was disappointed to learn Turquoise did that chore now.

Sometimes the pain of my loneliness was more than I could bear. I thought of my parents often during those days. Before I had been unable to understand taking such a desperate step to be together, but now I understood all too well. For when I saw the empty years stretch before me, happiness with Imih—however brief the time—seemed a fair trade indeed.

I would spend hours walking through the wilderness of Menethshir filling my eyes with its sunlight and colors, and my ears with the song of its birds and running streams. But even in this beauty there was a kind of sadness, for this was Imih's world, and I would soon be leaving it.

During one of my walks, I came across Jevetura and Nejo resting beneath the trees. Both were part-time, but skilled lapidaries and had been collecting stones together to make jewelry. I had seen the Jevetchev girl many times at Imih's house helping Tejalura with the account books.

"Don't look so morbid, Nejo. Imih will come around as soon as she gets that priest out of her mind. And that shouldn't take too long."

"I hope you are right, Jevetura," he said.

"Of course I am. Can you imagine a girl like Imih loving a dull fish like that Tehmu? He has the coldest eyes I have ever seen, and I don't suppose he has ever laughed in his life."

I decided to back off before they noted my presence. I shouldn't have been hurt by what Jevetura said—eavesdroppers never hear good about themselves—but I couldn't help wondering if Imih thought the same of me. Like all men in love, I wished her to see me as a hero, not a "dull fish."

I wanted everything to be different. I wanted Nejo to be my friend and approve of my love for Imih. I wanted Jevetura to admire me and perhaps be a little envious of Imih. Could I laugh? Yes, Neve would have been able to tell them that at one time I could, but Neve was dead.

The council met that winter on the Itan-shir Island. By then, of course, I had learned there was no king of Meneth-shir. How absurd Metul and I must have sounded at Cela Pass, demanding audience with a non-existent king. I was asked to deliver Queen Ceymar's message so they might take care of it along with the other pressing business. I was glad for the disruption in the monotony of my days. I had to collect my thoughts and think of how I was best to present the queen's request. I must keep it brief and to the point, for the Nejimenets were not fond of long, flowery phrases as we Zenadishj were. I must be honest, we were bankrupt, and we needed money desperately. I felt that if I were open about our circumstances they would be more inclined to help than if I were to become concerned with false pride. And I was right, for our request for money was granted immediately.

"But I think a condition should be established," Tejalura brought up. "A representative should be sent with the money to ensure that it is spent appropriately and is not pocketed by a select few."

I spread my hands.

"We would agree to these terms eagerly."

My uncle would have strangled me at such a weak approach to my negotiations, but I felt it was a fair enough request. These people had won my respect; I could at least be honest with them.

"Now all that remains is the choice of representative," one of the council members said. "Since Tejalura is treasurer, and since she suggested it in the first place, she should be the one to go."

Tejalura's mouth fell open in surprise. She had not expected this turn of events.

"But I have only just returned from five years among the Enavians. You can't expect me to leave Meneth-shir so soon. This may take years to resolve."

"No one will force you to go, Daughter." Zarkhon said. "But your experience with foreigners and handling money, as well as your fluent Zenadishj, makes you the obvious choice. Besides," he added wickedly, "We'll let you take Yari with you."

The others laughed. Tejalura smiled ruefully and said she would think the matter over. After a little more discussion, the meeting was adjourned and we went home. How efficient the Nejimenets were.

This same matter would have taken the priesthood weeks if not months to reach a decision.

After the meeting, my cottage seemed even more empty than ever. I hesitated a few moments, then put my coat back on and went to the Tehalchev household. Through the window I could see the fire was lit. I heard their laughter and friendly talk as I approached. Immediate silence followed my entrance. Imih looked away from me and started to leave the room.

"Imih, don't leave!" I hesitated, not knowing what to say next. Feeling like the greatest of fools, I plunged ahead: "I don't know the Nejimenet way for a man to ask a woman to be his wife. But that is what I am here to do. Will you be my wife?"

Silence.

Then Tejalura caught my arm and brought me to the fireplace.

"Of course she will," she assured me. "But it is our custom for the man to approach the father and offer for the bride. But you are Zenadishj, and I suppose allowances must be made for a foreigner. Here, sit with Geysan and discuss the bride-price."

Dear Tejalura, in her own offhanded way, she had managed to lighten an awkward moment. Geysan, taking her cue proceeded to ask me what I wished to offer for Imih.

"Geysan, were I the richest man in Narit, I would gladly offer all I owned. But as you well know, I have but the clothes on my back and my horse, and even they are owned by the priesthood."

Geysan shrugged philosophically.

"I supposed a man in my position can't afford to be choosey. I have been trying to rid myself of this worthless daughter for years." He slapped Imih smartly on her rear. "Take her lad, she's all yours."

Imih looked far from happy. After all, this should be the most romantic moment in her life.

"Come here, Imih," I said.

Hesitantly, she came forward. I took off my brotherhood ring and placed it on her finger. Tejalura, who knew the meaning of it, gasped in surprise.

"Tehmu," she said in Zenadishj. "Are you sure you want to do this?"

I nodded and answered in the same language.

"In this way she will be my wife before my gods as well as hers."

"What are the two of you talking about?" asked Imih whose Zenadishj was not as fluent enough to follow what we had said.

Tejalura hugged her fondly.

"Nothing darling," she told her. "Tehmu was just telling me how much he loved you."

Nejo was watching me intently. He also knew what the brotherhood ring signified. We would never be friends, but there was a respect between us and we would deal well enough with each other for the sake of the woman we both loved.

Imih informed me we would have a child in autumn. I was happy, but sad at the same time, for I would never see the child. I had planned to leave Meneth-shir that spring, and who would know when I would be able to return. It was Zarkhon who persuaded me to stay.

"For who's to know the council hasn't reached a decision on the loan yet?" he reasoned. "Besides, a representative hasn't been chosen yet, though it will probably be Taji. Stay another winter, at least to be with Imih when the baby comes."

So I stayed that summer and worked in the fields of the Tehalchev family. It was good to work beside Geysan and the others, while in the distance I could see my wife, heavy with child, working with the other woman. It was a peasant's existence, beneath the dignity of a priest, but I can't remember a time in my life when I had been more happy. I enjoyed the privacy of my cottage, but I agreed to move into the main house, because Imih missed her family. To my surprise, I found I enjoyed being a member of a large household. I wondered why extended families exist only among the poor in Narit.

That winter I was asked to show their potters some techniques in making Zenadishj ceramic ware. As I have said before, I am not gifted, but I am skilled, and was happy to show them the various sacred designs and glazes that have been secrets of the priesthood for centuries. When they showed an interest in the symbolic meaning behind the colors and the patterns, I gladly explained them in detail. The punishment for this sacrilege was death, but Narit seemed far away to me then, and I was not afraid.

THE PRIEST: TEHMU

"You don't believe all that nonsense, do you?" asked Yanahna Jevetchev, a pretty girl of sixteen who, in my opinion, was one of the most talented potters of all.

"Yana!" exclaimed her older cousin, Telein. "He probably doesn't, but that was very rude."

I smiled tolerantly at the bickering cousins. "Telein is right. I do not believe the traditions, nor do I think any Zenadishj priest with a reasonable amount of intelligence believes them either. And," I continued sternly for Yanahna's sake, "Telein was also right; you were rude. You're going to have to learn to be a little more tactful."

She gave a careless toss to her pretty curls. She was vain and a little too smug concerning her talent and beauty, but for the most part, she was a pleasant girl to be around.

"Well—if nobody believes in the traditions, why have them? Why not just get rid of them? It seems like such a waste of time and silly."

"And I agree with you, Yanahna. But change takes time in Narit. We are not so democratic as you Nejimenets are. Weeding out old, outdated traditions is a slow and painful process."

I tried to explain the differences between our cultures, but I don't think they entirely believed me. How different this school was from the one I had attended. Their bright, young faces were heart-warming; so eager to learn, but never hesitating to question my statements. How I wished for Neve to be with me, for here, in Meneth-shir, was his dream come true.

Yanahna escorted me home, accompanied by her disapproving older cousin. Imih had told me once that Yana had a schoolgirl crush on me, and lately I had come to think she might be right. Except for out-and-out rudeness, there was no way to keep her from following me around. Imih and Tejalura were gardening in front of the house. Imih stood to greet me, her eyes twinkled with amusement when she saw me being relentlessly followed by Yanahna.

"Hello, Imih," Yana said with false brightness. "My, but your stomach is getting big."

My wife ignored her cattiness and smiled warmly.

"Yes," she said. "It won't be long now."

I kissed her on the cheek and hugged her fondly.

"And then I'll have to get you pregnant again just as fast as I can, because you've never looked more beautiful."

"Well, I suppose that's all right," Yana remarked airily. "So long as a woman doesn't mind losing her figure and getting stretch marks. Come on Telein, let's go home."

Tejalura shook her head.

"That Yana is really getting impossible. Why don't you do something, Tehmu? She keeps following you around. People are starting to say it won't be long until you take a second wife."

"Maybe you have something there, Tejalura," I said as I studied Imih carefully, which is always a delight. "She is starting to loose her figure, and who knows what damage stretch marks will cause. Maybe a second wife is what I need."

"Tehmu! You can't be serious."

I smiled to show them that Jevetura and Nejo were wrong. I could laugh.

"Of course not," I said. "My first wife would kill me."

Two days later our baby was born. It was a girl, and we named her Khiseleh, because Imih insisted our daughter have a Zenadishj name. But the others called her Khiselay or Khiseh. She was a beautiful baby with hair the color of wine; there was no other hair like hers in the valley.

One morning I found myself alone. Imih and the others had left for the fields without bothering to wake me. Tejalura was downstairs watching the babies and toddlers of the family. This is a rare event, for she avoids this job whenever possible. I went downstairs to share a cup of tea with her. I had long since gotten out of the habit of eating breakfast.

As I sat there, looking outside, a deep feeling of peace and utter contentment filled me. The spring sunlight washed in through our windows. Did the Nejimenets know who blessed they were? I glanced at Tejalura's serene face. Yes, she knew. I realized then it would be hard, very hard to leave now.

"There is no reason to leave," she said. "We can always send a messenger to Halia Tehal."

How tempting that was. Yet I remembered my uncle and his plans for our country. I suspected he was grooming me to succeed him as high priest when he died. On the other hand, how could I, in honor, desert my wife and child?

It was Zarkhon again who persuaded me to stay.

"The roads are muddy," he reasoned. "Stay a while yet."
And when the roads cleared:
"Why don't you stay and help us in the fields? We could use an extra hand."
And as the summer ended and autumn approached:
"Why not help us with harvest? There is no hurry for you to go."
But after harvest, I knew I couldn't delay my departure any longer. If I were to accomplish any good for my people, I must return now.

Winter 1345 EE

When I arrived in Halia Tehal, I was immediately called in for a private interview with my uncle. He was grayer and leaner than I remembered him two years ago, but he still presented a powerful figure. He was pleased we were given the money and agreed that sending a representative was a reasonable request.

"The others will object to the representative on principle, but in the end they'll go along with it," he said with confidence. "And two years is a fair enough time for such an action, although I had expected the Nejimenets to work a little faster than we do down here in Narit."

"They do, Uncle, much faster. I took them only one night to decide to give us the money, and only a week to draw up the papers."

"And when did this take place?"

"During the first winter I was in Meneth-shir."

"So you could have returned the following spring, yet you stayed another year and a half. Why?"

"Because I wanted to," I answered simply. "No other Zenadishj has had such an opportunity to live among them. They are a fascinating people, we could learn much from them."

I paused to take a breath at this point. I decided then to be honest with him about Imih, for if anyone could help, my uncle could.

"And because I had taken a wife."

It took a moment for my statement to register.

"A wife! What for?"

"I suppose for the same reason my father married my mother."

He was really angry.

"Fool, fool!" he exploded. "As if I didn't need all the liberal-minded priests I can get, one of them has to get married. I suppose you were fool enough to give her your ring—yes, I see that you were. How many years do you have left? Three?"

"Three-and-a-half."

He was silent for a moment. "Well, there is only one thing to be done. You'll have to get another ring. You lost the other one, do you understand? Lost it. And I command you as your uncle, as well as your high priest, not to say a word about your Nejimenet wife. Is that clear?"

"Yes, Uncle."

There was a moment's silence while he mastered his anger.

"Well, so now you're married," he said in a voice that struggled for lightness. "Marihe will be disappointed to hear that."

"Marihe? Why?"

"I managed to get the priesthood to select her to be your wife. And believe me, it was no easy thing for me to accomplish."

I smiled thoughtfully as the bright image of Neve's younger sister came to mind. What was she now? Fifteen? Sixteen? When I last saw her, she had been a child of twelve or thirteen with rosy cheeks and thick, magenta hair in braids long enough to sit on. For years the Sisters had tried to subdue their high-spirited charge, but she was a fearless little thing and had always had my uncle's protection. Now I knew why.

"Thank you, Uncle. If I had not met Imih I would have been very pleased with your choice."

He shrugged off my thanks as if to say it was nothing. But I knew that taken a lot to arrange this for me.

"Tell me, Uncle," I said in a baiting tone. "How is little Marihe and the other wives in your harem?"

This was an utterly private joke between us, and I was rewarded by the sight of a twinkle in his eye which would have been equivalent to a belly laugh in a man like Zarkhon. The priesthood, as a matter of course, will sacrifice any child who shows signs of independent thought. My uncle has countered this by claiming the most promising of these victims for his harem. To date he has over eighteen hundred "catamites" and "concubines" among the pretty boys and girls of the brotherhood youth. They remain as untouched and pure as the day they entered his protection because they were never meant for his pleasure. They are the priesthood of tomorrow.

THE PRIEST: TEHMU

"They are well," he answered with a faint smile. "Now, tell me what you've learned about the people of Meneth-shir. Or did you spend all of your time with your wife? On second thought, tell me of your wife first."

I smiled.

"She is wonderful, Uncle, and very beautiful. Her name is Imih."

I paused.

"Well, go on, Tehmu. Tell me more."

"What more can I say? She is special. I have never known another woman like her. We have a child, a daughter named Khiseleh."

I dwindled off into silence again.

"Well, since you are too shy to talk about your wife, tell me about the people of Meneth-shir. What are they like?"

"They are a happy, cheerful, generous, industrious," I paused, for all of these words were true, but they came so short in describing them. "They live in households of extended families like our poor do, but they are rich—there are no poor among them. No orphans or beggars. All are taken care of."

I was still fumbling and grasping for adequate words, so my uncle took me in hand.

"Tell me of their religion. As a priest, that should have been your first topic. What of their gods?"

"They have only one, and their whole lives are dedicated to Him."

"So? It is the same with us."

"No, Uncle. There is a difference, but I am not sure how I can make the difference clear to you. As I have said, they have only one God, and He has no name. They worship Him, but there are no temples."

"Then where do they keep His image?"

"There is no image of Him. They believe His spirit to be larger than the universe itself, so what use could He have for a temple?"

I remembered the words of Tejalura: "The earth, the sky, the mountains, our homes, our farms—they are His temple." I tried to get this concept across to my Uncle, but I felt I was failing miserably.

"But they must have special days to worship their God," he insisted. "Where do they meet on these holy days?"

"There are no special days. Everyday belongs to Him."

"There is no priesthood? No holy men?"

"None."

"And sacrifices?"

"No, they say there is no need for sacrificing; their lives already belong to Him. Their lives, their work, their possessions all belong to Him."

"And their money?"

"Yes. Each year all the households have the treasurer calculate what ten percent of their profits were that year, and that is what they are expected to give, but they usually give much more."

"Who keeps this money?"

"No one does. It is kept in the storehouse until someone had need of it. As a matter of fact, that is where our loan is coming from."

"Yes, but there must be someone who controls the storehouse," he persisted.

"Of course. The treasurer does."

"Ah," my uncle was at last satisfied. "So now we come to the ruler, the man who holds the real power of Meneth-shir."

I laughed, as I now understood what information he had been seeking. He couldn't comprehend a society so simple and pure it had no need of kings and rulers.

"No," I said. "As a matter of fact, the treasurer is a woman, a simple housewife. In school she showed a love for math and bookkeeping, so she was assigned to this position. I believe this business of having a treasurer is an experiment, Tejalura is the first one ever appointed."

"So she has no real political power?"

"No, Uncle. She is not even that good of a mathematician. Someone else has to look over the records and correct her mistakes."

"I see."

"By the way, Tejalura is the representative they are sending."

He shook his head.

"The priesthood will tear her apart."

"I think not, Uncle," I said remembering the way she had stood up to Metul two years ago. "I forgot to mention she is also a *nutevek narashan*. Her teacher was General Kiakashe. You remember her don't you?"

He smiled with some amusement.

"A simple housewife, eh? I think I am beginning to understand the Nejimenets. A little, anyway. When are we to expect the treasurer and the money?"

"This spring, after the roads are cleared."

His next question caught me completely off guard.

"What would our chances be of overcoming the Nejimenets by military force?"

I felt cold.

"None, Uncle. Absolutely none. I still don't know where the entrance is and the valley is impregnable. The Nejimenets may be peace loving but they are trained warriors. It would be sheer suicide."

"It is just as well, for I prefer the Nejimenets remain our allies rather than become subjects, just on principle. As our subjects they would be only be an added burden at this point."

After the interview was concluded, I was dismissed, and once again I found myself in Metul's charge. My first task was to do penance for the "lost" ring and perform the purification ceremony to rid myself of the contamination from being among nonbelievers.

I was alone again. There would be days on end that I wouldn't say a word to another soul. I never realized how lonely I had been before I had gone to Meneth-shir. I would have to learn all over again not to care. But it was hard, cruelly hard. I saw injustice being done daily, and at last I understood Neve's anger, for it was now my own. It was such a simple thing to be happy, yet it seemed the Zenadishj only found pleasure in the misery of others.

Spring 1345

Tejalura and her family received a poor welcome when they arrived that spring. First of all, the guards would not let her enter the city because she was unveiled. When the guards discovered who they were, they sent a message to the temple for instructions. My uncle sent me, along with Metul, to smooth the way for them. Entering the customs room, Metul went straight to Yari and bowed low.

"Lord Tehalchev, Treasurer of Meneth-shir," he addressed the giant Nejimenet royally. "I, Metul Div, a senior priest of the temple of Zenedh of the city of Halia Tehal, bid you welcome. If there is any way I may be of service to you in the future during your stay, you have but to ask."

Yari grinned.

"That's all very nice," he said in perfect High Zenadishj, "But I am not the treasurer. I'm just the treasurer's husband. Here is my wife, Lady Tehalchev. She's the one you want to talk to."

Metul glared at me, blaming me for the whole embarrassing incident. Not only because I hadn't told him Tejalura was a woman, but I also had neglected to mention they spoke fluent Zenadishj. He turned to Tejalura who was smiling, greatly amused at the episode.

"Lady Tehalchev," he amended. "As I have told your husband, you are most welcome to our city, but you must be properly dressed to enter it. Our laws are most strict in this matter."

"Of course, Metul Div," she was all smiles and graciousness. "I understand completely."

She removed her outer traveling robe, revealing the full dress uniform of the Nejimenet warlord, which she was entitled to wear as a *nutevek narashan*. Warlords do not wear veils—not even Metul could demand such a thing.

And Uncle Bari Usul had worried the priesthood would eat her alive! She winked at me.

"Kiakashe gave me her old uniform because she knew some stuffy priest would try to make me wear the veil out of spite. How do you like it, Tehmu?"

She had spoken directly to me in Nejimenet, deliberately excluding Metul. She did not know it yet, but she had made a powerful enemy in those first few moments.

"It looks very well on you, Tejalura," I said with a slight bow. "It would be a shame to cover such a beautiful face."

Metul cut into our conversation almost rudely.

"I realize you are old friends, Lady Tehalchev, but this is Narit, not Meneth-shir. Tehmu is merely a junior priest. It is not fitting for one of your rank to associate with him nor is it good for one of his spiritual immaturity to have close contact with one of the secular world. Please remember that in the future. He only accompanied me because of his fluent Nejimenet, but as your knowledge of Zenadishj is such that a translator is unnecessary, he will now return to his quarters. Tehmu, you may go."

"Wait, Tehmu!" she called out as I turned to leave.

Metul should have learned his lesson at the Cela Pass two years ago.

THE PRIEST: TEHMU

Nejimenet women, especially Tejalura, are not to be pushed around. She rounded on him with a vengeance.

"No one, Metul, I mean no one tells me who I may or may not associate with, nor who is or is not beneath my dignity to speak with. I will speak and I will associate with whomever I choose. Please remember that in the future! I have a difficult job ahead of me, and I will need all the help I can get. You flatter me in saying my Zenadishj is fluent, but I will remind you it is not my native tongue and there are bound to be gaps in my knowledge, so Tehmu will be invaluable to me. He is also an adopted member of my household; this makes him my relative. A highly regarded relative whom my husband and I would seek out even if he were not of any use to my assignment here."

She turned to me.

"Tehmu, you will escort my husband and myself to the palace. I believe the queen is expecting us."

As haughty as a queen herself, she walked past Metul to her horse, mounted it and rode down the main street of Halia Tehal. Her wild barbaric beauty had a strong impact on the populace. We had no trouble making our way through the congested avenues, for the crowds parted of their own accord. The people loved her from the very beginning.

It seemed Tejalura could do no wrong that day, for she made a favorable impression on Ceymar, who had been getting rather difficult in her old age. Upon seeing Tejalura, the graying queen smiled with the brightness of a young girl.

"I've seen you before," the queen insisted. "Yes! I've got it. I saw you at a Nejimenet wedding I attended once. You were the little dark-haired *veshe* with the black eye. Oh, this is wonderful! Come sit down beside me." With a graceful gesture of her hand, she entreated us to come near her. "Bring chairs for her husband and the children," she ordered the servants briskly.

"Your majesty, I am flattered that you remember such an insignificant person as myself. That must have been twenty-five years ago."

"That is the way it is when you are old. Things that occurred fifty, sixty years ago can be remembered in great detail, while yesterday and the day before are completely forgotten. I have often thought of you these last years and wondered what became of you. You caught my eye that day—it may have been your black hair and your bruised eye. I fancied I saw myself as a child in you. Did you know I was sold as a slave when I was a young girl? Well, I was and I can tell you I got into many a scrape and received many a black eye in those days."

Metul coughed.

"My lady, it is not necessary to dwell on such unhappy days. Especially considering your present glory."

"Don't be so damned stuffy, Metul," the queen said impatiently. "It is necessary to remember those 'unhappy days', especially considering my 'present glory'. Otherwise, I might become as pompous and boorish as you are. There is no reason for me to be ashamed of having once been a slave. As a matter of fact, I found those years to be the most instructive in my life. I learned a great deal about human nature. I also learned just how transitory the possession of political power is. One day I had been the heir-apparent, my father's pampered darling; the next day I stood on the auction block. I wasn't even twelve yet, but I knew then there was no one I could depend on save myself."

"And God?" asked Tejalura.

Ceymar smiled. "There is no god, Tejalura. That is another thing I learned during those years. But now I am being a boring old woman. There are other things we need to discuss."

"Yes," said Tejalura. "But there is no hurry, no hurry at all."

The two women chatted away like old friends and the pleasant, though somewhat dull, afternoon continued. As I glanced around me, I could see my own politely bored expression plastered on the faces of Yari and the boys. Still, Tejalura managed to accomplish a great deal during that tedious afternoon. I was made their family priest, their quarters were established within the palace itself and Tejalura was given complete access to all temple and palace records. Not even my uncle has such freedom of the archives. She had no diplomatic experience, but it seemed, in those first days, fate smiled on her. There was only one unpleasant moment when Metul asked Tejalura outright where the money was.

"Oh, didn't you know?" she blinked her eyes innocently. "The money will come as soon as a thorough study of your records has been made. Actually, it was just as well. Did you know that we were attacked on the way over here? By the way, that reminds me—"

She untied a coin purse from her belt and handed it to Metul. Opening it, he found the purse contained seven brotherhood rings.

"I took them from the bodies of the 'thieves'. Perhaps they stole them from a group of your missionaries?"

There was a heavy silence.

"Perhaps," Metul said evenly.

General Neve tried to break the tension.

"Now that we know of the danger, let us know when you are bringing the money from Meneth-shir and we will send a military escort to safeguard it."

Tejalura smiled thinly.

"I've no doubt of that," she said. "But the money will remain in Meneth-shir until I have gone over the records."

"But why?"

"There is no point in giving you money to solve your problem until we discover just exactly what the problem is."

"Our problem is that we have no money," Metul said sarcastically.

"Yes, but why? Narit has the richest farmland on Ceytal. Yours is a feudal system, so labor does not have to be hired. Where is your money going?"

The queen laughed.

"I like you, Tejalura," she said. "You don't play around, you get right to the heart of the matter. If we had a few ministers like you in court, we wouldn't be in this mess."

As soon as we were all settled in our new quarters, Tejalura asked to see the financial records, but they were in such a snarled mess she could make no sense of them. Even I, who was familiar with the bookkeeping system, found it hard to decipher them. But after a few weeks of careful study and research, a pattern began to emerge. Over the years, the wealth of Narit had been transferred to important members of the priesthood, who by law could not be taxed; yet, at the same time the government was supporting all of their needs. The largest expense was reconstruction of the temple every fifty-two years. Layer upon layer of new stone facing had been added until the construction has become so monstrous we will not be able to do it many more times simply because it would be too large for our technology to cope with.

"Why every fifty-two years?" Tejalura said. "Why not fifty or one hundred?"

"Because every fifty-two years the lunar and solar calendar end at the same time, and a new cycle begins."

"So why do you to reface the whole temple? Do you know if the refacing of the temple could be put off during the next cycle, all debts would be eliminated and there would be money left over?"

I shook my head.

"Don't even suggest such a thing," I said. "Temples mean nothing to you Nejimenets, but to my people it is different. Your position with the priesthood is unpopular as it is, don't make things worse. Especially over something that has no possibility of success."

"Children are starving, but the refacing of the temple must go on, is that it?" She sighed. "Well, if another layer is constructed over the temple, all of the money we give you will be used up and your country will be further bankrupt. The priesthood must loosen its hold on the money. Would Bari Usul help? You said he wanted to make changes in Narit. Perhaps something could be worked out."

I spoke with my uncle about it, and he was more than willing. He had been present the day Tejalura met with the queen and had liked the way she handled Metul.

"But tell her that for every proposal she wants passed, she has to think of ten others I can veto. The priesthood must not know we are working together. In fact, when I do pass one of her proposals, I want to leave the distinct impression it is a temporary measure only, that I am humoring the Nejimenet treasurer until we get the money. Is that understood?"

And so, many changes were brought about with Tejalura's help that otherwise would have taken my uncle years to accomplish.

My being assigned as their family priest was merely an excuse for me to become a member of their household during their stay in Narit. As they had taught me of their culture, I now taught them mine. Tejalura demanded to see and experience every aspect of our society. I have never seen a woman with such energy. Often by the end of the day, the boys and I were barely able to stand, but she was ready for more.

She never tired of riding through the streets of Halia Tehal. The broad avenues were immaculate, for the trash collectors were constantly cleaning the streets of litter and animal waste. The walls were constructed of pure white sand and nearly blinded one with the reflected sunlight. The process of constructing buildings with sand had been lost to us, only the monumental works of those long-dead architects remained.

"Why are you squinting like that?" I asked as we rode down the Avenue of the Seven Stars.

"I'm squinting because . . . because if you blur your vision just a little, the city looks like upside-down icicles. Go on, Tehmu. You try it."

I shook my head. I had seen the curious looks some of the passersby had given her. Quite often she forgot the dignity of her position as representative of Meneth-shir. Even so, I liked Tejalura. She had an enthusiasm for life that was contagious. I found I was glad I didn't have to share her company with the others that day. Yari and the boys were hunting with General Neve on his country estate. For a man with no official position or duty, Yari was certainly spending a great deal of time with General Neve—not to mention several key members of the priesthood and the queen herself.

"It is like a dream city," she said. "I can hardly believe it is real. Not even the Enavians can produce such architecture." She paused thoughtfully. "Do you know, Tehmu, there are times when I question our right to bring change to Narit?"

"I hope it isn't because of our architecture. We didn't even build Halia Tehal."

"Oh? Who did?"

"No one knows. For lack of a better term, we call them the Nehimtehal, the People of the Moon. We don't even know the real name of this city, we ourselves named it Silver Moon in honor of our moon-goddess. Our ancestors found it centuries ago completely deserted. In the library there is an account of it written by our founding high priest, Neve Ce. He was one of the first to enter the city. You might find it interesting."

"Is he the Neve who all the mothers name their children after? I swear there isn't a family in Halia Tehal that doesn't have two or three Neves."

I smiled.

"Yes, he is the one."

"I'll probably never get around to reading his book. Why don't you give me a brief summary."

"Very well," I said agreeably. "A little over six hundred years ago, Neve Ce and his followers discovered Halia Tehal. As I have said before, it was empty of human life, yet everywhere there was evidence of daily activity that had been interrupted. In some of the homes, the tables were spread with partially eaten meals; in the streets and gardens there were the toys and unfinished games of the children. In the marketplace, stalls were being torn down and unsold merchandise was being packed away, but the traders and animals of the caravan had disappeared. In the temple, a ceremony had taken place, but all that remained was the knife and the blood drying on the alter. The priest and sacrifice were gone. Half-written letters, partially sewn garments, instruments of minstrels disturbed in song, that was all that was left of the Nehimtehal. The city might have been abandoned moments before Neve entered for everything was fresh and there was no dust anywhere. There was no sign of struggle, it was as if they had vanished into thin air."

Tejalura's eyes were bright with excitement.

"An enchanted city," she said. "I never thought such a thing existed."

I laughed at her.

"That's what I like about you, Tejalura. You are always ready to believe any tale told by anyone."

"You mean you just made that up?"

"No, it's there in the library. But whether it's true or not, well, who can say?"

"That's the trouble with you, Tehmu. You have no vision. At least this Neve Ce had the ability to dream, a characteristic sadly lacking in the modern-day Zenadishj."

"You are wrong, Tejalura, we do have dreams. We dream of enough food to feed our children. We dream of saying to a woman we love: 'I want you for my wife.' We dream of choosing our own occupation, our own place of residence. We dream of freedom, but we dare not dream aloud."

"Yes, changes need to be made but, again, I question my right to bring them about. I am not God, I am not even a citizen of Narit."

"With or without your help, change will come anyway, for the people are tired of seeing every hero who champions their cause

THE PRIEST: TEHMU

sacrificed by the priesthood. The only difference is that with your help, change may be brought about without a bloody revolution."

"If only I could be sure."

"Do you have doubts? Then come with me tonight to the temple of Halia Liet. We celebrate the Night of the New Moon."

·→※←·→※←·→※←·

Neve Beltehal, the Night of the New Moon, is one of the most ancient ceremonies of the Zenadishj religion. All of the city lights are put out and the only illumination there is comes from the candles of the worshipers as they make their pilgrimage to the temple. As soon as it is dark, the streets become glowing rivers of fire.

All of Halia Tehal, and a few of the surrounding villages, had come to the temple of our moon-goddess to pay homage to her dark sister, Divneve. Each month Divneve died so the silvery Halia Liet could continue to rule the night. Her death also serves as atonement for the sins of her worshipers. For the price of a silverpiece one may receive forgiveness of the gods each Neve Beltehal. As a boy, when I still believed in the gods, I loved her above all others because of her self-sacrificing nature. Our gods are cruel, and her compassion for mankind, as well as for her sister, made her stand out in that heartless lot.

I glanced at Tejalura, who walked close beside me as if afraid to get separated in such a crowd. With her dark beauty, she was the image of Divneve. Being the only unveiled woman in the crowd, she attracted attention but not once was she accosted. If the men of Narit did not respect her wedding ring, they did respect the tattoo of a *nutevek narashan*.

She shivered and hugged the green material of her *mactil* closer to her body.

"How much further, Tehmu? I'm nearly frozen."

"Not much. Did you bring a silver coin like I told you to?"

She nodded.

"One with the image of Halia Liet on it?" I persisted. "It would be just our luck for you to bring Nejimenet currency."

Wordlessly, she showed me the coin. On it was stamped the graceful figure of our moon-goddess.

We entered the temple and were ushered to our places of honor beside the queen. Ceymar smiled at us as we joined her. We waited silently while my uncle's rich voice sang the song of purification. When the temple was filled, he stopped, and the song was taken up again by the priestess who had been chosen to play the part of Divneve.

The priestess was Marihe.

She was nude except for the wide jeweled collar of rubies that dripped blood red over her shoulders. Her magenta hair had been dyed black so that she would more closely resemble the goddess of the dark moon. Her staring eyes were cold and empty of all feeling because she had been heavily drugged, but her voice was clear and beautiful.

O Silverwoman, make us pure
With silver make us pure
With the light of your pale throne
O Silverwoman, make us pure

I, Divneve, make you pure
With my blood I make you pure
On the night of my dark reign
I, Divneve, make you pure

As I handed her my silverpiece, there wasn't the slightest flicker of recognition in her eyes. Those eyes that were once so warm and golden, now were the eyes of one dead. Her dilated pupils had the appearance of bored holes in cold brass coins.

Oh, Marihe! my heart cried out silently. Why have they done this to you? You were the lovely one, the brilliant one, the favorite. What terrible compromise has my uncle been forced to make with the brotherhood that would cause him to give you up?

After all of the silverpieces had been collected from the worshipers within and without the temple, Marihe was led to the altar where my uncle waited. She stood, arms outstretched as if to embrace us all, and sang the last verse of the song:

I, Divneve, make you pure
With my blood I make you pure ...

THE PRIEST: TEHMU

How young she looked, how alive. She seemed as graceful as a bird ready to take flight. The warmth of her golden skin contrasted against the metallic glitter of the cold silver behind her. My uncle gathered her hair away from her neck and with one swift motion, cut her head off with his sword. Metul and another senior priest grasped her by the shoulders and held her so the piled coins would receive the baptism of her blood.

The grip of Tejalura's hand nearly crushed my own.

"Oh my dear God!" she whispered in horror.

I studied her anxiously. She was pale with shock, but she would not faint. Mingled with her horror there was also a burning anger that would give her the needed strength to stay in control. I saw something else I hadn't noticed before. There was a streak of gray in her hair.

· → ※ ← · → ※ ← · → ※ ← ·

There was a midnight gathering at the palace after the sacrifice. I suggested to Tejalura that she return to her quarters but she insisted on attending. I didn't argue because I also wanted to go. I needed to speak with my uncle and this might be my last chance for some time to come. I saw him standing by the queen, smiling as if he hadn't a care in the world.

"Uncle, I need to speak with you privately."

As soon as we were far enough away from the others, I landed on him.

"Why Marihe, Uncle? Why?"

"I had no choice. Keep smiling! Do you want the whole room to know you're upset?"

I didn't smile, but I managed to compose my features into a pleasant enough expression.

"What do you mean you had no choice?"

"The winter solstice is coming up, and you were nominated by the priesthood to be the sacrifice. Metul is gaining power within the brotherhood. In the end I was forced to compromise and give them Marihe. She never knew what was happening. I've had her drugged since the last council meeting adjourned."

We were silent for a moment.

"There was nothing else to be done, Tehmu. I loved Marihe, but I need you now more than ever. Power is shifting to the other side. Now let us return to the queen so you can pay your respects to her."

As I approached Ceymar, I could not help thinking what an attractive old woman she was. When she came to the throne as a young woman, songs were written about her dark, exotic beauty. At last old age had caught up with her, as it does with us all, but she proved that, black hair or gray, she was magnificent.

"Hello, Tehmu," she said smiling graciously. "Metul and I were just speaking of you."

I glanced at Tejalura's flushed and angry face and guessed whatever was being said about me, it couldn't have been good.

"Yes," said Metul with the confident smile of the man with the advantage. "Your assignment to act as household priest for Lady Tehalchev's family is illegal."

"You see, Tehmu," the queen explained, "When I allowed you to be Tejalura's priest, I had no idea you were a junior priest. We can't have this sort of thing going on in the palace. You understand, don't you, dear?"

Of course I understood. Perfectly. Not only did Metul have the priesthood's support, he also had the queen's.

"Oh, he understands, all right," Metul answered for me. The smugness of Metul's voice made my hands itch for his throat. "If it would please Your Highness, I might suggest a few good men. Any one of whom would make an excellent replacement."

Ceymar's eyes blinked with innocent surprise. How often I had seen that same expression on Tejalura's face when she had baited and trapped Metul.

"Replacement?" she seemed puzzled. "Whatever for?"

"Why, Your Highness, for Tehmu of course."

"Oh, no. That isn't what I had in mind at all. I was thinking of promoting him." She smiled. "To senior priest."

"But my lady," he babbled nervously. "There won't be any vacancies until the next senior priest dies."

She fixed a look on him as hard as yellow diamonds.

"That shouldn't be too hard to arrange. The winter solstice is coming up and I hear that a sacrifice has not been chosen yet. I could think of one." She paused. "Easily."

It was painful to watch the usually glib Metul stutter and fumble over his words in an attempt to worm his way out of the corner he had backed himself into.

"Metul," she cut into his awkward speech. "Your presence must be wanted elsewhere, for it certainly isn't wanted here."

"Y-yes, My Lady."

The corners of her mouth twitched as she watched his retreating figure.

"Got the little bastard, didn't I?"

Abruptly she turned to look at me.

"I meant what I said earlier. You are now senior priest, so tomorrow get your ear pierced and from now on you are to attend the conferences." She smiled at my uncle. "That should help even things up for you at the next meeting."

The next day Yari and the boys returned from their hunting expedition. I gave them a day to unwind and relate to me their experiences, but after that I put them back to their former schedule. Tejalura wanted them to receive a Zenadishj education and I was teaching them what I could. They were bright boys. Akashe picked things up faster but had a tendency to forget what he had learned. Khai, on the other hand, had trouble grasping even the simplest of new concepts, but the boy was determined to learn. He had his mother's stubbornness and his father's patience, and once he had learned a certain lesson, I was positive he would take it to the grave.

While the boys worked on their assignments and Tejalura continued her research in the archives, Yari and I had the chance to spend some time together. My excursions with Yari were quite different from the ones with Tejalura. Tejalura, who was much in the public eye, avoided crowds while Yari sought the company of the Naritian aristocrats by indulging in a bit of gentleman's gambling.

Yari only gambled a certain amount, joking that "My wife, the Treasurer" kept him on a budget. He didn't seem to mind his wife being the center of attention and always treated her fondly and with a respect the Zenadishj thought unusual, however admirable. He was pleasant to be around, he was easy to talk to. He was relaxed when Tejalura was harried; he was impartial when Tejalura had political considerations. Quite often the lords who were dissatisfied with their negotiations with Tejalura would seek him out. Among his most constant companions were General Neve Ce and his son Tarim Anen.

I was acquainted with Tarim for we had studied under the same *nutevek narashan* instructor as boys. I noticed he wore a blue ring of unusual design.

"My father gave it to me," he said when I remarked on its beauty.

"Yes, I obtained it during a raid on the Enavian Outpost during my youth," Neve added. "In fact, I captured two slaves which I sold to the Nejimenets at that time. One of them I sold to your household, Yari. A young Enavian girl with black hair. Whatever became of her?"

There was a small silence.

"There are no slaves among our people," Yari said quietly. "It is your turn to play, my lord."

There was something hidden in their words. Whatever their true interest was, it had nothing to do with slaves and rings. The game was resumed and as quite often happened, Yari lost. He accepted his defeat with a casual smile and a shrug. He never seemed concerned about winning or losing; whatever he was there to win, it wasn't money.

· →✦← · →✦← · →✦← ·

One afternoon Tejalura asked me to walk with her to the public park called the Garden of Roses.

"But that is where lovers meet!" I jokingly protested.

She shrugged.

"Half the palace believes we are having an affair anyway. What does it matter?"

I didn't argue with her further. There was something odd about her that day, I had never seen her so tense before.

I have always been fond of the park where we met. Throughout the year it is filled with the heavy scent of cela roses in bloom. In Meneth-shir there would be snow, I remembered suddenly. My heart ached at the sight of a young mother with her child. I wondered how Imih and Khiseh were.

"This morning Khai tried to make an appointment to see the queen," Tejalura said, breaking into my thoughts. "He was refused admittance."

"Perhaps she was busy."

"You know Ceymar. She's never too busy to see the boys. Especially Khai. Tehmu, I'm worried. Would you ask your uncle to check on her and see what's going on?"

"Of course. Why didn't you go to him yourself?"

"I hardly know the man. We're supposed to be enemies, remember. I have never gone to his offices except on appointment. It would look more natural for you to see him."

"All right, I will. But I think you are making a great deal over nothing. She's an old woman, after all. She may be sick."

"Ceymar? You saw her yesterday afternoon. She's as healthy as a horse. She'll dance on all our graves if she's allowed to die of natural causes."

She shot me a look.

"All right, I'm over-reacting, I know. But I would rather be too careful than not careful enough. If there is nothing wrong, well, no harm done. At least we'll be sure."

As we made our way back to the palace, the people in the streets called out to her and waved. Since the arrival of the money from Meneth-shir and the passing of new laws, she had become very popular with the citizens of Halia Tehal. Our Lady of Hope, they called her. Dark Lady or Daughter of Divneve, but she found no pleasure in that last name. Not after having witnessed Marihe's death.

"You see," I tried to reassure her, "The people love you. You have nothing to fear from the priesthood."

"I have everything to fear from the priesthood. The people? They are cattle who will choose the easiest path. If the queen were to order my death today, they wouldn't lift a finger to help me. I may love them, I may care about them, but I have no illusions about them."

In a way she was right, she did have reason to fear the priesthood. One of the biggest holds they have had over the populace is their complex calendar. It is so confusing only a trained priest can read it, and the general public has no idea when to sacrifice to the gods, when to plant their crops, when to baptize their babies unless there is a priest to tell them. Tejalura, after many months of research, simplified it. She has not been allowed to publish and distribute it—it would take my uncle a long time to manage that one—but someday her accurate but easy-to-read calendar will mean the liberation of the Zenadishj.

A woman came forward and begged Tejalura to kiss her baby. She has never been fond of babies, but she agreed to without hesitation. At that moment a village priest from the country held out a beautifully carved wooden box.

"If it would please you, Dark Lady, touch this box and bless it. Our village is starving. We need your help."

The priest seemed to have caught her off guard.

"Well if it's food and money you need, apply at the office . . . "

"No, Divneve, it is your blessing that we need. If you would but touch the box."

"I'm no priest, touch it yourselves!"

"But Lady Divneve . . . "

The name touched a raw nerve in Tejalura. She grabbed the box and flung it across the street. The priest's assistant ran after the box and had to fight the crowd for possession of it. Meanwhile, the priest had thrown himself down and was showering Tejalura's feet with kisses.

"O Lady, thank you! Thank you!"

For a moment I thought she would kick him, but her sense of humor came through, and she benevolently touched his head, recited a blessing and walked on.

"From now on, Tehmu, we ride horses or go in a carriage. I'll kiss their babies, but I draw the line at touching relics!"

We parted at the palace gates. She would return to her quarters and check on the boys, and I promised to join them when I had learned from my uncle just how matters were with the queen. When I reached my uncle's office, I nodded politely to the guard as I entered the door, but he blocked me off with his spear.

"The high priest is not to be disturbed."

"Since when? I am Tehmu Bari, senior priest, and am not accustomed to being questioned at the door of Bari Usul Ce."

The use of my uncle's personal name did not impress him in the least.

"Orders are orders."

It was on the tip of my tongue to ask whose orders he was talking about, but I knew: Metul.

THE PRIEST: TEHMU

"Carry on then," I said curtly, and left.

I had to reach Tejalura's quarters and warn them. We had to leave Halia Tehal immediately, for without the protection of the queen or my uncle, we didn't have a prayer. There was always General Neve. He and Yari had spent a great deal of time together, but I had no way of knowing just where the general stood in all of this, he would have helped by now if he were going to. For all I knew, the guard I had just spoken to was one of his personal men.

I entered their quarters without ceremony.

"Yari! Tejalura!"

Silence.

"Khai! Akashe!"

I saw their schoolbooks spread out on the table where they had been studying. Their quarters were deserted, even the servants were gone. I left the room, but I had no idea where I should go. *Think, Tehmu, think!*

"Tehmu Bari!"

I stopped and turned, and saw two members of the temple guard coming after me. One of them, Chev, I knew quite well.

"Tehmu Bari, you are under arrest."

"By whose orders?"

"The high priest, of course."

Chev saw my look of disbelief and taking pity on me, explained.

"No, son, not your uncle—the new high priest, Metul Div Ce."

·→※←··→※←··→※←·

They put us all together in the same cell; Yari, the boys, Tejalura and myself. We were all as good as dead, and with the winter solstice being tomorrow, I had no doubt as to how Metul would eliminate us. I thought of several escape plans, but none of them were very good. At last I chose the least impossible one and decided to act on it: I asked the guard to take me to Metul.

How it galled me to see him using my uncle's chair, the old and worn one that had always been his favorite, as if it were his personal throne. He greeted me as if I were a visiting prince he needed to curry favor with.

"Sit down, Little Nephew," he mocked me. "What can I do for you?"

"Let the Nejimenet woman and her family go."

"Ah, yes. I've often wondered if there was something dirty going on between you and Lady Tehalchev. Did her husband ever guess?"

I remained silent and refused to be drawn. I wasn't there to debate. I was there the save the lives of my friends.

"So now you want me to let them go, just like that?" he said unbelieving. "Why should I? Tell me that."

"So that you can sacrifice me to the sun tomorrow."

He seemed really amused by this.

"But my dear Tehmu, I had planned to sacrifice all of you. Why should I let four potential offerings go?"

"Although the Nejimenets are a peace-loving people, they are also a nation of trained warriors. I know, I've lived with them. If you killed their representative and her family, they would smash Narit as if it were a fly." I let that sink in. "Also, if they go, I will be a willing sacrifice. If you don't agree to this, you will have five unwilling sacrifices to wrestle with tomorrow. Come Metul, there is nothing less inspiring to the public eye than to watch priests dragging their sacrifices to the alter, kicking and screaming all the way."

I began to breath easier. Having said it aloud, it all began to sound quite reasonable.

"You have a point, Little Nephew," he said thoughtfully as I held my breath. "Very well, I'll let them go."

I turned to leave.

"Tehmu?"

I looked back at him.

"Aren't you going to inquire about your uncle and the queen?"

"I know they are dead," I said. "That is enough."

"Oh, the queen is. But your uncle—" he paused, "Not yet. He's taking such a long time to die."

If it wasn't for the fact that Yari and Tejalura were still in prison, I would have killed him with my bare hands. I think he saw it in my eyes.

"Chev!" he called out to the guard. "Escort Tehmu back to his cell and release Lady Tehalchev and her family."

As soon as I told them the news, Tejalura started to argue with me.

"We're not going without you, Tehmu," she said stubbornly.

"This is no time to be noble," I brushed her words away. "I'm a dead man already, whether you and your family leave or not. It makes no difference to Metul."

"But Tehmu—"

Yari silenced her. He knew what the situation was, and I would get no empty heroics from him.

"He is right, Tejalura," he said. "There is nothing we can do. Now, we'd better go."

Mercifully, the good-byes were short. Yari was the last to leave.

"What can I say, Tehmu? You have given us our lives. I wish there was something I could do for you."

"There is," I said. "Get out of Narit as fast as you can. Good-bye, Yari."

At last the door to my cell shut with a hollow thud. I closed my eyes tightly.

Now I am alone as I have always been, I thought. No. No, not always.

I leaned back and felt the damp surface of the stone wall press against my skin. It was cold as ice, just as it had been in all of my dreams. Now it occurred to me that the nightmares of my childhood had suddenly and horribly come true. Hot tears squeezed between my closed lids and coursed down my cheeks.

"Damn you, Metul!" I whispered. "Damn you! I don't want to die!"

I had never had much faith in the Nejimenet teachings of heaven and hell but now I prayed they were true. There should be a hell for the Metuls of this world.

All at once I felt my hate melt away. I saw Imih running barefoot through a dark forest. The grass was covered with morning dew that reflected shattered pieces of the dawn; each drop contained an unborn rainbow. She was running to me, her hair blown by the wind like a blue flame.

Imih, there were so many things I left unsaid. I don't believe I ever told you I loved you with words, but I did, so very much!

Even long after I made peace with myself, I did not sleep. I could not bear to dream my nightmare, the reality would come soon enough with the dawn. Instead I contented myself with watching the stars as they made their way across the sky. When a memory came to me, whether it was pleasant or not, I would savor it, every word, every color every touch that was a part of it. Incidents from my childhood that I hadn't thought of in years, came to me vividly as if they were yesterday.

The first light of dawn spread across the sky like a sheet of blue lilac. It was a pretty enough sunrise, I thought, as the brilliant colors came into view, but I had seen far prettier in Meneth-shir.

"You in there!" the guard's harsh voice cut into my thoughts. "Do you want breakfast?"

Breakfast. The people of Meneth-shir did not even have a word for it in their language. How long had it been since I had eaten a breakfast? Years . . .

"You, Priest! I asked you if you wanted your breakfast."

"No," I said quietly.

"Well, here. You had better take this. It's drugged. I saw Metul prepare it himself. It'll make the going a little easier."

He set the steaming coffee in front of me and left. As I looked into the dark liquid, the rich, warm smell of it brought the Tehalchev's household to mind as nothing else could. I remembered the many morning talks I had with Tejalura and her father, Zarkhon, and there, in the background, was sullen Barije poking at the fire. How many cups of coffee had we shared in that warm, friendly kitchen?

So, Metul had sent me the mercy cup. I was surprised that he was capable of such a humane gesture. I debated whether or not to drink it. In my early training for the priesthood, I had achieved mind control, and I was certain I could die without loss of face, but on the other hand I had never taken a drug in my life—here was my last chance to experience its effect. I saw Marihe's vacant eyes, and I poured the dark liquid on the ground. I had nothing left now save my memories, so I wished to keep my mind clear and enjoy them as long as possible.

At last it was time for me to go, and I walked down the Avenue of the Temple of Zenedh, as I had a hundred times in my dreams. The scent of the fresh morning air, the clear blue sky, the brilliant colors of the garments of those who were a part of the procession as well as the citizens in the crowd, it was all so familiar that I expected to awaken at any moment.

But there were differences. Metul looked older, nervous, not quite in control. As I marched along the avenue and sensed the

THE PRIEST: TEHMU

discontent of the crowd as well as the unease of the guards flanking me, I knew why.

Worried, Metul? I don't blame you. Look at the crowd. They are not the same ignorant rabble they were before their Dark Lady came to them. They know why she left and they know why I must die. Taxes have been raised again, and they know the reason for that, too. Soon they will know how to count the days, when to plant their crops and worship the gods. Yes, they will know and will no longer have any use for your parasitic brotherhood. A change is in the wind, Metul, and my only regret about dying today is that I won't be there to see it when it comes. But, it is enough to know that it comes.

Yes, it is enough.

Ah, here's another familiar part from my dreams. The steps that led up to the alter. There were fifty-two of them, all made of rose-colored marble that faded into orange at the top like the dawn, and were veined throughout with gold pyrite. As I climbed the stairs, I felt a cool but gentle northern breeze on my face. Knowing that it came from the direction of Meneth-shir gave me strength with each step. My heart felt light and free.

At the last minute I had given Tejalura a piece of my hair to bury in Meneth-shir. Yari had frowned but she understood, pagan though the gesture had been. Forgive me, Father of the Nejimenets, it is the only way I know. I have tried to do things for the good. I know that I have made mistakes, but I have tried. I do not want the afterlife my gods offer, give me Yours instead for I know Imih will be there. And when You consider this, please remember I have saved the lives of four of Your people.

I paused in my prayer. Somehow I did not believe the God of the Nejimenets was a god one could bargain with. I could only trust He would make things right.

At the top the air was so utterly still that silence became sound itself. I have never felt so alive and strong. Metul could see by the clearness of my eyes that I had not taken the drug. Odd ... by the expression on his face, one would have thought he, not I, was the condemned man.

TEJALURA

Chapter 18
The Queen: Divneve Ce 1348 EE

> I, Divneve, make you pure
> With silver, make you pure
>
> — *The Song of Neve Beltehal*

Winter 1348 EE

"Believe me, Tejalura, there was nothing we could have done."
Was it me or was it himself he was trying to convince?
"I know, Yari. But what are we going to tell Imih?"
My voice trailed off into sobs. Yari knew how much I hated to cry. He touched my shoulder gently.
"There, Taji. Dry your eyes, there's plenty of time to worry about that when we reach Meneth-shir."
It would be impossible to return through Cela Pass until next spring, so we spent the winter with Chevari and Tzeri. We arrived without warning, cold wet and hungry but we were welcomed without question. I had not seen Tzeri in years. She had grown rather plump but appeared to be happy and Chevari seemed well pleased with her.
Yanahna-Khai was a beautiful girl of fourteen now. She still resembled Terez a great deal in appearance as well as temperament. She was good-natured and loving, but always there was mischief lurking in the depths of her golden eyes. She had forgotten most of her Nejimenet, apparently Tzeri only spoke Zenadishj to her.
Akashe and Khai, now sixteen, helped Chevari with the horses and often as not Yanahna-Khai would be with them.
"Seeing them together like that reminds me of you, Yari and Hushé when you were children," Tzeri commented. "Yana and Akashe fight just like you and Yari did at that age."
"Don't Tzeri!" I begged. "It's too soon for that yet. They're still babies."
"All right. Listen, why don't we go in and start getting dinner ready."
Tzeri was a bit put out with me when I went to the corral instead of following her into the house, but I was in no mood for housework.

Anyway, she had servants to help her; I wanted to see the horses. I stood beside Yari and we talked about the new additions to the herd, judging them and offering a hand to the workman when they needed it.

Off in the distance we saw three Erteyan riders approaching, one of them was Lev Kedhari. My heart stopped at the sight of him. They had to buy horses for their community and, of course, Chevari offered them the hospitality of his home for the next few days while they bargained with him for the ones they had chosen. When I introduced Lev to Yari as "an old Enavian friend of mine," my husband favored me with a shrewd look. He knew.

I don't remember what we spoke of during those few minutes before we went to the house for dinner. I just remembered feeling so ashamed I wanted to die. Yari walked beside me as we followed the rest of the group in.

"Tejalura—" he began.

"Yari, please! I don't want to hear it."

I tried to rush ahead, but he held me back.

"Taji," he said fondly. "Have I ever told you what excellent taste you have in men?"

How like him to tease me at a time like this.

"Oh, Yari," I cried in a voice choked with tears. "Have I ever told you know much I love you?"

He laughed and hugged me tighter.

"Not often enough," he said.

That evening Lev and his brother-in-law did most of the talking. It was good to hear news of the community, but most of all I enjoyed hearing about Jack.

"He has grown into a fine young man," Lev said. "I can't believe how much he and Khai look alike. Do you know that he is attending the university in Naritjina? Yes, he is an honor student, you would be proud of him. During most of his vacations he comes to the community to help out. His major is agriculture and he has helped us with our farming methods. But he insists we have helped him more by allowing him to gain practical experience towards his career. He has won a scholarship to attend the university on Taen."

I couldn't be happier if this were news of my own son.

"That's wonderful," I said. "Give him my love the next time you see him and tell him to visit me before he leaves Ceytal. Tell him that I'll meet him at Cela Pass."

"You haven't told me who your friends are, Lev," Chevari interrupted.

"Oh, forgive me. This is Rayert," he indicated the man on his left. Then turned to the man on his right. "And this is Tal, Irima's husband."

"I didn't know that Irima was married. How long ago was this?"

"Two years ago," Lev answered.

"And how about you, Lev?"

He smiled quietly.

"No, not yet."

There was a small silence before Tal dispelled it with a laugh.

"Irima and I are threatening to buy him an Urthic slave girl from the Zenadishj if he doesn't marry soon."

There were no other uncomfortable moments during their visit, still I was glad to see them leave two days later.

On our return to Meneth-shir, we learned of Imih's death. She had died in her sleep, without warning or reason. She simply went to sleep and never woke up. She had died on the day of the winter solstice as Tehmu had. Their death occurred five years after their marriage, just as Tehmu told me would happen to the Chosen of the Gods. It may have been a coincidence but to this day I have never made a pledge or vow in the name of a foreign god.

The years I spent away from Meneth-shir taught me to value the life I had among the Nejimenet people. It was a life of peace and blessings without number. Never again would I desire to leave. But Ce had other plans.

It was almost dark, that final moment when the last traces of blue-gray were all that remained of daylight. Yari burst into the house shouting:

"Tejalura! Tejalura!" he saw me in the kitchen. "Oh, there you are. You'll never guess who's at Cela Pass."

"Jack?" I ventured, although I didn't think Yari would be that excited about my nephew's arrival.

"No, it's Metul."

"Metul? What on earth could he want?"

"He wants to talk to us. Well, me actually, but I think you should be there with me."

"Why?"

"Because he specifically asked that you *not* be there."

"Well, I'm not going. If he wants more money, that's too bad. I'll see him rot before I give him so much as a tenthpiece. He murdered Tehmu and he would have murdered us as well if he thought he could have gotten away with it."

"Taji, do you know your way?"

"Don't you dare lecture to me about knowing 'my way,' Yari Tehalchev! My way is not to have anymore dealings with that monster Metul."

I saw his mouth tighten in anger, but he forced himself to be patient.

"Taji, please understand, this is very important to me. Now which one is your newest dress?"

"The red one you bought me last week," I said quietly.

"You'd better wear the yellow one," he decided. "A few generals of the Naritian Army will be there and I don't want you wearing their national colors. Your jewelry, wear every piece of it you possibly can."

"Yari," I interrupted. "You must tell me what's going on. I don't have the faintest idea of what you are talking about."

"Never mind," he said. "Just look absolutely beautiful in the next few minutes."

Men!

"How am I supposed to know what to wear. Yari, you've got to tell me what's happening."

"I'm not sure myself, I can only guess. But whatever this means, you must look like a queen for the occasion. The impression you first make on the Naritian generals is very important."

"Then I should wear Aunt Kiakashe's uniform."

He hugged me and spun me around.

"Taji, you're a genius! By all means, wear the uniform. But don't forget to look beautiful."

It was almost spring and the air was bitterly cold as we rode down the pass. My teeth chattered, I think it was due more to excitement than the temperature. What could the Naritians possibly want with us? They must know what they would have little chance of getting any more money after the way they had treated us in Halia Tehal.

It was daylight when we came to their camp and they looked as if they had been up for hours waiting for us. Beside Metul stood General Neve whose aide carried a long pole of scalps. I pressed my lips together with impatience. How ridiculous these Zenadishj were to show off these scalps. Did they think to intimidate Yari with them? As soon as we had come as close as protocol would allow, we halted our horses and dismounted. The aid stepped forward and thrust the pole between us for Yari's inspection.

The scalps were many in number, in varying shades of red, blue, black, white and even a few Enavian blond ones. But there was one that caught my attention. I stared at it fixed, unable to tear my eyes away from it. It was as black as my own hair and its braid would have hung past my waist. A gold wire caught it at the end, a gold wire I had seen many times as a little girl. I noticed the blue ring Tarim Anen, General Neve's son, wore on his left hand. Although it had been nearly thirty years since I had seen it, I knew immediately it was the same ring that Mheftu had given my Enavian brother Jack many years ago. I knew then, it was General Neve who sold me to the Nejimenets.

I looked again at my mother's scalp. I tightened my grip on Yari's arm to keep from swaying. He couldn't have known for sure the reason of my weakness but I think he guessed.

"I see you Metul Div," my husband said at last.

"I see you Yaremida Tehalchev Ce," Metul returned politely enough for a man who had wanted to kill us a few months earlier. "And I see also your charming wife. I had not expected to see her this day."

"She is here."

"She seems a little pale. Perhaps she is not feeling well?"

I glared at him. Yes, he had brought them here on purpose. He knew my mother's scalp hung on General Neve's pole so he knew that I was Enavian and he is letting me know that he knows. But of what importance is my Enavian ancestry? Why should he make such an issue of it?

"The scalps," Yari said bluntly. "They displease her. They displease me as well." He turned to the general. "We knew each other well during our stay in Halia Tehal and had been acquainted long before that time. You need not intimidate us by waiving your trophies in our faces. Please ask your aide to set them aside."

The aide stood back, General Neve continued to study me closely. All at once I recognized him as the warrior whose thumb I had bitten over thirty years ago. I felt completely out of my depth.

"I have not had the pleasure of seeing your wife so close until this moment. Her hair is uncommonly dark, so dark one might say it is nearly black."

"One might say so," Yari returned stiffly, "Because it is black. The blood of the Black Water tribe runs strong among our people," he said.

"Then she is perhaps a relative of Ceymar Ce?"

Yari shrugged.

"Perhaps. Who can be sure?"

Yari had lied by telling the truth. It was true some of Ceymar's relatives had married into the Tehalchev household. But I was an Enavian captive of simple pioneer stock, not a born Nejimenet with connections of Urthic royalty. We all knew that. Yari fooled no one and he knew that. What was the purpose to all of this?

"I am impressed," General Neve said at last. "The blood of your sons must indeed be noble."

Neve bowed first to me then to Yari. Yari bowed slightly in acknowledgment of the compliment. It seemed he had scored some great victory.

"But we waste much time," my husband said to Metul. "Tell me why you wished to see me."

"We have come to offer you the crown of Halia Tehal."

I was stunned but Yari didn't even bat an eye. He seemed to expect it.

"I am flattered of course," he said smoothly. "But why? Surely the people of Narit would prefer one of their own race. Would they accept a Nejimenet ruler?"

Metul shrugged.

"Now they would accept a beggar from the street. Whether you retain the crown or not depends on your actions from the moment you become *zivu*. Queen Ceymar and her father, Div Kassar, were Urthic, yet they were our most able rulers. A precedent has already been set, it will not arouse much comment."

"But why me? There is no love lost between us. In fact, you tried to kill me and my family. But now you would make me *zivu*. Why?"

"It was General Neve's idea, not mine. But I have come to agree with him these past months. There have been five pretenders to the throne since Ceymar's death. Narit needs a time of peace and a chance to rebuild. We need strong leadership, and with the support of the Naritian Army, you could provide that."

Yari smiled, it was a smile I had never seen before. It made him look rather hard and grim. Now I understood the various friendships he had cultivated while we lived in Narit. I realized the evenings he had spent with General Neve, the queen and others were the real meetings and the ones I attended were merely a display to impress the priesthood. Yari had worked very hard for this moment. It had been his plan to live among the Enavians in the White Desert. The circumstances that forced me to live as an Enavian citizen, as well as my appointment as a representative in Narit, had been perceived as unexpected opportunities to be taken advantage of. It was all very clear to me now.

"Very well, Metul. Narit has itself a *zivu*. Expect us in Halia Tehal this fall, just before the snow falls. Come Tejalura, let's go back."

Without giving the priest a chance to say anything else, we mounted our horses and rode away. When we were far enough away, I said:

"You could have at least looked a little surprised, Yari. You acted as if you knew about it all along," I said to test him. How much would he share with me now?

"I did. The queen and General Neve approached me about it during our stay in Narit. It took me a while to believe they were serious."

"But Metul put us in prison. He tried to kill us!"

"Of course he arrested us, it was the only thing he could do to prevent me from becoming *zivu*. But now that the military under General Neve is in power, Metul has no choice."

"You said General Neve and the queen spoke of this to you. Why didn't you tell me about it?"

"I had to give them my word I wouldn't."

"Why?"

He glanced at me and smiled as if something amused him.

"One of the things we discussed was you. You noticed the interest General Neve showed in your black hair?"

"Yes that puzzled me. Why should it matter whether I am Urthic or Enavian?"

"They felt my position on the throne would be strengthened if I were to marry a Zenadishj princess. They suggested Princes Liet."

A cold fear gripped me. And to think I had counted Ceymar my friend. Well, that is the way with politicians, I thought, and now it would appear I was married to one.

"And what did you say?" I managed to ask in the normal voice.

"I told them they were probably right," he said with a teasing smile, "But I could barely manage the one wife I had, let alone two."

I looked at him seriously.

"You took a great risk, Yari."

"Not really, I told them I saw no advantage in marrying Princess Liet. I was already married to the people's beloved Dark Lady. What could endear me more to the Zenadishj people? Even for political reasons, my decision was a good one."

"But if they should disagree with you, what then?"

"Then they disagree with me. The worst they could do is not appoint me *zivu*. I have no intentions of setting up a dynasty. My goal is to give those people their freedom. Do you realize in ten years, twenty or thirty at the most, the people of Narit could be self-governing? When that day comes, I intend to return to Meneth-shir. What good would a Zenadishj princess be to me then?"

I smiled weakly with relief. For a moment I thought I had lost the old, familiar Yari. But he was still there, simple and strong, as he always would be.

"Oh, by the way," he said. "You are to rule beside me with equal power. Your throne name is Divneve Ce. Queen Divneve. How do you like that?"

"Oh, no. Yari, please. I hate that name."

He looked at me with surprise. I had never told him about the time Tehmu and I had gone to the temple to celebrate Neve Beltehal.

"That's odd. I thought it was a pretty name myself. It rather suits you. Divneve was the goddess of—"

"Yari, please! I know what she's the goddess of."

We were silent for a moment.

"I won't force you into anything, Tejalura. But, well, that's the name the people have given you. It is a name they understand and I think it would be a mistake not to use it. There are going to be times when I seem very foreign to them, they have never had a Nejimenet ruler before. But you, they see you as their favorite goddess incarnate. They can identify with you. It would help me a great deal, Tejalura."

I shrugged. What was in an name? I'd had so many during my life, why not Divneve also?

"Very well, Yari. I'll use the name if you think it best."

· →✸← · →✸← · →✸← ·

Late in the afternoon I sat under the tree watched Melia while she practiced the new dance she was learning in school. My chubby little sister had grown into a skinny ten-year old. I smiled as she paced herself through the unfamiliar steps as graceful as an uncertain fawn.

Melia fell again, her laughter mingling with the wind as it stirred the leaves above me.

"Oh, Taji. I'll never get this dance right."

"Yes you will, keep trying."

"But I've been trying and trying."

"Well, why don't you rest a while and try later?"

Before I had finished wording my suggestion she had already stretched herself on her back and was gazing up at the clouds with her hands behind her head.

"Taji?"

"What?"

"Am I too old for stories?"

"No, what ever gave you that idea?"

"I asked Barije to tell me one the other day and she told me I was too old for them anymore."

"Oh, you know Barije. She was just too lazy to tell you one, that's all. If you want, I'll tell you one tonight."

"An Oramaklete one? Please Taji, those are the best."

"All right then, an Oramaklete one."

"Taji?"

"Hmm?" I was beginning to think I would never get my afternoon nap.

"Can't you stay? I mean, do you really have to go to Narit?"

"Yes and no."

She wrinkled her freckled nose.

"You're the meanest sister anyone ever had. What do you mean 'yes and no?'"

"No, I don't have to go, but yes I do if I want to be with Yari. Once we were separated for three years and I'm not going to let that happen again."

Especially with Princess Liet waiting for him in Halia Tehal.

"But why does Yari have to go to Narit?"

"Because he feels he must," I said gently. "Don't worry, Melia, we'll be back."

"When?"

"I don't know."

What had Yari said? Ten or twenty years. Thirty at the most. In that case I would be sixty or seventy before I returned.

"Will it be more than a year?"

"Melia, please! I don't know."

That's it, I scolded myself. Snap at your sister and ruin what little time you do have together. But it all seemed so unfair, I began to feel sorry for myself. Leaving Meneth-shir was the last thing I wanted to do. I can't bear it, I thought. I can't.

I remembered Tehmu the day he left, Imih had been so unhappy to see him go.

"Imih, please. Don't worry about me, I'll be fine. I'll be back just as soon as I am able."

"But what if you can't come back? What if something happens?"

"What will happen will happen. You, your people, the valley; they all have become a part of me. I have Meneth-shir with me always, nothing can change that. One thing I have learned during my time with your people: Meneth-shir is nothing if it does not live within our hearts."

Tehmu had been more Nejimenet than I. I felt ashamed. I remembered something Terez had said years ago.

"I cannot forget about the way things are down here because I have a mountain refuge in which to hide. You are right in saying the land is ours only as a gift from Ce; but unless we love this land enough to fight for the right to keep it, Ce will give it to the Enavians who love it enough to fight for the right to take it."

Terez was right, we must fight the Enavians but not with weapons. We have so much, if we could share our wealth and help unite Ceytal, all would be well.

And as for myself? I glanced at the tree above me. It looked the same as it had thirty years ago when I sat under it with Laughter and Geysan, it would look the same thirty years from now. Meneth-shir would be waiting for us when we finished our work in Narit. And if I never returned? Well, as Tehmu had said, I would have Meneth-shir with me always and that in itself made me rich.

"Come, Melia," I said holding my arms out to her. "Sit beside me. I didn't mean to snap at you like that."

"And I'm sorry, too," she sniffed. "I didn't mean to make you angry. I just don't want you to go."

"Well, I'm not going yet, not until next autumn at least."

She brightened. "Not 'til autumn? You mean we have a whole summer?" She threw her arms around me. "That's wonderful, Tejalura."

I smiled remembering when I was ten and summer stretched before me like a small eternity.

"Yes, Melia. A whole summer. Now let me tell you a story."

"Do I still get to hear one tonight?"

"Of course."

As I was deciding which story to tell, I glanced around me and I saw the edge of a cliff. In the evening light it had the appearance of an old woman's profile carved in stone, it was a face that was familiar and dear. I hadn't thought of Ancient in years, but then I felt her presence as strong as a physical touch.

"Melia, do you see that cliff over there? Well, there is a story about it . . ."

Chapter 19
The Ambassador: Erten Zemmer 1349 EE

> They crowned the midnight of her hair
> With all the stars of heaven
>
> — *The Coronation of Divneve,*
> *Zenadishj Hymn*

Winter Solstice 1349 EE

I had been ordered by Senator Neral Tariv to attend the coronation of the new king and queen of Halia Tehal. If it had been possible to avoid the journey to Narit, I would have. Life with Pallas had tamed me. I had become all I had despised in my youth: a middle-aged man, who could be content to warm himself by the fire, watching the news rather than making it, while his wife fixed him a smooth drink to relax him after a hard day's work. Adventures in distant Ceytalian kingdoms held little allure for me.

"With the discovery of mineral wealth on Ceytal, relations with the Ceytalians have been a top priority with the emperor," Tariv explained during our meeting. "The coronation of an Enavian citizen, adopted and raised by Ceytalians isn't something to be ignored."

I couldn't protest the assignment because Pallas knew she had been included in the invitation. Now there were plans for a new hairstyle as well as a new wardrobe—a must, she insisted, even though her closet was crammed to bursting with dresses and each and every one looked enchanting on her. That, and a chance to visit Tejalura and Yari, and suddenly I found the happiness of my marriage depending on our attendance at the Naritian court. Though he had denied it, I knew it was Tariv who had informed her she was on the royal guest list. I complained to Tariv, but it did me little good.

"Everyone knows you're the expert on Ceytalian culture. Without your assistance I might make some social blunder that would cause us to loose what little ground we've gained with them. Or worse, I might miss untold opportunities and contracts."

I smiled. It was impossible to imagine that Tariv, with all his urbane nonchalance, would make a social blunder or let a profitable opportunity pass by. His was the coolest brain in the empire. He was one of the few competent politicians we had.

"You're so good with the natives," he continued. "And this is a job that requires special handling. Your language skills and intimate knowledge of Ceytalian culture will be invaluable."

"You know, Tariv," I said lightly, "For over thirty years I've been hearing the same thing. It doesn't seem as though I've made much progress in my career since coming to Ceytal."

"You've made it to general, that should count for something. However much you try to minimize it, you've made powerful connections among the influential people on Ceytal. Queen Ceymar spoke quite highly of you during our previous negotiations with her. Not to mention your personal friendship with the new king and queen. It wasn't our government that requested your presence; it was Lord Tehalchev and his wife. This thing is too important, Erten. A lot hinges on this meeting. Taen, it seems, wants to secure its previous claim on Ceytal, which had been neglected during the Nevaran Revolution."

So I had no choice but to make the best of it and go to Narit. Pallas was overjoyed. Although I thought her desire for a new dress frivolous, I indulged her. After all, one didn't attend a coronation every day. Besides, she deserved it and even if she didn't, I enjoy spoiling her. At an age when other men are losing possession of or interest in their wives, I discover myself growing more in love with mine every day. It isn't something I am conscious of in the normal course of the day. But occasionally it will come to me that I am a happy man and Pallas is largely responsible for it.

The dress she purchased was a rather bold and glittering affair of black, silver and gold that was well worth the small fortune it cost. The jewelry her father had loaned her was a barbaric creation of diamond, black onyx, and gold, which blazed at her throat and wrists. They looked so stunning on her I decided, whatever the cost, I would purchase them for her—an end I'm sure my father-in-law had in mind all along.

From the Enavian standpoint, the coronation was not a political success, but Pallas and I enjoyed ourselves. I'd like to think the power and influence of my position were why we found ourselves surrounded by so many of the Naritian royalty, but I knew it was Pallas they were paying court to, not me. A wife is an important part of a man's career. There are no bachelor generals—no successful ones anyway.

THE AMBASSADOR: ERTEN ZEMMER

The Naritian court had changed little since my previous visit with Tariv to negotiate with Queen Ceymar the release of Enavian captives. It still had the same ornate splendor and high vaulted ceilings that made me feel diminished in size. The elaborate dress of the aristocratic Zenadishj made me feel quite unremarkable.

I as relieved to see the high priest, Metul Div Ce, there. He was another familiar face from my previous visit. He was a genial man who neither tried to curry favor with us nor cut us cold. Because he had taken the trouble to learn something of our culture, he understood our perspective. He was a comfortable man to be around—more so than the other Naritian nobles. He greeted us with friendly interest.

"I was flattered to hear the Enavian Empire would be represented and pleased when I discovered you would be among their party."

"But not surprised," I said.

"No, not surprised." He turned to the young man beside him. "Ce Aten, I would like to introduce you to General Erten Zemmer."

Ce Aten bowed with the correct ease of one born to nobility.

"We are indeed honored by the presence of the Enavians," his greeting possessed thinly veiled sarcasm. "Your reasons, of course are purely social. Surely the discovery of mineral wealth could have nothing to do with your presence."

Metul silenced him with a look.

"Youth must never display rudeness in the presence of their seniors—especially when one of them is a guest and another is their superior officer." There was a steely edge to Metul's voice, leaving no doubt who the superior officer was. "The renewed interest of the Enavian Empire in Ceytal at the same time of those discoveries is merely a coincidence—a fortuitous coincidence that must be taken full advantage of. That is why the king and queen personally invited General Zemmer."

Although the young lord was silenced, the glittering gold of his eyes spoke volumes. Not all Naritians were as appreciative of the renewed interest of the Enavians as Metul was—and even Metul's sincerity was not to be completely trusted. That didn't stop me from enjoying Metul's company as a pleasant diversion from the politically centered conversations around me, but I had far more respect for the open hostility of Lord Ce Aten.

The king and queen stood near the center of the room speaking with the other Naritian aristocrats. When Yari saw me he acknowledged me with a polite nod, but continued his conversation with General Neve. We could speak later and when we did it would be of personal, rather than political, matters. Let Tariv attempt to extract Yari's commitment and fail. My own friendship with Yari was something I could depend, but never presume upon. I would never use it as leverage.

The Enavian Empire's assumption that Yari would be easy to manipulate because of his Enavian wife was a serious misjudgment. It was no accident Yari had been declared king, I was certain of that. I had observed Yari for years and his appointment to the Naritian throne was deliberate and calculated—something he had been cultivating for years. To what end I couldn't be certain. What could balanced goodness, backed by real political power, accomplish in this world? It would be interesting to see.

A magenta-haired servant girl dressed in purple refilled my wine cup. Having accurately placed me as a faithful husband, she favored me with an alluring smile that was without promise before turning to Ce Aten. I glanced guiltily at Pallas who, secure in the knowledge of my love, had watched the exchange with amusement.

Yari might be dignified and distant, but not so Tejalura. She smiled at me broadly and waved openly as if we were still in the White Desert. She abandoned her conversation and came to join me.

"Pallas—Erten," Tejalura hugged us each in turn. "It's so good to see you both."

"Erten," Pallas prompted. "You have a gift for Tejalura. Why don't you give it to her now."

I smiled a little embarrassed. At the time it had seemed a good idea—now in this formal gathering I wasn't so sure.

"I'm afraid it is of little monetary value, your highness."

"And I'm afraid you are going to have to stop calling me 'your highness.' That isn't necessary between us in private."

I handed the small package to her. With uninhibited eagerness, she opened the package. It was the picture of her and Gabrielle I had carried for so many years. I'd had it professionally restored and framed. It made a pretty piece.

"Why, I haven't seen this in years. I'd forgotten all about it. Oh, Erten, it's a lovely gift. I shall treasure it always."

"I was afraid it might be inappropriate."

She continued to smile and shook her head.

"It couldn't possibly be, especially with you as the giver. It will remind me where I came from and I will remember I am a queen by chance, not by right. Then I shall never forget or become too proud."

The musicians, in honor of their Enavian guests, were playing a waltz, the same one I had danced with her sister many years ago. What a treacherous thing a memory can be. I loved Pallas, but I have often wondered what my life might have been if Gabrielle hadn't died.

I saw the glittering image of my wife glide by in the arms of no less than the king himself, and I pushed the thought away. What was the point? Gabrielle probably would have married one of the neighboring landowner's sons. Only a fool would lament unlikely possibilities when his own reality was as happy as mine was.

"General Zemmer," Tejalura's words broke into my thoughts. "It is very rude to leave a lady standing alone when there is music playing."

I smiled into her teasing eyes that were so much like Gabrielle's, and held out my arm to escort Queen Divneve to the dance floor.

TEJALURA

Appendix

The following is a list of foreign terms, geographic locations and historical biographies referred to in this novel. Abbreviation code: Ceytalian = *c.*; Enavian = *en.*; Enavian Era = *EE*; Erteyan = *er.*; Erteyan-Enavian = *er/en.*; = Nejimenet = *n.*; Nejimenet-Zenadishj = *n/z.*; Oramaklete = *o.*; Urthic = *u.*; Zenadishj = *z.*

akashe (ah-kah-SHAY) *n.* bear.

Akashechev (ah-kah-SHAY-chev) is a Nejimenet family name "Bear Household".

Akashechev, Gan (ah-kah-SHAY-chev, gahn) *n.* 1273-1351. Father: Nejo Akashechev. Mother: Metahali Rakura (Ancient). Sisters: Silverwoman and Kiakashe. Wife: Turquoise. Stepchildren: Laughter and Hushé. Served for twenty years in the Zenadishj Army. Considered a hero by even his enemies, the Enavians. Returned to Meneth-shir in 1321 with the rank of general.

Akashechev, Ki "Kiakashe" (ah-kah-SHAY-chev, kee "KEE-AH-kah-shay") *n.* 1275-1351. Father: Nejo Akashechev. Mother: Metahali Rakura (Ancient). Brother: Gan. Sister: Silverwoman. Husband (divorced): Neve Bari. Adopted son: Nejo. She served for ten years in the Zenadishj Army, retired to Meneth-shir in 1311 with the rank of general.

Akashechev, Melia "Turquoise" (ah-kah-SHAY-chev, may-LEE-ah) *n.* Born 1283. First husband: Huri Tehalchev. Second husband: Gan Akashechev. Daughter: Laughter. Son: Hushé.

Akashechev, Metahali Rakura "Ancient" (ah-kah-SHAY-chev, MA-ta-ha-lee RAH-ku-ra) *o.* 1253-1331. First husband: Kura Zhat. Second husband: Nejo Akashechev. Daughters: Silverwoman and Kiakashe. Son: Gan. Born in the Oramaklete village of Yalangi. Killed her first husband to save the life of their daughter, Silverwoman. Escaped to Narit and was adopted by the Nejimenets by marrying into the Akashechev household. She was also the adopted grandmother of Tejalura.

Akashechev, Nejo (ah-kah-SHAY-chev, NEE-ho) *n.* Born 1312. Adopted mother: Ki Akashechev. Father: Lev Aleksandar. Mother: Seraine Aleksandar. Brother: Jack. Sisters: Gabrielle and Lillian (Tejalura). Nejo was Tejalura's Enavian brother Johnny Aleksandar.

Aleksandar, Gabrielle (al-ek-SAN-dar, ga-BREE-EL) *er/en.* 1300-1317. Father: Lev Aleksandar. Mother: Seraine Aleksandar. Brothers: Jack and Johnny. Sister: Lillian (Tejalura). Gabrielle was a casualty of the Market Place Bombing.

Aleksandar, Jr., Jack "Aleshe" (al-ek-SAN-dar, jack "al-eh-SHAY") *er/en*. Born (uncubed) 1330. Father: Jack Aleksandar, Sr. Mother: Cia Anset. Wife: Melia Tehalchev. Children: Tejalura, Lillian and Yari Aleksandar. Jack Aleksandar received a general education at the Enavian University of Naritjina in 1348. He transferred to King's University of Taen and majored in agriculture then changed to anthropology and briefly to political science before dropping out. He returned to Ceytal in 1350 and served as an advisor to the Minister of Agriculture in Narit where his uncle, Yaremida Tehalchev, ruled as *zivu*.

Aleksandar, Sr., Jack (al-ek-SAN-dar, jack) *er/en*. 1293-1317. Father: Lev Aleksandar. Mother: Seraine Aleksandar. Brother: Johnny. Sisters: Gabrielle and Lillian (Tejalura). Wife: Cia Anset. Son: Jack Aleksandar, Jr. (uncubed 1330). Jack was a casualty of the Market Place Bombing.

Aleksandar, Johnny See: Akashechev, Nejo.

Aleksandar, Lev (al-ek-SAN-dar, lev) *er/en*. 1270-1317. Wife: Seraine Hershem. Sons: Jack and Johnny. Daughters: Gabrielle and Lillian (Tejalura). Before immigrating to Ceytal he was employed by Hershem & Hershem of the Royal Court of Taen as a senior financial advisor. He was a casualty of the Market Place Bombing.

Aleksandar, Lillian See: Tehalchev, Ura "Tejalura".

Aleksandar, Seraine (al-ek-SAN-dar, su-RAYN) *er/en*. 1274-1317. Husband: Lev Aleksandar. Sons: Jack and Johnny. Daughters: Gabrielle and Lillian (Tejalura). She was a music instructor at the University of Taen. She immigrated with her husband to Ceytal in 1301. She was a casualty of the 1317 Market Place Bombing.

Ancient See: Akashechev, Metahali Rakura "Ancient".

anen (ah-NEN) *z*. jump.

arae (ah-RAY) *n*. silver.

Arae Shjina (AH-RAY SHJEE-nah) *n*. Silver Falls, a waterfall marking the southwestern entrance to Meneth-shir.

aten (ah-TEN) *z*. tower.

aza (AH-zah) *n*. red.

Azakhanis (ah-ZAH-kah-nees) *z*. Redhawks, a tribe of Zenadishj who once inhabited the Naritian Prairies.

bari (bah-ree) *z*. gypsy.

Bari, Tehmu (bah-ree, tay-MU) *z*. 1319-1348. Wife: Imih Leyi. Daughter: Khiseleh. Zenadishj representative sent by the priesthood of Halia Tehal to Meneth-shir.

APPENDIX

Bari Usul Ce (bah-ree yu-SUL say) *z*. 1281-1347. Served as high priest during the last nineteen years of Queen Ceymar's reign. Naritian history records very little about him except that at the time of his death he had 1,837 concubines and catamites in his harem. Apparently this set some sort of record. Later it was learned that his harem was actually a refuge for the priesthood youth from being sacrificed.

barije (bah-REE-hay) *z*. firelight.

Barije (bah-REE-hay) *z*. Zenadishj captive who became the second wife of Geysan Leyi after the death of his first wife, Laughter.

bel (bel) *z*. new.

beltehal (bel-tay-HAL) *z*. new moon.

besari (bay-SAH-ree) *z*. all right, fine, good.

besedi (bay-SAY-dee) *n*. all right, fine, good.

Black Water River also known as Khai Zishuni.

Blue Mountain River also known as Khai Yarashji.

ce (say) *n/z*. god, one, first, lord, lady, sir, a term of respect.

ced (sed) *er/en*. total, complete, goal.

cela (SAY-lah) *n/z*. Creative, wicked, evil, seductively beautiful, treacherous, deceptive, sinful, different, original thinking.

Cela Pass is the entrance to Meneth-shir the permanent home of the Nejimenet people.

Cela Rose, The began as an ancient tea house on Mactil Street. Currently a fine food restaurant able to cater to clientele ranging from casual to elegant. Galactic travel agencies consider it a "must see" location for all who visit Ceytal.

Ceremony of the Chosen is a wedding feast that occurs every third year. The Nejimenets of Meneth-shir and the Mountain Zenadishj of Zeneshtu meet outside the city of Halia Tehal to celebrate a group wedding ceremony. The origins of this ceremony can be traced back to the days when Ceytalian warriors chose their wives from war captives.

ceven (KEH-ven) *en*. white bear.

Ceven, Jr., Dr. Halumne Ral (KEH-ven, ha-LUM-nay rahl) *en*. 1309-1403. Father: General Halumne R. Ceven, Sr. Mother: Seraine Duval. Wife: Halia Liet Ceven. Children: Tehal and Neve. Received a dishonorable discharge (which was later revoked) due to his defeat at the Blue Mountain Massacre. He served two terms as mayor of Naritjina.

ceymar (SAY-mar) or (KAY-mar) *u*. vivacious, lively, a flirt.

Ceymar Ce (SAY-mar say) or (KAY-mar say) *u.* 1275-1347. Father: Div Kassar Ce. Mother: Zishu Ce. Half-brother and husband: Padhari Kassar Ce. Div Kassar's queen, Marihe Ce, was unable to produce an heir so he took Zishu, a princess of the Black Water tribe, to be his concubine and she bore him a daughter, Ceymar. In less than a year Queen Marihe became pregnant. Div Kassar against his wishes, was forced to formally declare his daughter, Ceymar, as his heir to keep peace with Zishu's warlike relatives who feared the queen's pregnancy would displace her as the mother of the heir apparent. After Div Kassar's death in 1284, Ceymar was sold into slavery and her half-brother was placed on the throne. As *zivu*, King Padhari was ineffective and when his party lost power, Ceymar led a rebellion against him and won. To prevent further civil war she married King Padhari but, after his death in 1294, she remained the political power of Narit until her assassination in 1347.

Ceytal (say-TAL) is a territorial planet of the Enavian Empire and the native home of the Ceytalian races. The word Ceytal is the Enavian interpretation of *tzetl*, which means water jewel. The Tzetlis were a tribe of cannibal Oramakletes whom the Enavian explorers first encountered on Ceytal. For many years Enavians believed all peoples of Ceytal practiced cannibalism, but in fact, Ceytal has as much ethnic diversity as any planet in the Enavian Empire.

chev (chev) *n/z.* them, theirs, household, home.

Chevari, Nateheh (che-VAH-ree, NAH-tay-heh) *z.* Husband: Neve Chevari. Son: Terez. Granddaughter: Yanahna-Khai.

Chevari, Neve (che-VAH-ree, NEH-vay) *z.* 1277-1391. First wife: Nateheh. Second wife: Telein. Third wife: Tzeri Jevetura. Son: Terez. Granddaughter: Yanahna-Khai. Horse trader who sells horses to the Naritian royalty. Has a ranch in Zeneshtu and a horse trading office in Halia Tehal.

Chevari, Terez (che-VAH-ree, teh-REZ) *z.* 1302-1335. Father: Neve Chevari. Mother: Nateheh. Wife: Tamai. Daughter: Yanahna-Khai. Zenadishj guerrilla fighter who led attacks on Enavian settlements in the Naritian Prairie. He was Tejalura's first love.

Chief Wolf Winter See: Tehalchev, Yaremida "Yari".

cia (SEE-yah) *er/en.* cobalt blue.

creda (CRAY-dah) *n.* understand, realize, to be aware of.

dasha (DAH-shah) *n.* thank you.

dassar (DAH-sar) *z.* gratitude.

APPENDIX

dax (dax) *er/en*. flag pole, standard.
DCNA See: Department of Ceytalian Native Affairs.
dejo (DEE-ho) *n*. man.

Department of Ceytalian Native Affairs was established in 1306 initially to negotiate the return of Enavian captives. Attempts to negotiate terms were unsuccessful until Senator Tariv, Erten Zemmer and Dr. Mheftu Padhari met with Queen Ceymar in 1322. DCNA representatives were responsible for tracking the progress of assimilation of released Enavian captives as well as Ceytalian refugees into the Enavian society.

dev (dev) *n*. black.
di (dee) *n*. I, me.
dimma (DEE-mah) *z*. come.
dimmeh (DEE-mey) n. come.
dinge derogatory term for natives on colonial planets.
div (deev) *z*. black.

Div Kassar Ce (deev KAH-sar say) *u*. Died 1284. An Urthic desert prince who became the first non-Zenadishj zivu to rule Narit. His son, Padhari Ce and daughter Ceymar Ce ruled after his death in 1284.

Divneve (deev-NEH-vay) *z*. "Dark night" the name of the dark-haired sister of the moon-goddess, Halia Liet or Silverwoman. Divneve was the protector of all hunted things. Each month Divneve died to atone for the sins of man during the celebration of Neve Beltehal.

Divneve Ce (deev-NEH-vay say) *z*. See: Tehalchev, Ura "Tejalura".

Earth is the ancient name for Ceytal and, according to Erteyans, the planet where all human life originated.

EE Enavian Era.

Eia (AY-yah) *en*. is a popular name among Enavian royalty which means "light" in Ancient Enavian. It is also a title of respect, e.g., lady, your highness, your majesty.

Eialise (ay-yah-LEES) *en*. is a popular Enavian name among royalty which means "bright light" in Ancient Enavian.

Enavian Empire (ay-NAH-vee-an) *en*. Solar industrial society that has achieved intergalactic space travel; the true Enavian is blond (dark blond to towhead) and light colored eyes (blue, green or gray), although they have become more heterogeneous since any human can apply for citizenship as long as they live in Enavia proper. Humans born on Taen, the center of the Enavian government, are automatically Enavian citizens unless they are slaves, debtors or criminals. They are the major political power in the galaxy and the most recent immigrants to Ceytal.

Enavian Plague (ay-NAH-vee-an) Although imperial scientists established strict protocols to ensure Ceytalians would not be exposed to Enavian diseases they had no immunity. At least one outbreak occurred 1316-1317 killing millions of Ceytalians before it could be contained.

erevna (er-EV-nah) *n.* "I see you" Nejimenet greeting.

Erten (ER-ten) *er.* is a popular name among the Erteyan-Enavians which means "a man of Earth" in Ancient Enavian.

Erteyan (er-TAY-an) or Erteyan-Enavian (er-TAY-an - ay-NAV-ee-an) a minority group of Enavians who recently immigrated to Ceytal under the Erteyan Homestead Act of 1301. A large percent of Enavia's scientists, businessmen and artists are Erteyan, but because they are a minority of the population they have had little voice in their government. One of the reasons they left Taen was to create another better life for themselves and their children. They chose Ceytal because there was a tradition that Ceytal was the Earth of their legends where the human race was to have originated. Surprisingly, there is a great deal of evidence to back this theory up.

evimeh (ay-VEE-mah) *z.* lady, mistress.

Frontier Guard is the auxiliary branch of the Enavian military.

gan (gahn) *n.* ten.

Gan Akashe (gahn ah-kah-SHAY) *n.* See: Akashechev, Gan.

Gavin, Eialise (GAY-ven, ay-yah-LEES) *en.* Born 1282. Celebrated beauty of the Enavian court. Married a rancher on Ceytal named Ral Gavin. They have one daughter, Melisanne.

Gavin, Lemmer Helt (GAY-ven, lem-mer helt) *en.* 1315-1412. Father: Senn Gavin. Mother: Leta Mandt. Brothers: Sen, Lev, Mandt, Kelen and Redin. Sisters: Talamy, Kisahna, Nia and Eia. Wife: Ina Khai. Children: Lemmer, Talamy and Khai. Received his general education at the Blue Mountain School and served six years in the Frontier Guard. In 1360 he was elected Erteyan representative in Naritjina City. In 1363 he resigned from office to join the Ceytalian Guard and served throughout the revolution. After the war he returned to the Blue Mountains.

Gavin, Melisanne (GAY-ven, mel-is-AN) *en.* Born 1308. The daughter of Ral and Eialise Gavin.

Gavin, Ral (GAY-ven, rahl) *en.* Born 1287. Wife: Eialise. Daughter: Melisanne. Owned a ranch on Ceytal near the Blue Mountain River.

APPENDIX

General She Bear See: Akashechev, Ki "Kiakashe".
General Ten Bears See: Akashechev, Gan.
geysan (gay-SAN) *n.* water hole, spring.
Geysan Leyi See: Leyi, Geysan.
halia (hah-LEE-ah) *z.* silver.
Halia Liet (hah-LEE-ah lee-ET) *z.* Silverwoman, the Zenadishj moon-goddess.
Halia Tehal (hah-LEE-ah tay-HAL) *z.* Silver Moon, capital city of the Zenadishj Empire.
halim (hah-LEEM) *n.* silversmith.
halumne (hah-LU-nay) *en.* shield.
Helt, Lemmer, General (helt, lem-mer) *en.* 1219-1312. Enavinan general who led the first expedition to Ceytal to allow the establishment of the Outpost and Enavian settlements along the Khai Melia, later renamed the Lemmer Helt River in his honor.
helvah (hel-VAH) *en.* fawn.
Hershem, Cia (HER-shem, SEE-yah) *er/en.* 1296-1391. Maiden name Cia Anset. First husband: Jack Aleksandar, Sr. Second Husband: Ral Hershem. Mother of Jack Aleksandar, Jr., and Enavian aunt of Tejalura.
Hershem, Ral (HER-shem, ral) *er/en.* 1287-1389. Father: Lev Hershem. Mother: Nera Helt. Sister: Seraine. Wife: Cia Anset Aleksandar. Stepson: Jack Aleksandar, Jr. Graduated with honors from the Mylande University of Law in 1312. Immigrated to Ceytal in 1317 and in 1365 served as a member of the committee that outlined the Erteyan-Ceytalian Constitution.
hessante (hay-SAN-tay) *z.* silence.
huri (HU-ree) *n.* tree.
hushé (hu-SHAY) *n.* near, close, dear, valuable.
Hushé Tehalchev See: Tehalchev, Hushé.
ijeh (EE-hay) *n.* blue.
imih (ih-mih) *n.* song.
Imih Leyi See: Leyi, Imih.
iraveh (EER-ah-vay) *n.* activity.
irima (EER-eem-ah) *er.* quick intelligence.
Irima Kedhari See: Kedhari, Irima.
itan (ee-TAN) *n/z.* center middle.
Itan (ee-TAN) *c.* is the queen and mother of all the gods according to Ceytalian mythology.

Itan-shir Island (ee-tan SHEER) *n/z.* "Center Place" is an island on the east side of Lake Melia in Meneth-shir. In ancient times it was the Nejimenet center of worship where the priesthood and the ruling class administered control. Currently it is the cultural center where schools are held and community matters are discussed and resolved.

ja (yah) *n.* I, me, my, mine.

jamesh (yah-MESH) *n.* my own, an endearment.

jameshe (yah-me-SHAY) *n.* my flesh, my blood, my relative.

jevema (je-VEE-ma) *n.* lady.

jevet (je-VET) *n.* sun.

Jevetchev (je-VET-chev) *n.* Nejimenet family name "Sun Household".

Jevetchev, Dejo (je-VET-chev, DEE-ho) *n.* 1260-1351. Was the great-great-grandfather Dr. Ura Jevetchev and is her primary reference for oral histories she documented of the Nejimenet people.

Jevetchev, Tzeri (je-VET-chev, TSER-ee) *n.* Born 1308. First husband: Hushé Tehelchev. Second Husband: Neve Chevari. Stepdaughter: Yanahna-Khai. Great-great-granddaughter of Dejo Jevetchev and cousin of Dr. Ura Jevetchev. Childhood friend of Tejalura. Her first husband was killed in the Blue Mountain Massacre. She remarried and lives with her second husband, Neve Chevari, on a horse farm in Zeneshtu Valley.

Jevetchev, Dr. Ura "Jevetura" (je-VET-chev, U-rah "je-veh-TU-rah") *n.* 1302-1395. Father: Gan Jevetchev. Mother: Melia. Sisters: Arae and Imih. Brothers: Nevi, Yaremida and Khai. Served as a Nejimenet representative during the 1351-52 Peace Conference. She published many books on Ceytalian folklore, the most popular being about her childhood in Meneth-shir as well as the recorded stories and memories of her grandfather, Dejo Jevetchev.

jevetura (je-veh-TU-rah) *n.* sunlight.

Jevetura (je-veh-TU-rah) *n.* See: Jevetchev, Dr. Ura "Jevetura".

jevim (je-VEEM) n. sir, lord.

ji (jee) *n.* Suffix indicating possession. Example: Tejalura Zarkhonji means Zarkhon's Tejalura.

kassar (KAH-sar) *u.* nomad.

kedhari (kay-DAH-ree) *er/en.* athlete.

Kedhari, Irima (kay-DAH-ree, EER-eem-ah) *er/en.* Born 1316. First generation Erteyan-Enavian born at the Blue Mountain Community. Served in the Frontier Guard with her brother Lev. A friend of Tejalura.

APPENDIX

Kedhari, Lev (kay-DAH-ree, lev) *er/en*. Born 1313. First generation Erteyan-Enavian born at the Blue Mountain Community. Served in the Frontier Guard. A friend of Tejalura.
  khai (kiy) *n/z*. long, river, rope, tall.
  Khai Melia (kiy may-LEE-ah) *n*. See: Lemmer Helt River.
  Khai Yalangi (kiy yah-LANG-gee) *z*. See: Yalangi River.
  Khai Yarashji (kiy yah-RAH-shjee) *z*. See: Blue Mountain River.
  Khai Zeneshtu (kiy zen-ESH-tu) *z*. See: North River.
  Khai Zishuni (kiy zih-SHU-nee) *u*. See: Black Water River.
  khiseh (KEE-say) *n*. girl.
  khiseleh (KEE-seh-leh) *z*. little girl.
  khiseley (KEE-say-lay) *n*. little girl.
  ki (kee) *n*. she, hers, also indicates gender.
  kiakashe (kee-AH-kah-shay) *n*. she bear.
  Kiakashe See: Akashechev, Ki "Kiakashe".
  kimeneth (kim-EH-net) *n*. strategic, a person who plans ahead.
  King Yaremida (yah-ray-MEE-da) *n*. See: Tehalchev, Yaremida "Yari".
  kiral (KEER-al) *en*. tailor.
  kirat (KEER-at) *er/en*. noble.
  Laughter See: Tehalchev, Uralai "Laughter".
  Lake Melia (may-LEE-ah) *n*. is located in the center of the Nejimenet kingdom of Meneth-shir.
  lemmer (lem-mer) *en*. anvil.
  Lemmer Helt River (lem-mer helt) *en*. is a river that runs east through the Naritian Prairie, a.k.a., Khai Melia.
  lev (lev) *er/en*. measure.
  Lev Kedhari See: Kedhari, Lev.
  Leyi, Geysan (ley-EE, gay-SAN) *n*. Born 1300. First wife: Laughter Tehalchev. Daughter: Imih. Son: Teve. Second wife: Barije.
  Leyi, Imih (ley-EE, ih-mih) *n*. 1320-1348. Mother: Laughter Tehalchev. Father: Geysan Leyi. Brother: Teve. Husband: Tehmu Bari. Daughter: Khiseleh.
  Leyi, Teve (ley-EE, TE-ve) *n*. Born 1320. Mother: Laughter Tehalchev. Father: Geysan Leyi. Sister: Imih.
  leyimeh (ley-EE-mah) *z*. lady, ladylike.
  liamet (lee-ah-MET) *n*. belonging to or having the characteristics of women.

Liamet Negezos (lee-ah-MET nay-GAY-zos) *n.* The proper name of the Negezos Mountains, the Negezos are located on the northern border of the Naritian prairie lands.

liet (lee-ET) *z.* woman.

lonnor (LAH-nor) *er/en.* rope, braid.

mactil (mak-TEEL) *z.* shawl, rebozo, scarf.

Mactil Street (mak-TEEL) *z.* is a popular tourist attraction in the city of Naritjina on the planet of Ceytal. It boasts of many quality restaurants and cafés located near an authentic Ceytalian market place. The market place dates back to pre-Ceytalian times and was the original location of the Enavian Outpost.

mahtil (MAH-teel) *n.* shawl, rebozo, scarf.

marihe (mah-REE-hay) *z.* turquoise.

meiklei (MEE-klee) *o.* A mirage nymph. According to Oramaklete mythology mekleis are the illegitimate offspring of the desert god, Hactl, and the water goddess, Tzetl-Marihe. Meiklei is also Ceytalian slang for crazy, insane, or mad.

melia (may-LEE-ah) *n.* turquoise, sky, blue.

melisanne (mel-is-AN) *er/en.* the course of a river.

meneth (MEN-eth) *n.* stone.

Meneth-shir (MEN-eth-SHEER) *n.* "Stone Place," a large caldera in the Liamet Negezos Mountains that is the permanent home of the Nejimenet people.

metul (me-TUL) *z.* integrity, truth and honesty.

Metul Div Ce (me-TUL deev say) *z.* 1286-1381. Served as high priest after engineering the deaths of Queen Ceymar and her high priest, Bari Usul Ce. Metul Div, with the help of General Neve kept the Naritian government stable during the quick succession of incompetent zivus until King Yaremida and his wife, Queen Divneve, were crowned in Halia Tehal in 1349. He continued to serve Narit well during the reigns of the Nejimenet king, Yaremida, and his son King Tehmu. Metul Div Ce died peacefully in his sleep after thirty-four years as high priest of Halia Tehal.

mheftu (MEF-tu) *n.* agility.

mheftuli (mef-TU-lee) *n.* kick ball, soccer.

narashan (nah-rah-SHAN) *n/z.* warrior.

Narit (nah-REET) *z.* "Beauty," the name of the Zenadishj prairie lands.

APPENDIX

Naritian Prairie (nah-REE-shan) *z.* is known for its beauty throughout the Enavian empire. Imperial laws were put into place to preserve areas of it for future generations.

Naritjina (nah-REET-SHJEEN-ah) *z.* City built on original site of the Enavian Outpost. Underground ruins of pre-Ceytalian cities have been discovered and are currently being excavated.

Naritjina Highway (nah-REET-SHJEEN-ah) *z.* runs along the length of the Lemmer Helt River.

nateheh (NAH-tay-heh) *z.* Golden prairie flower prevalent along the southern foothills of the Liamet Negezos Mountains that is used by Ceytalians in medicines and poisons. Also known as cela rose.

nathaja (NAH-thah-jah) *n.* Golden prairie flower prevalent along the southern foothills of the Liamet Negezos Mountains that is used by Ceytalians in medicines and poisons. Also known as cela rose.

negezos (nay-GAY-zos) n. grindstone.

Negezos Mountains (nay-GAY-zos) *n.* See: Liamet Negezos Mountains.

Nehimtehal (ne-HEEM-tay-hal) *z.* People of the Moon, term for the unknown race who built Halia Tehal.

Nejimenet (ne-JIM-eh-net) *n.* "Stone People" inhabitants of Meneth-shir. The Nejimenets live in Meneth-shir, an ancient caldera on the southwestern edge of the Negezos Mountains. They are an unusually tall race, much taller than the average Enavian citizen. They are dark skinned with golden eyes and blue hair. They are an agrarian, semi-nomadic and monotheistic society. Polygamy is allowed but they are generally monogamous and live in households of extended families.

Nejimenet numbers 1 = ce; 2 = ti; 3 = ki; 4 = gi; 5 = tan; 6 = har; 7 = gar; 8 = sar; 9 = mar; 10 = gan; 11 = gan-ce; 12 = gan-ti

nejo (NEE-ho) *n.* friend.

neral (NER-al) *er/en.* champion.

Neshamin (NESH-ah-men) *er/en.* Enavian term for Nejimenet.

Nevara (ne-VAR-ah) territorial planet of the Enavian Empire.

neve (NEH-vay) *z.* night.

Neve Beltehal (NEH-vay bel-tay-HAL) *z.* Night of the New Moon, purification ceremony of the Zenadishj celebrated each month.

Neve Ce (NEH-vay say) *z.* 704-798. He discovered the deserted city of Halia Tehal in 736 and became its first Naritian zivu.

Neve Ce (NEH-vay say) *z.* 1295-1383. Father: Halu Usul. Mother: Emme Liet. Brother: Hari Han. Sisters: Marihe, Aza, Halia and Tejalura.

Received no formal education outside the Naritian military. He became Warlord of Halia Tehal when he was forty-two and served Queen Ceymar, King Yaremida and King Tehmu with equal loyalty until his death. In the history of Narit there is no other personality who's memory is more venerated, unless it be that of Queen Divneve.

nevi (NEH-vee) *n.* night.

N'jim-aza (ne-jim-AH-zah) *n.* Red Human Being, term for Zenadishj.

N'jim-ijeh (ne-jim-EE-hah) *n.* Blue Human Being, term for Nejimenet.

Nor (nor) *c.* is the king and father of all the gods according to Ceytalian mythology.

North River also known as Khai Zeneshtu flows from the Valley of Zeneshtu across the Naritian Prairie where it joins the Lemmer Helt River.

nu (nu) *n/z.* no.

nul (nul) *z.* eyebrow.

Nul, Dassar (nul, DAH-sar) *z.* Zenadishj slave trader. His relationship with the Enavian authorities shifted without warning from consultant to person of interest for various crimes.

nutevek narashan ce (nu-te-VEK nah-rah-SHAN say) *n/z.* "No blood warrior," an elite caste of warriors able to kill their opponent without any bloodletting.

narashan (nah-rah-SHAN) *n/z.* warrior.

Oramaklete (OR-ah-MAH-kleet) *o.* tribesmen may be found living in the White Desert and the Naritian Prairie. There are also small communities along the Lemmer Helt River and in the Negezos Mountains. They are white haired with gray eyes and light brown skin. The slave traders of Ceytal prize them for their physical beauty but prefer captive children as the adults are too savage to control. Although Oramakletes worship the same gods, the Zenadishj do not recognize them as part of their culture because they practice cannibalism.

otain (O-tan) *en.* accountable, dependable, measures up to standards.

padhar (pah-DAR) *n.* horse.

Padhari, Mheftu (pah-DAR-ree, MEF-tu) *n.* 1273-1398. Wife: Talamy Anset. He was born to a wealthy, politically well-connected Nejimenet family and raised in the Naritian court during Div Kassar Ce's reign. He studied medicine at Taen University, an uncommon privilege for a Ceytalian. He made a career of leading tourist excursions and scientific expeditions into the Ceytalian wilderness. He also served as an advisor to the Enavians during times of political conflict.

pallas (PAL-as) *en.* ancient Enavian for "lioness".
perren (PER-en) *er/en.* eagle.
Queen Ceymar See: Ceymar Ce.
Queen Divneve See: Tehalchev, Ura "Tejalura".
ral (rahl) *en.* goal, target.
rayert (ray-ert) *er/en.* to connect, join, bridge.
seraine (su-RAYN) *er/en.* dancer.
shemetul (shem-e-TUL) *n.* lowlander, outsider.
shir (sheer) *n/z.* place.
shjina (SHJEE-nah) *n.* waterfall.
silverpiece is a coin worth one-sixteenth of an Enavian credit.
sleevan (SLEE-van) *er/en.* baker.
Sleevan, Kirat (SLEE-van, KEER-at) *er/en.* Born 1312. DCNA agent assigned to White Desert refugee camp 1336-1338.

Taen (tay-EN) *en.* Ruling planet of the Enavian Empire. Cultural as well as political center.

talamy (TAL-ah-mee) *er/en.* honey.
tamai (tah-MIY) *u.* gypsy.
tarim (tah-REEM) *u.* dancer.
tariv (tah-REEV) *er/en.* warrior.

Tariv, Senator Neral (tah-REEV, NER-al) *er/en.* 1292-1389. Father: Andel Tariv III. Mother: Mala Kurt. Sisters: Gelita and Eia. Wife (divorced): Eia Melia Tehalchev. Adopted daughter: Eia Nathaja. He served as a senator in the Enavian court for thirty-five years during which time he was the one most responsible for mediating peace on Ceytal during the Erteyan-Zenadishj Wars. Successfully negotiated the release of enslaved Enavian captives in Narit.

tehal (te-HAL) *n/z.* moon.

Tehalchev (te-hal-CHEV) *n.* Nejimenet family name "Moon Household".

Tehalchev, Halia Liet "Silverwoman" (te-hal-CHEV, ha-LEE-a lee-ET) *n.* Born 1271. Mother: Metahali Rakura (Ancient). Father: Kura Zhat. Adopted father: Nejo Akashechev. Brother: General Gan Akashechev. Sister: General Ki Akashechev. Husband: Zarkhon Tehalchev. Daughters: Tejalura (adopted) and Melia.

Tehalchev, Hushé (tay-hal-CHEV, hu-SHAY) *n.* 1306-1335. Father: Huri Tehalchev. Mother: Turquoise. Sister: Laughter. Wife: Tzeri Jevetchev. Tejalura's cousin by adoption. He was killed in the Blue Mountain Massacre.

Tehalchev, Melia (tay-hal-CHEV, may-LEE-ah) *n.* Born 1338. Father: Zarkhon Tehalchev. Mother: Silverwoman Akashechev. Tejalura's sister by adoption.

Tehalchev, Ura "Tejalura" (tay-hal-CHEV, U-rah "Te-jah-LU-rah") *n.* Born 1310. Father: Lev Aleksandar. Mother: Seraine Hershem. Brothers: Jack and John. sister: Gabrielle. Adopted Father: Zarkhon Tehalchev. Adopted Mother: Silverwoman Akashechev. Adopted Sister: Melia. Husband: Yaremida Tehalchev. Children: Ceymar (Trista), Khai and Akashe. At the age of seven her family was killed in 1317 Market Place Bombing and was adopted by a Nejimenet family. In 1344 she served as a financial advisor to the Naritian kingdom. In 1349 she was crowned queen of Narit and given the throne name of Divneve Ce.

Tehalchev, Uralai "Laughter" (tay-hal-CHEV, U-rah-li) *n.* 1302-1335. Father: Huri Tehalchev. Mother: Turquoise. Brother: Hushé. Husband: Geysan Leyi. Daughter: Imih. Son: Teve. Tejalura's cousin by adoption. She was killed in the Blue Mountain Massacre.

Tehalchev, Yaremida "Yari" (tay-hal-CHEV, yah-ray-MEE-da "YAH-ree") *n.* Born 1305. Father: Kassar Tehalchev. Mother: Leyimeh. Brothers: Zarkhon and Huri. Wife: Ura Tehalchev. Children: Ceymar (Trista), Khai and Akashe. He was crowned king of Narit in 1349.

Tehalchev, Zarkhon (tay-hal-CHEV, ZAR-kan) *n.* Born 1274. Father: Kassar Tehalchev. Mother: Leyimeh. Brothers: Huri and Yaremida "Yari". Wife: Silverwoman. Daughters: Tejalura (adopted) and Melia.

tehmu (tay-MU) *z.* gypsy.

Tehmu Bari See: Bari, Tehmu.

tejalura (te-jah-LU-rah) *n.* moonlight.

Tejalura (te-jah-LU-rah) *n.* See: Tehalchev, Ura "Tejalura".

telein (teh-LAYN) *n.* kitten.

tenukeh (teh-NU-kah) *z.* challenge, trouble, difficulty.

terez (teh-REZ) *z.* leader.

Terez Chevari See: Chevari, Terez.

teve (TE-ve) *n.* blood, life.

teyadinj (tay-yah-DINJ) *u.* animal dung.

teyado (tay-YAH-do) *u.* The dung of an unclean animal. A derogatory term for the Urthics and Erteyans.

trista (TREES-tah) *n.* thirsty.

Turquoise See: Akashechev, Melia "Turquoise".

tzeri (TSER-ee) *n.* star.

APPENDIX

Tzeri Jevetchev See: Jevetchev, Tzeri.
tzetl (TSAY-tl) *o.* water jewel.
ura (U-rah) *n.* light.
uralai (U-rah-li) laughter.

Urthic (ER-thic) tribesmen are the true aborigines of Ceytal, all other races have immigrated during historical times. They are a dwindling race of olive-skinned brunettes who live at the fork of the Lemmer Helt River and Black Water River. They are polygamous, polytheistic and nomadic. The most famous tribe of Urthics is the Black Water tribe (Zishuni). Queen Ceymar's mother was a Zishuni princess who was the concubine of Div Kassar, zivu of Halia Tehal.

usul (yu-SUL) *n/z.* pale blue corn gown on Ceytal.
Usul, Bari See: Bari Usul Ce.

veshe (VEH-shay) *n/z.* a young boy or girl who stands beside the wedding couple during the Ceremony of the Chosen; also, a homosexual male.

White Desert lies south of the Naritian Prairie.

White Desert Camp was established to contain the Nejimenet refugees during 1336-1341.

Winters, Ced and Mar *er/en.* owners of a general store near the Blue Mountain River.

Wolf, Lillian See: Tehalchev, Ura "Tejalura".

Yalangi (yah-LANG-gee) *o.* is an Oramaklete word for "Prosperity"; also, an Oramaklete village located in the Negezos Mountains.

Yalangi River (yah-LANG-gee) *o.* also known as Khai Yalangi flows from the foothills of the Negezos Mountains and joins North River (Khai Zeneshtu).

yanahna (yah-NAN-ah) *n.* to replace, replacement.

Yanahna (yah-NAN-ah) *n.* is a name Nejimenets often give to an adopted girl or a daughter whose mother has died in childbirth. On a planet where most Ceytalians place little value on female children, it is a name meant to expresses deep affection and to communicate how much she is cherished.

yarashji (yar-rah-SHJEE) *n/z.* dark blue.

Yarashji-shir (yar-rah-SHJEE-shir) *n/z.* An open field located along the Lemmer Helt River where it joins the Blue Mountain River. Used as campground by various Ceytalian tribes and considered neutral ground.

yaremida (yah-ray-MEE-da) *n.* wolf winter. One of the long-range effects of pre-Ceytalian chemical warfare that is currently impacting Ceytal. The Great Yaremida Spot which is believed to be the residue of one of those ancient bombs. This invisible mass completes its orbit around Ceytal every three years, causing extremely cold winters on the surface it covers.

Yaremida Zivu Ce See: Tehalchev, Yaremida "Yari".

yari (YAH-ree) *n*. wolf.

Yari Tehalchev See: Tehalchev, Yaremida "Yari".

zar (zar) *c*. goldpiece, Ceytalian currency worth approximately one-fourth of an Enavian credit.

zarkhon (ZAR-kahn) *n/z*. red hawk.

Zarkhon Tehalchev See: Tehalchev, Zarkhon.

Zemmer, General Erten (ZEM-mer, ER-ten) *er/en*. Born 1291. Father: Eled Zemmer. Mother: Vita Karel-Zemmer. Brother: Alac. Wife: Pallas Taen. The first seven years of his military career he was stationed on Ceytal. He was transferred to Nevara to help suppress the Nevaran Revolution. He returned to Ceytal with the rank of general and served as imperial advisor during the simultaneous revolts of Ceytal and Nevara. After fifty-four years of service he retired as one of the most highly decorated soldiers in Enavian history.

Zenadishj (ze-ne-DEESH) *z*. "Chosen of Zenedh" are the dominant race on Ceytal. The Zenadishj are dark skinned with magenta hair and golden eyes. They are found in the White Desert, the Naritian Prairie, the Valley of Zeneshtu, the Negezos Mountains and the small communities along the Lemmer Helt River and the Blue Mountain River. The pre-industrial Naritian Zenadishj of Halia Tehal have been most receptive to the modern technology of the Enavians, but still they cling to the traditions of their ancestors. They are polytheistic and practice human sacrifice. Being polygamous, their women are kept in harems and are veiled when in public. They are governed by two elite factions of aristocrats and priests with one or the other gaining most of the power. Occasionally the two groups unite under a priest-king. They have complete control over all Zenadishj nations except for the Mountain Zeneshtu who are closely linked with the Nejimenets of Meneth-shir.

Zenedh (zen-NED) *z*. Zenadishj sun god.

zeneshtu (ze-NESH-tu) *z*. spring.

Zevlin (ZEV-lin) *er/en*. is a laser gun developed by Hirim Zevlin, a Nevaran immigrant from Lyria. It was inexpensive to produce and was immediately embraced by his fellow immigrants to Ceytal. Because of its immediate popularity, the gun as well as individual parts have always been well stocked making it easy to purchase and repair. It's popularity spread throughout the Enavian empire and remains the personal weapon of choice by civilians and professionals alike.

zishu (zi-SHU) *u.* black water.

Zishuni (zi-SHU-nee) *u.* tribe of Urthic natives of Ceytal who once inhabited the area where the Enavians established the Black Water Community.

zivu (ZIH-vu) *z.* king.

TEJALURA

Bibliography

Akashechev, General Gan. *A Song of Meneth-shir: Poems and Reflections of the Great General*, Gan Akashechev. Translation by Dr. Ura Jevetchev. Taen, Enavia: King's University Publications, 1369.

Akashechev, Ki. *Ten Years Service in the Naritian Army*. Translation by Dr. Ura Jevetchev. Taen, Enavia: King's University Publications, 1371.

Horvak, Thes. *Through Another Man's Eyes: A Collection of Interviews of Famous Ceytalians by Thes Horvak*. Taen, Enavia: King's University Publications, 1389.

Horvak, Thes. *The 1390 Encyclopedia of Ceytalian History*. Taen, Enavia: King's University Publications, 1390.

Jevetchev, Dr. Ura. *Ceytalian Folklore*. Taen, Enavia: King's University Publications, 1354.

Neve Ce. *The Book of Zenedh*. Translation by Dr. Yanahna-Khai Chevari. Naritjina, Ceytal: Oramak, 1363.

Neve Ce. Halia Tehal: *The Mystery of the Nehimtehal*. Translation by Dr. Yanahna-Khai Chevari. Naritjina, Ceytal: Oramak, 1361.

Neve Ce. *The Nine Books of Wisdom*. Translation by Dr. Yanahna-Khai Chevari. Naritjina, Ceytal: Oramak, 1362.

Made in the USA
Charleston, SC
31 December 2011